GOD
OF
PAIN

RINA KENT

To a love that's nurtured by pleasure and intensified by pain.

AUTHOR NOTE

Hello reader friend,

If you haven't read my books before, you might not know this, but I write darker stories that can be upsetting and disturbing. My books and main characters aren't for the faint of heart.

This book contains a talk of child abuse and suicidal thoughts. I trust you know your triggers before you proceed.

God of Pain is a complete STANDALONE.

For more things Rina Kent, visit www.rinakent.com

LEGACY OF GODS TREE

ROYAL ELITE UNIVERSITY

COUSINS

LEVI KING ┬ ASTRID KING

LANDON KING (28) BRANDON KING (23) GLYNDON KING (19)

XANDER KNIGHT ┬ KIMBERLY REED

CECILY KNIGHT (20)

AIDEN KING ┬ ELSA STEEL

ELI KING (25) CREIGHTON KING (20)

RONAN ASTOR ┬ TEAL VAN DOREN

REMINGTON ASTOR (22)

COLE NASH ┬ SILVER QUEENS

AVA NASH (19) ARIELLA NASH (16)

THE KING'S U'S COLLEGE

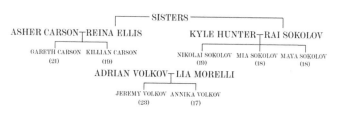

SISTERS

ASHER CARSON ┬ REINA ELLIS

GARETH CARSON (21) KILLIAN CARSON (19)

KYLE HUNTER ┬ RAI SOKOLOV

NIKOLAI SOKOLOV (19) MIA SOKOLOV (18) MAYA SOKOLOV (18)

ADRIAN VOLKOV ┬ LIA MORELLI

JEREMY VOLKOV (23) ANNIKA VOLKOV (17)

ABOUT THIS BOOK

I made a terrible mistake.

Being a mafia princess, I knew my fate was already decided.

But I went ahead and longed for the wrong one.

Creighton King is bad news with a gorgeous exterior.

He's silent, brooding, and obviously emotionally unavailable.

So I thought it's over.

Until he awakens a beast inside me.

My name is Annika Volkov and I'm Creighton's worst enemy.

He won't stop until he breaks me.

Or I break him.

PLAYLIST

"The Death of Peace of Mind"—Bad Omens
"Karma Police"—Radiohead
"Therapy"—VOILA
"Drinking with Cupid"—VOILA
"Bad Habits"—Ed Sheeran & Bring Me The Horizon
"A Way to Restart"—Colours in the Street
"In Circles"—Holding Absence
"Same Team"—Alice Merton
"All the King's Men"—The Rigs
"Empty"—Letdown
"Half the World"—Arcane Roots
"Beyond Today"—James Gilespie

You can find the complete playlist on Spotify.

GOD

OF

PAIN

ONE

Annika

THERE'S SOMEONE OUT THERE.

Or some*ones*.

The sound of their harsh breathing slips from outside the room, going up and up in staccato, resembling a trapped injured animal.

A feral animal.

My eyes fly open and I stumble out of bed, smoothing my hair so it falls to my lower back. Then I tug down on my purple sleep shirt that barely covers my ass.

Shadows linger in the corner, twisting and groaning like starved beasts. The only light comes from the balcony bulb that I always leave on. I don't reach out to the lamp's switch or even attempt to touch it.

Something tells me that if I shed light on whatever animal is lurking out there, the situation will diverge in an ugly direction.

My steps are inaudible, which comes naturally to me. But the remaining calm part doesn't.

It's impossible to control the tremors that slash through my limbs or the sweat that trickles down my back, making my shirt stick to my overheated skin.

This isn't right.

My brother's mansion should be the safest place on campus and the second safest on earth after our home back in New York.

It's why he insists I spend *certain* nights here. I don't meddle in his business, but I know what those nights entail—mayhem, chaos, the butchering of poor souls.

So the best place to keep me protected is right under his wing with a dozen guards watching me.

You know that ivory tower Rapunzel stayed in? My room in the Heathens' compound—my brother's anarchy-infested club—is the personification of that.

Hell, there are even guards beneath the balcony, so even if I actually attempted to climb down the tree, they'd be the ones to catch me. They'd scowl, grunt, and report my actions to both my brother and my father.

Yikes.

On the bright side, however, I'm protected. I've been protected since the day I was born into the Volkov family.

And I *am* a Volkov.

I nearly laugh at the shiver of fear that refuses to be purged from my system. I don't know about anywhere else, but I'm safe here.

Okay, whatever is lurking out there, you better be some injured bird or something trivial. Otherwise, be ready to die.

The balcony curtains flap inside, the white material soaked in the color of the night and the dim light.

I pause once I'm a few steps away. Did I open the balcony door last night?

No. No, I didn't.

The logical approach would be to turn around and run to the door, call for my brother or any of his men, and hide in my gilded cage.

But here's the thing.

My toxic trait is curiosity, like I really can't sleep at night if I don't satisfy that thirst for knowledge.

The spacious room with its fluffy pillows, purple sheets, glittery wallpaper, and everything glam and pretty slowly fades to the background.

The soft light from the balcony is my only compass as I take a step forward.

Fate works in mysterious ways.

Ever since I was little, I've known that I wouldn't always be a sheltered little princess fighting for her family's approval. That one day, something would come for me when I least expect it. I just didn't know what it would be or what it would entail.

I sure as hell didn't think it'd start in my brother's mega-secured, guard-filled mansion.

The moment I reach a hand to the half-open glass door, a dark figure slowly slides inside.

I jump back, slapping a hand to my chest.

If I hadn't seen the slick movement through my balcony sliding door, I would've thought this person—a man, judging by his build—was cut from the night.

He's in all black. Sweatpants, a long-sleeved shirt, shoes, gloves, and a half-smiling, half-crying mask.

A shiver snakes beneath my flesh as I stare at the details of the mask. The crying half is black and the smiling part is white. The mixture of both is creepily haunting.

All of him is.

The bleak color of his clothes doesn't conceal the bulging of his muscles beneath the shirt or reduce the sheer power of his quiet presence. He's someone who works out, his chest filled with planes of muscles and a defined abdomen, but he's not bulky.

Just muscular enough to exude power by merely standing there.

He's also tall. So tall that I have to crane my head to take in the entirety of him.

Well, I'm a bit on the short, petite side. But still. I don't usually have to go to such an extent to look at people.

We stare at each other for a beat, like two animals before they go at each other's throats.

The two holes in the creepy mask serve as his eyes, which are dark, but not black or brown, more like the darkness of the ocean.

And I latch onto that color, to that disruption of the black aura.

It's also my toxic trait to see the good in people, to not let the world harden me until I can no longer empathize with anyone.

It's a promise I made to myself when I figured out what type of world I was born into.

My limbs continue trembling, the rhythm matching my skyrocketing heartbeat.

Still, I force my super cheerful, super casual tone. "You might want to leave before the guards find you—"

The words die in my throat when he advances toward me.

One imposing step at a time.

So, remember the fact that his presence has power? I'm witnessing the effects of it firsthand.

I was wrong.

It's not only power; it's intimidation in its purest form.

An ocean that's groaning and roaring to release its wildness.

I don't even notice I've stepped back until he advances again. This time, I stand my ground and stare up at him. "As I was saying, you should probably go—"

His chest nearly collides with mine as he swiftly kills the distance between us. Warmth mixes with something spicy and the smell of soot. Was he near a fire or something?

He steps forward again and I automatically step back. Either that or I let him crash into me and sweep me over like a tornado.

"Seriously, do you know whose house this is?" My voice is no longer cheerful and has long since matched the shaking of my limbs. "Do you have a death wish—"

I'm not ready for what happens next.

In a flash of movement, he slams his gloved hand against my mouth and shoves me back.

My spine hits the wall with a jerk and I yelp, but it's muffled. The sound echoes in the air with the spookiness of a haunted lullaby.

The mask rests a few inches from my face like an episode from my deepest, darkest nightmares.

It's accentuated by the proximity of his body against mine and the strong leather smell.

It's all I can breathe.

And he's all I can see. His eyes are indeed blue, but they're black-rimmed.

Like a mythical creature.

I've seen these eyes somewhere. But where?

Is it wrong that I want to see what's beneath the mask? To just pluck it off and find out if he's the crying or the smiling half? Maybe both?

The longer I watch him, the more my breath hitches and his warmth seeps into my bones.

No. It can't be.

It's simply not who I'm thinking about.

Just to make sure, I lift a hand to his mask, fully expecting him to swat it away.

To my surprise, he doesn't make a move. My fingers slide over the edge of the frozen smile. But I don't see it as petrifying anymore—it's just a cover for someone.

A monstrous edge.

A conundrum of feelings.

Is it you? I ask with my eyes, and his slightly narrow in return.

So I try to peel off the mask, but before I can do so, he shoves my hand away. It falls limp by my side, but I'm almost sure my hunch is correct.

I don't know about anything else, but I would recognize these eyes anywhere, including in an alternative universe.

A bang comes from outside.

We both go still.

It comes again, and I realize it's on the door of my room.

"Miss, are you awake?"

A guard.

The Russian-accented voice comes again, coupled with another bang. "There has been a breach in security. Are you okay?"

I meet the masked stranger's eyes.

No, not a stranger.

He's way more than a stranger.

I'm still shaking, but it's for a completely different reason.

"Mmm," I let out a small, muffled sound.

He tightens his hold on my mouth, sweeping into my space with the sureness of a hurricane. My breasts brush against the hardness of his chest with every inhale.

"Miss? I'm coming in."

I grab hold of the intruder's arm and implore him with my eyes. He narrows his to slits but slowly slides his hand from my mouth. He keeps it hovering, ghosting close, probably to shut me up again if I scream for help.

But that's the thing, I don't need help, because he's not a threat.

Or at least, he wasn't in the past. I'm not quite sure in this situation.

"I'm okay!" I say loud enough for the guard to hear. I'm surprised I don't stammer or sound nervous, considering the situation.

The door opens a bit, but it remains in that position as the guard's voice drifts in. "I'm coming in to make sure, miss."

"Don't! I'm... I'm naked."

The clearing of a throat comes from the guard and I can almost imagine his flustered face. He knows his head would be on a stick if he saw me nude.

Unless my life was in jeopardy.

Which isn't the case.

I don't think.

"I'm really cool. I'm going back to sleep now. Don't wake me up."

Silence for one, two, three seconds—

"Very well, miss. If there's anything, the boss will come to see you."

The door closes and I release a long breath.

My next inhale causes my chest to brush against the not-stranger, and I pause, staring up at him.

"The boss he just mentioned is my brother, and I can't keep him out with the 'I'm naked' excuse. He'll just come in, eyes closed, pick up a sheet or something, and throw it on me, then do his search. He's brutal like that, so you really want to go before he comes if you don't want to have 'Beaten to death' written on your tombstone. Oh, also, are you going to stay glued to me for a long time? I might seem cool, but it's actually hard to breathe when you're around."

He stares at me blankly, absolutely not impressed nor derailed by my word vomit. It's a habit I'm trying to get rid of, but it's actually harder than it sounds.

"What are you waiting for?" I whisper. "Seriously, go before Jeremy shows up. If you came through the balcony door unnoticed, then return the same way. And uh, maybe give me my space back sometime soon?"

He reaches a gloved hand to my face and I think he'll shut me up again, but his fingers wrap around my jaw.

It's not threatening, but power simmers beneath the gesture.

No, not power.

Control.

He oozes with it to the point of suffocation.

His thumb strokes my bottom lip and it parts, just like that.

My heart hammers, and I think maybe I'm dreaming or something.

Maybe I've conjured so many scenarios in my twisted brain that one of them is actually coming true.

Otherwise, why would he touch me when he never has before?

And he's not just touching any part of me. It's my lips.

Is he going to kiss me?

Before the thought is fully formed, his rich, deep, and absolutely familiar voice rings in the air.

"You talk too much. One day, this mouth will get you in trouble."

Then he releases me, steps back, and slips out the balcony door as easily as he got in.

My limbs finally fail me and I slide down the wall and to the floor.

There's no doubt about it.

My fingers touch where he did a second ago. Well, he had a glove on, so it wasn't a direct touch, but it still counts, right?

Only, now, my lips quiver and my heart falls in disarray.

It is him.

The one I shouldn't want.

TWO

Annika

"ARE YOU SURE NO ONE CAME IN HERE?"

Am I sure this is, in fact, an alternative reality and I will soon wake up? Am I surprised no one sees my trembling insides?

Sure thing.

I'm totally certain something is wrong with me, because I plaster on my brightest smile as I face my brother.

Jeremy, who's barged into my room and is now towering over me, is tall, muscular, a bit bulky, and is the perfect clone of our father. Like, seriously, Papa gets an A+ for the copy-and-paste efforts.

He's also six years older than me, so I'm like a baby at only seventeen. I'll be eighteen in about a month and a half, so mentally, I'm already at that age.

Besides, due to my stellar academics, I got to skip a grade and attend college at this age. A fact my brother isn't fond of.

He's always been like a lethal tiger who stands guard in front of my door. I was only able to breathe when he left the States for college a few years before me.

Well, *able to breathe* is an exaggeration, because I was still under Papa's even more suffocating attention and protection.

That's why I worked hard to get into college. But naturally, I could only apply to where Jeremy is. That, or I had to stay in New York.

My brain voted my brother as the lesser of two evils.

I came to Brighton Island at the start of this semester. It's an island near the south coast of the United Kingdom. Ever since I reunited with my brother, that subtle feeling of suffocation, of being watched and monitored every second has returned.

I pull my sweater over my shirt, because, heck no, I'm not going to stroll around in my short-as-sin shirt in front of my brother.

That didn't seem like a problem earlier.

I hush that tiny little voice and throw up a dismissive hand. "I was totally deep asleep until that guard woke me up. Can't a girl have her beauty sleep around here?"

Nailed that.

Seriously.

If it were anyone else, they'd leave me be, but this is Jer. President of the Heathens, dubbed a devil, and the heir to Papa's mafia empire.

People at home are waiting for him to finish his master's degree and go back to his awaiting position in the heart of the New York Bratva.

This whole college experience is just a stepping stone for him, a way to soak in as much power as possible before going back to where he belongs.

His hawk-like gaze flits all over my room, stopping now and again as if he can see traces of *him*.

As if he can smell the leather from his gloves and feel the warmth emanating off his body.

My lips tremble at the reminder of how the intruder touched them, and my ears ring. The good type of ring. The type where I can still hear his voice in my head.

His words.

My Tchaikovsky—that's my god, by the way, because he's the root of my spirituality.

Get it together, me.

"You haven't heard any commotion?" Jer pushes with the persistence of a hound that's sniffing for prey.

"Aside from the guard's loud voice, not really. What's going on? He said there was a breach?"

"Yes. There was an attempted arson in the annexed house."

"A-arson?"

Holy shit on a stick. I knew that the smell of soot had something to do with a fire. Does that mean he was the one behind it?

Instead of asking that and flaring Jer's suspicious radar, I go with, "Is everyone okay?"

The fact remains, this mansion is the compound of the Heathens, and the founding members of the club, who are my brother's friends, use it as a home. Not to mention the live-in guards and some staff.

I'm preoccupied with the intrusion, but not enough to forget about other people. Even if they rival my brother's savageness.

"No one was hurt and we put out the fire before it ate up the annex," Jeremy offers.

"Phew! So glad there were no casualties." For more reasons than one. "Do you know who did it?"

"Not yet, but I will find them." He steps forward. "Are you sure everything's okay? You don't need anything?"

"Beauty sleep, remember?"

He ruffles my hair, a rare smile grazing his lips. I can't help but grin in return, knowing full well that my brother is a hard man and I shouldn't take his warmth for granted.

I'm lucky enough to be on the short list of people Jeremy cares for.

"Sorry for interrupting your beauty sleep, Anoushka."

That's what he and Papa call me. *Anoushka.* A Russian endearment derived from my name, Annika.

"Apology accepted, but stop messing up my hair. I'm not a kid anymore."

"You're a cute little baby to me."

"Jer!"

"What?"

"I'm really old enough to take care of myself."

"Not hearing that."

I snort. "Okay, but can I go back to the dorm tomorrow?"

Jeremy studies at The King's U, one of the two titan universities on Brighton Island, which is fueled by mafia money. The other university, Royal Elite University, was founded and is funded by old British money.

The two universities and their students can't stand each other. That animosity bleeds into sports and secret club rivalries.

To say they're at each other's throats would be the understatement of the century.

So the fact that I study at the art school at Royal Elite University—or REU—and stay in their dorm doesn't sit right with my brother.

Which is why he sometimes insists that I stay here—in the Heathens' mansion that he shares with his three friends.

He says it's to protect me, but it's more to keep an eye on me.

"Not yet," he says, confirming my thoughts. "Stay here for a few more days."

"But, Jer—"

"It's for your safety."

I want to groan in frustration, but I'm interrupted when a gruff voice comes from the other side of the door.

"The fucking fuck is wrong with people in the middle of the night? Can't anyone get some sleep in this godforsaken hole?"

A tall, muscular, half-naked guy waltzes inside my room, kicks away a fluffy pen, and peers through his bloodshot eyes at us.

Or more like at Jeremy.

My status and last name erased me from Nikolai's eyes a long time ago.

Thank you, Tchaikovsky.

He's a scary mofo, has a mafia princehood, and belongs to the New York Bratva just like us. His body is inked with more tattoos than can be counted, and he's always shirtless. Seriously, I wonder if he wears more than shorts to classes or if he bestows them with his half-nakedness status, too.

He lets his heavy body lean against the wall. "The fuck is going on?"

"Fire." My brother tilts his head in his friend's direction. "And put a shirt on."

"Shirts are overrated. And did you say fire? Why didn't anyone wake me up?"

"You were nowhere to be found."

"You sure? Because I was sleeping at the bottom of the stairs. Or maybe behind the stairs. Can't fucking remember."

"That's if you were asleep."

"The fuck is that supposed to mean?"

Jeremy ruffles my hair one more time and gets out of my room with Nikolai in tow. Despite the fact that Nikolai is younger than Jeremy by a few years, they've been close friends for as long as they've known each other.

My brother is the silent strategist who only uses violence when absolutely necessary, while Nikolai is the unhinged, bloodthirsty monster.

As I watch their backs, I can't help feeling a tinge of discomfort at knowing the type of future that awaits them.

One filled with blood, mafia wars, and brutal encounters. While Nikolai fits that image perfectly, and even strives for it, I don't want to imagine Jeremy in that light.

Even if I know he can be much worse.

"Who was the fucker?" Nikolai asks Jeremy on their way out. "I'm going to fuck up his life, burn his corpse, and spread the ashes in blood."

"I have a hunch."

I subconsciously step to the door, but Jeremy flashes me a glance I can't quite decipher, then closes it behind him.

Cutting off any chance I had to hear his hunch.

He couldn't have possibly figured out it's *him*.

Right?

Hushed whispers float around me with the perseverance of buzzing bees.

My name and Jeremy's, as well as our last name, have been murmured a dozen times.

I still smile at whoever meets my eyes and even ask them how they're doing. I comment on their fashion and tell them I loved their last TikTok or Instagram.

Every last one of them smiles back, and even if they still murmur about me, it's all along the lines of:

I can't believe she's the Jeremy Volkov's sister. She's such a darling. A doll.

A sweetheart.

A good sport.

I'm the people person, the PR of Jer's reputation, and the number one candidate to be the family's spokesperson.

They say the only way to be popular or loved is to stomp on others and be mean, but I believe in being nice.

I believe in being social for the greater good.

Now, if I could just not let other people's opinions eat me up from the inside, that would be perfect.

I come to a halt when an arm wraps around my shoulder. "Oh. Em. Gee. You're alive, thank the gods and all religions."

Ava does a whole tour around me, and it looks kind of funny, considering the huge cello strapped to her back.

She inspects every inch of my body, even patting my face to make sure it's the same.

Today, she's dressed in a pink skirt and a white top with a fashionable cut. She's the most elegant person I know, after my mom, and she resembles me in personality, too.

We clicked the moment we first met about two months ago when I first enrolled in REU. As a result, I became close with all her friends, too. She and the girls even allowed me to move into their private apartment in the dorm, despite the fact that I'm the 'American' who simply doesn't understand their obsession with fish and chips.

I grin. "Hi, missed you."

She hugs me and kisses my cheek. "Missed the shit out of you, bitch. What are the chances of your brother dropping the lame patriarchy and letting you come back to the dorm?"

"At the moment? Zero."

She groans and hooks her arm with mine. "You really okay? Everyone keeps talking about the fire in the Heathens' mansion."

"I was dead asleep." I lie through my teeth. "Until they woke me up with all the noise."

"That must've been so scary. I can't imagine waking up in the middle of the night at the news of an attack."

"I wouldn't exactly call it an attack."

"Totally was. They were probably after your brother or his heathen friends. Like, seriously, how does he think that place is safer for you than our little dorm?"

"No clue." Due to the fact that he has all the guards there, probably.

"Let's have Ces talk to him. She obviously isn't scared of the whole dark lord aura mojo he has going on… Speak of the devil!"

We arrive at the cafeteria we often eat lunch in. We, as in, Ava, Cecily, Glyndon—the girls I stay with—and Remington, Brandon, and…*him*.

The boy with ocean eyes and an intimidating presence.

Though when we get to the table, Cecily and Remi are bickering over some fries and Bran is trying to mediate. I don't see Glyndon and *him* anywhere.

I try to ignore the knot in my chest but fail.

Ava and I take the vacant seats and I smile at Bran when his eyes meet mine. "Where's Glyn?"

"I'm surprised you still ask about that traitor, honestly." Ava huffs. "She's probably out there getting the D."

Bran pushes his plate away, his nose scrunched. "Not the image I needed of my little sister."

Ava throws a French fry in her mouth. "That's why I said the D and not the dick."

Remi slides over super smoothly and grins. "Did someone mention a dick?"

"Oh, look at this. Someone recognizes they are one." Cecily crosses her arms over her shirt, on which there's a cute cat with a gun shooting the words *Pew, pew, mudafaka.*

"One?" Remi's lips pull up in a Cheshire cat grin, and it still doesn't take away from his symmetrically handsome face. "Say the word, Ces. D-I-C-K. Don't be a prude."

She flips her silver hair back. "Prude? I prefer boundaries."

"Yawn." Remi pretends to have fallen asleep. "Wake my lordship up when this nerd starts having a life."

That's what Remi calls himself, 'my lordship,' because of his noble blood. While everyone else sees it as arrogance, I find it super endearing.

He has the personality of a carefree angel—though Ava and Cecily would argue that he's a hedonist devil. Remi was one of the first people who warmed up to me instantly and I will never forget that.

"Stop it." Bran nudges him.

Cecily is ready for round one thousand of bickering but then sees me and backtracks. "Oh, Anni. Are you okay?"

"Totally cool. Physically examined by Ava herself."

"That's right." My friend strokes her cello. "She's okay from the outside."

"Do they know who did it?" Cecily asks.

"No idea. You know I don't get involved in that." I smile, pulling out my food container.

My OCD can be triggered by tiny, stupid details like how one of my salad containers isn't at the same level as the others.

My blood pushes against my rib cage and the sounds of the cafeteria start to get drowned out.

I quickly unclasp the containers full of healthy food, organize them in front of me, and only breathe when they're perfect.

The noise from the outside world slithers back in slowly but surely.

"Who else could it be?" Remi leans back in his chair, sipping from his iced coffee. "Probably the Serpents."

"Aren't they from the same uni?" Ava asks. "Our club is more likely to have a beef with them."

Bran shakes his head. "The Elites aren't really on bad terms with the Heathens currently. The Serpents, however, were humiliated by them, especially after the last raid on their mansion, and are more prone to take action."

"This whole thing is too messed up," Cecily says. "Someone could've been hurt in that fire."

"No one was," I relay Jeremy's words. "Don't worry."

"Still. I don't like this." She chews on her bottom lip, then reaches into her backpack and fishes out a purple pen with fluffy feathers. "I found this in my drawer, and I don't use it anymore, so I thought of you, Anni."

I grab it with both hands. "This is so cute, thanks!"

"Anytime."

The conversation goes on and on about the feuds between the three clubs, two from The King's U—Heathens and Serpents—and one from REU—Elites.

There are talks about war, rivalry, and payback, but I'm not really paying attention to that.

My gaze keeps flitting to the entrance for a hint of that familiar tall frame. I nearly finish my food, but there's no sign of him.

No one is talking about him either.

So I beam and ask in a casual tone, "By the way, where's Creighton?"

"Oh, Cray Cray?" Remi speaks between inaudible slurps. "Probably sleeping somewhere. That spawn of mine said he didn't sleep much last night."

I wonder why.

What I also find adorable about Remi's personality is how he calls Creighton a spawn. They're cousins from their mothers' side, but Remi is totally the extrovert who adopted him.

I let them go back to discussing the fire and the clubs' shenanigans, then say I'll be back.

I probably won't, but there's no harm in a little white lie.

Usually, I'd be on my way to volunteer at the local animal shelter since I don't have afternoon classes, but I'll do that later.

After tucking my containers back in my bag, I slip out of the cafeteria and head to the business school. On the way, I greet anyone who says hi or even looks at me.

A part of me knows all these people only want to get on my good side because of my brother's notorious reputation and my father's mafia status, but that's okay.

At least Ava and the others like me for me, and not for my last name.

Despite a few attempts by some students, I don't stop to chat.

See, I'm on a mission.

It takes me exactly ten minutes to reach the gazebo at the back of business school.

Sure enough, someone is lying on the bench, in the shadows. Hidden from passersby and onlookers.

The only reason I know about this is because Remi offers any information I ask for.

I stop and stare at the gloomy sky that blocks the sun every few seconds as if furious about its audacity to keep peeking through.

The wooden gazebo sits in a secluded area of the back garden where not many students mingle.

Exactly why I figure he likes it here.

Inhaling deeply, I walk as casually as possible. But even if the world can't see it, I feel the stiffness in my steps. The weight on my chest. The tremor in my lips.

Get it together, me.

The boy who lies on the bench, a leg bent and a hand under his head, looks peaceful.

He's dressed in jeans that hang low on his hips and a hoodie that's flung up, revealing a hint of his abs and his V-line.

I swallow, forcing my gaze to focus on his face instead.

That's totally not a better idea.

His face is nothing less than regal. He has the type of beauty that calls out to you without words. Sharp jawline, high cheekbones, and defined lips.

His brown hair that's short on the sides and long at the top is messy, finger-raked, and the most beautiful hairstyle I've ever seen. I've always wondered what those longer strands would feel like.

Wondered.

That's all I've done since I met this enigma. I've wondered and imagined and dreamed.

But they all came crashing down into one bleak reality.

He wants nothing to do with me. Or at least, that's what I thought.

Point is, his disinterest should make me happy. It's for the best, considering my fate was already sealed the day I was born.

I certainly don't want him to get hurt because of me.

But at moments like these, I find myself inching closer, reaching to ease that crease between his thick brows.

Make it go away.

In a flash, a hand grabs my own and I swallow as he slowly opens his eyes.

Rich blue, rimmed with black.

The same eyes of the masked man who paid me a visit last night.

THREE

Annika

I CAN'T BREATHE PROPERLY.

I can't even think properly.

I've been imagining this moment ever since I recognized those eyes. Chameleon, ocean eyes with rare heterochromia that I've never seen on anyone but him.

That's what the black rings surrounding his blue eyes are called. Heterochromia. A perfect imperfection that's part of who he is.

It was the first thing that tugged on my attention. And while many would say my attention is easy to get, no one knows it's impossible to keep.

Yes, I continue to treat people nicely, remember their names and ask about their last social media post, but it's all part of a feigned behavior. Whatever drew me to them in the first place has long since shriveled and died.

Creighton is the exception to that phenomenon. My interest in him started like with anyone else—mild, normal. Impersonal.

Little by little, it's expanded into this boundless powerful interest that's swept through me from the inside out.

My attention to him hasn't waned. If anything, it's grown more potent with every encounter, every stolen glance. Every touch.

Though they've never been sensual in nature.

As opposed to right now.

My hand tingles in Creighton's, or more like my finger that I reached out. That's all he's holding—or crushing in his palm. A mere finger.

He slides it away from his face and then drops it as if it's an insignificant object. Beneath the apparent detachment, a much worse feeling lingers in his gaze—disgust.

A familiar clamping clenches my chest, followed by a subtle ache behind my rib cage.

Oblivious to the tremble in the finger he just threw, Creighton springs up to a sitting position. I have to step back to keep from colliding with him.

My Tchaikovsky.

He really needs to stop moving so suddenly.

Or maybe I'm the one who should move less jerkily.

Hugging my bag, I sit beside him and put on my best smile. "Hi! I didn't see you at lunch, so I thought maybe you'd be hungry?"

He doesn't reply, but he doesn't need to. As much as I've tried to pull words out of him in the few weeks I've known him, I've come to the bitter realization that he just isn't the talkative type.

Worse, he takes the silent treatment game to the next level that makes you feel less than the dirt on his designer shoes.

For the record, my pride is wounded. Usually, I'm able to befriend anyone. I tell them witty stories and smile and they fall for me, just like that.

The only exception is this six-foot-four wall of muscle.

But it'll be a cold day in hell before I give up.

So I dig into my bag and retrieve the purple container—not the one I ate from—and place it on his lap. "I made extra lunch, not salad; I know you don't like those. Jer was starving this morning, so I fixed him some shrimp and there were leftovers."

It's actually the other way around, and my brother has the smallest portion—sorry, Jer—but Creighton doesn't need to know that.

He stares at the container with that edge of his usual disapproval. Creighton has this permanent blank stare that makes it impossible to figure out what he's feeling. It's worse than any mask and more effective than any camouflage.

And whenever he looks at something, you never know if he's considering touching it or flat-out murdering it with his bare hands.

My gaze strays to those hands that are hanging nonchalantly on his knees. So the thing is, Creighton made me unlock a new fetish—hands.

Or maybe I had that before and it just became more prominent when he came into the picture.

He has these big hands, long fingers, and veins. Lots of veins snake over the backs of his hands with the promise of something sinister.

I quickly derail my attention from them or else there will be an embarrassing event where I'll start drooling.

Creighton is still staring at the container, serious lines etched in his forehead, and I think he'll throw it away like he did my finger.

He doesn't.

But he doesn't open it either.

Just stares at it blankly. Then he grabs it, those veiny hands flexing on the lid, and starts to get up.

"You could've told me you were paying me a visit last night and I would've dressed up for the occasion. Unless…you wanted to see me half naked?"

He stops mid-rise, sits back down, and tilts his head in my direction. The blue of his eyes has subtly darkened and sharpened with a haunting edge.

I'm not used to this type of expression from Creighton. Indifference is the most I get from him, but this?

It's like he's picturing the best way to snap my neck.

Heat rises up my neck and to my ears, and I push down the tinge of fear that's gnawing on my insides.

I try to maintain my smile. "I know it was you. See, I might not have great attention to detail, but your eyes kind of gave you away. Don't worry, Jeremy is none the wiser. He did suspect that someone came into my room, but I was able to derail his attention and—"

One moment I'm talking, the next a hand slams against my mouth.

Like last night.

He physically jerks me sideways so that my back hits the wooden pillar of the gazebo.

Only, this time, it's his bare hand on my mouth and I'm breathing straight through his fingers. Gone is the scent of soot and leather. Right now, he smells like clean clothes out of the dryer mixed with his natural spicy scent.

"What do you want?"

His question takes me off guard. Not just because he spoke in that gravelly, deep, and hot British accent, but also due to the fact that he thinks I'm telling him all this because I want something.

"Mmm," I mumble against his hand.

"I'll only let you talk if you tell me what you want. If you chatter on, I'm going to shut you up again."

I nod once and he releases my mouth slowly. Though instead of stepping back, he remains so close, it's hard to breathe properly.

Sometimes, I think he knows exactly what type of effect he has on people—and me—and still does this on purpose.

He still barges in uninvited with the sole intention of leaving a trail of devastation behind.

"Why did you come to the Heathens' mansion last night? Why did you burn the annex house? I didn't think you had a problem with the club or its members. You're not even part of the Elites, so it doesn't make sense that you would want to do that, right?"

He reaches his palm out again, but I put both my hands up. "Okay, okay. There's no need to shut me up, but I can't tell you what I want unless you confess the reason."

He stares at me. Blankly. His 'no' is obvious.

I sigh. "Then I guess I'll tell Jeremy about how you not only burned his property but also snuck into his sister's room. *Le sigh*. I can't guarantee he won't be all savage."

"If you wanted to tell him, you would've already." The calm, rich timbre of his voice echoes around me like a song.

The one that haunts my waking and sleeping moments.

"I only wanted to give you a chance, and I did, but you chose not to take it. That's just sad. One last chance to change your mind?"

"Tell him."

"You…you're bluffing."

"You are."

"W-what?"

"You hate conflict so much that you hide from it like Little Miss Ostrich. That's also why you didn't let that guard come in last night, then covered for me. It's completely out of character for you to personally create conflict, so yes, you're bluffing, Annika."

My lips fall open.

Oh. My. Tchaikovsky.

Please tell me I'm not dreaming and that he actually said a whole paragraph. Oh, and he knows this much about me.

I didn't think he really knew anything about me, let alone my character.

Maybe I underestimated just how attuned to details he is.

"Okay, okay, you don't have to tell me the reason yet. We'll get to that someday." I link and unlink my fingers on my lap. "But you asked me what I want, right?"

He raises his brows, and why the hell is such a simple gesture enough to trigger a flutter in my stomach?

As if that's not enough, a little part of me is whispering, whining, and absolutely grouching about where I'm going with this.

It's wrong and you know it.

You'll only get him in trouble and regret it.

But I can't just ignore the other part, the one that's yearning, living on borrowed air and needing to feel what it's like to be alive.

To not just pretend I'm living, popular, and loved, but to actually breathe life into my sheltered existence.

Still, my voice comes out small, unsure. "I want you to spend an hour with me every day. Alone."

"Doing what?"

"I don't know, anything. Talking, just sitting here, reading, eating, maybe go shopping…" He scowls and I backtrack. "No shopping, got it. We can watch a movie."

"A movie lasts for more than an hour."

"Uh, okay. No movies either. But we can do everything else."

"No."

My heart shrinks behind my rib cage, but I force a smile. "Why not?"

"I will not date you."

"I…I'm not asking you to date me."

Okay, so maybe I was? But why the hell is he such a stone-cold asshole? Can't he hurt people more gently or something?

"All the better then." His face, expression, and tone are all caught in the freaking Arctic Ocean. "No dating will happen."

"Hypothetically speaking, and only hypothetically, because this isn't a real situation, why do you not want to date me?"

He reaches a hand to my face again and I freeze as he lifts my chin with two fingers. A charge of electricity rushes through me like a slowly brewing storm.

Tension rises, clings to my skin, and rips through my bones. I shiver, but I still can't tear my gaze away from those ocean eyes.

They're dark again, a manifestation of their owner's changing mood.

I don't know if the change is due to me or the fact that he's touched me more in the span of twelve hours than he has in all the weeks I've known him.

But I'm caught in his web.

Unable to move.

Absolutely trapped under the calloused touch of his lean fingers that dig into my sensitive skin with the lethality of a whip.

When he speaks, the low, deep words nearly paralyze me.

"Hypothetically speaking, I have deviant tastes and violent tendencies for the opposite sex. You're so fucking breakable, I'd crush you in no time."

"How are you, baby angel?"

I internally shake my head to focus on my mother's radiating features.

We're FaceTiming like the coolest mother-daughter pair because that's a thing.

If Jeremy counts as Papa's clone, I'm Mom's successful attempt at a 2.0. I'd like to point out that I would never be able to pull off her elegance, but we share the same petite features, the brown hair—though mine is longer—and the round eye shape. Though mine have a lot of gray—like Papa's.

Hers are more haunting, as if they're harboring a tragic story. And I know they are. A long time ago, before I was born, Mom wasn't as happy as she's been during my life.

Another thing Mom will always beat me at is ballet. Lia Volkov was one of New York City Ballet's most renowned prima ballerinas. I spent my childhood watching her performances—secretly, because she wouldn't have liked it—and being spellbound. I wanted to be like her at any price, to fly into the sky and know exactly where to fall.

Am I at that point? Not really. I'm at that crossroad where I have no clue whether I should focus on college or aim to be a professional ballerina instead. I fell in love with ballet at first sight at four years old, but I still find myself gravitating more toward academics. Since ballerinas have a short professional life, I don't want to be caught with nothing to do later on.

That is, if my future isn't already decided.

"Oh, you know. Same old, same old." I throw a hand in the general direction of my room in the Heathens' mansion. "Playing Jer's prisoner for shits and giggles. Ivory tower and gilded cage are taking their turns with me."

She does a horrible job of suppressing her smile.

"This isn't funny."

"I know, I know. You just look so adorable when you lash out all that sarcasm."

"Thanks, but I prefer beautiful instead of adorable. Considering my college status and my attempts to act older. And seriously, Mom, can't you talk to Jer so he'll give me some freedom? At this rate, I'll die young and my ghost will start posting inspirational videos on TikTok."

Laugh lines still linger on her face. "I did and his response was that he's just looking out for you."

"That's just an excuse to lock me up."

"One that your father wholeheartedly agrees with. You know he didn't want you out of his sight."

"Because I'm a girl?"

Her eyes soften to the lightest blue. "Because he has too many enemies and he's worried about your security."

My lip pushes forward, exaggeratingly pouty. "So I'm his weakness?"

"The three of us are, but we're his strength, too, Anni. You know that, right?"

"I do. But this still sucks."

"I know. I'm sorry."

"Don't be. It's not your fault, and I get it. This is how it's supposed to be. I'm just being grouchy. Enough about me. How are things at home? Are you guys okay? Do you miss me?"

"Like crazy. I'm currently convincing your father to find us a home on Brighton Island so we can live right beside you."

"Please don't. Papa will just bring an entire army along."

"You think?"

"Duh. Remember the last time we went to Russia for Christmas? I get chills thinking about all that security. And when I asked him, don't you think it's too much? He was like *absolutely not*." I mimic Papa's deadpan voice and Mom bursts out laughing. Even her laughter is as regal as she is.

"You're such a naughty hellion."

"You still love me."

"Oh, I do." She sighs, then I sigh, too.

The thought that's been plaguing my every waking and sleeping moment pushes to the forefront and I pause, measuring my words.

"Hey, Mom."

"Yes, baby angel?"

"Is Papa looking into possible suitors for me?"

A delicate frown appears between her brows. "What makes you think that?"

"Isn't that my destiny?"

"You're still young. Your father won't marry you off when you're just seventeen."

"Going on eighteen. And does it really matter if he does it now or a few years from now?"

"Oh, Anni. Is that why you were hell-bent on going to college? Did you think you only had a few years before your freedom was confiscated?"

"Isn't that the case?"

"Adrian would never make you marry someone against your will. Do you have that little faith in your papa?"

"I have little faith in his world. *Our* world. Women are just a flashy accessory and a currency for the highest bidder. I'm aware that I'm expected to strengthen the Bratva's alliances with anyone they deem worthy."

"They'd have to kill me before I'd let them use you as a pawn."

"Thanks, Mom. But I don't want to be the reason behind our family's misfortune. When the *Pakhan* orders Papa to marry me off to one of the other leader's sons or into one of the crime organizations, the only thing he can do is agree."

"He won't."

"Then he'll just be labeled a traitor and be driven out."

"Anni…"

"It's okay, Mom. I made peace with this fate a long time ago. Well, not really peace. Understanding, I guess."

"No, it's not okay." She inches closer to the phone, her expression serious. "Yes, the world we live in is brutal, but that doesn't mean your papa and I won't stand up for you. Besides, if you happen to fall in love, who would dare make you marry a stranger instead?"

My lips part.

That's it.

How come I've never thought about this before? Well, I have, but I didn't think it'd make a difference.

That is, until Mom just confirmed it.

Papa wouldn't make me marry anyone against my will, but he'll be more convinced if I actually have a boyfriend.

I've never had one before. Sure, I've flirted and made as many friends as possible, but I've never made it official. That would've meant putting the poor boy in direct conflict with Papa, Jeremy, and their equally ruthless guards.

Just thinking about the scowly face of Kolya, Papa's senior guard, makes me shiver. He'd rip the poor guy to pieces before he could even introduce himself to Papa.

Yikes.

But if it means I'd get out of my predestined cruel fate, then maybe it's worth a try.

"Anni? Are you still with me?" Mom's voice brings me out of my thoughts.

"Uh, yeah. What's up?"

"Don't tell your papa what you just told me or he'll be upset."

"I will be upset about what?"

Mom's face brightens with a wide grin as he comes up behind her, leans down, and kisses the top of her head.

Swoon.

I want a man like Papa. Yeah. He's mean to everyone and you really don't want to meet him in a dark alley—or even in broad daylight—but he's always treated Mom like a queen.

The mecca of his world.

The person who makes his darkness go away.

He strokes her cheek. "I've been looking for you, Lenochka."

"I was only gone for half an hour."

"Still too much time."

"Uh, hello? I'm right here, you guys. Thanks for noticing."

Papa finally looks at the phone Mom is holding and smiles. Or as much as it could be called a smile for a badass mafia leader.

Don't care what anyone says. Those suckers in the New York Bratva would all be done for if it weren't for Papa's strategic brain.

"Anoushka, isn't it late there?"

"No, and you're not dismissing me for alone time with Mom, Papa. Seriously, I'm wounded."

"You're being dramatic. You've been talking to her for half an hour."

"But, Papa!"

"Night, Anoushka. We love you."

He takes the phone from Mom's hand and she laughs, then squeals as the line is cut off.

Great. Now, I know what my parents are doing for the night.

I flop against my bed and stare at the glittering purple objects hanging from the ceiling.

My mind fills with all sorts of thoughts. The first is that I need to find a way out of my fate.

Okay, maybe that's not the first thing, because I haven't been able to stop thinking about Creighton's words from yesterday.

Violent tendencies.

Deviant tastes.

I can still feel his deep voice against my ear and the furious shiver that overtook me right afterward.

That was definitely not what I expected someone like Creighton to say. He could've been lying, but he doesn't have a reason to.

Besides, he's direct to a fault.

I was so stunned that I only snapped out of it after he took the lunch I made and strolled out of the gazebo.

In truth, I'm still stunned.

That was obviously his warning to make me stay away, so why the hell am I even more intrigued with him now?

Just what does a twenty-year-old consider deviant and twisted?

I guess there's only one way to find out.

FOUR

Creighton

THERE'S NO SUCH THING AS BEING TOO YOUNG TO REMEMBER. I was three years old when my life was turned upside down. Blood splattered, monsters' fangs showed, and I was caught between them, having the sole destiny to be crushed to death.

I was three years old, and I still remember every vicious word, every hateful stare and can still hear the gurgle of life leaving a body. I still have nightmares about a body hanging from the ceiling and looking at me with unblinking, bulging eyes.

I haven't been the same since.

Yes, I was adopted by a loving yet unconventional family and have the best parents alive, but that never managed to make me forget the past.

Thing is, some images just can't be erased.

Some images bleed into my subconscious and devour me from the inside out. Every night.

Every day.

Every second.

It's not just a distant memory; it's part of who I am.

I've ignored it all my life, tried to cope with it, to come to terms with the past, and to blend myself into my current life.

I've truly tried. My honest attempts have included doing

everything by the book, following the therapist's coping mechanisms, and learning to lead a normal life.

But I'm not normal.

And coping is never enough. And neither is convincing myself that time will make it better.

Seventeen years later and the images are still as vivid as back then, with their gruesome details and those bulging fucking eyes.

I learned to stop asking my parents about the past—not only do they avoid the subject like the plague, but Mum also gets this sad look in her eyes. The one where it feels as if I'm ripping her chest open and punching her fragile heart.

Luckily, I'm old enough now to pull the strings on my own.

Even if it means abandoning everything I've known for the seventeen years since the massacre.

That's what I've always called it in my head, even though only two people died. Make that three—including the three-year-old version of me.

He suffered the most, despite the fact that death chose to exempt him.

The time has come to finally do something about those hideous memories.

In the past, I couldn't be proactive due to living under my parents' roof and being under their constant scrutiny.

However, I'm at university now and I have enough freedom to seek the truth. The only barrier is the personification of my parents' hawk eyes—my annoying older brother, Eli.

As circumstances would have it, I know exactly the information to feed him so he'll remain preoccupied and leave me the fuck alone.

Because something changed recently.

I got a piece of information that flipped my perspective upside down.

It's not anything groundbreaking, but it's the tip of the iceberg—a little clue that will allow me to dig deeper.

This time, I won't stop until I unveil the whole truth.

"The arson didn't do much damage. I'm a little disappointed."

I slide my hand from my face to stare up at my cousin—second cousin—who's perched over my bed.

Landon is three years older than me and has the looks of a refined prince and the character of the devil himself.

Or more like Lucifer—the one who controls demons and every obscure creature.

His brown hair falls in a chaotic mess over his forehead, highlighting angular features that are no different from the stones he's obsessed with sculpting. He's even doing an art master's degree to be able to produce more stones that people weirdly call masterpieces while labeling him a genius.

Anarchist would fit him better.

Since I'm trying to sleep, I turn on my side and close my eyes again.

A creak comes from the chair beside the bed, indicating that Landon chose to stay, not caring about my clear 'Fuck off.'

"It could've been much better. What a loss of potential."

"And you could've left so I can sleep."

Landon *pffts*, a light chuckle spilling from him before he kicks my back. "Wake up. There are better things to do than sleep."

"Doubt it."

"What if I say I have the second piece of the puzzle for you?"

My eyes open and I slowly turn around.

Landon grins, knowing full well he's got me exactly where he wants me. "Happy to have your attention, baby cousin. Now, let's go."

Staring at him harshly, I don't move, and he rolls his eyes dramatically. "Your habit of trying to communicate with your eyes is annoying as fuck. Not all people are good with that language and they could—and will—misunderstand you. Lucky for you, I'm proficient in all languages. To answer your less-than-subtle demand, no. There will be no piece of the puzzle for you unless I get something in return. That was the deal, remember?"

So this is the downside behind my master plan of collecting information about my past. Somehow, Landon got wind of that and he's using it to make me do his bidding.

He tried to ask nicely at the beginning, I'll give him that, but those of us with the King last name just don't do things nicely.

We need to be kicked, provoked, and even threatened so that we're forced to do anything.

And that's exactly what Landon has done to have me on his chessboard.

I sit up, throwing my weight against the metal bedpost. "What do you want? Another fire?"

"Nah, that was fun on the first try, but their security has gotten better now. Let's give them some time to come to terms with the change, and just when their guard is down... *Boom*. We strike again."

"Then why are you bothering me now?"

"Don't be a little shit." He opens my wardrobe, flings out a hoodie from all the similar ones and throws it in my direction. "We're out to have fun."

"No."

"Or you can model for me? I'll make a masterpiece out of your features."

"Definitely not."

"We're going out then. Only when we're done will I tell you what the next step is."

I grab the piece of clothing and step past him. "You must be so lonely if you want to spend time with me."

He laughs, the sound genuinely amused. "Maybe. Your peaceful silence is hard to find in this loud world."

I lift a shoulder and pull on the hoodie. Landon and his twin brother, Brandon, are probably the only two who seek me out because of my silence. Everyone else just wants me to talk—not them.

They're tolerable, but only separately. They become annoying dicks in each other's company.

After I'm dressed, we leave my room and start down the hall. Elegant wallpaper extends for as far as the eye can see, giving the place a classical vibe.

We live in an off-campus mansion that Landon also uses as the compound for his club, the Elites.

A club that he has wanted me to be part of since I enrolled in REU, but I've refused his invitation every time.

I pledge loyalty to no one. Not even to myself.

We drive away from the mansion, or more like Landon does in his show-off one-of-a-kind McLaren. I spend the whole ride sleeping.

The opening of the door hauls me out of a light sleep. A man dressed in formal wear inclines his head in my direction. "Welcome back, sir."

I step out and cast a look at my cousin, who's already stepping onto the cobbled street. An easy expression is written all over his face, but it's just a camouflage for his twisted insides.

Only a few lights adorn the hidden alley that's situated in the least populated part of the island.

This is where Landon started to bug the fuck out of me. He somehow ran into me through our mutual fucked-up cravings and hasn't left me alone since.

Knowing him, he probably hunted me down like the creep he is.

The bouncer of the club lets us in with a smile and a curtsy. We're probably their youngest members but the most ruthless.

The most in-demand, too.

"What do you have for us?" Landon asks, pure sadism dripping from his voice.

He is a sadist.

I'm just an animal.

A man in a tux smiles with the shrewdness of a pimp. "There are two members who I believe will be to your liking. Room nine." He hands the key to my cousin, who slips him enough cash to make the man's beady eyes glow in the darkness.

We walk down the dark red halls, our steps making little to no noise on the carpet.

My blood pumps with the promise of inflicting pain.

Lots of pain.

Enough to drown the pain festering inside me.

Landon opens the door and we slide inside a red-lit room.

Two naked girls kneel on the carpet, collared in black leather, heads bowed, arms bound with black cuffs, a gag hanging around each of their necks, waiting to be shoved in place.

Whips, canes, and chains decorate both sides of the room, shining in the red light, all available for our use.

"Evening, ladies." Landon goes to the brunette and strokes a thumb under her jaw. "Are you ready for some fun?"

"Yes, please," she purrs.

Her friend, a leggy blonde who's at least five years older than me, licks her lips when she looks at me.

She's beautiful and will be even more exquisite when I engrave my welts in her pale skin.

She'll be enough for a little fun, like Landon said. Enough to stop the nightmares for one more sleep.

I start to approach her, then stop. Her face, older, mature, and a little sharp, morphs into a completely different one.

Just like in some fucked-up fantasy, her hair turns a rich brown. Her features soften, becoming smaller, more lively, more…irritating.

Her pouty lips are parted, begging to be stuffed with cock, and a pink hue covers her cheeks. Big blue-gray eyes glitter with life, happiness, and breakable innocence.

An innocence I want to tarnish with my darkness.

I shake my head with the sole purpose of ensuring I'm not going insane.

Sure enough, the blonde comes back into focus, staring between me and her friend, who's getting acquainted with Landon's ruthless cane.

I didn't even notice when he got the brunette on the floor and started his session. I didn't hear her muffled cries or see her tears— usually, those are the highlight of my nights of cravings.

The blonde arches her back, thrusting her big tits in my direction, an invitation for me to give her the same treatment as her friend. She doesn't move or crawl toward me, though, probably having been told by the waiter that I loathe disobedience.

Her face starts to blur again, changing, morphing into one that has no business being here.

I curse beneath my breath, turn around, and leave.

Not only the room but also the club and the street.

I walk all the way to the rocky side of the beach where a few people and couples are mingling about. I hop on a faraway rock and sit there, leaning back on my palms.

My gaze gets lost in the waves that slam against the jagged rocks in a symphony of violence.

I have always had an inclination toward brutality. Whether it's underground fighting or inflicting sexual pain. It's why I get along with morally black people such as Eli and Landon.

It's also why I usually participate in any adrenaline-induced mayhem they plot. I need that deranged energy and the pure unhingedness that comes with it. It's how I survive day-to-day.

I remain in the same position for over half an hour, but the pesky reason that I rushed out of the club is still plaguing my mind.

I fetch my phone and type a text to the one person who'd be able to explain the fuckery that just happened.

Creighton: What does it mean when you see another girl's face on the one you're about to fuck?

I say 'fuck' so I don't have to mention the whipping and caning part. He wouldn't judge, but he'd publish it in the *Daily Mail* for the world to see.

My cousin from my mother's side replies almost immediately.

Remington: It means you should've fucked the other girl. The one whose face you saw, because your dick wants her and we always let our dicks decide who they fancy. That's like the easiest and most logical explanation ever. Come on, spawn, my lordship taught you as much.

Creighton: I'm not even attracted to the other girl. She's not my type.

Remington: Types are overrated. They can change.

My jaw clenches and I refuse to take Remi's words as fact. After all, I'm the only one who considers him wise. Everyone else just seeks him out for fun times, not advice.

He's probably the most balanced out of us all, but then again, he's the only one in the house whose last name isn't King.

Remington: And rude, btw, you left me on Read last night.

I exit the chat, leaving him on Read again.

But before I close the app, I go to someone else I've been leaving on Read for the last couple of weeks.

Annika.

My finger hovers over her endless texts. Some are telling me about her favorite music—classical. Her favorite film—*Pride and Prejudice,* all versions. Her favorite food—pizza—that she doesn't get to eat a lot because of her disciplined routine. Some are selfies of her.

Those stopped after I ignored the first few.

Her last text was prior to the deliberate loss of control on my part.

Deliberate because I meant to push her away. So far away that she'd stop looking at me with those glittery eyes and parted lips.

It was my last bit of courtesy for someone who gave me food and didn't hand me over to her brother on a silver platter.

That incident happened a week ago.

She's kept her distance since—even during lunch. Before, she glued herself to my side and chattered happily until I got up and left.

Now, her chosen victims are either Remi or Bran. On and on, she talks to them about the last book she read or film she watched.

They listen to her, engage, and even reply.

Unlike me.

Ava even asked her if she's finally given up on me. She laughed and subtly changed the subject.

She did give up.

Finally.

If I'd known it would be that easy, I would've shown her a hint of who I truly am a long time ago. That way, I wouldn't have had to put up with her disturbing cheerfulness.

I click on the last selfie she sent two weeks ago. Her hair falls on either side of her face and she has both hands under her chin. She's too young, oozing with an irritating type of happiness that grates on my nerves.

Yes, I'm young, too, but only in age. I've never felt young since the massacre.

A notification of a text shows up at the top of my phone. Did I somehow send a reaction or something?

That's when I realize I've been staring at her selfie for about five minutes.

A long fucking time.

I scroll to the text she sent just now.

Annika: So I've been thinking.

Creighton: I'm surprised you do that before talking.

The dots indicating she's typing appear and disappear.

Screaming emoji

Dead sticker

It's happening GIF

Annika: OMT! Did you actually reply? Say the secret words or I'm reporting you for kidnapping Creighton.

What the fuck is she on about now?

Annika: I'm serious. I'll report you right now. I swear to Tchaikovsky. That's what OMT means if you were wondering. Oh my Tchaikovsky.

Creighton: You talk too much.

Annika: It's really you. Hi! Also, thanks for replying after a thousand years. Really appreciated.

Creighton: If I'd known this was what I was in for, I wouldn't have.

Annika: Wait, don't ghost me yet. You're seriously cold, did you know that? I wonder if you even have a heart beneath all that ice.

I don't reply.

Annika: Here we go again. You're leaving me on Read. But anyway, I've been thinking about what you said the other day and I'm curious about the 'deviant tastes' part. I tried searching and asking around your childhood friends, but I think either you keep that part of yourself under wraps or it's not true? At any rate, I want to know more. Can you tell me?

My hand flexes on the phone and I type with stiff fingers.

Creighton: This is my one and only warning, Annika. You have no clue what you're asking for. Be grateful that I have no interest in you and run the fuck away. If you let me catch you, I'll swallow you alive.

She reads my text immediately, but no dots appear.
Good.
"There you are."
I turn off my screen and slide my phone into my pocket as Landon sits beside me.

"Why did you disappear before the fun started?"

"Not in the mood." Which is putting it mildly. I was disgusted to the core.

Not by that girl.

By myself.

The fact that my thoughts veered in that direction made my skin crawl and softened any erection I could've gotten.

"I had my fun with both of them. Thanks for that." Landon leans back against his palms, not looking satiated in the least.

It's almost a routine for him now. It's probably starting to become the same way for me, too.

The satisfaction of flesh against flesh, of welts and canes, chains, and gags can only last for so long before it fades away.

Soon enough, it becomes an afterthought, a mere instinct to satisfy.

"Ready for what comes next?" Landon tilts his head. "Spoiler alert, it'll be brutal."

I give a sharp nod.

"Always a good fucking sport, Creigh. Listen up, in exchange for telling you who destroyed your biological family, here's what I want you to do…"

My muscles tighten at the prospect of finally having a name.

I never questioned what Landon's scheme behind all these little anarchies is. He's always plotting for chaos anyway, and I don't mind playing a part in it as long as I get what I want.

And to do that, I'll tune out any and all distractions.

Namely, Annika fucking Volkov.

FIVE

Annika

"ARE YOU SURE WE CAN DO THIS?"

I stare back at Cecily and grin. "Nope, but we can definitely try."

"You're going to get us killed, aren't you?" she whispers as we sneak along the mansion's garden.

"Don't be a bore, Ces. This is, like, our only chance to see inside the Heathens' place." Ava bumps her shoulder against mine and I nod, agreeing with her.

"I thought this was supposed to just be a party," Cecily whisper-yells even as she keeps her head down. Her steps are a lot more silent than ours. Like a ninja.

I peek around the corner of the mansion and then quicken my steps to the annexed house. "I know this will sound like blasphemy, but parties can get boring sometimes."

"Unless you're getting dicked down by a hot prick like Glyndon is." Ava waggles her brows.

"Are you sure you want to call someone hot when Eli has ears in the damn sky?" Cecily asks.

"Bitch, please. I couldn't care less about him."

"Shh, you guys. If any of the guards see us, they'll report back to Jer and we'll be done for. As in, expelled from the Heathens' mansion for life. Or *you* will be. I'll just go back to being a prisoner à la Rapunzel."

"Okay, okay. Is this where the fire happened?" Ava, who's wearing a gorgeous lacy pink dress that matches my purple one, leans closer to my side.

We're at that point in our friendship where we wear matching clothes in our favorite colors.

I throw a hand in the general direction of the annexed house. "Yup."

"It looks all clean, though."

"It's been more than a week. Besides, it wasn't a big fire."

"Oh!" Ava exclaims. "Show us where they do all that violent stuff. You know, where they chase people and hunt them down."

Cecily jams two fingers against her childhood friend's temple and pushes her. "There's a loose screw in your bloody head. Why would you want to see that?"

"Because it's fun, duh."

I lift a shoulder. "I don't really know the exact location for that. It can happen on the whole property."

"No, I heard the last one happened in the forest surrounding the mansion."

"You want to go to the forest at night?"

"Yes! That should be so fun."

"You're crazy." A rush of adrenaline seeps beneath my skin. "I love it."

"No, no." Cecily stops in front of us, hiking a slightly shaking hand up onto her hip. "We're not going to some doomed forest in the dark. That's where all the predators are."

"Oh, come on, Cecy, you've been studying so much psychology that you see the worst before the best. Besides, this is private property. No predators are allowed, isn't that right, Anni?"

"If you don't count the ones inside, sure. I mean, I'm not a big fan of the dark myself, but I'm open to adventures."

"Yes to adventures! Come on, Ces. It's going to be loads of fun."

"But—"

"Nuh-uh. Two to one, democracy wins."

Cecily looks like she wants to say something, but she slides her black-framed glasses up her nose and follows us down the path to the forest.

The music and chatter from the main house wanes and eventually disappears as we wander down the dirt path.

The tall trees watch our every movement like scowly guards. Due to the cloudy sky, no light illuminates our way and we have to use our phones' flashlights.

The leaves crush beneath our shoes with every step and this is seriously the worst occasion for heels.

"See? There's nothing interesting about roaming through the forest at night. Except for bad vibes and weird mojo," Cecily says fifteen minutes after we wander in. And is it just me or has she been trembling the whole time?

I've always known Cecily to be more badass than demons, so it's weird for her to shake. Maybe I'm imagining things due to my own paranoia.

"The weird mojo is probably because of all the blood that was spilt here at the initiation," Ava whispers, her tone spooked. "I heard a few participants had to go to the hospital because of how brutal it got. Maybe some even died. Do you think their souls might be here waiting for someone to possess? *Boo!*"

I jump and Cecily flinches.

Ava tips her head back in loud laughter. "You guys are such wimps, haha."

"You scared the bejesus out of me," I breathe out. "Also, isn't this scene too familiar? Oh, it's like in those horror movies when they wander into a desolate place and get killed one at a time—"

"Who's there?"

The three of us freeze at the older male voice coming from a short distance away.

Heavy footsteps crush leaves as they head in our direction.

"Shit, it must be the guards," Ava whispers.

"Run," I murmur back, and we do.

Or they do, because I'm the one with the highest heels of the bunch.

I fall behind in no time, struggling to keep up. Cecily stops and turns around, then offers her hand. "Remove the shoes."

"No way in hell. These are Gucci."

"You can just carry them, Anni," Ava says.

"But I'll hurt my feet." The thought of suffering any sort of injury and killing my potential ballet future gives me nightmares.

Though I shouldn't have worn heels in the first place. In my defense, heels are a rare indulgence, and I only own three pairs.

"I would rather be locked in my ivory tower for a few more days instead. You guys run. He's one of my brother's guards and won't do anything to me."

Cecily grabs my hand and pushes me forward, a weird expression on her face. It's how I look when I try to be brave. "We can't just leave you here."

"Jer might tolerate you now because I beg and stuff, but he will really ban you from entering the property if he finds out about this."

"I don't care."

"Well, I do. Heathens' parties are the shit. But they're not more important than Anni." Ava grabs at my other hand and I almost cry.

Due to my gilded cage and mafia princess status, most girls are simply scared to get too close to me. Not Cecily, Ava, and even Glyndon. Yes, they're scared of Jer, but not to the point where they'd avoid me because of him.

Renewed energy pulses through me and I run the rest of the way with their help. Cecily takes the lead in guiding us back to the house. She's so good with directions that she can find the way after one trip to the forest.

That and she's the only one wearing sneakers, so her movements are easier than ours.

The moment the music fills our ears again, we breathe in relief in unison. No more forest for a lifetime.

We sneak back into the main mansion and mingle with the crowd. The King's U's students are hardcore party people with a distinguished taste for debauchery. REU students love to party, too, but not in this extravagant way.

Almost everyone has shown up to this party held by the Heathens. It's even considered a privilege to be get in. Usually, Jeremy doesn't even allow me access, let alone invite my friends, but he's been somewhat lenient ever since I started showing depression signs.

I've had some growing up. Whenever I felt too suffocated, too sheltered I'd get these gray days where I can't see colors no matter how much I try.

Usually, ballet or a chance to wander outside is enough to lessen that burden.

The three of us huddle near a wall, catching our breaths, and that's when I catch glimpse of Jeremy across the room talking to Nikolai and his most trusted guard.

I hold my breath in preparation for when he'll barge in, disclose that he knows all about our sneaking about session and ground me like I'm twelve-year-old. However, he doesn't move. The gray of his eyes narrow, darkening on me.

No, not me.

Cecily?

I stare back at her and she's still slumped against the wall, breathing harshly, and completely oblivious to how my brother is looking at her as if she's at the top of his shit list.

Oh, no.

The look disappears as fast as it appeared and Jeremy climbs the stairs with his guard and Nikolai. That's when I actually release a breath.

We're safe. For *now*.

"No more wandering in the forest at night," Cecily grumbles. "I swear I lost a few years of my life."

"We'll do it in secret," Ava whispers to me.

"I heard that and it won't be happening."

Ava makes a face and Cecily just stares back. "Very mature."

"Sorry I want to live my youth to the fullest, *Mum*." Ava huffs and takes a glass from a passing waiter.

Yikes. That was probably a guard, considering the glare he threw her way. If I weren't around, he would've grabbed her by the neck and threw her out for the insolence.

She drinks a little, then stops and groans. "Holy shit. This is strong. What is it?"

"Probably pure vodka meant for Jer or Nikolai."

"I knew Heathens had the best stuff." She gathers me in a side hug. "We're lucky we didn't lose partying privileges."

"More like reckless," Cecily lets out under her breath, leaning against a pillar. Her shirt for the day has *I would rather be reading.* "Can we go back to the dorm now?"

"Hell to the no. You promised to come along, Cecy."

"Did you forget that we kind of have classes in the morning?"

"Yeah, so? Being a uni student doesn't conflict with having fun, you know. In fact, everyone but you does, Miss No-Fun."

"Don't come begging me to wake you up tomorrow when you're proper hammered."

"Pfft. Glyn will."

"Glyn, who's with her boyfriend doing God knows what?"

"It's called fucking, Ces. Repeat after me. F-U-C-K."

She gives her a blank look and Ava bursts out laughing and goes back to drinking. They all tease Cecily about being a nerd and a prude, but I find her super cool for having clear boundaries for what she likes and what she doesn't.

I wish I were as confident as she is.

"So…" I clear my throat. "I've been meaning to talk to you guys about something."

"Ooh, sounds juicy." Ava focuses on me. "What is it?"

"Remember that arranged marriage thingy that I was destined to do ever since they found out I have a vagina?"

"Those patriarchal pricks." Cecily's eyes shine with defiance.

"What she said." Ava bumps her friend's shoulder. "And? Did they pick up a husband for you at seventeen? Want us to riot in front of the US embassy? Maybe the Russian embassy, too?"

"No on all counts. Mom said she wouldn't allow it."

Cecily's expression eases. "I knew I liked your mum."

"What she said again. So is your mum going to cut a bitch in your name or should we do it?"

"I don't think any of that is needed. Mom said Papa won't let anyone force me into marriage if I have someone I love."

"Yes! Bitch, why didn't you say that before and why aren't we celebrating?"

"Hello? Because I have no one I love?"

"Well, you can find someone." Ava sighs. "Falling in love is actually easier than it sounds. Overrated, too, just saying. Not that I'm talking from experience or anything."

"Security, this one right here is a pathological liar," Cecily says.

"Am not!"

"Are, too!"

"You're delusional," Ava says, then focuses on me. "Back to the subject at hand. I'm telling you, Anni, you're like hot and smart, and I'd totally become gay for you if I had a choice. Point is, anyone can fall in love with you. All you have to do is love them back."

I lean on the pillar beside Cecily to ease the ache from my ankles and release a long sigh. "That's easier said than done. I was thinking about convincing someone to fake date me until my parents think I'm in a stable relationship. But then again, they'd see straight through my lies. Also, I would be putting the poor boy at the top of Papa and Jer's shit list. Also known as the hit list."

"You don't have to think that hard about it," Cecily says. "I'm sure if you explain it to any of your guy friends, they'll be willing to help. Jeremy won't kill them or anything."

"You obviously don't know how overprotective my brother can get."

"If the one you pick is a brilliant chap and has great conversational skills, he'll be able to win over your brother."

"And where do I find this Prince Charming, Ava?"

"Brandon! He's quite the looker, charismatic, and most importantly, he likes you. I think only as a friend, but that's enough to convince Jeremy and fly under his radar."

"I don't know. I don't want to get him hurt."

"Talk to him and see." Cecily smiles. "Remi would be willing to help, too. He's an infuriating prick, but he has a great sense of loyalty. And he can become an eloquent conversationalist when the situation requires it."

I did think about that option when I first came up with this plan, but I'm hesitant about getting someone hurt for my benefit.

"Oh, Creigh!" Ava stares ahead behind us. "What are you doing here alone? Where's your designated shadow, Remi?"

The hairs on the back of my neck stand on end and wildfire explodes on my skin.

I don't dare look behind the pillar or even take a breath.

But just because I'm hiding doesn't mean the world pauses.

Creighton strides to our small circle, one hand in his pocket and the other grasping a bottle of water.

His black T-shirt and jeans do nothing to conceal his muscular build or the power shimmering beneath the surface.

Nor does the signature blank look on his face or the coolness in his expressionless eyes.

"Remi's shagging," he announces coolly, easily.

He nods at Cecily and spares a glance in my direction. But it can't actually be called that. It's a tenth of a glance.

A mere inch of a glance.

"Ugh. That pig." Cecily shakes her head. "We're crossing Remi off the potential candidates list."

"We can add Creigh instead!" Ava grins, wrapping an arm around his shoulder. When he gives her a look, she goes on, "Anni needs a fake boyfriend to convince her family not to arrange her with some evil mafia chap. Bran is our number one candidate because he's like the best. You are, too, Creigh, but your lack of words can be a deal breaker for some."

"Yeah, not him." I force a smile and rub my foot against my calf. "That just leaves Bran. I'll go beg him on my knees."

Something flashes through Creighton's eyes. Not sure what it is, but it's raw enough to send a chill down my spine—like his text two days ago.

For the first time ever, I, Annika Volkov, found no words to type back. Not even an emoji or a GIF. I was stunned into silence.

Partly because I knew not to push when someone set clear boundaries and partly because I'm starting to think Creighton is nothing like the façade he shows to the outside world.

And while that intrigued me, it terrified me to the core as well, and I have enough self-preservation instinct to stay away from muddy situations the moment I sense them.

That feeling is repeating again, and it tunes out all the noise around us as if we're trapped in a bubble.

"We'll help," Ava says. "Bran is like my bestie."

"Everyone is your bestie," Cecily points out.

"And you're at the top and you love me." She blows her kisses to which Cecily shakes her head again.

"Why not me?"

We all pause at Creighton's calmly spoken words. He's staring at me.

Dead on.

With those darkening heterochromia eyes and that stone-cold face.

I've never been under his scrutiny to this point of suffocating intensity.

The way he looks at me now is different.

He used to regard me with annoyance, blankness, or pure indifference.

There's certainly no indifference now. It's interest, but not the good type. Hell, it might as well be the dangerous type.

"Do you want it to be you?" Cecily asks slowly, almost carefully.

"Why not me?" he repeats, still staring at me, drilling holes in my face.

"I'm sure you wouldn't be interested." I'm surprised I sound collected, considering the war raging inside me.

"What if I am?"

I almost choke on my own drool. What is wrong with him tonight? He obviously did his best to scare me away, but now he wants to be my fake boyfriend?

"No," I speak with more determination. "Bran is a better fit."

"Why?"

"Because he says more than a few clipped words per month." I smile at Ava. "I'm going to get something to drink. Want to come?"

"Sure." She interlinks her arm with mine, and once we're walking away, she whispers in my ear, "That was such a low blow. He's glaring."

I glance behind me, and sure enough, Creighton's cold gaze follows my movements, his jaw set, his wicked lips thinned in a line and his arms taut.

I can't help feeling a sense of apprehension or the lash of his anger that rolls over my skin.

It's not like I did anything wrong. I only gave him a taste of his own medicine.

Still, I cut off eye contact first, willingly losing the battle.

Something tells me I poked the monster in his cave and he might come after me.

SIX

Annika

TWO SMALL POINTY EARS, BABY WHISKERS, AND A PINK NOSE are the definition of my weakness.

I hold up the tiny striped cat in my hand and pet his head. He rubs himself against my hand and a fuzzy feeling shoots down to the marrow of my bones.

He releases a soft mewl, a cry for affection, and my heart bleeds. "I'm so sorry you lost your mommy, Tiger. I promise to take care of you until you start to wreak havoc around here."

I found him a few days ago on the side of the road in a box with three other kittens. The pouring rain and probably hunger killed all of them except for this tiny fighter. I hid him in my pocket and brought him to the animal shelter where I volunteer.

Dr. Stephanie was surprised Tiger didn't meet his siblings' tragic fate, but I was sure the little baby would survive.

"You're a fighter, aren't you?" I speak to him in a child's voice, trying not to cry at the reminder of what happened to the other kittens.

I did cry at that time. They were so small and helpless and without a mother. I'm commissioning a voodoo doll to curse the heartless monster who threw them to the side of the road.

In the meantime, I'm pledging to protect this baby with my life.

Every day, I come to help Dr. Stephanie with all the stray animals we get in the shelter, and when it's my break time, I play with Tiger.

Cecily volunteers with me—she's all for humanitarian activities—but she usually comes later, while I have to leave early or else guards would swamp this place.

But oh well, I can just talk to the animals. They're better friends than people anyway and I'd cut any bitch who tries to hurt them.

I place baby Tiger on my thigh and he tugs on my dress with his claws in his attempt to climb up. "I specifically wore cotton, you little fashion terrorist, so you won't be able to ruin it like you did the other dress."

"Are you talking to a hamster?"

My head whips up and I cease breathing.

The last person I expected to see at the shelter is standing in the doorway, or more like blocking it.

For a moment, I think maybe I'm imagining things, like that cryptic dream I had last night in which he glared at me and then disappeared.

Considering how things went down yesterday, I expected Creighton to come after me again—there was just something strange in his gaze, something absolutely nefarious—but I didn't think it'd be this soon.

"It's not a hamster, it's a cat, and his name is Tiger." I clear my throat. "What are you doing here?"

"Volunteering."

"Why?"

"Cecily asked me to."

"And you just listened?"

He doesn't reply, which is his cue that the conversation is over. But you know what? I'm done trying to impress him or get on his good side. That didn't work anyway, and I seriously want to cut ties right now, so why the hell is he making it harder?

"I find it hard to believe that you decided to volunteer just because Cecily asked you to."

"She said you were short on staff, but if that's not the case, then I can tell Dr. Stephanie you don't want me around."

"I didn't say that."

"You implied it."

I narrow my eyes and he stares at Tiger, who's fallen asleep on my lap, curled up in a ball.

He slowly slides his attention from the cat to my face. "What should I help with?"

"Ask Dr. Stephanie."

"She said to ask you."

"You can lift the bags of food and litter from the truck outside and put them with the stock."

He doesn't make a move to leave, and I desperately need to get out of his vicinity. Surely he knows that he sucks all the air out of the room whenever he's around.

Creighton might be tall, muscular, and a renowned fighter at REU, but it's his freezing stare and cold eyes that are intimidating.

"What?" I ask when he remains in place.

"What about you?"

"Me?"

"What will you do?"

"I'll go check on the animals and finish some paperwork."

"And then?"

"You're awfully talkative today."

His blank expression doesn't falter. If anything, it's cemented. "What will you do after you check on the animals?"

I purse my lips, and he regards me with that shimmering intensity again. The one that brims under the surface with the promise of exploding in a supernova of colors.

No, not colors. Probably just gray.

"Don't make me ask the question again." His voice deepens, brimming with authority.

And usually, I'd hate it. I'd try to subtly rebel against any form of a command. Not now, though.

This is different.

And I really don't want to see what happens if he asks again.

"I'll go back to school," I let out in a low murmur.

He shoves a hand in his pocket, his jaw clenching.

What is he getting mad about now? I answered his question, didn't I?

After what seems like forever, Creighton throws a glance at Tiger, who's still peacefully sleeping on my lap, then heads to the exit.

I release a long breath and hug Tiger to my chest. "What the hell is wrong with him, huh?"

The cat gives me a yawn as an answer and I shake my head before putting him back into his cage.

I get busy with work and manage to ignore the nagging emotion scratching at a corner of my heart.

After I finish some paperwork, I stretch my arms and stand up. We're really short on staff, so if I miss a day, administrative things would pile up to the point of being overwhelming.

I'm about to grab the smoothie I brought with me when a commotion from outside catches my attention.

Which is weird. Besides me, Cecily, and a few others, we barely get any volunteers. If ever. Dr. Stephanie and the two other technicians don't come out much either.

Hearing noises or conversations is rare.

Unless something happened to one of the animals?

I dash out of the small office and head to the patio leading outside.

Bubbling energy reaches me in waves as the two technicians, Harry and Zoey, and one of the volunteers, Sandy, an American who studies at my brother's university, stand there with their noses practically glued to the glass.

I inch closer to them and stop when I find the scene that's put them in a state of spellbound shock.

Outside, Creighton has removed his shirt and is lifting two heavy bags of pet food at a time.

His abs ripple with the effort and sweat glistens over honed muscles. A spider tattoo covers his left side, bleeding into the

Adonis-shaped lines on his abs. Usually, spiders would look gruesome, but on him, it's…mysterious, camouflaging something a lot deeper.

His jeans hang low on his hips, revealing defined V-lines that go down…

Down…

I force my gaze up as Sandy whistles. "If I'd known he'd volunteer, I would've come more often. Look at those lickable abs."

"I know he's a few years younger than me," Harry says in a British accent. "But I'd gladly choke on his cock."

"He looks like he has big dick energy." Zoey fans herself. "I'd be open to backdoor action any day."

"You wish, girl." Sandy nudges her shoulder with hers. "We don't study at the same college, but I go to watch him fight in the underground ring all the time. He's like at the top of the food chain. Right under Jesus."

"I wouldn't be so sure." No clue how I sound detached when a strange fire rattles my bones. "He's cold, indifferent, has the personality of the North and South Pole combined, and wouldn't talk more than two sentences, even if the queen personally conversed with him."

The three of them turn in my direction and Harry rolls his eyes. "He doesn't need to talk if he has the D. Fucking speaks louder than words, Anni."

"He's straight, Harry." *I think.*

"So? Let a guy have his crush. Don't be a spoilsport."

"Except you keep crushing on straight guys and getting your heart broken, poor lad." Zoey laughs.

He flips her off and they all focus back on Creighton, whose abs flex as he carries another bag.

The truck is almost empty.

No shit. Did he actually carry all of those bags on his own? I only meant for him to help with some. I didn't think he'd do it all himself.

A few moments later, he emerges from the building just as the sun peeks from between the clouds.

He uses his hand as a shield and stares up, one of his eyes half closed, the other becoming a glittering, liquid blue.

"Let's go give him something to drink!" Zoey exclaims. "I reckon he's thirsty from all that lifting."

"Not as much as I am." Sandy laughs.

"I'll give him my energy drink." Harry winks and the girls go back to talking about Creighton's dick.

I slowly slip from their circle, the whole scene leaving a bad taste in my mouth.

It's not a secret that Creighton is popular without even trying. Ava told me that's been the case ever since they were kids. Girls have flocked to his silent personality and stellar looks since elementary school.

That's me. I'm girls. Girls is me.

Or were me. I'm totally over him now.

Totally.

I work for some time, then I make sure the animals have their food. After I kiss Tiger goodbye, I leave the shelter.

The distance to campus is about ten minutes by car, but I prefer to walk the half hour and clear my head.

It helps that the seaside is on the way and I can get lost in its beauty. It's violent today, considering how the giant waves crash against the rocks.

I try not to think about the scene I left back at the shelter, but it keeps niggling at the edge of my consciousness.

So I pull out my AirPods and put on Tchaikovsky's third symphony on the highest volume, hoping it'll be able to drown out the restlessness.

Ten minutes later, I feel more balanced. No surprise there. Only my Tchaikovsky is able to do that.

A presence appears behind me and warmth radiates off my back. I whirl around, my breath catching when my eyes clash with Creighton's chest—that's covered with a shirt, thank Tchaikovsky.

I pull out an AirPod and breathe harshly. "You scared me."

"You didn't wait so we could go back to campus together." His low, rich voice vibrates through me as he falls in step beside me.

"We never said we'd go back together."

"Why else would I ask you what you were doing?"

"I don't know. Making conversation?"

"I don't talk without purpose."

Oh, so that's what this is all about? I mean, yeah, he doesn't talk, no matter how much I try to push him, but maybe that's really because he finds no purpose in speaking for the sake of speaking.

"There was a purpose behind all those questions?"

He nods, his dark lashes lowering like a prison against ocean eyes.

"And what was it?" I pull out my second AirPod and place them back in their case, then throw them in my bag.

"Don't ask Bran to be your fake boyfriend."

My hand pauses on the zipper before I slowly close it, and my steps falter until I fall behind. My face feels frozen as I stare up at him. "What?"

"You heard me."

"Yeah, I did. Which brings on the question: what makes you think you have the right to tell me what to do?"

He comes to an abrupt halt and I crash against him before I jump back. When he spins around and stares down at me, his face has tightened and his hand is in his pocket again.

As if he's stopping it from doing something.

What, I don't know.

"I won't repeat myself another time."

My breath catches. Just how the hell does he manage to pack so much punch and dominance behind his words?

"Seriously, what do you want from me, Creighton? You pushed me away, didn't you?"

"And you pushed back."

"What?" When he remains silent, I insist, "I did no such thing. I put distance between us as you so eloquently instructed. I don't even text you anymore. This isn't how it's supposed to work."

"*This?*"

"Scaring me away, then talking to me and volunteering at the shelter I go to. Is this like a game of push and pull or something?"

"Were you scared away?"

"Wasn't I supposed to be?"

"You were, but I'm surprised it took that little to scare you."

"Yeah, well, pain frightens me."

His eyes shine with something similar to…excitement.

And that right there scares the bejesus out of me. It's not normal excitement like the type I get whenever I go shopping or when I practice ballet. It's nothing that innocent or harmless.

That look in his eyes is downright demented.

Is he supposed to be thrilled at the prospect of frightening someone?

"Don't ask Bran or anyone else to be your fake boyfriend," he repeats, with an edge this time.

"And if I refuse to follow your demands, which are super illogical, by the way?"

He steps closer until his chest nearly brushes against mine and grabs my jaw with his thumb and forefinger, imprisoning me in place. "Then you'll be acquainted with the pain you're so scared of."

SEVEN

Creighton

OVER THE PAST WEEK, I'VE BEEN ON THE EDGE OF something dark and absolutely nefarious.

The urge I've controlled so well ever since I hit puberty has been seeping into my nightmares, my meal time, and my fighting time.

All my time.

It has heightened, magnified, and reached altitudes that even I am unable to shove into the hollowness of my soul.

And the reason is none other than the girl sitting across from me.

The guardian of her hell, Jeremy, allowed her to spend the night in REU's dorm. We're in the apartment she shares with my cousin, the silver angel, and the girl my brother is obsessed with.

Usually, Remi drags me to these nights with a lot of begging and a bribe in the form of fish and chips. Tonight, however, no begging happened.

The fish and chips are nonnegotiable, though.

I take a bite and slap Lan's hand when he tries to snag a piece.

"Stingy bitch," he mutters under his breath.

"And what are you doing here?" Bran asks him from the other side of me after they deliberately put me between them.

"Can't I hang out with my brother and sister and friends?"

"Friends?" Bran tuts, seeming disgusted. "Since when do you have those?"

"I have a friend." He nudges my shoulder, but I ignore him, so he stares at the opposite side where Cecily and Ava are bickering with Remi while Glyn tries to mediate. "Isn't that right, Ces?"

She stops in the middle of cursing Remi, drags her fingers through her grandma-like hair, and smiles. "Sure."

Hopelessly pathetic.

I've gone out of my way to warn her about Landon ever since we were in secondary school. But the chances of her actually listening are slim to zero.

Due to the fact that I only speak when it's absolutely necessary and after I allow my brain to mull over my words, I notice things. Patterns, lingering gazes, and unresolved obsessions.

It's how I knew Glyn was into Killian long before he staked a public claim on her. Hell, long before she admitted it to herself.

Despite her reserved nature, Cecily actually yearns for Ava's openness and what Glyn has with the Heathens' psychopath.

She just went the wrong way about it. She still is.

In spite of my warnings.

Cecily is one of the purest souls to ever exist with enough heart to fit the globe. When we were young, she defended me every time someone made fun of me. Not that I cared, but I won't forget how she told me 'I'll protect you, Creigh. That's what friends are for.'

I tried to protect her, too, from the monster on my right, to no avail.

This is why I make it my mission not to get involved in anything that doesn't concern me. People call it heartless; I call it preserving my time.

"See." Landon grins at his brother. "I have a friend, so I'm staying for Cecily's beautiful eyes."

She blushes. I fix her with my signature blank look and she lowers her head.

"If you're not leaving, I will," the nicer of the twins says.

"Bran, don't." Glyn leaves her plate and goes to her brother's side, then strokes his arm. "Come on, it's so rare for us to get together."

"You heard our little princess." Landon pats his sister's head.

She makes a face at him and he grins back.

Bran is half convinced but keeps throwing daggers at a terribly amused Lan.

The more they show disgust or any sort of hostility, the more he enjoys tormenting the hell out of them. Just because he can.

Chaos ensues, more talking, more dramatics, more fucking noise.

My gaze fixates on the reason behind my sour mood and the darkness that's been slowly but surely occupying my every waking and sleeping moment.

Annika nibbles on some chips as she sits elegantly on the sofa, both legs bent to the side. She's wearing a fluffy pajama set that has a cat on it.

Her hair is gathered in a ponytail with a matching purple band.

A ponytail that I've been imagining all the ways I can grab onto it as I throw her down on the nearest surface and mark that flawless skin with red welts. They'd look striking against her dewy pale skin.

She'd look at me with that tangible fear and maybe tears.

She'd be so scared, she'd cry and beg me to stop, but I'd do everything except for stopping.

I've had these depraved fantasies for the opposite sex ever since I hit puberty, but they were never about a specific woman.

Any female would do as long as she was ready to take the lash of my whips and submit to my chains.

This is the first time I've had a face for all those fantasies. And a body I've imagined in all positions as my cock pounded and pounded, and fucking pounded until she screamed.

Annika isn't supposed to be the face of my twisted fantasies. I meant it when I tried to scare her away.

She's an innocent girl who's not fit for my taste of fucked up.

But then she had the fucking audacity to say that she'll take a boyfriend. A fake one—not that it mattered—and will be playing Hollywood with him in front of her brother.

And the little fucking minx also dared to exclude me from her unorthodox arrangement.

She was the one who roamed around me with the perseverance of a bee for weeks on end, suffocating me with her violet scent and blinding me with all the purple. And now, she pretends I'm not even on the menu?

Not on my watch.

And yes, the change of attitude might have started when I imagined another man touching her and my vision became red. The need for violence scratched and clawed at the surface of my sanity, demanding retribution. And no, it didn't matter that the ones I would've been committing murder against were Remi and Bran.

As if feeling my gaze on her, Annika lifts her head and her glittering blue-gray eyes clash with mine. They're so innocent, so full of life, and it shouldn't be right that I want to fill them with tears. Pleasure tears. Fear tears. I don't give a fuck at this point.

Her pouty lips fall open, probably at seeing whatever emotion slipped to my face, and it takes all my control not to stuff them with my fingers and watch as they quiver.

She swiftly cuts off eye contact and takes over Glyn's mediating position in the never-ending cat and mouse game Remi, Ava, and Cecily like to play.

"Come on, spawn, help me with these crazy cougars," Remi calls for me for the thousandth time tonight.

I ignore him. Again.

"I swear on my lordship's name that I'm revoking parental rights. Go look for someone else to translate your thoughts without you having to speak."

"Hmph. I can do that just fine." Cecily lifts her nose into the air. "Creigh and I volunteer at the same shelter and I always talk to the other staff on his behalf."

What started as a decision on the spur of the moment has become part of my schedule now.

At first, I only went to that shelter to learn more about the doll-like girl who's actually a mafia princess but has not one criminal trait in her bones.

The girl treats animals like a mother would treat her baby, for fuck's sake.

Then I noticed that the more I showed up, the more annoyed she became. And I like getting on her last nerve, catching her glaring at me, or watching me with that puzzled expression.

Besides, many students started volunteering at the shelter soon after I joined. Cecily said it's because of me and that I should stay.

Who am I to say no to such a great cause?

It's been almost a week, and I've been going there every single day, deliberately sacrificing my sleeping time.

"Spawn! You have it in you to betray me with this me wannabe? You can try for an eternity to dress like me, walk, talk and act like me. You might be the next best thing, but not quite me."

"Wait. Isn't that Eminem?" Ava asks.

"Point is, I'm wounded, spawn," he says in his overdramatic voice. "And here I thought I was your favorite. Now I need to go find me another spawn who's willing to follow my lordship's teachings. I'll take candidates starting now. No pushing, I can't accept everyone."

No one comes forward and he laughs. "Don't be shy. I know I'm intimidating, but I can be cool as fuck."

Annika inches forward and opens her mouth. There's a tidbit I've learned about her during the time we've spent together in this unholy group. She doesn't like seeing anyone in a vulnerable state and is always game to sacrifice herself for it.

Either that or she's seriously considering Remi for the position of her fake prick.

I'm not ready to find out which it is. Before any words come out, I say, "You already have me. Why would you look for someone else?"

"Right!" He points at me with a laugh. "I knew I was still your favorite and no attempts from the crazy cougars will be able to tear us apart. Hear that, nerd? You mean *nothing*."

"And you think you do?" Cecily throws right back.

Ava holds out both hands. "Time out! Ces, don't you think we have something more important to discuss, especially now that everyone is here?"

"Oh, right, of course." Cecily sits beside Annika and Ava takes the other side. "We're gathered here today for an important reason that's a bit more pressing than choking the life out of Remi. Our friend, Anni, needs someone to pretend to be her boyfriend for enough time to convince her family not to arrange a marriage for her. Who's up for it?"

Annika stares at me with wide eyes and I narrow mine. I specifically told her to erase this idea out of her head, and by association, out of Cecily's and Ava's heads.

"No funny business in the fake dating." Ava points a finger at my cousin. "I'm talking about you, Remi."

"Define funny business, love." He grins mischievously, and I can feel that tension rising in my compressed throat.

The darkness shimmers from the background, threatening to devour everything in its wake.

"No, you're out," Cecily tells Remi. "Like, totally out."

"Why the hell are you the one who decides that? It should be Anni! From the potential candidates present, I'm the most handsome, duh, and would make the best boyfriend material."

"Your arrogance is astounding."

"Thanks, my lady."

"That wasn't a compliment, Remi."

"Whatever. All I'm saying is that the girl of the hour should choose. Out of everyone present, who do you want to be your fake boyfriend, Anni?"

Her eyes meet mine again, bright, so fucking bright that it's blinding. She sinks her teeth into her bottom lip, chewing, biting, waiting.

My jaw tightens as other images fill my mind. All of them start with her trapped beneath me with no way out.

There won't be any nibbling or chewing. There'll be slapping, throwing, choking, flogging, gagging, fucking, fucking, and more fucking until I tear her tiny little cunt.

Christ.

The fuck is wrong with me lately?

She releases her lip, all red and plump from how much she bit on it. "If he's willing to help, and it's in no way an obligation, of course, but if I had to choose, it'd be Brandon."

My fist tightens on the fork and I'm surprised it doesn't snap in two from the ferocity of my grip. My jaw flexes and my muscles stiffen until I'm no different than a rock.

The only thing stopping me from hauling her onto my lap right at this moment is the knowledge that I would break her skin. No doubt about it.

The clever little minx avoids my gaze completely, knowing full well that she fucked up.

But she doesn't know to what extent.

Annika just unleashed the last bit of control I've been conjuring for weeks.

My soul craves the darkness and that's exactly what I'll give it.

"I'm sorry to say this, but you have a terrible taste in men, Anni." Remi flips his hair back. "But then again, my lordship was never meant for fake anything."

"I'm honored you chose me." Bran smiles. "I'd be happy to help—"

He's cut off when I stand up abruptly. This time, Annika looks at me with terrified eyes.

The right eyes.

I don't say a word as I turn around and leave.

She can have her fun all she wants—or think she is.

It won't matter one bit once I have her at my mercy.

One thing's for certain. I'll keep my promise.

Annika Volkov's pain will be mine.

EIGHT

Annika

I'M LOSING IT.

My pulse quickens, my ears prickle, and my limbs shake at the faintest sound.

It's been this way since last night.

Ever since Creighton looked at me with that frightening heat, metaphorically stripped me, and then stood and left.

But not before he issued that warning with a mere gaze.

It's crazy how expressive his eyes can get when he puts in the effort. In a fraction of a second, they'll morph from blank and absolutely indifferent to scorching lava.

I kept tossing and turning in bed last night, staring at the window and the door. For some reason, I thought he'd ambush at night, when the world sleeps and he's camouflaged by the darkness.

Like the night he committed arson in my brother's house.

The anticipation kept me awake, tossing and turning in bed with my heart pulsing in my throat.

I refuse to address or put a name to the feeling that's been sinking in my stomach since this morning.

After school, I go to the shelter with Tchaikovsky's *Swan Lake* blasting in my ear. It takes an inhuman effort to stop myself from dancing in sync with the music.

It's quiet today, with dejection floating in the air because their resident 'Hot Stuff' didn't show up. Yes, we have more volunteers, thanks to him, but it's inconvenient when their entire work ethic is centered on his presence—or lack thereof. Oh, and his six-pack. Harry started a whole group chat where they share half-naked pictures of him and bicker over who's going to worship his 'huge dick' first. Seriously, not one of them has seen his dick, so that's a total overstatement.

In no time, he has a fan club, fanatics, and antis—the latter being only me at the moment. I'm just in that group to grasp hold of the situation, nothing more.

And he does get half naked a lot. If I didn't know he was aloof to a fault, I would swear he's doing it on purpose.

If it were up to me, I'd kick him out of the shelter so that we can get our peaceful atmosphere back. However, if I do voice that thought, I'll be stoned to death by the fanatics.

Even Dr. Stephanie appreciates all the helping hands.

I play with Tiger for a bit, exchange some small talk with the other volunteers, and then I get busy list-checking the stock in the storage room.

Since no one usually comes in here, I put my Tchaikovsky on speaker and twirl as I move from one aisle to the other.

My feet tingle and burst with inexplicable energy. I've always loved dancing, to the point that Mom had no choice but to teach me and enroll me in ballet classes when I was four years old.

Sometimes, it feels like I'm putting that talent to waste by choosing to go to college. Other times, I remember that I love ballet for ballet, for moments like these where it allows me to purge negative energy. It's not for stardom or for people to watch me.

Yes, I'm a people person, but not in that sense.

As the music reaches a crescendo, I open my arms and twirl on pointe across the aisle.

Then, in that moment of excitement, I slam into a wall.

No, not a physical wall—a wall of muscle.

The music starts a slow descent, completely at odds with the chaos brewing inside me.

A merciless hand grabs my elbow to stop me from toppling over. I stare up at his ethereally gorgeous face, at the lips that rest in a line, completely devoid of emotion.

He's a cold god whose only language is disapproval.

A predator whose sole purpose is trapping prey.

That's currently me.

My breasts are smashed against the hard muscles of his chest. Our bodies have collided in a mesh of strength against softness.

In this position, the difference in size is too great to ignore. I'm so small compared to him that he could easily break and stomp all over me.

Leave me absolutely wrecked.

The skin where his fingers are touching my elbow sparks in a million fires, expanding all the way to my chest.

I've always heard about overwhelming tension, the type that lingers like a weight at the back of one's throat and robs them any semblance of sanity and logical thinking.

But I never imagined it would be this…frightening.

This powerful.

And I need out of his orbit. *Now.*

I try to pull my elbow free, but it might as well be caught in a trap.

So I force my lips into a smile that probably looks awkward at best. "Oh, hi. I didn't know you were coming today. You should probably go out and greet the fangirls and fanboy, Harry. They've been dejected thinking you wouldn't be here—"

"Shut up."

My lips slam shut in an attempt to actually stay quiet. Just two words are enough to stiffen my spine. All the anxiety from tossing and turning and staring at my balcony last night crashes back into me.

"You truly fucked up, Annika." He pushes me backward with his commanding hold on my elbow. "I told you to give up on the fake boyfriend idea, but you went ahead and provoked me. You. Fucked. Up. You're lucky I didn't jump through your window and turn your skin red."

A gasp echoes in the air and I realize it's mine as my back hits one of the shelves. Creighton still has my elbow hostage, his body pressed against mine.

I'm sure he can feel my heaving chest and hear my choked breaths that rise over the sound of the music.

This is the first time I've witnessed this side of him, and it's eliciting all sorts of emotions—fear, dread, but also thrill and anticipation.

The type I've never experienced before.

"What did I say would happen if you didn't do as you were told?" His deep voice floats in the air and lands on my constricting chest.

I gulp the saliva that's gathered in my mouth. For the first time, he's the talkative one and I'm speechless, grappling for words and finding nothing.

"What the fuck did I say, Annika?"

I flinch at the whip of his commanding words and blurt, "That you would acquaint me with pain."

The words are barely out of my mouth when he spins me around. A yelp escapes me as he grabs hold of my ponytail and shoves my head against a plastic bag of dog food.

That's when I realize that I'm bent over, ass in the air, with him right behind me.

Strong fingers lift the skirt of my dress to my waist and a gust of air hits my bottom. Goosebumps erupt on my skin in terrifying succession and my temperature rises until I'm boiling.

"You should've listened, little purple. You really shouldn't have provoked me." He strokes his hand across my ass cheek and over my lace panties. His touch is sure, dominant, disallowing even an ounce of resistance.

I try to stare back, wanting—no, *needing*—to see his expression. The grip on my hair tightens, letting me know who's in complete control here.

"You've been wiggling this little arse for weeks and it's time to discipline it." His chest covers my back—heavy, hot, and powerful. Then his whisper follows in my ear, "And you."

"Creigh…" His name comes out like a haunted whisper. "Please."

I don't know what I'm begging for. For him to stop? To take this a step further? Test my limits to the point where I won't be able to come back from this?

What exactly?

He pushes off me, his body heat leaving mine, but his merciless grip remains on my ponytail. "I didn't ask you to beg yet. When I do, it'll be much worse than this."

What—

My thoughts are interrupted by his firm command, "Now, count to ten or we'll start from scratch."

A slap echoes in the air and my mouth opens in a wordless gasp. Pain erupts on my ass cheek, hot and fierce. But I don't even focus on that when his hand meets my flesh again, harder than the first time.

So hard that my front bumps against the shelves and my legs shake.

"I don't hear you counting." His voice has darkened, becoming shadowy and rich with dominance. "We'll go again."

The slap collides with the mounting music and I whimper, "One."

He smacks my ass again and a sob tears from my throat, mixed with the crescendo of the song and my raw breathing.

"T-two."

The air is weighed down with a cloak of depravity and twisted emotions. I never imagined I would be in this position, held down, ass in the air, being spanked.

But maybe this is exactly what I've been yearning to learn ever since he warned me away.

Ever since he told me about his deviant tastes.

Maybe this is why I provoked him. I didn't do it on purpose, but deep down, in the black corners of my mind, I wanted to see him... *snap*.

I just had no idea that it'd be this brutal. Or that I would have this foggy reaction to it.

His hand comes down on my flesh again with the ruthlessness of a whip.

"From now on, when I tell you to do something, you do it." *Slap.*

"If I warn you, you don't ignore me." *Slap.* "You'll listen to fucking orders." *Slap.* "You *will* obey me." *Slap.*

"Three, f-four, five, six." I grab onto the shelves with a death grip. My nails dig into the metal as sweat trickles down my back.

My pretty purple dress is all crumpled and squashed by his overwhelming ruthlessness, but that's the least of my worries.

Tears sting my eyes, and it's not only because of the pain.

Tchaikovsky almighty. I really hope it's only due to the throbbing of my assaulted ass.

My thighs clench and my core aches, pulsating with an animalistic need. When he slaps me three times in a row again, I rock forward, bumping my clit against the shelf below.

Bursts of pleasure knot the base of my stomach and I close my eyes, my voice turning deeper, erotic. "Seven, eight, nine."

My breaths form condensation on the metal and I welcome the small reprieve and the break from pain.

He slaps my ass, and I haven't even finished whispering "Ten" when he shoves my thighs apart in one motion. His fingers dig into my skull and he yanks me back with his grip on my hair, forcing my eyes to shoot open.

The back of my head rests on his hard chest as he whispers in my ear with chill-inducing intensity, "You haven't earned the right to come."

I twist my head the slightest bit, and for the first time since he started his 'punishment,' I'm able to see his face.

And I'm not ready for the scene.

It's like I'm looking at an entirely different person. His breaths are ragged, causing his chest to inflate and deflate in a rapid rhythm that still simmers with calm, and his face—damn his stone-cold face that's caught in eternal blankness and oozes control to the brim.

His eyes, however, tell a completely different story. Yes, there's that display of dominance, sadism even, but they're masking something a lot deeper.

An emotion a lot darker.

And I wish I could reach inside him and tug those emotions out. Even if that means I'd get swooped up in the process.

My assaulted ass rubs against his jeans and I whimper, both at the pain and the expression on his face.

Though the first has dimmed compared to the throbbing between my legs.

His jaw clenches and his eyes flash to my parted lips. "I thought pain scared you, so how come you get off on it?"

I try to shake my head, but it's impossible with his grip on my hair.

"I can smell your arousal. It's permeating the fucking air." His fingers spread against my panties. "When did you become this soaking wet, hmm? Was it before or after I spanked your little arse? Maybe during? Did you get turned on by the thought of being owned by me? Did you picture my cock tearing through your cunt until you screamed and choked on my name?"

My lips part.

Holy. *Shit.*

Who thought the quiet Creighton had such a dirty mouth? It's almost like I'm meeting another version of him.

One whose every secret I want to unwrap and flounder in every splash of its darkness.

My hips rock against his hand, basically dry humping him, and he doesn't remove it. Instead, his fingers push my panties to the side and glide against my folds.

His voice lowers against my earlobe. "Now is the time to beg."

My heart nearly jumps in my throat as I murmur, "Please."

"Please what? Say the whole sentence."

Damn it. I've never spoken such vulgar words out loud, but I don't really have a choice now.

He has me completely at his mercy.

"P-please make me come."

His jaw tics once, twice, and then he shoves two fingers inside me. I reel from the pressure as it mounts and mounts until I'm unable to breathe.

The stimulation from earlier rushes to the surface and I reach a hand out and grab onto his side, my nails sinking in his shirt.

"Hand down," he orders in a frigid voice, and I let go. My arms lie limp at my sides as a knot forms in my chest.

His thumb teases my clit with staggering expertise. He's not only dominant, but he also knows exactly what he's doing and how. I've used a few toys and my fingers before, but none of them compare to the wild intensity that's shaking my limbs.

Pleasure bursts through me all at once and I have no hope to last. My raw moans overlap with the music as I fall apart around his fingers.

The wave submerges me and the pulsing welts on my ass elongate the pleasure, making it more potent.

By the time I come down from it, Creighton is staring at me with that suffocating darkness again.

That need for more.

More.

And *more*.

At this point, I'm not sure I can stop him from taking what he wants.

Hell, maybe I'll even enjoy it.

His lashes lower, blocking his emotions, as he slides his fingers out and steps back. My legs wobble and I use the shelves as an anchor to remain standing.

My harsh breathing fills the storage room and it's only then I realize someone could've walked in and seen the entire unorthodox scene.

Shit.

Creighton shoves a hand in his jeans pocket and glares at me, and the look is enough to make me shiver.

What's wrong with him now? He looks even more tense than when he walked into the storage room.

And he's suppressing something again. What, I don't know.

"Defy me again and this punishment will look like child's play in comparison to what I'll do to you."

NINE

Annika

IT'S A MIRACLE THAT I MANAGE TO REACH THE DORM WITHOUT having an accident.

I haven't been able to focus on anything except for the throbbing pain in my ass, the clenching of my thighs in remembrance, and the tightening in my chest.

Something must be wrong with me.

Seriously wrong.

Because I can't help replaying what happened in the storage room over and over until I choke on the carnal memories.

Until my heart threatens to burst and my head fills with all sorts of depraved theories.

And images.

His hand on my ass, his fingers inside me, my hair at his mercy. My whole body homed in on his ruthless dominance.

I've always thought I would be the type who likes respectful sex, the 'can we do it tonight' sex, the 'we'll have a date, then eat and touch each other in the dark' type.

So what if I somehow ended up watching hardcore porn once or twice—okay, maybe a few times. That was only curiosity, a fantasy, and had nothing to do with my real-life preferences.

But those preferences and every single perception I had about myself have been shattered to pieces in a single encounter with Creighton.

He reached inside and yanked out a part of me I didn't even know existed. It was hidden right beneath the surface, waiting for a natural disaster of Creighton's caliber to finally show itself.

I tiptoe inside the apartment I share with the girls, then stop just past the threshold. Why do I need to sneak around as if I'm doing something wrong?

Truth is, a sense of corruption reeks from my every pore, not to mention that I'm a little bit filthy in the best ways possible.

"Anni!"

I jump slightly, then school my reaction and smile as Ava waltzes in my direction, holding something in her hand.

"Someone dropped this in the mailbox with your name on it. Do you think it's poison?"

My lips part and my vision fills with the tube of ointment in her hand. No one else would know I need this except for the one person who gave me a reason to use it.

"Earth to Anni?" Ava waves a hand in front of my face.

"Uh, I don't think so." I subtly pull it from between her fingers. "I'll throw it away, just in case."

"Yeah, good call. Looks fishy as hell."

"I'll go change." I step past her, thankful that she doesn't see the emotion on my face. Hell, I would've sworn she'd comment on my crumpled dress and possibly see the handprints her childhood friend gave me.

"Wait."

My breath catches in my throat. Please don't tell me she's seen something more incriminating.

I hold on to my cool as I turn around to face her with my usual smile. "What's up?"

"I know I'm supposed to fix something for dinner, but I don't want to. Can we order instead?"

Phew. "Sure thing. I can cook if you want."

"No, definitely not, I mean no." She's quick to wave my offer away.

I narrow my eyes. "My food is edible, you know."

"Not to humans. Seriously, Anni, I love you, but you're not made for cooking. Just stick with your fresh salads."

"Creighton ate my food just fine," I grumble. Though it was only once and not in front of me.

"That one eats anything, including dog food if he finds it."

I tuck my hair behind my ear. "Do you know why he has that weird fixation about food?"

"Not really. It's been there since we were kids."

Sometimes, I envy Ava and the others for having known a younger Creighton. But then again, Cecily said his personality isn't drastically different, so on second thought, it's probably better that I didn't meet him back then.

He would've either friend-zoned me to death or broken my heart into irreparable pieces.

He could still break it now.

I smother that thought in the dark corners of my mind and focus on Ava. "Like his silence, I assume."

"Totally. Creigh is a man of few words because he simply doesn't feel like talking. And I know he might seem standoffish and cold, but he can be super caring."

My ass throbs and I mutter, "You must be talking about a different Creighton than the one I know."

"Nope." Ava leans against the wall and tilts her head back, eyes seeming lost in another universe. "He was there for me during a dark moment. He didn't say anything, just sat beside me and let me use his shoulder to cry my eyes out on, like a brother would, and I will never forget that."

This is the first time I've seen Ava so pensive. In pain, even. I want to ask what that dark moment was, but I don't want to come on too strong or to intrude.

My friend shakes her head and narrows her eyes on me. "Wait a minute, you flirt. Why are we talking about Creigh when you wanted to fake date Bran last night? Ces and I even put in a good word for you, you know. Bran doesn't like dating that much, since all the girls go to him because they can't get Lan. And if they actually liked him for himself, they'd change lanes to the evil twin as soon as they meet Lan. I'm on a mission to stab those blind little bitches in the eyes for hurting Bran."

I bite the corner of my lip. "So…uh, I've thought about it and I don't want Bran hurt by my brother, after all. He doesn't deserve it."

And he's definitely not the one who haunts my nightmares. Last night, I texted him and told him that he doesn't have to be my fake boyfriend, and he replied that he's always around if I need him.

Seriously, the world doesn't deserve such a gentle soul like Brandon. Now, if his cousin were a bit similar, things would be way easier.

But no, I had to be interested in the resident mute of the King family.

"Bran is, like, the most eloquent ever," Ava argues. "He could totally convince Jeremy."

"That means he'd be dragged into the Heathens' games."

"So? He's a big boy. He can handle himself."

"Have you seen the way Nikolai looks at him?"

Ava visibly shudders. "That psycho looks at everyone like they're on his shit list."

"Yeah, but it's different with Bran."

"Different how?"

"Bad different. Nikolai has a serious thirst for blood and violence, and he might be my brother's close friend, but I keep as far away from him as possible. I'm simply not putting Bran in his path. I'd never forgive myself if he were to end up being hurt because of me."

"Aww. You're like the sweetest." Ava strokes my arm, then steps back. "I'm telling you this because I really love you, Anni. Creigh is like the hardest nut to crack, after his stone of a brother, but I think you're getting there."

"I-I am?"

"Hello? He was super pissed when you didn't consider him for the fake boyfriend position *and* then picked Brandon."

"That's nothing."

"That's interest, bitch. And believe me, Creigh never shows that in anything that isn't food." She caresses my arm again. "Not sure if gaining his interest is a good or a bad thing. Scratch that, totally bad. He's a King, after all, and they kind of have a twisted family aura, except for Glyn and Bran."

The handprints on my ass tingle in pain as if agreeing with Ava's words.

"Good luck. You're totally going to need it." She steps away from me and grins. "Be right back. I'll go convince Cecily to let us order in tonight."

As she jogs to our friend's room, I disappear into mine and close the door behind me. I let my bag fall to the ground and stand facing the full-length mirror with a neon purple frame.

I lift the skirt of my dress and wince when the fabric rubs against my sore bottom. Turning sideways, I inspect the angry red handprints Creighton left on my ass and my upper thighs.

My fingers subconsciously ghost over them and I wince again when my cold skin makes contact. I continue to touch them, gently poke at them, reveling in the small bursts of pain and the memories they trigger.

I can still smell him, that spiciness and clean scent. I can feel his weight, his sheer size, and the absolute dominance he held over me.

My core pulses back to life, recalling the methodical way he brought me pleasure I've never experienced before.

Hell, I didn't know that type of carnal claiming even existed.

I flinch when I touch an especially painful spot. It'll hurt like a mother to sit or sleep on my backside for days to come.

And yet, for some reason, I'm looking forward to it.

The ache will bring back those fresh memories that somehow refuse to leave my subconscious.

I stare at the tube in my palm, open it, and apply some ointment on my ass. The pain becomes too much sometimes and I get on my tiptoes, inhale deeply, and then continue.

By the time I'm done, I think I'll either cry or come again.

After changing into comfy pajamas, I grab my phone and lie on the bed on my stomach with my legs in the air.

I check my notifications, reply to Mom's daily text and to a few others, then I open my Instagram.

After sending a few likes and typing some comments, I click on Remi's profile.

Since Creighton is completely, absolutely, and irrevocably against having any sort of social media, Remi's account is the closest thing to getting updates on him.

Considering Remi's religious nature about posting updates, I'm sure there'll be something there…

Sure enough, he shares a selfie where he's in the middle of three guys. Two of them are the twins, Landon and Brandon. One is smirking, the other is smiling. The fourth is the mysterious Eli King, Creighton's oldest brother and the reason Ava gets defensive whenever his name is mentioned.

In the background, Creighton sleeps while sitting on a chair.

I pinch the picture to zoom in on him. How can someone look criminally gorgeous even when he's sleeping? I've always found Creighton hot, but that has long since bypassed the superficial beauty and reached new depths.

Dangerous depths.

He's wearing the same clothes from earlier and since the picture was posted ten minutes ago, that means he got home.

Ava told me the five of them live in the mansion that's dedicated to the Elites. They throw parties, too, or more like Remi does, but neither Ava, Cecily, nor Glyn ever wants to go there.

Not even when I told them I was curious about what their mansion looked like.

Seriously, they're okay with tagging along with me to go to The King's U, but when it's their own club, they're suddenly not interested.

I release the picture to read Remi's caption.

Rare as fuck picture of these fuckers together. Thank me later, fangirls. Also, we're so going to paint Creigh's face with a permanent marker. Think he'll look good with a mustache?

Smiling, I like the picture and comment.

annika-volkov: I'm sure he will. Share pictures.

It's only fair after the map of handprints he left on my ass then went to sleep as if nothing had happened. How dare he?

Remi replies to my comment immediately.

lord-remington-astor: Your wish is my command, my lady. Stay tuned.

I smile and go back to scrolling through my IG feed, then switch to TikTok. I'm about to post one of my drafts when a text appears at the top of my screen.

My heart skips a beat at his name and I'm seriously wondering if this is even a logical reaction anymore?

The text is a photo of Remi. Sulking. Wearing an ugly mustache drawn with a marker.

Creighton: I heard you wanted pictures.

Annika: I didn't suggest it, he did, and I only played along.

Creighton: Don't play along next time.

Annika: Or what?

My heart beats in my ears as I type the words.

Creighton: Your arse knows the exact answer to that. Don't be a brat.

Well, damn.

He has no right to sound so hot when telling me not to be a brat. I can even imagine his lowered tone if he were to say the words.

In an attempt to ease the ache that's blossomed between my thighs, I slide onto the bed and retrieve the ointment, then take a picture and send it over.

Annika: Do you give these to everyone you spank?

Creighton: Only the brats.

My chest aches and I refuse to honor the feeling crawling inside me with a name. Or even my attention.

And no, I'm not going to think about how many women have experienced what I did. That what I consider an awakening of sorts is a normal occurrence for him.

I'm simply *not* going there.

Annika: I thought the whole purpose of punishment was me feeling pain.

Creighton: It is. But I don't want it to bruise. Not for long, at least. That way, I can mark it again.

Annika: That started swoony and turned creepy real fast. Oh, and by the way, I'm better. Still sore as hell, but I'll survive. Thanks for asking.

Creighton: Watch it.

Annika: So I'm just supposed to take it and shut up?

Creighton: Preferably.

Annika: Well, that's not me.

Creighton: Don't I know it.

Annika: And you're okay with it?

Creighton: I'm not.

My chest aches again, that familiar pain becoming more potent than the one on my ass.

Annika: But you still insist on pursuing me.

Creighton: I wouldn't call it pursuing.

Annika: Then what is it?

Creighton: I'm punishing you, little purple, and I'm getting off on every moment of putting my mark on your translucent skin.

I rub my foot again on my leg. Somehow, the throbbing between my legs has gotten worse and my ass feels like it's on fire.

He's a true sadist, isn't he?

Then why am I not more scared? Hell, the least I can do is stop being intrigued.

Creighton: Is that smart mouth of yours finally speechless?

Annika: Not in this lifetime. I was just thinking.

Creighton: About?

Annika: One: Why do you call me little purple?

Creighton: Aren't you obsessed with that color?

Annika: But you aren't.

Creighton: In my mind, you are the personification of that color.

I try not to blush, but considering the heat in my cheeks, I've definitely failed.

Creighton: That's one. What's two?

Annika: When did you start having these...singular tastes?

Creighton: Since I hit puberty.

Annika: So you've been experimenting since?

Though I wouldn't call his lashes experimental. He knew exactly what he was doing. Despite the pain from his handprints, they're not meant to leave a permanent mark.

Which means he's done this countless times before.

To a dozen other girls. Maybe more.

Nope, no. I'm simply not going there.

Creighton: Not experimenting, engaging.

Annika: With girlfriends?

Creighton: With sex partners.

Annika: As in, whores?

Annika: Sorry, I mean sex workers?

Creighton: No. Willing submissives.

My fist tightens at the thought of how many submissives have gotten on their knees, taken his beatings, and thanked him for it later.

Hell, if the fangirls at the shelter knew he was this kinky, they'd be like 'Choke me, Daddy.'

Annika: And are you still seeing these willing submissives?

Creighton: Why are you asking?

Annika: I don't want to compete with girls who are already into your stuff.

Creighton: Stuff?

Annika: You know. At any rate, they need to go.

Creighton: Will you take their place as my plaything?

Annika: Aren't I already?

Creighton: What happened today was a mere demonstration, a little taste of what I'm capable of. It's by no means the entirety of my 'singular tastes.' You think you can handle me? Think again.

Well, shit.

If that was only a taste, then what else does he plan to do to me?

This is probably that moment where I should backpedal and abort whatever twisted feelings I have for the sadist.

One small problem, though.

No matter how much it hurt, no matter how painful it will be to sit at all, there's something else. I've never felt as empowered and free as in the moment when he held me down and 'punished' me.

When he threw me against those shelves and dominated me, I never thought to fight or escape his savage hold.

For some reason, it felt…right.

And my toxic trait is definitely curiosity because I type.

Annika: I'll never know until I try. And don't be a hypocrite. You don't get to tell me not to take Bran as a fake boyfriend, then go and have other people. If you're going to unleash your inner sadist, unleash it on me.

His next text steals my air and leaves me gasping.

Creighton: You've fucked up again. I've given you an opening to try and run away, but you went ahead and refused to take it. Don't blame me for what'll happen next. You're now mine to punish and discipline, little purple.

TEN

Creighton

A RED HAND TUGS ON MY SMALL FINGERS AND I'M SENT flying into a pool of blood.

My vision reddens, then gradually blackens as my limbs soak in the hot crimson liquid.

A low, haunting moan of pain saturates my ears and clashes against my bones.

I'm frozen, bound, helpless, and trapped in the middle of an intricate web.

Her web. The spider.

Soft hands grab hold of my face, but she's only a blurry shadow due to all the red.

She squeezes my fingers with brute force and I scream, but the only sound that echoes in the air is an unintelligible muffle.

"Shh, Creigh. It'll all end soon."

I jerk awake, my heartbeat hammering in my ears.

My hands are still metaphorically bound and I can't move.

For a moment, I think I'm back in that dark room, dripping with blood, while a giant black spider hovers over me like a looming Grim Reaper.

I snatch my hand away, only to find that it's in a fist and someone has grabbed it.

My brother.

Eli stands by the side of my bed, looking as regal as usual in his casual black trousers and white button-down. His hair is styled, his demeanor is sharp, and his face is caught in eternal boredom.

Soft light illuminates the room and casts a gloomy edge on his angular features.

He's five years older than me. At twenty-five, he's the oldest of all of us. The first child of godlike parents, and the first grandchild of even godlier grandparents.

Grandpa Jonathan—from Dad's side—is constantly warring with Grandpa Ethan and Grandpa Agnus—from Mum's side—about whose fortune Eli is going to manage once he finishes his PhD.

Eli slowly releases his grip on my fist that I nearly pummeled him with, casually drops it, and sits beside me. And just like that, his true nature dissipates with a bright smile.

After pulling his phone up to face him, he unmutes it. "Sorry about that, Mum. I think there's a problem with the Wi-Fi. Remi's probably downloading his stash of porn."

From my view of the screen, I can see Mum holding a hand to her chest. "Stop it, Eli. You're so bad."

He winks. "The best type of bad you'll ever meet. Also, look who I have here. A rare sight of your baby boy."

A feminine gasp reaches me first before Eli tilts the phone so it's facing us both.

Elsa Steel King is the epitome of an elegant woman. Nude-colored lips, shiny blonde hair gathered in a neat ponytail, and a face that's both beautiful and wise.

"Creigh!" she cries with her hand still at her chest. "Oh my, have you been asleep?"

"Yes, and your insolent son woke me up."

Eli elbows me. "I was only looking out for his sleeping schedule, Mum. This punk sleeps more hours than is considered healthy, suffers from serious Sleeping Beauty syndrome, aka narcolepsy, and is prone to skip class because of it."

"Still have perfect scores."

"Still sleep in class so often that my professors tell me about it. Don't go tainting my reputation."

"And you think you have a good one?"

"At least people actually know me."

"And that's positive because…"

"Boys!" Mum chuckles from the other end of the phone. "Have you called me to bicker? And leave your brother alone, Eli. As long as he studies, it's all fine."

I raise a brow in his direction.

Hear that, fucker?

"Stop spoiling him rotten, Mum. This is why you only FaceTime him once in a year or if your favorite son, aka me, plans a surprise and wakes him up from hibernation. Where's my thank-you?"

"Outside." I grab the phone from his hand and bring it closer so that I'm the only one in the frame. "Mum and I don't need to speak every day to have a connection."

"That's right." She smiles, her eyes sliding all over my face with veiled desperation. "I just miss you so much, Creigh."

"Miss you, too, Mum."

"What's with all the sappiness? You're acting like it's been years since you last met, when the fact is, we visited home a month ago." Eli snatches his phone back so that he's front and center of the screen.

"I still miss you boys every day." She releases a long sigh. "I miss the nights when I used to tuck you in bed and tell you stories."

"We can recreate that, say on our next visit home. One condition, though." Eli grins. "Kick Dad out first."

"I'll be kicking you outside the solar system, punk." Dad strolls inside the room, appearing in the frame behind Mum.

The phone shakes in her hold as she slightly turns around to look at him. Her expression radiates and her features brighten with a rosy emotion.

Love.

A feeling Mum has been trying, and failing, to instill in both me and my brother for years.

My father sits on the armrest of Mum's chair and wraps a possessive arm around her shoulder.

Aiden King is everything his last name exemplifies—a monarch with a ruthless iron grip, the media's notorious devil, and the love of Mum's life.

He's tall, dark, handsome, and absolutely merciless with anyone who crosses him—or us.

Since we were kids, Dad has taught us to prevent others from stepping on us and unintentionally, or intentionally, made us as cutthroat as he is.

Eli inherited more than just his personality. He has his black hair, dark gray eyes, and similar facial features—a fact that Mum secretly loves but is openly jealous of, complaining that her eldest looks nothing like her.

"Hi, Dad." Eli's eyes shine with the promise of a challenge. He's always been in some sort of weird rivalry with our father. "I called Mum so we could have her all to ourselves."

"Not even if you're reincarnated ten times in a row."

Mum laughs, strokes Dad's hand that's on her shoulder, and looks at Eli. "Really, now. Stop antagonizing your father. You're so bad."

"Hear that, Dad? I'm bad. Probably worse than you, huh?"

"Not even close." Dad tilts his head to look at me. "Look who we have here."

"Hi, Dad."

"Is everything okay with you, son?"

I nod, and Mum tells him that I've been getting perfect scores, completely omitting the part about how I sleep in most classes and don't attend the other half.

That's what mothers do. They play the role of a bridge, a mediator. An anchor.

Or at least, Mum does.

That can't be said about my other mother.

"I'm glad you could pop in, Creigh," Dad says. "You, too, Eli."

My brother points a thumb at himself. "Creighton's rare appearance is all thanks to me. Besides, we both miss Mum."

"And Dad," I finish, earning a rare smile from my father.

He completely ignores Eli's attempts to rile him. After a few more minutes of catching up, he decides we've had enough of Mum's time and ends the call.

As soon as the screen goes black, I kick Eli in the ribs, sending him flying to the other side of the bed.

Once I have enough room, I lie back down with a palm beneath my nape and close my eyes.

A petite brunette with an infuriating mouth barges into my mind.

Or more like the images of the red handprints I left on her arse do. All bright against that pale skin that's begging to be marked and bruised and *owned*.

That was two days ago.

And she's tactfully avoided me for as long. Always making sure we're in a group, as if she's scared I'll pounce on her.

I would.

Thing is, Annika tests my control, edging it to limits I didn't think were possible.

And the more she tests it, the more my beast screeches with the need to own her.

That's what started it all.

After she defied me despite my clear warnings, I had to teach her a lesson.

When I shoved her against those shelves, I had every intention to punish the fuck out of her, but what I received was way past my expectations.

Her submission.

I thought I'd glimpsed the secret submissive in her whenever my tone turned authoritative, but I never thought she was a natural.

Annika not only took my lashes of pain, but she reveled in them as well. The moment she came apart all over my fingers, it took every ounce of control I had not to ram my cock into her sweet heat.

I would've broken her. No doubt about it.

So I gave her and myself a temporary reprieve. I simply can't predict what I'm capable of when it comes to that girl.

The mattress dips beside me.

I expected Eli to bugger off, but he kicks me in the side and stretches out next to me. "Seriously, the fuck is wrong with you and sleeping? Pretty sure the doctor Mum took you to said there were no hormonal imbalances. Open your eyes."

"Sleeping is better than peopling. Sod off."

He nudges my side again. "Your big brother is bestowing you with a rare bonding moment, peasant. Wake the fuck up."

"Go to Lan or Bran."

"I don't like Lan sometimes and Bran doesn't like me sometimes."

"Remi."

"Shagging two blondes as we speak. Also, the fuck? You'd throw me at them instead of entertaining me?"

"I'm not a bloody clown."

"No, but you're my cute little brother." He wiggles his fingers under my chin like he used to do when we were kids.

I shove his hand away. "If you're so bored, go to Ava."

Sweet silence fills the air and I think I've managed to finally get rid of the sod, but then his voice echoes in the silence. It's lower, deadlier, and has lost the nonchalance from earlier.

"If I go to her, I'll fucking kill her." The darkness vanishes as fast as it appeared. "But this is neither the time nor the place. Wake up before I drench you with water."

He goes back to tapping his fingers beneath my chin and I'm so close to punching him to the next planet.

Eli is detached, Machiavellian, and downright psychopathic, but ever since I accidentally became the sidekick of his destructive energy, he weirdly dotes on me.

He fought my battles, taught me how to fight my own—by knocking me down a few times, and turned psycho on anyone who attempted to bully me.

And by psycho, I don't mean violent. But conniving. He hid stashes of drugs in their closet, made them doubt their own existence, and even drove them to change schools.

He's always been discreet but highly effective.

That reputation has given him a lone wolf status. No matter how many people surround him, I know that, deep down, Eli is as lonely as me.

Probably worse.

So I let him play with my chin. Maybe then he'll leave me alone.

"Jesus. You sleep like the mummies, did you know that?"

I don't reply, hoping he'll think I'm already asleep.

"Maybe I should've tagged along with Lan. He's got an up-close location to watch the Heathens fall in their own compound."

My eyes fly open and clash with Eli's muted ones. He slowly grins, fingers pausing at my chin. "Finally. I was so close to kicking you in the nuts."

"The Elites are going against the Heathens?"

"No, I think the Serpents are raiding their mansion. Lan grabbed the popcorn to watch the internal war unfold after he probably instigated it. He made sure Glyn was at the dorm and not with Killian first, though."

I sit up so abruptly that Eli is forced to release me and back away.

"The fuck is wrong with you now?"

In a flash, I get up, my bare feet sinking into the carpet as I grab my phone.

The moment I click on Ava's contact, Eli appears behind me emanating Lucifer's dark energy, his voice lowering to that edge again. "This is why I don't like Lan sometimes, you know."

"Shut up." I shoo him away, but he remains there, waiting, watching, his attention no different than a hawk's.

Creighton: Is Annika with you?

I could've texted Cecily or Glyn, but they're not as obsessed with their phones as Ava is.

Sure enough, the reply is immediate.

Ava: OMG. Did you just text me? Who are you and why have you kidnapped our Cray Cray?

Creighton: Answer the question, is Annika there?

Ava: Jesus. Slow down, no hi, how are you? Or maybe an attempt to answer my previous dozen texts that you left on Read. I'm wounded, you know. Beg me and I might consider answering.

I feel my brother's demeanor turning rigid behind me. Worst part is that Ava meant it about the begging. I have no doubt that she'd be cheeky just for the fun of it.

So I go for the jugular.

Creighton: Eli is reading this conversation as we speak. Answer my question.

The dots appear and disappear a few times before her reply comes.

Ava: Anni had to spend the night at her brother's mansion.

My hand tightens around my phone as my whole body stiffens. I dial Annika's number and place it to my ear, listening to the long, haunting rings.

No reply.

Fuck.

Yes, she usually goes to bed early for 'beauty sleep' or what-the-fuck-ever, but this is too early.

I throw on my hoodie, put on the first shoes I see, and storm out.

"You're welcome!" Eli shouts behind my back, but I'm already jogging down the stairs.

I call Annika again, but it goes to voicemail.

"Hi, this is Annika. Leave a message and I'll call you back ASAP."

The more times I get her voicemail, the more my temperature rises.

I hop into my car and drive out of the property at high speed, then dial my cousin.

He picks up almost immediately. "Weren't you in your Sleeping Beauty phase?"

"Where are you?"

"Currently watching a live show of a wildfire that's eating the Heathens like holy water. May all their sins trap them in hell for eternity. Amen."

"There's fire?"

"Did you miss the wildfire part?" Pure sadism shines in his voice. "I've got to applaud the mastermind for the immaculate planning and execution—"

I press the End button and hit the gas.

A feeling I've never felt before spreads through me with suffocating intensity.

And it's all because of her.

The girl who shouldn't have been part of my plans yet somehow managed to sneak inside.

The thought of something happening to her turns me into a feral beast.

ELEVEN

Annika

THE SOUND OF AN ALARM GOES OFF AND COLD LIQUID splashes all over my face.

I jerk up, gasping as the spray from the fire sprinklers drenches my sleep shirt in seconds.

It takes me a few more seconds to shake the disorientation out of my head and focus on my surroundings.

The smell of smoke clogs my nostrils as shadows and bright light spill in from outside.

I stumble out of bed and peek through the window, fingers clenching the sill. The view that materializes in front of me traps my breath in the back of my throat.

The brightness isn't actually light. A huge fire is eating up the upper western half of the mansion.

The half where I am.

Where my brother is.

A deep sense of terror lodges itself into my soul and I remain frozen in place.

Being Adrian Volkov's only daughter has put me in danger more times than I can count. There have been at least three kidnapping attempts and a few shootings. Some scum would try anything to hurt my father, and that includes targeting me, Jer, and Mom since they think we're his weakness.

Because we have the best guards, all those attempts ended in failure and were followed by the assailants' eventual deaths.

I've never really been scared of outside threats, because I knew Papa, Jeremy, or their men would be there every time.

But that doesn't apply to a fire.

Namely, the one that's currently devouring the mansion.

My eyes widen as I continue to watch the scene unfolding in front of me. Guards run in different directions, some with hoses, others with fire extinguishers.

Judging by their exerted expressions, it seems the fire has gotten out of control.

I spot Gareth and Killian with them, but there's no sight of Jeremy or Nikolai.

A different type of horror seeps into my bloodstream as I bolt toward the door.

My bare feet slip on the water that's filled the floor and I step on something, but I don't pay it any attention.

The moment I'm out the door, a heatwave slaps me across the face. The dark corridor is crowded with so much smoke that it's impossible to see or breathe properly.

I place my hand against my nose and mouth and inhale toxic air through them.

My brother's room is on the other side of this smoke, but I'm not sure if I'll be able to find it in this hell.

It's as if the flames have swallowed the entire place.

"Annika, come down!"

My spine jerks at the loud voice. When I turn toward the stairs, I make out a half-naked Nikolai holding a hose.

"Where's Jeremy?" I shout back.

"We haven't seen him. You just get out for now. I'll go find him."

No, no, no…

I sprint in the direction of the smoke, ignoring Nikolai's curses.

My eyes water from the thickness of the toxic air and I cough as I grab the wall for balance.

This won't do.

I rip the hem of my shirt, bend over, and soak it with the water from the floor, then hold it to my nose.

The humid cold offers a small reprieve, but the smoke still clogs my throat. My eyes burn and I cough until I think I'll throw up.

Still, I keep going, using the wall as balance. The moment I touch a door, I try to open it, but it's locked.

I bang on it with my free hand. "Jeremy!"

My voice is so weak and muffled that I can hardly hear it myself.

So I hit the door again while having a coughing fit. "Jer!"

"Anoushka?" His low question comes from the other side, equally weak. "What the fuck are you doing here? Get out."

"I came for you!"

"I'm all right. You go."

I keep coughing as dizziness assaults me. "If you're all right, then let's go together."

"Get the fuck out of here, Annika." There's a strain in his voice that's so similar to pain.

My heartbeat thunders as I choke on my cough. "Open the door."

There are more coughs from his and my side, but there's no reply.

"Jer?" My voice is spooked. "Open up—"

"I can't." I barely hear his low words. "I'm trapped. You need to go, Anoushka. *Now.*"

"No, no." I hit the door with my shoulder, tears streaming down my cheeks, and they're not only due to the smoke.

So this is why he didn't come to find me as soon as the fire hit. I found it weird that my overprotective brother didn't break down my door or haul me out of sleep.

It's not that he didn't think of me, it's that he couldn't come to my rescue.

"Go!"

"No!" I scream back through my coughs. "I'm not leaving you to die."

My vision becomes blurry and I sway on my feet, but I don't stop hitting the door over and over. It takes all of my strength, but it does nothing to move the fucking shit.

So I kick the handle with all my might and throw myself at it repeatedly.

"Anoushka…go…please…"

"Shut up." I'm sobbing through my coughs as I kick and punch and hit the handle. My feet sting, my hand screams in pain, and my vision has filled with tears, but I refuse to give in.

"If you stay…we'll both die…" Jeremy sounds far away, almost like he's in another realm.

"I'm not leaving you." I kick the handle again, my strength waning. "I'd rather die with you than live knowing I could've saved you but didn't."

I pack all my energy in one final kick against the handle and it comes off, falling to the ground.

My heart leaps as I push the door open. A hot wave of heat physically jerks me backward and I tighten my grip on the cloth.

The room is completely gray, reeking of smoke. The fire has eaten up the northern wall and is advancing with creepily easy speed.

"Jer?"

No reply.

My fist clenches and I can feel the emotions clogging my throat as I cough.

I call my brother's name again, spooked this time, and getting weaker. I'm swaying and I don't think I'll be able to stand on my feet for much longer.

He was right, after all. Maybe we were meant to die together tonight.

I snort. Jer is always right.

Tears stream down my face as I lose my footing, and the fabric falls to the ground. "Jer…"

My side hits a wall—no, not a wall.

It's warm, but not with the lethality of the flames. It's suffocating, but not like the deadliness of the smoke.

Strong arms pull me up effortlessly and I end up flush against a rock-hard chest.

My vision slowly focuses on Creighton's beautiful face that's half covered by a gas mask. Despite that fact, I would recognize him anywhere.

And it's all because of these piercing light eyes that haunt me everywhere I go.

For a moment, I think this is a figment of my imagination and I'm making him up in my most dire situation.

But he is here.

For me.

Creighton removes the mask, revealing his tight, sharp features. He straps it to my face. I inhale the clean air deeply, then pull it away, my other hand fisting his shirt.

"Jer…is over here."

"We have to go."

"Not without Jeremy." I don't recognize the heat in my voice.

Because I will not move from here until my brother is safe.

Creighton shoves the mask back onto my face and pushes me toward the exit. "Leave."

"No—"

My word is interrupted when a body shoves against mine. "Get out of the way, bitches."

Nikolai storms inside wearing a mask and carrying a few more in a sheet that he's morphed into a messenger bag and strapped around his waist.

I take one and slam it against Creighton's chest and glare. He shakes his head, but he wears it.

Despite the possibility of being able to breathe, the hot air is unbearable. Still, when I point Nikolai and Creighton in the direction of where the fire is spreading, they don't hesitate.

We run there, but Creighton keeps me shielded by his body at all times.

"Annika…" Jer's low voice barely reaches us. "Leave…"

We follow the sound until we finally find my brother trapped beneath a table. Probably caused by a blast or the spreading of the fire.

I snatch a gas mask from Nikolai's sheet and strap it on my brother's face. His eyes are closed, and his body is limp, but he's breathing.

He's still here.

While I push Jeremy's hair away from his face, calling his name but getting no reply, Creighton and Nikolai lift the table.

Then they carry him out just as the fire is about to devour the room.

My brother's feet drag against the ground, his weight pulling him down even as they swiftly carry him away from the danger.

I stay close behind them, trying and failing not to get tense whenever Creighton throws a glance at me. He continues to keep an eye on me until we reach the bottom of the stairs.

Once we're outside, chaos of different proportions greets us. Guards, firefighters, onlookers. The whole of The King's U campus seems to be here to watch.

I tune them out, choosing to focus on my brother.

Gareth takes over from Creighton, then he and Nikolai carry an unconscious but breathing Jeremy to get medical attention.

I take off my mask and start to follow behind them, when a wall of muscle blocks my path.

Creighton glares at me with that silent broodiness of his and it's downright terrifying.

It's like he's blaming me for what happened. Or maybe he's blaming me for having somehow ended up in the fire.

He removes his mask and throws it to the ground, revealing a clenched jaw. Both his hands and his face are smudged with soot, and I want to wipe it away.

I don't, though, completely entrapped by the dark expression covering his features.

His punishing gaze glides from my face to my breasts and then to my waist with heated anger.

That's when I realize I've been roaming around wearing a wet shirt. A ripped wet shirt. Not only does it barely cover my ass, but it's also molded to my body, leaving little to the imagination.

Even my nipples are hard, pushing against the fabric.

And Creighton doesn't seem pleased with the view, but if he is, the displeasure and anger have cut open any sense of appreciation.

He takes off his hoodie and slides it over my head. I help by putting my hands through the oversized sleeves. The thing swallows me whole and almost reaches my knees. And just like that, I'm surrounded by his warmth and soothing smell.

But despite the reprieve from the cold, I can't help shivering at the view of his half-nakedness, the bulging muscles, and the spider tattoo.

Something gets stuck in my scratchy throat and I cough a few times. "Thanks."

A savage hand grips my upper arm. "What the fuck were you thinking staying in the house in the middle of the fire?"

I swallow and flinch a little at the raw power behind his words. I thought he was mad because of how I looked, but maybe that's not the case.

"Jer was trapped," I say slowly. "I couldn't leave him alone."

"So you decided to die along with him?"

"If need be." I lift my chin. "Besides, it all worked out fine in the end. What are you so mad about?"

"The fact that you put your life in jeopardy." He tightens his grip on my arm until I wince. "That won't be happening again, is that clear?"

I purse my lips.

"Is that fucking clear, Annika?"

"I won't leave the people I care about to die," I murmur. "That's just not me."

Creighton's nostrils flare with the force of his inhales and exhales, but before he can say anything else, something hits him from behind.

At first, he remains frozen, but then a trickle of blood trails down the side of his head.

I shriek as he tumbles forward, but I don't get out of the way. Before he can fall against me, a savage hand grabs his hair and wrenches him back.

Nikolai throws down his baseball bat and grins like a maniac. "Time to punish the cunt who burned our property."

TWELVE

Annika

THEY TRY TO STOP ME FROM FOLLOWING.

Nikolai, Killian, Gareth, and all the guards, I mean.

However, I'm apparently a force to be reckoned with today.

After I make sure Jeremy's getting medical care and is recuperating in the safe eastern end of the house, I catch up with them.

The fire has been put out, but the whole western end of the house has been eaten by the flames. All that remains is dark soot, walls, and the occasional firefighter. After witnessing the show, or some of it, the students, who weren't supposed to be here in the first place, were kicked off the property.

My brother's friends have carried Creighton into the annexed house that wasn't touched by the fire. Probably because the guards and all their equipment and security gadgets are here.

Obviously, the main house was the assailants' target.

A guard stands in front of the door, burly and big, and all but blocks the entire entrance.

"Please go back to the main house, miss," he says in a Russian accent, not bothering to even look at me.

If it were any other time, I'd tuck my tail between my legs and do as I'm told. It's all part of my sheltered upbringing and the harsh world that my father and brother tried their hardest to keep me away from.

Avoiding conflict and living in my pretty purple-colored bubble isn't only good for my sake but also for everyone else's.

But something changed tonight.

It happened sometime between the time when I could no longer hear Jeremy's voice and when he passed out and couldn't save himself.

I realized that neither Jeremy nor Papa will always be there. The time has come for me to regain control over my own life.

Usually, I don't glare at people. Hell, I don't even know how, but I manage to as I speak in a nonnegotiable tone. "Move."

"I have orders to not allow anyone inside, miss."

I cross my arms over my chest. "You'll have no orders to obey if I tell Papa you failed to protect Jeremy and me. We are your priority, not whatever invalid orders you're trying to follow. So unless you want to be kicked out of Papa's close circle, I suggest you move out of my way right this instant."

This time, the guard stares down at me, brows lifted as if he's seeing me for the first time. Then he steps aside with the sluggishness of an opening gate.

I storm inside and head to where the voices are coming from.

Yes, Jeremy has made sure to keep me away from his club and whatever nefarious activities he does in the dark, but that doesn't mean I'm clueless about what's going on.

Papa has always said that knowledge is power, so I made sure to accumulate as much of it as possible and tucked that information into neat boxes at the back of my head in case I needed it someday.

That day is now.

My ability to gain comes naturally. The guards like it when I treat them to meals the cook has made—not mine, since apparently no one likes my cooking. As a reward for treating them, they tell me things.

Gareth freely divulges some information, too, when I probe a little—the right amount of little that won't trigger his suspicion.

So I know a lot more than the Heathens would let out.

I arrive at the half-open metal door at the end of the hall. Ordinarily, they'd close it to dispel any unwanted attention, but they must've been in a hurry this time.

My steps are inaudible as I push the door open and step inside.

The scene I find freezes me in place.

The room is stark white from the walls to the floor and to the shelves on either side. It's almost blinding.

And those shelves? They're full of all types of knives, metal objects, canes, and baseball bats. And those are just the ones I recognize. There are other different tools I can't begin to name that shine with bad mojo and the promise of torture.

My gaze flits to the reason I defied all rules and reason and came here.

Creighton.

Thick rope straps him to a metal chair as he sits there, unconscious, his head lolled forward at an awkward angle.

Nikolai picks up what looks like a cane and glides his fingers over it. "I vote for caning him and paying tribute to his Middle Age ancestors."

Killian presses on a Taser, creating a spark that echoes in the silence. "This will be more effective in making him talk."

At that, Nikolai swings the cane in the air and it makes a whooshing sound before he slaps it on his hand. "This will leave a mark and that's more important in teaching the motherfucker a lesson."

"Whatever you're doing, get to it." Gareth leans against the wall, arms and ankles crossed, appearing bored with the whole conversation between his brother, Killian, and his cousin.

"We can't push violence, Gaz." Nikolai breathes heavily. "There needs to be the right preparation."

I take a few seconds to lock up the strong emotions roaring inside me. If I let them loose, I'll only be emotional, and feelings don't work on these guys.

If anything, they'll use them against me.

After putting on my cool façade, I stroll inside, easing my previously clenched fists. "Whatever you're thinking about doing, stop it."

Three pairs of eyes slide in my direction, all dark and intimidating. Usually, that would give me immediate anxiety.

I can feel the pang of discomfort rushing through my chest and clogging my throat, but I squash it down.

"And what are you doing here?" Nikolai tilts his head in my direction, still stroking his weapon of choice. His state of half-nakedness coupled with all the tattoos and the deadly look in his eyes would've made me bolt not too long ago.

Not today.

"I know you'll torture Creighton, and I'm here to tell you it's not going to happen."

"This is not the place for you, *princess*," Killian says, voice becoming mocking at the princess part. "Go play with your dolls. That is, if they didn't get burned in the fire."

"The dolls can wait." I match his mocking tone. "And I'm not leaving."

Gareth pushes off the wall, walks to me, and takes his time to sound calm—human. "This is a lot more serious than you think, Annika. You shouldn't concern yourself with it or waste your breath on it. How about you go check on Jeremy?"

"Not until you let Creighton go."

"No can do." Nikolai swings his weapon in the air. "This motherfucker thought he could burn our compound and walk away as if nothing happened."

I take a step backward, my back nearly meeting the wall.

Doubt slaps me across the face when his words and the events sink in.

What Nikolai is saying could be true.

After all, Creighton attempted arson in this same place before. What's stopping him from widening his scope and going after the whole house?

My limbs tremble at the thought of him doing that and not caring if Jeremy and I died.

If everyone in the house died.

I internally shake my head. I'm not going to believe those suspicions unless there are hard facts.

Besides, Creighton wouldn't burn the house while I'm in it, right? True, we haven't known each other for a long time, but he doesn't hate me.

I hope.

So instead of falling into whatever black hole my brain is forming, I laugh, head tilting back for extra effect.

"What's gotten into you?" Nikolai watches me as if I'm an alien. "Did you hit your head earlier?"

"I'm just laughing at how ridiculous all of that sounds." I wipe the tears from the corners of my eyes, pretending to make a huge effort to stop being amused. "Creighton was with me from the time I went to bed."

Gareth raises a brow. "With you?"

I throw a hand in the air. "You know, *with* me."

Silence falls over the room for a beat too long and I do my best to appear unaffected. I didn't have enough time to think of a solution to save Creighton from certain torture, and this was the best idea that popped into my head.

Here's to hoping my storytelling skills will be able to convince these three.

Killian presses the Taser against Creighton's cheek without breaking eye contact with me.

I've studied in the same private schools as these guys, and Killian has always been the scariest, along with Nikolai. But while his cousin is open about his methods, Kill is discreet, and the only evidence he leaves behind is a trail of destruction.

While Gareth is approachable with prince-like looks, Killian has a serial killer's beauty with his dark hair and somber blue eyes that only shine when Glyn is around.

I'm pretty sure he's a psychopath, and that makes him the

hardest to convince. Not to mention, looking straight into his eyes is similar to being dissected alive.

"Did he now?" he muses. "Pray tell, how did he manage to bypass security? The only way he can come inside the property is if he hacks into our system and stops our camera feed. Like say…the perpetrator of the fire."

"Right!" Nikolai agrees with his cousin. "Let me beat the fuck out of this motherfucker."

I step forward, feeling less and less nervous. "Why would he go to such lengths and hack the system when I gave him my access card?"

Killian presses the Taser against Creighton's cheek harder and it takes everything in me not to flinch. "You're trying to tell us you invited a guy over under Jeremy's roof?"

"Why wouldn't I? Jer is watching my every move, so the best way to go unnoticed is to meet Creighton where he wouldn't suspect it."

I remain standing strong under the scrutiny of their watchful eyes. I'm pretty sure I've convinced them, or at least, I've opened up their tunnel vision.

Nikolai's gaze bounces between me and Creighton. "Wait a minute. If he was in your room, how come I didn't see him with you when the fire first broke out?"

"I told him to stay put until I investigated the situation since I didn't want him to run into you guys." I'd high five myself if I could. Now, that's a believable lie.

"Still…" Gareth starts.

"Still what?" I lift my chin. "Creighton saved my and Jeremy's lives. You should be rewarding him instead of beating him up for it. Besides, if you're worried this is the Elites' doing, it still doesn't make sense to threaten Creighton. He was never a part of that club."

"His cousin is," Killian says matter-of-factly.

"But he isn't. Never was and never will be. The time you're wasting here could've been used to worry about the Serpents that you so thoroughly offended, Kill. Surely you realize they're the most likely culprits behind this mess?"

I can tell that I'm getting to them, considering the subtle change in their expressions. They must've thought about the Serpents' angle, too, but since they had Creighton in their grip, they chose to believe it would be the Elites instead.

Nikolai tosses away his weapon, appearing dejected that his fun has been ruined.

"I must admit, the whole story sounds convoluted," Killian says. "You're not even worried that Jeremy can and will hear about this incident?"

I swallow, not feeling so brave anymore. Still, I try my best to preserve the façade. "I'll talk to my brother when he wakes up. In the meantime, let Creighton go."

Both Killian and Nikolai step out of the room.

Only Gareth stays behind and helps me untie him. The dried trail of blood looks gruesome against his ethereally beautiful face.

The lack of light gives his features harsh angles, almost sinister to the eye. His lips are slightly parted and I can't help reaching a hand out to touch them, or touch him. But then I recall he doesn't like being touched, so I let it drop to my side.

After we're done removing the ropes, I crouch by his chair. "Is he going to be okay?"

Gareth leans back against the wall, arms crossed, expression nonchalant but alert. Dirt smudges his wet shirt, neck, and face as lingering evidence of the fire. "He's just unconscious. Will probably wake up in a few."

"I'll call Remi and Lan to come pick him up."

"Or you can wait until he wakes up and leaves on his own."

"I don't trust Kill or Niko not to come back here and finish what they started."

Gareth smiles. "That's true. Call away, but instead of Landon, make it Brandon. Elites aren't welcome here."

"Okay. Thanks, Gareth."

"Don't thank me yet. Jeremy will find out about this one way or another. Before anyone else opens their mouth, I'll be the one to tell him about this whole scene."

"I understand."

I think I've gotten myself in worse trouble than I bargained for.

So I might have overestimated my abilities to deal with the fallout from the fire.

After Jeremy woke up and found out about the thing with Creighton, he downright forced me into house arrest.

I'm escorted back and forth between REU and the mansion. I'm not even allowed to volunteer at the shelter.

His excuse: it's dangerous.

And this time, Mom is on his and Papa's side. She even told me that it was a good idea to come home for a while.

It's been a week of constant security, boundaries, and stupid locked-up prison.

I can only talk to the girls via texts or sometimes when I beg the guards to let me have lunch with them.

Well, not really beg. I've learned to threaten, too.

The silver lining about this situation is that Jeremy didn't personally go against Creighton. Probably because he knows he saved his life.

But he still told me he'll be a dead man if he sees him in my company.

Which is why I've kept my distance.

Remi and Bran picked him up that day, and Remi said to absolutely not let Eli know about the incident of his brother's kidnapping or torture attempt.

"If the psycho Eli finds out this happened to Cray Cray, he'll burn the entire mansion down after making sure all the Heathens are in it this time," Remi said.

"And he'll make sure no one escapes his wrath," Bran continued in a sympathizing tone. "Take it from us, Anni. Eli and Lan are the two people you want to avoid and never, under any circumstances, get on their bad side."

I haven't seen or talked to Creighton since they took him away.

He sent me a few texts soon after, mostly asking if I was okay and how I managed to get him out, and this time, I'm the one who left him on Read.

I may have embraced the courageous me, but she can't be reckless. Not when I'm sure Jeremy's threats could become reality in no time.

And maybe it's for the best anyway. I'd never forgive myself if something were to happen to him because of me.

Besides, since the fire, it's been getting absolutely dirty between the three clubs.

It's still unknown whether the Serpents or the Elites were behind the fire, or if it was a joint effort.

Tension has been rising in the air at both universities and it's very similar to the Cold War. All three of the clubs are packing their forces and no one knows when mayhem might strike.

Today, I managed to convince Jeremy to let me go to the shelter without the guards.

He only allowed it if the guards remained outside, so I couldn't really complain.

The first thing I do as soon as I arrive is go to check on Tiger. I jog to his cage, grinning for the first time in a week. "Missed you, baby! How have you—"

I stop short when I find a small hamster where Tiger is supposed to be.

My heartbeat picks up and I back away slowly. Harry, who's walking down the hall, catches a glimpse of me and comes running.

"Where have you been, girl? We missed the shit out of your face." He gathers me in a hug and I return it, still stupefied about my find.

"I was busy with school," I offer as we break apart. "Hey, Harry, where's Tiger?"

"Tiger?" he repeats. "Oh, Tiger, the cat you let ride your face? He's gone."

I nearly faint, my feet taking a step back. Harry grabs my arm and slaps his forehead. "Jesus, me and my mouth. I don't mean gone as in dead gone. No, nope. I would have told you that and we would've had a proper funeral and shit. He's gone, as in, he was adopted."

"Oh." My breathing slowly returns to normal, but the stab of pain doesn't subside. I'm glad he found a loving owner, but I wish I could've said goodbye. "Do you know who adopted him?"

"No clue. Heard about it from Dr. Stephanie when I went to feed him this morning." He playfully tugs on my cheek. "Now, spill the actual reason you've been gone. And don't give me the 'busy with school' bullshit. Did you go on a beauty retreat without taking me? I'm gonna need deets on where you do your facials, because, sweet Jesus, you don't only look like a doll, but your skin also feels like a doll's."

I smile. "Shh, don't tell anyone about the beauty retreat. It'll be our little secret."

"I knew it. This little bitch, I swear." He teasingly pinches my cheek more. "Take me with you next time?"

"Can you let go of me first?" I laugh.

"Not until you promise. Just the two of us so none of the others find out the secret."

One moment, I'm laughing at Harry's antics, the next, I'm pulled back by a savage grip on my waist.

I slam against a hard chest as an all-encompassing presence looms over me.

Creighton's fingers dig into the fabric of my dress at the waist as if he's intending to burn it and engrave his fingerprints on my skin.

My head whips up to get a glimpse of his face. There's no trail of blood now, no soot or impurities over his criminally attractive features.

There's darkness, though, the slow, simmering type that could and would transform into a hurricane.

Despite my resolution to stay away, malevolent butterflies erupt in my stomach with the intention of devouring me from the inside out.

It's unfair that he's in his usual jeans and hoodie but still looks straight out of a fashion show. It's even more unfair that he has the superpower of snatching my attention without even trying.

"She said to let her go." His deep voice is laced with a timbre of anger and I shiver, even though it's not directed at me.

Harry, who is forced to release me, seems oblivious to the tension and merely gawks at him. "Oh my, hi there, handsome. Didn't know you actually talked. And we missed you this whole week! Wait a minute, do you only come for Anni?"

My lips part. Don't tell me Creighton hasn't been at the shelter when I wasn't around?

Instead of answering him, Creighton basically drags me with him to the small nook I use as an office, leaving Harry behind.

"Nice talking to you!" he shouts behind us. "And don't forget about our deal, Anni, or I'll sacrifice you to Jesus and start calling you Nika."

"Don't you dare!" I glare at him over my shoulder.

He just makes a face, grins, then forms a hole with his fingers and slides the index finger of his other hand in and out of it in a suggestive way.

My cheeks heat as Creighton pushes me into the room and slams the door shut behind us.

All the embarrassment is forgotten when his chest crashes against mine.

My feet falter backward until I hit the wall. I open my mouth to speak, but even that is put to a halt when he grabs my hands and throws them above my head against the wall.

The deep gravel of his voice reverberates on my skin when he whispers too close to my face, "I'm going to ask you a few questions and you'll answer them, Annika. Lie to me, and you'll be punished. Are we clear?"

THIRTEEN

Annika

THE LONGER I STARE INTO CREIGHTON'S EYES, THE MORE MY breathing shatters and splinters into pieces.

Harsh eyes.

Completely-devoid-of-emotions eyes.

I've always seen him as detached, with ice in his veins instead of blood, but this is the first time I've witnessed it firsthand.

And that iciness? It's currently seeping underneath my skin and hooking against my darkest part.

"Are we fucking clear, Annika?" The lethal sound of his voice hits my skin like a whip.

I can't help the slight jump in my shoulders or the dryness in my throat, despite my attempts to stand strong.

Swallowing, I nod slowly.

"You have a voice. Use it."

Tchaikovsky.

Come have a word with this guy because he has no business sounding so infuriatingly hot when he's bossy and controlling.

"Yeah," I murmur and attempt to smile. "Can you let me go now?"

"Quit that fucking habit of smiling when you're uncomfortable. You're not a bloody doll."

How...*the hell* does he know that?

I've perfected my fake smile so well that no one can read through it, so why can he?

The act has become so subconscious that I don't pay it any attention anymore.

So why does he?

A cloud of disapproval cloaks around him like a second skin as he presses closer, the length of his body crushing against mine. "Tell me, Annika. Why haven't you answered any of my calls or texts?"

My chest saturates with a carnal urge that even I can't put a name to, and I have to clear my throat to be able to speak. "You know, it was crazy after the fire, and Jeremy kind of confiscated my freedom."

"He didn't confiscate your phone, which you used to talk to everyone else but me just fine."

Shit.

Considering his nature, I was so sure that he wouldn't focus on that detail, so I didn't pay attention to that angle.

Apparently, that was a mistake.

His fingers dig into the soft flesh of my wrists and the rich timbre of his voice lowers further. "Answer me."

"Feels bad to be left on Read, doesn't it?" I deflect, grabbing onto my composure with bloodied fingers.

"Don't fuck with me."

"What? I didn't realize you were the only one with Read privileges. I thought I'd try and see how it feels, and it's safe to say, your reaction kind of sucks. Might keep it up if I'm in the mood. Also, can you speak without touching me?"

He grips me tighter, not only disregarding my last request, but also doing the exact opposite. I'm assaulted by his otherworldly presence, striking warmth, and addictive scent all while trying to remain unaffected.

Chances of actually succeeding? In the negative.

"What are you playing now, little purple?"

My heart and mind war for an appropriate reaction to his words. A part of me wants to pull out of this charade, save everyone the trouble and bury myself in my bubble.

But the other part, the part that falters at the little purple nickname, claws and bangs, demanding to be set free.

"Can you remove the little before purple?"

"You *are* little." His fingers flex on my flesh and the air shimmers with his assertive intensity.

"I'm going to be eighteen soon, you know."

"It's not about your age."

"Then…what is it about?"

His eyes shift, growing hot as he rakes them over my face and heaving chest. "You're so small and breakable that I'm always craving to bite, bruise, mark, and pound the fuck out of your tiny cunt while you cry because you can't take it anymore."

I should be a lot of things right now, including horrified, petrified, creeped out, but standing here so shamelessly hot and embarrassingly wet is definitely not one of them.

Damn him and his surprisingly dirty mouth. It's like I'm getting to know a completely different Creighton.

"I'm asking you for the final time. What are you playing at, Annika?"

"No games," I murmur. "I've just been thinking about your warnings and decided to take them seriously. I won't bother you anymore. I swear on Tchaikovsky's grave, cross my heart and hope to die."

His expression remains the same, short of a slight tic in his jaw. "Too late."

"What?"

"I'm not letting you go."

My heartbeat skyrockets and my whole body seems to mold into his hold. "But—"

"Shut up."

"Shouldn't you want me gone? That's what you've been campaigning for since we met."

"Shut the fuck up, Annika."

My lips purse and I tighten my thighs. This controlling side of him affects me in ways I refuse to admit and rushes to places I refuse to name.

He releases my hands and steps back. My stomach sinks as I consider that maybe he thought things through and decided it's not worth it, after all.

But Creighton doesn't leave.

Instead, he shoves a hand in his pocket, and I realize he does that when it seems like he's stopping himself from doing something.

Like a storm that comes to an abrupt ending.

"Sit on the table."

My gaze flicks to the only table in the space—my small desk that's pushed against the wall with a stack of paperwork on top.

"W-why?"

"Quit asking questions. When I say sit on the table, you sit on the fucking table."

I startle, hating and loving the tightening between my legs. It's impossible to be in control of my body when he's around, not when he confiscates and incinerates that control as if it's his birth right.

After a futile attempt at calming myself, I climb onto the table. Once I'm sitting, he tuts.

"Open your legs as wide as you can. Feet and palms on the table."

My cheeks heat and I can feel the thudding pulse in my neck. A part of me wants to fight this, but I'm unable to under his scrutinizing gaze, so I lift my legs and get into the position he asked.

My dress pushes back to my middle, revealing my bare thighs and the lace of my panties.

Panties that Creighton sees as soon as he walks in front of me. He remains there, as still as a statue, while I tremble and feel completely out of my element.

I start to close my legs, but a mere stern look from him is enough to make me abort the idea.

Damn it.

Why does he look like a completely different person right now and why am I reacting this strongly to it?

"That's one." He pulls the chair from my desk and throws his weight on it, sitting at eye level with my pussy. "Disobey me again, and it'll be ten."

This close, I'm drowning in his intoxicating scent while his dark eyes devour what's between my legs.

"You said you were taking my warnings seriously, no?"

I nod, trying and failing not to focus on the angle he's seeing me from. This is so intimate, the type of intimacy that leaves my lungs heaving for air.

His hand shoots up between my legs and I gasp when he cups me through my panties, fingers digging into the sensitive flesh.

"So how come you're soaking wet, little purple?"

My palms turn sweaty as I purse my lips.

"Where's that smart mouth now?" He tugs on my panties so the seam rubs against my folds. "Or is that only saved for spouting lies?"

The friction from the taut fabric on my overstimulated folds is both pleasurable and painful. I'm starting to think maybe those two sensations go hand in hand with Creighton.

"You're such a cocktease, walking around with your little skirts and lace panties, begging to be disciplined." His hand comes down on my pussy. *Hard.* "But you can't pull out now. That's not how this works. Do you know why?"

My whole body jerks from the power of his hit, tears spring into my eyes, and more arousal coats my panties and his hand.

His savage eyes meet mine, dripping with carnal, animalistic sadism. "Because I've decided you'll be my toy."

And then he's on me.

His veiny hand wraps around my thigh, making it look so small as he dives between my legs. His stubbled jaw scratches my sensitive inner flesh when his teeth nibble on my pussy through my panties, then he all but tears them from my core.

My body trembles, but it goes into a full shock when he thrusts his sharp tongue inside my opening.

I arch off the table, jerking, but his hold brings me back down.

Holy. Hell.

It takes everything in me to not move too much. I try to clench my legs together for some friction. Something, anything, but his ruthless grip on my thigh forbids me to.

My head rolls back as sparks of pleasure spread from my core and across my whole body.

He expertly rolls my clit between his thumb and forefinger at the same insane pace that he tongue-fucks me.

My hips jerk forward and I only realize it once the frantic rhythm of his tongue nearly unravels me. I lift my hands to grab onto his hair and I basically ride his face as stars dance across my vision.

A powerful orgasm washes over me.

It's more desperate this time, so absolutely unhinged in its strength that I'm surprised I don't pass out.

My lids lower, camouflaged by my lashes as I attempt to muffle my shameless moans.

Creighton's head peeks from between my legs and he slaps my pussy so ruthlessly that I yelp.

Pleasure mixes with pain and I have no clue if the tears clinging to my eyes are due to the former or the latter.

"Did I say that you could remove your hand from the table?"

I shake my head and he glares.

"No," I murmur as my sweaty palm falls back on the table.

"And what did I say your punishment would be?"

"Oh."

"Oh isn't an answer."

"Ten."

Frightening excitement covers his features at the promise of punishing me. He gets off on the knowledge that he'll inflict pain, that my flesh will bear a map of his making.

"Start counting." His hand comes down on my pussy again and I flinch, gasping.

The pain of his slaps mounts with each one, offering a minimal amount of pleasure, enough to make me want to come yet not enough to allow me to.

He's savage, absolutely merciless, in the delivery of his punishment. He doesn't stop when I yelp, scream, or sob.

Especially not when I sob.

My tears deepen that sadistic glint in his eyes, the need for more, more, and so much...*more.*

A beast.

That's what he is right now with his sharp features, set jaw, and thinned lips.

And control.

He drips with it. Every time my legs falter or fall, he straightens them back up so that I'm in the right position.

So I'm at his disposal to do with as he wishes.

By the time he's finished, I'm crying my eyes out. My pussy feels like it's on fire, even as arousal coats my inner thighs.

Creighton pushes off his chair and towers over me. My legs are still bent, my whole body shakes, and tears cover my cheeks. However, I don't dare to wipe them in case that'll get me in more trouble.

I'm still not sure how this works, but I know that despite the pain and the discomfort, I'm drawn to it in inexplicable ways.

His hand reaches to my face, colder than my heated cheek, bigger and...safe.

He strokes his thumb beneath my lids, gliding the tears over my skin as I sniffle silently.

Pure sadism shines in his ocean eyes, seeming to eradicate any noble feelings he could have. "I love the sight of your tears."

My breath catches as a shudder rips through me. "That...sounds sick."

"I *am* sick. You should've stayed away while you had the chance."

He slides his thumb all over my face again, the darkness shifting, morphing, and simmering on the surface.

I watch it with keen interest.

Just like the other time, it seems that whenever he punishes me, something inside him claws to the surface.

Fighting.

Biting.

Hitting.

It's like he's...warring for control. But against whom? And for what?

As if validating my thoughts, he shoves his hand in his pocket and steps back.

He's leaving.

Again.

I can't help feeling the tinge of emptiness at the dysfunctionality of it all.

But I won't have him throw me away like this. I wanted the way out he offered, but he didn't let me take it.

The least he can do is treat me like I matter.

I let my legs fall and swing from the table. "Will I find an ointment for a sore pussy in my mailbox this time?"

He stops a few steps away from the door and spins around, his eyes narrowed. "Don't be a brat."

"Don't be a jerk. I'm not a sex doll that you use and discard."

"No, you're not. I haven't fucked you yet."

My neck and cheeks heat, but I carry on, "Either give me the respect I deserve or let me go."

"I told you it's too late to let you go."

"The answer is simple then."

He raises a brow.

"I mean it, Creighton. If you think I'm bluffing, try me. I'll go fake date Brandon. Just make sure you don't regret it afterward, because there's a trope in romance novels that's called fake dating and it always becomes the real thing."

His brows dip and his eyes taper as his cold voice rings in the air. "There will be no dating Brandon, fake or not."

"Then give me what I want."

"And what do you want, little purple?"

I hop from the table and, dammit, I totally overestimated my abilities, because my pussy throbs like crazy.

Creighton must see the change on my face, too, because his darkened gaze slides to my now covered pussy before his eyes finally meet mine.

Waiting.

Intimidating.

I step toward him. "Take me on a date and I'll tell you what I want."

"I don't do dates."

My face must look monstrous with all the tears, but I still flip my hair. "In that case, I guess you'll have to start."

Then I brush past him with my head held high.

FOURTEEN

Creighton

"IS THIS YOUR IDEA OF A DATE?" I RUN MY GAZE OVER THE picnic-like setting on the roof of the shelter.

When Annika demanded a date yesterday, I was ready to ignore her.

But that's the thing about this infuriating girl. She's impossible to ignore.

Every time I pretend she's not there, she barges in with her colorful, chatty, and absolutely bratty presence.

Today, she came to volunteer with a huge carryall bag slung over her shoulder. Now, I see what it was for.

A checkered purple sheet lies on the ground and on top of it rests countless dishes. Pasta, meatballs, three types of salad, fish and chips, and a basket of fruits.

Annika is on her knees pouring what looks like apple juice into a glittery cup with an even more glittery straw.

I try but fail not to focus on her position. I'm almost sure she doesn't mean to be a cocktease, but that's exactly what happens when she naturally gets into these submissive positions and looks downright elegant while doing it.

Heat rushes to below my belt, and my cock slowly but surely

awakens. It thickens at the thought of stretching and tearing her tiny cunt from the inside out.

Too soon.

She's not used to pain.

Fuck, she didn't even know pain before I came along. I have to remind myself that I can't break her...*yet.*

Her fashion today doesn't help, though. She's wearing a ruffled skirt that stops above her knees and an off-the-shoulder crop top that reveals her belly button. With the way I'm looking down at her, she appears so small that I could ruin her with a flogging.

No, mere biting would do.

Her translucent skin would become red, then purple—like her favorite fucking color.

"Unfortunately, I'm like the first daughter and have to be watched at all times, so this is the only type of date we can have until further notice." She smiles up at me, the blue-gray of her eyes sparkling under the hint of sun. "Are you going to just stand there all day?"

With a sigh, I lower myself onto the edge of the blanket and grab some utensils. "Do you have to make everything so...*purple?*"

"Do you have to be grumpy about everything? Besides, purple is superior. Sorry, I don't make the rules."

I stare at her, and usually, she'd break eye contact or try to talk her way out of the situation, but this time, she simply shakes her head as if I'm the one being unreasonable.

Then she pushes the fish and chips in my direction. "Look, I made your favorite. Totally had to beg Ces to teach me how to cook it over FaceTime, and it wasn't really that hard. Also, people say I'm a horrible cook, and by people, I mean my family is included. Ava also says I should stick to salad, so I totally understand if you don't want to eat it."

Should've said that before she gave me that cursed lunch box. I opened the container and took a bite of food and basically swallowed it without chewing. I'm the number one non-picky eater on the planet. As long as it's food, I'll devour it, but Annika is a certified food terrorizer.

She should be banned from the kitchen.

I'm surprised my expression doesn't change as the salty thing rolls down my throat. I take another bite before the first one is gone.

When I grab a bottle of water, I realize she's watching me with big eyes and parted lips.

"How is it?"

"Not bad." An overstatement. It's the worst thing I've ever consumed and that's saying something, considering Mum isn't that great of a cook either.

But just like my mum, Annika made the effort for me. So that's a positive, I think.

Her face falls and she toys with the straw in her cup. "Oh."

Is it normal that I hate that type of expression on her face? It's even more noticeable when it drastically changes from all bright and fucking glittery to complete dejection.

"It's good." I continue eating. "Just a little bit excessive on salt." *Another understatement.*

"Really?" She reaches a hand out but then stops. "Can I try it?"

"No."

"Stop being so stingy. I just want to see how bad the salt is."

"Still a no."

She stabs the fork in her salad and stuffs her face with it, glaring at me from beneath her lashes.

I resist the urge to smile at her absolutely comical expression and open my water. It's the first time I've seen someone with their emotions so out there that it's become a bit intoxicating.

It's so entertaining to provoke or rile her up just to see the noticeable change in her face.

We eat in silence for a beat, or more like I eat, then drink water almost at the same time.

Still, I wait for the peaceful phase to end in three, two, and *one*—

"I thought this would be a date, but apparently, I just set you up with food. Maybe I shouldn't include anything to eat in the future."

You shouldn't cook anything in the future.

But I don't say that and, instead, move on to the meatballs after I finish the first dish.

Annika's still holding on to her salad for dear life.

"I've been meaning to ask you, why do you enjoy food so much? Actually, I don't know if you really enjoy it or if you just like the act of eating."

I swallow the mouthful of the equally horrific meatballs and lift my head. "Why are you asking?"

"I want to get to know you better."

What's there to know?

Having been acquainted with her personality, I have no doubt she'll bolt at the first sign of darkness.

She didn't run from your fucked-up side yesterday. Or the time before that.

I ignore that small voice and mutter, "There's no need to."

"Uh, no. That's not up to you to decide. Although I'm not sure what we are exactly, I am sure we're something, and the rules say we have to open up to each other. So you might want to tell me or I'll bug you."

I raise a brow. "You'll bug me, huh?"

"To death, mister. You can count on it. I'm nothing short of persistent. In fact, persistent should probably be my middle name.

"Pretty sure it should be brat," I grumble. She grins and I narrow my eyes. "What?"

"Nothing. I like that you have a sense of humor, as dry as it is."

"Did you just call me dry, brat?"

She slaps a hand to her chest in pure mock reaction. "Did you just call me a brat?"

"Watch it or I might start counting."

She purses her lips, and a slight jerk lifts her shoulders. At least the promise of pain has an effect on her.

For now.

I take a sip of water and stare at the buildings in the distance. "There was a time in my childhood when I nearly starved to death. Ever since then, it's always felt as if there's a black hole in my stomach that can't be filled or satiated, so whenever there's food, I have this need to just…consume it all."

Her hold weakens around her fork and she stares at me with puppy eyes.

Innocent eyes.

That I'm tempted to fill with tears all over again.

"Are your parents aware of this?"

"They saved me from that eternal starvation."

"I'm sorry—"

"Don't pity me or this will be the last time I share anything with you."

"You're right. I'm sorry. I had no business pitying you, and I didn't really mean to. Empathizing just comes naturally to me. But I swear to Tchaikovsky, I won't do it again."

I have known a lot of people. Some are secretive as fuck, others are fake, some are real, but all of them, without a doubt, hide a piece of themselves.

Annika is the only one who's been this upfront about herself. What you see is literally what you get—most of the time.

I have a feeling that I can pull out the darkness lurking beneath the surface if I dig deeper and tug harder.

The fact remains, she's the only one who'd admit to doing wrong without bothering to offer excuses.

And I might like that a bit too much.

She pushes the third dish, pasta, in front of me.

I take it, swallow a salty-as-fuck bite, then lean back on a hand with the plate on my lap. "What's with you and Tchaikovsky?"

She beams, her face brightening as if she's meeting her idol. "He's my god. You know how people worship Jesus, Allah, and Buddha? I listen to Tchaikovsky's ballets, concertos, and symphonies. They give me the same spirituality that religions strive for. It started when I was maybe four and Mom took me to my first ballet. I legit cried watching *Swan Lake* and got lost in Tchaikovsky's brilliance. As soon as we got home, I told her, 'We need to talk, Mom. I decided that I'm totally gonna be a swan when I grow up, so convince Papa and make it happen. Pretty please.'"

I glide my fork on the plate without eating. It's not that I hate the saltiness so much, but her storytelling in that soft, energetic voice is more entertaining than food.

That's a first.

"I assume she did make it happen?" I ask for no other reason than to keep her talking.

"At the beginning? She was totally against it. So, the thing is, and I found out more about this as I grew up from Mom's favorite guard and best friend, Yan—he happens to be Papa's least fave, by the way, because Papa can be petty and jealous. Anyway, Mom was like an iconic prima ballerina in the New York City Ballet, but her career ended abruptly. After that, she kind of hated the whole scene and only began coming to terms with her career ending when I was young, which is why she took me to that show in the first place. She has friends there—big-name directors, choreographers, and ballerinas. Still, she didn't want me to experience that life. So instead of helping me convince Papa, he had to be the one to convince *her*. Shocker, I know. Couldn't believe it myself. In the end, it all worked out and she agreed to let me start taking classes a few months after my first trip to ballet." She sighs and sips on her juice. "I was so sure I wanted to be a ballerina. I even managed to get into several shows in high school and did so well, but Mom convinced me to try college for a year, study art from an academic perspective and see if maybe I like it better than ballet. I agreed more for the adventure than anything, and the chance to leave Papa's watchful gaze, even temporarily. I'm not sure which one I like the best. I'll just decide at the end of the year." She lifts her head, eyes widening. "Sorry about that. I got carried away, I guess."

"About what?"

"You…won't say I talk too much?"

"You do talk too much."

"Oh."

"I'm used to it."

"*Oh.*" This one comes with a grin. "But, you know, I feel like I talk too much around you because you talk too little. Someone has to fill the silence."

"Why does it have to be filled?"

"Isn't it human nature to socialize and form connections?"

"Not all humans are the same."

"That's true. I didn't realize your type existed before."

"My type?"

"Looks like a prince and has the tastes of the devil. Totally caught me off guard and blindsided the hell out of me."

My lips tilt in a smirk. "The tastes of the devil, huh?"

"Duh, have you seen your face when you inflict pain—wait a minute, are you smiling?" She pulls out her phone and snaps what seems like a thousand pictures, long after I return to my blank face.

Still, she grins, looking pleased with her accomplishment as she scrolls through her phone.

I shift in my place to ease the sudden thickening beneath my belt. "You said you hate the pain. Is that still the case?"

"Totally. Who wants to be in pain?" She's still focused on her phone.

My jaw clenches and I tighten my hold on the container. I thought she'd come around if I took it easy on her at the beginning, but maybe I'm wasting my time with someone who'll only want vanilla.

But I couldn't have mistaken her tastes.

Annika has an inner submissive that peeks out now and again, especially when she's not paying attention.

"Part of my devil's taste is that I can only feel pleasure if I inflict pain."

"Don't I know it." She shakes her head in mock reaction. "I'm still sore from yesterday's stupid punishment."

"Look at me."

"One sec."

I reach out, grab her phone, and fling it from her hold. "When I say to look at me, you look at me."

She swallows thickly and a red hue creeps up her cheeks. I want to lick that blush, gnaw at it, grind it between my teeth.

I lift her chin with my index and middle fingers so that I'm the center of her attention. "If you think this is a temporary game or experimenting, then you have no fucking clue what you're dealing with, little purple. I'll eat your life up for breakfast and leave no leftovers for anyone to pick at. When I order you to do something, you don't question it, you don't give me attitude, and you certainly don't be a brat about it. Is that clear?"

Her lips tremble before she purses them together.

"Where's your answer?"

"I'm still thinking about it."

"There's nothing to think about in a 'yes, I understand' reply."

"Nope, I'm not going to agree with everything you say. That's not how relationships work. There's give and take and all that stuff. You can google it."

"Annika."

She beams even as the tremble remains. "What, Creighton?"

"You're pushing it."

"And you're being oppressive. I'm cool with your dominance in sex, and even with the pain, because it brings pleasure, too, but you're simply not going to dictate my life or make me live it according to your rules. That's like Papa and Jeremy 2.0 and I'm not a fan."

I release her jaw and push back. "That's one."

"You can't possibly be serious?"

"Two."

"Oh, come on. I can't express my opinion?"

"Not when you're defying me, no. Three."

"Stop counting, damn you."

"Not if you don't stop talking. Four."

"You—"

"Five."

She opens her lips to say something but promptly seals them shut and glares at me with her arms crossed over her chest.

Seems that I found the perfect method to make her keep her mouth shut.

I finish my meal in silence while she stabs her salad over and over yet barely eats anything. I suppress a smile.

Only Annika would try to make noise, even if solely through her actions.

She opens her mouth a few times, then upon remembering that she'll add to her punishments, she seals it shut and groans softly.

I watch her struggle for a few minutes, loving the sight a bit too much, before I finally speak, "You have something to say?"

"I hate you right now."

My jaw clenches. "Six. Next time, think before you speak."

"I still hate you. I can't believe I sacrificed my freedom for you last week."

"Seven." I tilt my head. "And what do you mean, you sacrificed your freedom?"

"Did you really think Kill, Niko, and Gaz let you leave out of the goodness of their hearts?"

I narrow my eyes. "Don't use nicknames. They have names."

"Oh, please. Besides, that's not the point. It's that they thought you burned the mansion, and you were the most likely candidate, too, considering your closeness with the Elites, so to deflect the blame, I told them you were with me all night long. Naturally, Jeremy found out and put me on house and campus arrest."

I place the utensils and the container on the ground. When I woke up back at the Elites' mansion, Remi was being hyper, calling me his favorite spawn and asking me not to worry him anymore.

He also said that they got a call from the Heathens to come fetch me, so I thought Nikolai realized he'd made a mistake by knocking me out and they decided to let me go. Never would I have believed that Annika had something to do with it. The good girl Annika. The 'conflict is evil' Annika.

No shit, I actually heard her tell Ava that exact sentence once. Conflict is evil and should be avoided at all costs.

I thought Jeremy tightened the security around her and stopped her from coming to REU's dorm due to worrying about her safety.

Turns out, he was specifically keeping her away from me.

"Why are you only telling me this now?"

She throws a hand in the air. "I didn't think it was important."

"It is. Didn't I warn you against putting yourself in danger? I could've dealt with your brother."

"And when would you have done that? Before or after the Heathens beat you to a pulp?"

"Doesn't matter. I mean it, Annika. Stop sacrificing yourself for others. No one is worth it, me included."

"I get to decide that, not you."

"Annika," I warn.

"Eight? Whatever."

"Make it a nine."

She releases a frustrated breath, but she eyes me with that innocence again. "Did you do it?"

"Do what?"

"Burn the mansion?"

"You think I did?"

"I don't know what to think. You have a history of arson at the Heathens' compound. Why did you do that, by the way?"

"Nothing you need to know about."

"Then how about showing up in my room? I think I have the right to know why you showed up there of all places."

"I was trying to find an escape." And I could've used any balcony, but I subconsciously jumped into hers.

It was easier to spot considering the purple cushions and girly Plushies in the patio.

Back then, I wasn't sure why I made that snap decision to get into her balcony, but now I do.

Even when I thought I had absolutely no interest in Annika Volkov and her annoying, chattering presence, I still looked for her when she wasn't around. I never voiced it aloud, but I noticed when she wasn't there.

Despite myself.

Back then, she didn't come to the girls' apartment for three days and was confined to her brother's mansion.

And a part of me wanted to see her.

Her shoulders drop at my answer, but she says, "Is that what the second fire was all about? You couldn't finish the job with the annex so you decided to widen your scope?"

"And risk your life in the process?"

"Small sacrifices for the greater good, right?" Her whole body goes rigid and her fingers tremble. She doesn't want to believe her words even as she says them.

"If that's what you think, we're done here." I get up.

Annika jumps up with me and grabs my arm. "Is it true?"

"I don't know. You tell me. Do you believe I would hurt you, then save you *and* your brother?"

She remains silent.

"Do you fucking believe that, Annika?"

"No," she lets out in a small murmur. "But I want to hear it from you."

"I would never hurt you."

A long breath rushes out of her, and the light slowly returns to her eyes. She smiles a little and stands in front of me, close enough that I'm dwarfing her. "Outside of sex, you mean."

"Outside of sex, brat."

"What if it gets to be too much and I really can't take it anymore? What do I do then?"

"Pick a word and say it. I'll stop."

"Ohh, like a safe word?"

More like a break from my darkness. But I nod. "Yeah, a safe word. What do you want it to be?"

"Violet," she says without thinking. "I don't like it as a color. It's less superior than purple."

"Why am I not surprised?"

"Because you're starting to get to know me. Congrats on becoming a VIP."

I flick her across the forehead teasingly, not hard enough to hurt.

She slaps a palm on the assaulted skin. "What was that for?"

"For your smart little mouth."

"I'll take that as a compliment—oh no!" She stares up at the sky as it opens and rain pours out. "My hair. Come on, England. Damn it."

She runs to the door that leads downstairs with her hands covering her head.

Upon finding refuge in the doorway, she looks behind her to find me standing where she left me.

I'm staring up at the sky, letting the rain soak me in seconds. I close my eyes and allow it to wash over me.

I've always loved the rain.

It rained when I woke up in the hospital that day and the day I met Mum and Dad for the first time. In a way, rain rinses away everything.

Including a bloody past.

It gave me a new beginning, even if only temporarily.

"Creighton, what are you doing?"

"Feeling the rain."

"But you're all wet!"

My lips tilt in a smirk. "Is that comment supposed to be about me or you? Last I checked, your cunt was all wet after I punished it."

"You…damn sadistic pervert."

"And that's ten." I open my eyes, cock my head in her direction, and extend my hand. "Come here."

"If you think I'm stepping out in the middle of that rain, you're crazy."

"Isn't craziness normal in this crazy world?"

"Nuh-uh. I spent two hours fixing my hair to look this gorgeous."

"If you keep hiding from the rain, you'll miss out."

"I'd rather miss out than ruin my hair and clothes. Even all the food is destroyed."

I lift my shoulder and close my eyes again.

Annika's probably flying downstairs to dry her hair. I wouldn't be surprised if she has a change of clothes lying around somewhere. She's always prepared for these types of situations.

Always strives to look her best, as if anything less is a direct insult to her personality.

Slow classical music fills the air before a small hand slips into mine and the scent of soft violet fills my nostrils. "If I'm going to ruin my hair, you better dance with me."

I open my eyes and stare down at her petite face that's all soaked. Droplets of water slip across her cheeks and to her neck. Her white top has become transparent, molding against her strapless bra and revealing a hint of her round, perky tits.

I make a mental note to give her my hoodie before we go down so that no one gets to see her like this.

"I don't dance," I tell her.

"Don't worry. I'll teach you." She places her hand on my shoulder and plants mine on her waist, then starts to move slowly to the rhythm of the music.

She feels so small and right in my arms.

The need to feast on her, devour her, eat her the fuck up pulses inside me like an urge.

On.

And on.

And fucking *on*.

She must see the animalistic need on my face, because her lips part. The air constricts, shifting with unbearable tension that's been growing ever since I spanked her and she came from it.

Not only did she not mind the pain, but she was also turned on by it.

I wonder how far I can push her before eventually finding her limits.

I wonder if I'll stop at such limits.

"Now you make me spin," she whispers, her voice sounding too loud in the silence. Then she uses my hand to twirl her body with the grace of a feather.

I'm trapped by her elegance and how right she feels in my arms, how I want to keep her pressed up against me, so I pull her back and she crashes against my chest.

The moment she gasps, I lower my head and capture her lips with mine. Annika goes slack against me, her mouth slightly open, probably due to shock, and I use the chance to thrust my tongue inside.

I feast on her as if I've been starving for a taste, a sip.

A kiss.

My lips pressing into hers, my tongue confiscating hers, licking, sucking, biting and biting and *biting*.

She whimpers, her hands going limp on my shoulders, and that might as well be an invitation to eat her alive.

I kiss her like I've never kissed before, because I have never kissed before, never considered the act of any value—not until this wrecking ball bulldozed through my life.

My lips feast on hers with the energy of an unsatiated beast until she's gasping, until her body molds against mine. Until I can no longer decipher where she starts and I end.

The rain beats down on us like a witness of this moment.

The moment I decide that Annika Volkov won't be able to escape me.

Not even if she wants to.

FIFTEEN

Annika

TWO WEEKS HAVE PASSED SINCE THE DAY MY LIFE WAS flipped upside down.

Since the day I danced with Creighton in the rain and then he kissed me.

Or more like swallowed me whole and feasted on the remains until I thought I would pass out.

I never knew kissing could be a life-or-death experience, but Creighton is obviously making it his mission to revoke each and every one of my convictions.

Before him, I thought I was too sensitive to pain, but with every punishment, every slap of his hand, I'm beginning to think maybe I enjoy this depravity. Maybe my sensitiveness is one more reason why I like it so much.

Or maybe I enjoy what comes after—the controlling touches, the earth-shattering orgasm.

Even the tears.

Before him, I thought crying was a weakness. Now, whenever I cry, Creighton's intensity burns a notch higher and he devours me whole.

He's a sadist like that.

But he's *my* sadist.

Over the past two weeks, he's been introducing me to concepts I didn't know about. Like gagging my mouth with my panties or his fingers while he spanks me—he totally enjoyed that one a bit too much. Or making me beg for an orgasm, edging me on and on until I become a mess.

But he's also taught me to embrace the pain, to stop fighting it, and the moment I do, pleasure comes a lot more easily.

Partly because I'm becoming accustomed to his ministrations.

Partly because he's the one behind the pain. Not anyone else—Creighton.

Though I stopped idolizing him a long time ago. Not only is he an imperfect human, but I also dislike him sometimes. Especially when he goes into his tyrant mode and refuses basic requests.

If I say no, I'm punished.

If I defy him, I'm also punished.

If he feels like I'm being a brat? Yeah, that one gets me in deep trouble.

Sometimes, it seems that his immaculate control is his way to keeping parts of him sealed inside.

That theory has been getting more plausible the further he deepens my punishment whenever he feels a rebellion building inside me.

After that kiss, I felt a wall between us had been demolished. The sad news is that I'm discovering more and more walls.

It's like he's keeping me an arm's length away, far enough to not peek at his true nature.

Beyond the sadist who can't feel pleasure without inflicting pain, I mean.

Which is why I've been pushing to get him out of his comfort zone. And that's basically by demanding dates. Yes, I get punished for them, but it's worth it.

At first, we often met up on the roof of the shelter and had lunch, but Jeremy loosened the security last week.

No more guards follow me around and I don't have to look over my shoulder. I even go to hang out with the girls—still not at the stage where I spend nights at the dorm, though.

I had to put my foot down for my freedom, called Papa and Mom, and told them I was going to run away if they keep shackling me.

"That is, if you can run away," is what Papa said matter-of-factly, but then he told Jeremy to grant me freedom.

Papa is all about tough love, I tell you.

But anyway, after gaining my long-awaited freedom, Creighton and I went out to see a movie, and he surprisingly didn't fall asleep during it.

We also went jogging up the mountains, or more like he dragged me up. *What?* I don't like hiking. That's what it's called. It's not jogging, it's damn hiking.

He just smiled and shook his head as I struggled, turned red, and demanded a break every ten minutes.

The discomfort may have been worth it since I got to see his smile. They're as rare as special editions and have the ability to cause heart issues. So maybe it's a blessing that he doesn't show them often.

Besides, I don't want to share them or him.

But I kind of have to today.

Ava, Cecily, and I have gone to the fight club. This is where REU and The King's U students beat each other up. They even have a championship for it. It's like a venting outlet for all the rivalries they have going on.

Since the Heathens are regulars in the championship, Jeremy made it blatantly clear that I'm not allowed here.

The last time he found me, he escorted me out before I even watched any fighting and put me under house arrest.

So I had to sneak in this time. I made sure to wear an oversized hoodie, hide my hair, and even put on sunglasses.

My vision isn't the best, considering it's nighttime and the glaring lights, but it's better than being kicked out before I can watch Creighton fight in the semifinals against none other than Nikolai.

The same Nikolai who always appears ready to fuck up someone's face and end another person's life.

"Have you guys tried to stop him?" I ask the girls with a half-spooked voice.

"No one can stop Creighton from fighting," Cecily says.

"Not even Uncle Aiden." Ava gets on her tiptoes to get a better view of the crowd. "And Uncle Aiden is, like, the most ruthless person I know, no kidding."

"Maybe he got his ruthlessness from his father?" I ask, catching a glimpse of Creighton talking to Remi on the side of the ring, or more like listening as Remi does all the talking.

He's only wearing black shorts, putting his physique and the spider tattoo on display. And I can't help watching it closely, getting lost in the striking details.

I've seen more models than I could count, but in my eyes, Creighton is the most beautiful man alive.

And yes, I'm biased.

"Nope," Cecily says. "Uncle Aiden isn't violent. Not even close. He's just calculative and methodical to a fault."

"Totes, but he can become violent if need be. Dad always says he can't believe Creigh is Uncle Aiden's son. Like, he's so sweet and well-mannered and actually fits Dad's personality."

Sweet? I stare at Ava, dumbfounded. Are we talking about the same Creighton or does he somehow have a twin?

Cecily smirks. "Yeah, your father obviously prefers Creigh over his older brother."

"Shh. Don't bring up bad mojo when I'm having fun." She points at Cecily's T-shirt that says, *Violence isn't the answer. Violence is the question, and the answer is yes.* "And you totally came here for fun."

"You're the one who bought me this."

"Looks perfect on you." She grins. "I should've made that wuss Glyn wear it. Can't believe she ditched us again."

"Doesn't she hate violence?" I supply.

"More like she's more interested in Killian. I'm rooting for her, though. That girl needed to get shagged a long time ago."

"Still wish that she'd gotten with someone other than a student from The King's U," Cecily mutters under her breath, then smiles at me. "No offense."

"None taken." I wave a hand absentmindedly while focused on Creighton.

On the other side of the ring, Nikolai flings his arms out and tilts his head back, eyes closed.

His black satin robe flies wide open, revealing his red shorts and the extravagant tattoos covering his chest.

It's like he's doing a satanic ritual.

The silver lining is that both Jeremy and Gareth are by his side, so I can keep an eye on them and bolt if they come in this direction.

My brother is scheduled to fight against Landon in the second semifinal match next week, and I'm definitely not going to be around to watch that.

Nikolai's eyes flash open and stare directly at me.

Shit.

I half hide behind Ava, but his gaze remains the same. If he tells Jer I came here despite his clear warnings, I'm doomed to another episode in the ivory tower.

Wait.

I move sideways and Nikolai's gaze doesn't track me.

It's on…

I follow his line of vision to find a stiffening Brandon who's standing behind us. His hand pulls at the back of his hair as he meets Nikolai's savage gaze, lips pursed, eyes hard.

It's the first time I've ever seen him look so upset, so…perturbed.

"Bran!" Ava jumps him in a half hug. "What are you doing here?"

His expression reverts back to normal and he drops his hand from his nape. "Remi begged us via the group chat."

"He did?" Cecily asks. "How much do I have to bribe you to show us that?"

"No need for a bribe." He fishes out his phone and scrolls to a group chat called *Lord Remi's Sidekicks.*

Remington: My favorite—and only, might I add—spawn will be fighting in the semifinals tonight! I'm going to need you all to come and cheer for our youngest little shit. I have tears in my eyes, I swear. When did he become all grown up?

Eli: Stop talking about him as if he's a kid.

Remington: Fuck off, psycho. You call him baby brother all the time.

Eli: But only I get to do that.

Landon: We can always do it behind your back.

Eli: Not if you wish to live another day. He's my brother.

Landon: And my baby cousin.

Creighton left the chat

Remington: Blah, blah, blah. You scared my spawn away with all your ramblings. He's my cousin and my spawn, but you don't see me bragging about that, though I totally should. Anyway, who's going to be at the fight club?

Remington added Creighton to the chat

Brandon: You know violence isn't my scene.

Landon: Beg first, your lordship.

Eli: Yes, beg. And make it worth our while.

Remington: What kind of fucked-up kink is this? The only time I'll beg is when both of you are shoved into hell. That's when I'll get on my knees and plead with Satan to skin you alive and let me watch.

Landon: I guess that means you'll go alone.

Eli: We would hate for you to look sad, Remi.

Landon: The fangirls wouldn't approve.

Eli: You might lose shagging rights.

Remington: Fine, you fuckers. Please come.

Landon: Pun intended?

Remington: Fuck you, Psycho 2.0. Tell anyone about this and I'll kill you. Okay? Okay.

Creighton has left the chat

Cecily laughs and Ava stares blankly at the screen for a while before she chuckles, too.

"I'll pay you to send me screenshots," Cecily says.

"You can get them for free."

"Awe, we don't deserve Bran." She grabs him by the arm.

"Bitch, the whole world doesn't deserve Bran." Ava wraps an arm around his free shoulder.

He subtly slings it off him. "Thanks for the compliment, but I kind of still want to live another day."

She rolls her eyes and steps back.

"Does Creighton always leave the chat?" I ask.

Bran smiles. "Yeah, and Remi adds him back in. It's like a cat and mouse game."

"Does he talk to you guys?"

"Rarely."

"OMG." Ava watches me intently.

"What?"

"You little bitch! All this time, you said you were putting Operation Fake Boyfriend on hiatus because you're hung up on Creigh, aren't you?"

"Now that you mention it." Cecily narrows her eyes on me. "Maybe the reason she doesn't glue herself to Creigh's side anymore is because they're having alone time in private."

"Also, Creigh did ask me what the best film at the cinema is these days," Bran supplies to my horror.

"A date?" Ava's eyes nearly bug out. "Cray Cray on a *date*? This is huge. We need deets, like *all* of them, and in order. Did you kiss? Did you fuck?"

My face must look crimson, but I still clear my throat. "I…don't know what you guys are talking about."

The three of them close in on me, but before they can grill me for answers, the fight begins.

That definitely gets their attention.

I release a long breath, but it's caught in my throat when Nikolai all but lunges at Creighton as soon as the referee announces the start.

Most fighters spend the first few seconds carefully circling each other.

Not Nikolai.

He was born to inflict violence. A mafia prince through and through.

The King's U's crowd goes wild as he lands the first blow, sending Creighton's face flying sideways.

A gasp falls from my lips and my whole body stiffens.

REU's crowd starts chanting Creighton's last name in unison. Ava and even Cecily join in.

"King, King, King!"

I'm unable to breathe properly, let alone speak.

Creighton sways back, but he doesn't fall. He swings his fist and it lands straight in Nikolai's face. Blood trickles from his nose, and he groans, then wipes at it with his wrapped hand.

They go at it for some time, one hitting and the other jumping back before punching harder.

All the shouts, screams, and cries from the crowd mingle together until they become one.

It takes everything in me to stay and watch as they punch and send each other flying. But I do because this is also a part of Creighton.

There must be a reason why he is the way he is. Why he's so intent on inflicting sexual pain and violence.

And I need to be acquainted with it.

Only then will I be able to understand Creighton.

And I want that more than anything. I can't just take his lashes of pain and hide from the reason he became like this.

Remington jumps by the side of the ring, calling out and cheering him on. Soon after, Landon joins him, a bored expression covering his face.

Both Cecily and Bran go still at the sight of him. Only Ava continues jumping up and down. "Get him, Cray Cray! We love you!"

"Do you now?"

Ava comes to an abrupt halt, and her mouth remains slightly parted as we all turn toward the gravelly voice.

The newcomer is none other than Eli. I've never met him, but I've seen him around, and Ava made me follow him on IG so she could stalk him.

He followed me back, so we're in that awkward situation where we're mutuals but have never spoken.

Besides, he's Creighton's brother and his IG is one of the few places where there are any updates of him. Some of them are within family settings, but most are selfies where Creighton is sleeping in the background and Eli has captions like:

Documenting the Sleeping Beauty chronicles. Day 100.

The cheeky bastard fell asleep while I was talking. The audacity is presumptuous.

I asked him to choose between me and sleep. He covered his head with the sheet. Revoking brotherly rights as we speak.

Eli King looks nothing like his younger brother. They're both handsome, but while Creigh looks like a beautiful prince, Eli is more like a serial killer prince. His build is leaner, his features sharper, cutting even. And he has black hair and dark gray eyes that could compete with pure metal.

I thought maybe the drastic difference in their looks was a case of someone taking more after one of the parents, and that's true in Eli's case. He does look like a carbon copy of their father. Creighton looks nothing like their mother, though, so maybe he resembles someone else from the family.

Ava's face has gone red in the span of seconds, but she still says, "Shouldn't you be hiding in the dark to do some satanic rituals?"

"I'm missing an important ingredient." His expression doesn't change. "Blood."

Wow. Okay. Maybe the King brothers are more alike than I initially thought.

"Annika, right?" He offers me a hand and I shake it. "I'm sure Creigh talks about me all the time."

"He actually doesn't." I grin, then follow up with, "But I've heard about you."

His brow furrows. "Not from him?"

"No?" I answer awkwardly, thinking that's probably not what he wants to hear.

"That cheeky bastard." His gaze flits to the fight that's getting heated. "Want to get out of here?"

I cast a glance at Cecily, but she pretends the fight is more important than the nuclear war currently happening.

Ava grinds her teeth, but she stares ahead, too.

Brandon has been so engrossed in the fight that he hasn't moved an inch. Hell, he's been so silent that I'd forgotten he was here in the first place.

"Leave her alone," Ava finally grits out.

A cruel smirk curves Eli's lips. "I have a few things to ask Annika. It won't take long."

The two of them glare at each other, or more like Ava does, while he keeps that perfect smirk in place.

I'm distracted away from whatever is going on between them, because something's changed in the ring.

The crowd goes wild and it's because Creighton has backed Nikolai in a corner.

Punch.

Punch.

Punch.

His expression has turned savage as he plows over and over. Nikolai bursts out laughing, maniacally, not even attempting to protect himself.

I catch a glimpse of Bran lifting his hand to his nape and tugging at the short hairs so violently, I wince.

The harder Nikolai laughs, the more savage Bran's hair pulling turns.

The referee announces that Creighton has won by points. REU's crowd goes crazy, shouting his last name.

Cecily claps. Bran turns around and leaves without a word.

Eli and Ava are still in that weird stance that even made her lose focus on the fight—and that says something since she's the most enthusiastic about these types of scenes.

I throw a glance behind me and gasp when Creighton jumps from one of the ring posts. He completely ignores Remi and Landon and jogs in our direction.

The crowd parts for him, and some slap him on the back while others attempt to shake his hand. He pays none of them any attention. His sole focus is on me.

There's a cut on his lip and his face looks like that of an underworld lord who's fresh out of a battle.

"Oh, hi—" Whatever I had to say dies in my throat when he grabs me by the waist and slams me to his side.

Creighton's voice is clipped at best as he glares at his brother. "Stay the fuck away from what's mine."

And then he drags me out of the club.

SIXTEEN

Annika

"**H**EY, SLOW DOWN…"

I practically jog to keep up with Creighton's wide strides. We fly past the gaping students who are probably as shocked as I am by his actions.

Or maybe it's because he's half naked, his honed muscles on display and only shorts hang low on his hips.

Even though I've never come to watch any of his fights before, it's a known fact that Creighton King is a reigning champion. His detachment is his power and the reason he won last year's championship and has won every match since.

So to have him lose his cool at the end of the fight must have looked like some sort of blasphemy.

His grip on my wrist forbids me from entertaining the thought of fighting. All I can do is keep up—or try to. When I remove my sunglasses to see better, they fall to the ground, but he doesn't let me pick them up.

We walk on and on, flashing past students and locals, and then we're going down the empty streets and past closed shops. I attempt to talk in a soothing tone, to tell him to slow down, but he's not hearing me.

He's a beast with the sole purpose of sweeping me off my feet.

The night air seeps into my bones and I'm thankful I wore a hoodie, not only does it keep me warm, but it also allows me much-needed anonymity.

"I'm fine with being kidnapped and all, but can you please walk slower?" I try to joke. "It's impossible to keep going at this pace."

He glances at me over his shoulder, eyes dark and tension rippling through his frame. "Shut up."

My words die in my throat. I guess that means he's angry. No, maybe it's a step beyond that.

But why are these destructive emotions directed at me? It's not like I did anything wrong.

To prevent unknowingly worsening my case, I bite my tongue and let him drag me to God knows where.

After what seems like forever, we arrive at the beach. People usually go to where there's sand so they can enjoy the water and the view.

Definitely not Creighton.

He leads me to a rocky area where the pointy parts look like savage animal fangs.

I struggle to get free. "No, nope. I'm not going there."

He pulls on my hand and I plant my feet on the ground. "I said I'm not going there. Weird things live on those rocks, waiting for their next victim. Who knows what type of animal would jump at me in the dark?"

"The only animal you need to worry about is me."

My lips part and he uses my moment of bewilderment to tug on my wrist, bringing me along with him to the top of a huge rock.

I carefully watch my surroundings. It's dark around here, the sky is cloudy, and only a distant streetlight offers a break in the night.

The waves crash against the shore with a ferociousness that causes a shudder to trickle down my spine.

Creighton flings me forward so that I'm standing with my back to the water and he's towering over me.

He appears monstrous in the dark, a piece cut from the night and custom-made to inflict punishment.

He's dangerous violence wrapped in beautiful skin. Dry blood sticks to his hairline, the corner of his lip is cut, and a bruise decorates his cheekbone.

I'm still studying him when he presses against me in a single motion, his hungry gaze stripping me bare and his intensity rippling with every intake of oxygen.

My foot slips and I yelp as I grab onto his taut arm. "What the hell are you thinking?"

"I should be the one to ask you that."

"Me?"

He says nothing, continuing to glare at me, probably figuring out how he'll lay me on his lap and spank me.

I shiver at the image but ignore the throb between my legs. "If you don't tell me what you think I did wrong, I won't be able to figure it out. As much as I would love to mind read, I, unfortunately, don't have that superpower."

"One."

"Oh, come on. You're just being spiteful and unfair right now."

"Two."

"Creighton!" Anger bubbles in my veins, but I know that if I continue to be guided by that emotion, I'll only be digging myself into a hole.

Especially with the way he's watching me as if he's at the point of explosion.

So I smooth my tone, stepping closer to him, my voice softening. "Can you please tell me what's going on?"

"Stay away from Eli."

My brows crease. "Isn't he your brother?"

"Doesn't mean you get to be close with him."

"Why not?"

"Stop asking questions and do as you're told."

This is one of the times when I'd usually shoot out a barely thought-out reply and get myself in trouble. But I force myself to remain calm. In the few weeks I've spent in Creighton's company, I've come to the realization that he doesn't deal with human emotions like the rest of us do.

He's not soulless like, say, Killian, Nikolai, or even Jeremy. It's not that he doesn't care. He just chooses not to. It's a conscious decision he must've made a long time ago.

Which means that he does have feelings, imperfections, and secrets—that I've been trying to unravel.

And to do that, I can't be guided by emotions. Not only does he not react well to them, but the more I escalate, the deeper he escapes into his sadistic mind.

So the only way to bust down his sturdy walls is to willingly open my own and show him the vulnerable part of me.

"You know I'm on your side, right?"

His grip softens on my wrist. "You are?"

"Sure as hell. I'm your number one fan and currently sabotaging all the other fangirls and fanboys, namely Harry, so they'll stop thirsting after you. I'll bribe him with luxurious skincare products and let you know how it works."

His lips twitch and that's the nearest thing to a smile he offers, so I snatch it, lock in the corner of my heart with his name all over it, and press my body even closer. "Point is, since I'm on your side, I kind of need you to trust me, put your faith in me and tell me things. I swear to Tchaikovsky's grave that I'll keep it a secret."

"Is that so?"

"Totally."

"Okay."

"R-really? Okay?"

"Yeah. In return, you'll stop bringing up Tchaikovsky."

I pause. "But why?"

"I don't like it when you admire other men."

"But he's dead. He's been dead for over a century."

"Don't care."

I can't help the snort that escapes me. "Are you perhaps...jealous of a dead old man?"

"Guess that means you're not interested in this trade." He releases me and goes to sit on a nearby rock.

I follow after and pull the hood of my sweatshirt away from my hair, letting it fly in the wind. I spend a few minutes observing my sur-roundings, searching for a creepy animal. When I see nothing suspi-cious, I wipe the ugly, dirty surface and I settle beside him. "Fine, fine. No more Tchaikovsky."

Except in my head.

He gives me an approving glance, then focuses back on the ocean, remaining as silent as the night.

But his lack of words never undermine his imposing presence. He's prone to turning into a lethal weapon if he chooses. No, it's not a choice. He has destructive energy that needs a breathing outlet. He's like the rock he's sitting on, unmovable and solid. But the waves still slam against its hard surface, trying on and on to eventually reach its core with the sheer power of their persistence.

It's me. I'm waves. Waves is me.

I bump my shoulder against his. "This is where you keep your part of the deal."

"You need to learn some patience."

"Totally have been doing that since you dragged me out of the club like a caveman."

His head tilts in my direction. "A caveman, huh?"

"Hello? Did you see the expression on your face?"

His gaze gets lost in the violent water again. "I always have this inexplicable need to protect you."

"I can shoot a gun better than a pro, you know. Papa trained me from the time I was little, after a lunatic tried to kidnap me, so I have a perfect shooting score and never miss. And Jeremy often tells me to carry a gun. Point is, I can protect myself and kick some ass. Well, shoot some ass, but semantics. Besides, I wasn't in a dangerous situ-ation at the club."

"I don't like it when others touch what's mine. Especially Eli."

My heart jolts at that word. *Mine.* He said it earlier at the club, but I was more concerned with being kidnapped in front of all those onlookers whom Creighton was paying no attention to.

"Why especially Eli?"

"He's an anarchist. The type who has no purpose other than to watch the world being flipped upside down. If he puts you in his sights, you're done for."

Oh. "I think he was just offended that you never mentioned him to me."

"He's clingy like that."

"Eli? Clingy?"

"Yeah, he won't leave me alone and it isn't due to lack of effort on my part."

"From what I've seen on his IG, he's only like that with you. Otherwise, he's more like Kill, absolutely detached while giving the exact opposite image."

"And how do you know that?"

"We're mutuals."

"Mutuals?"

"Oh, right. I forgot you don't do social media. Being mutuals means we follow each other."

"You *follow* him?"

"Why not? The point of social media is to follow people."

He narrows his eyes. "Unfollow him."

"No."

"Annika." The sound of my name in his deep, rough voice is nothing short of a command.

"Stop being a tyrant. Besides, I'm following Remi, Bran, and even Landon. Not to mention Nikolai, Gareth, and Killian. Do I have to unfollow them, too?"

"Preferably."

"Might as well tell me to delete my socials."

"Preferably."

I snort. "You're impossible."

"And you're so out there that it pisses me the fuck off." In a flash, his fingers squeeze my jaw.

I can see the darkness creeping into his features. The air shifts with his earnest stare, and his not-so-subtle plan of laying me on his lap and extracting his punishments from my skin.

But we're not done talking.

"You can always start your own social media and stalk me," I suggest. "That way you'll know everyone I'm interacting with."

"Not in this lifetime." His thumb strokes my chin, back and forth, with heightening intensity.

"Worth a try." I pull the sleeve of my hoodie over my hand and wipe at the dry blood. "Why do you fight?"

"I have too much excess energy that I can only purge through inflicting violence and pain."

A craving.

An impulse.

Part of who he is.

But why is he the way he is?

Instead of asking that, I go for, "What happens if you don't purge it?"

"Nothing good comes from pent-up pressure." His lips thin in a line. "If you're considering options to change who I am, save it."

"I don't want to change you." *I want to understand you.*

The last words get stuck in my throat before I can relay them and I stroke my finger over the cut on his lip. "Does it hurt?"

He makes an affirmative noise, his eyes getting lost in mine as his thumb continues the maddening back and forth on my chin.

Back and forth.

"Really?" I start to pull my hand away.

Creighton grabs it and places it back on his face. "You can continue."

I grin. "Are you sure it hurts or do you just want me to touch you?"

"The second."

"Wow. You've come a long way from when you refused to let me touch you."

"I don't like giving up control," he admits in a low voice that gets carried by the wind.

"It's in good hands with me."

"Doubt it."

"Why?"

"You're a brat."

"I can be good, too." An idea springs to mind and I perk up. "What if I prove it?"

"Prove what?"

"That you can give up control for me and I'll treat it well."

"I don't like where this is going."

"Trust me." I drop to my knees between his legs.

The harsh surface of the rock hurts my skin, but I don't pay attention to that and, instead, focus on my mission.

In the semi-darkness, Creighton shares the aura of a warlord, half naked, bloody, and fresh out of a battle.

Not to mention that we're in a public place where anyone can walk by. Yes, we're hidden from the main street, but someone could wander back here.

The old Annika would be freaked out, but I couldn't care less.

Not when Creighton is here.

My fingers latch onto the elastic of his shorts, a bit shaky, but not to the point of being a fumbling mess.

At first, he lets me pull at the material, but then his hard voice vibrates in the air. "What do you think you're doing?"

"Bringing you pleasure." It takes me a few moments to free his cock.

I pause as my small hand barely contains his girth.

What the...

I've never seen a cock in real life, aside from some unsolicited dick pics. Or some porn—don't judge, I was curious.

But I knew those porn stars' dicks didn't reflect reality.

However, Creighton is totally porn-star level. Both in girth and length. Now, I'm having second thoughts about my earlier plans.

His index and middle finger slip beneath my jaw, lifting it, trapping me in the darkness of his eyes. "You going to wrap these lips around my cock and let me choke your pretty throat with my cum, little purple?"

Holy shit.

My heart jacks up in speed. He's supposed to be silent, so how come he has the best dirty talk?

"Have you deep-throated another cock before, Annika? Have you let another prick fuck your mouth and turn your lips all swollen?"

My thighs clench together.

Seriously, he needs to stop talking like this. My actions are supposed to be about him, but I'm the one who's getting shamelessly wet.

"Answer the question."

"No, it's…my first." Like it's *his* first.

I know because once, we played 'never have I ever' with everyone else, and he admitted to never having his dick sucked. A fact that made Remi throw a dramatic fit.

Ever since then, I think I've secretly fantasized about being the first girl to give him a blowjob.

Especially now that I realize he's probably never allowed himself to receive oral because it takes away his control.

But he's not stopping me now.

If anything, he's watching me with fiery eyes and a lust-filled expression.

The fingers that were beneath my jaw push against my lips. "Open."

I do, and he glides his middle and ring fingers all the way inside. He pushes them against my tongue, smears them with my saliva over and over.

I start to gag, spluttering around them.

"Breathe. If you can't handle my fingers, how will you take my cock?"

I use his eyes as an anchor as I inhale through my nose. Slowly, the pressure eases and I lick his fingers. A low humming sound falls from his lips as he wraps his other hand around mine that's on his cock.

Then he uses my grip to slide it up and down his length in a twisting motion, making me jerk him off. "Don't just lick. Be a good girl, and use your tongue between my fingers."

I do tentative thrusts between his fingers and quicken my rhythm. The more he releases pleasure sounds, the harder I go. My head turns dizzy from the overstimulation, and my thighs become so wet that I wish I could reach a hand down to touch myself.

Creighton pulls his fingers from between my lips and from around my hand. "Put my cock in your mouth."

My lips wrap around his length, his authoritativeness adding heat and tension to the act. But my mouth is so small that I struggle. And he enjoys that, judging by the light sparkling in his ocean blue eyes.

I do as he taught me with his fingers, though they don't compare to his monster cock. I breathe deeply, trying not to gag, and I lick the sides over and over.

He groans and my pulse picks up. Is it normal that I'm soaking my panties at the thought of his arousal?

That I want to deepen that look in his eyes, to trap it, and make sure I'm the only one he gives it to?

Creighton slides his fingers in my hair, fists it and wraps it around his hand, then stands.

I stare up at him as his other hand strokes my face with a sinister edge. "So beautiful and innocent, my little purple. So...breakable."

My body goes rigid, but I still try to lick, to prove that I can give him pleasure the same as he can give me.

"I'm going to fuck your face until you choke on my cock. This might hurt."

He thrusts his length all the way in and I gag, for real this time. I'm not ready for the onslaught of his power, for the way he's using me like I'm a fuckable hole.

Tears sting my eyes and I'm not sure if it's because of that realization, the suffocation, or the wetness smearing my thighs.

He uses his merciless hold on my hair as he thrusts in and out of my mouth. I choke and splutter, tears, drool, and precum trickling down my chin.

The erotic sound of his in-and-out mixes with the violent waves and crashes against my rib cage.

Creighton can't feel pleasure without inflicting pain, so the more I gag and cry, the deeper he groans.

The harder he goes.

The more twisted he becomes.

This is so screwed up, but I must be as deviant as he is, because the further he takes it, the more brutal he gets, and the wetter I become.

He goes on and on, each of his thrusts like a direct stimulation to my starved core. Then when I think I'll come from being deep-throated, a salty taste explodes all over my tongue.

Creighton pulls out and stuffs his fingers into my mouth, authority dripping from his every move. "Swallow."

I have no choice but to do so. He gathers the cum that streams down my chin and thrusts it between my lips, forcing me to lick every drop.

When he finishes, he lifts me up by the hair and slams my body against his as he kisses me.

No, he devours me.

He licks every last bit of cum off my lips, my tongue, and then some. He ravages me, eats me, detonates me from the inside out.

I try to kiss him back, but he's like a beast. There's no way I could match his intensity. So I let him feast on me, and I sink into the perverse, erotic way he drinks his taste off my lips.

When we finally break apart, I sway back and his hand wraps around my waist, keeping me standing.

His nose rubs over my hair and an appreciative groan spills from his lips. "Good girl."

The hairs on my body stand on end and I'm surprised I don't melt in his embrace.

Damn it. Are those two words supposed to be such a turn-on?

"You owe me at least three dates for that," I grumble.

My body goes still when something I've never witnessed before happens.

Creighton throws his head back and laughs.

It's heartfelt and happy and causes my toes to curl.

And I think maybe, just maybe, I'm in too deep with this beast.

I'm in so deep that I will try everything in my power to understand him.

Even if he doesn't like it.

SEVENTEEN

Creighton

"**A**RE YOU GHOSTING ME?"

The question is accompanied by a kick to my side, a poke, and a subtle shove, tumbling me out of bed.

I fall to the ground with a thud and I groan as I sit up, then glare at my deranged cousin.

Landon grins and makes a rectangle with his thumbs and forefingers. "Perfect expression. You're art material, Cray Cray. How about you model for me?"

"How about you give up asking me that?"

"Not when you could change your mind." He sits on my bed—the one he kicked me out of—and stares down his nose at me. "You didn't answer my question. I sense ghosting vibes."

"Shouldn't it be me who senses those?" I stand, punch him out of my bed, watch as he falls down, then sit so that I'm the one staring down at him. "You've been stalling for the information we agreed on."

"Not the face, you bloody sod," he curses while smiling. "And I wasn't stalling, I was just piecing the puzzle together to form the bigger picture. I can't reveal anything until all the pieces are where they're supposed to be."

Ever since we were kids, Landon and Eli have been obsessed with chess and have done everything under the sun to win. They've gone as far as challenging Dad, Uncle, and Grandpa Jonathan. As in, the strongest chess players we know.

They each managed to win against both Uncle and Grandpa—the latter, I think, because he let them.

Dad remains the reigning champion, though.

They also never win against each other. In fact, Eli and Lan are still playing a game they started years ago.

Landon, in particular, has always viewed the world as his chess-board and the people in it as his pawns.

Me included.

And while I don't give a fuck about that as long as I get what I want, something's been bugging me since the fire.

Lan watches me carefully before he throws his weight on the bed across from me. Once he's sure I won't kick him, he smiles like a creep.

"I've been thinking," I say.

"Oh? How did you find time for that between the excessive sleeping and eating enough for an army?"

"Were you behind the fire that burned the Heathens' compound?"

"Haven't you heard? They're blaming it on the Serpents. Nasty bunch, those ones. Venomous, too, last I checked."

"Did you set them up?"

"Do I look capable of such satanic acts?" When I remain silent, he grins. "Fine, I am capable of that and more, so who knows? If events can be falsified, why can't the truth?"

I spring to a standing position and haul him with me, nearly choking him with my grip on his collar. "I don't give a fuck about your plans, or lack thereof, but you will not, under any circumstances, put Annika in danger again."

His face turns blue from the lack of oxygen, but instead of fighting, his grin widens, turning proper monstrous.

I release him when I'm on the verge of strangling him to death. This fucker is abnormal, and if I hadn't let him go, I would've probably killed him and he wouldn't have moved a muscle.

It's not that Landon isn't violent, he is, but that happens on his terms, not anyone else's.

I honest to fuck have no clue what Dad sees in him and why he chose to personally nurture him. He's deranged.

And that's saying something, considering my and Eli's character.

Landon falls on the bed, that creepy permanent grin still plastered on his face. "How would you have had the chance to be a Prince Charming if she hadn't been in danger?"

"So you *were* behind it?" I reach out to him again and he ducks and rolls out of bed.

"Once was me being courteous, twice and I'll fucking kill you, Cray Cray. We don't want Uncle Aiden sad, now do we?"

"I mean it. Play your games far away from what's fucking mine."

My lungs burn with the words and how true they are. Annika is mine. She was mine long before I even considered it, and I'll fuck up anyone who attempts to hurt her.

No, I'll destroy anyone who causes her discomfort. That's enough to land anyone on my shit list.

I'm not sure where this obsession with her will lead, but I'm committed to seeing it through until the very end.

Especially after the semifinals fight last night.

I was thinking of ways to chain her to me, but she went ahead and got on her knees for me. To Remi's horror, I've never been interested in getting head before, but the moment Annika put my cock in her mouth, I turned into an animal who's solely driven by primal instinct. And when she let me face-fuck her and swallowed my cum, my beast soared to the surface.

Landon circles me slowly, taking his time with the act. "I thought you were no longer interested in pain, but it seems you've found a permanent purging outlet. As I thought, Annika Volkov is the reason you've been absent from our bonding time. Is that interesting or what?"

"Erase whatever you're thinking."

"Oh? This is way worse than I could've anticipated." He taps his lips with a forefinger. "Take my advice. Stay away from her and her brother and her whole fucked-up entourage. It'll only screw you up."

If he thinks that whatever the Heathens do would scare me away, he has no clue what lengths I would go to keep what's mine.

"Want to go to the club? Vary your tastes?"

I shake my head. The thought of touching anyone but her makes me physically ill.

He shrugs, heads to the door, then stops and speaks over his shoulder, "Still don't want to join the Elites?"

"No."

"One of these days, you'll change your mind. Oh, and you might want to check your phone."

Then he's out.

I lie back on the bed and retrieve my phone.

Usually, I do that only to find out if Annika has sent me any texts. She's the type who likes to take pictures of all the little things she encounters in her daily life and send them over with 'Isn't this so cute?' or 'I wish I could take this home with me.'

They're typically cats or dogs or any small creature.

So imagine my surprise when I find no text from her in the past... two hours.

Now, that's rare.

Normally, she'd be demanding a date or she'd lure me in for a conversation.

Not tonight.

I scroll to the group chat that Remi insists I stay part of. I mute them whenever they start blowing up my phone with notifications.

Remington: Who wants to partyyy?

Eli: Don't throw it in the house and you can do whatever you want.

Remington: But why? I have privileges in the house.

Eli: Not unless you want to put your balls in jeopardy.

Remington: Bloody hell, mate, no threatening the family jewels. I have a title that I need to keep alive.

Landon: You can always go to a club.

Remington: Be right back. Let me go get my spawn.

Brandon: Creighton's sleeping.

Remington: Never stopped me before.

Brandon: Don't wake him up. If you need someone to go with you, I will.

Remington: Awe, I just got tears in my eyes. I knew you were my favorite, Bran.

Remington: Don't tell Cray Cray.

Landon: @Creighton King

Remington: I'm going to fucking kill you.

What the hell did Landon want me to see? Remi being a clown? Or the fact that he's out to shag and has successfully dragged Bran along as a sidekick?

A notification appears at the top.

Landon: Forgot you're a hermit.

Attached is a screenshot from Remington's Instagram.

He's posted a selfie where Ava, Cecily, and Annika are standing between him and Bran. And he has an arm around Annika's shoulders as they smile brightly.

My favorite party people. Join us?

My fingers clench around the phone and wildfire spreads across my chest as I continue to look at her. And Remi's arm around her bare shoulders, since she's wearing a strapless dress.

So this is the reason she didn't text me. Apparently, being busy partying is able to wipe her memories.

I text her.

Creighton: Where are you?

No reply comes in...five minutes. Which I spend pacing the length of the room.

When her name pops up on my screen, I lean against the wall.

Annika: Um, hi.

Annika: I mean hiiii.

Annika: Hi :)

Annika: That's what people say before asking questions. Hi :)

Creighton: Are you drunk, Annika?

Annika: Nah, nope. No.

Creighton: Are you sure?

Annika: Uh-huh. Though I did have a drink.

Creighton: Only one?

Annika: Maybe two. I like drinking. I'm gonna ask him to bring me another.

Creighton: Who's him?

Annika: My favorite drinking buddy, of course.

Creighton: Name.

Annika: You guess :)

Creighton: Remi or Bran?

Annika: Maybe both. Maybe it's someone different.

My grip tightens on the phone and it takes all my control not to throw it against the wall.

Creighton: Where are you?

Annika: No, nope. I'm not telling you so you can come and spoil my fun. You prefer sleep anyway. Nightyyy.

I send her a few more texts, but she doesn't even read them.
The little fucking—
I spring up, throw on a hoodie, and text Landon.

Creighton: Address.

Landon: That was fast. Can I bring popcorn and come watch?

Creighton: Address.

Landon: We need to work on your conversational skills, baby cousin. Here you go. Don't murder my brother. Remi's life, however, is all yours.

It takes me fifteen minutes I don't have to arrive at the club. I step out of my car and head inside with rigid steps.

The loud music, shouts, and the fucking noise are similar to having a machine prowl inside my head.

I push through the wiggling, twisting bodies as they jump and sway and drink and snort drugs.

After some time of shoving people out of my way, I arrive at the top level of the club. I grab the railing and cast a glance at everyone jumping around downstairs.

The colorful lights dim my vision, making them look like a copy of a copy.

In the midst of the chaos, my eyes are drawn to a girl in a light purple dress. Her rich brown hair falls to her half-naked back.

Annika, Ava, and Remi jump together to the music and point at a corner of the room across from them. It's where Brandon and Cecily sit together, watching them with smiles and a lot of shaking their heads.

The emotions from earlier heighten in intensity as I practically jog down the stairs and to where they are.

When I arrive, it takes all my restraint not to punch Remi in his aristocratic nose and potentially start a dramatic saga.

But I do barge into their circle and shove him away with my shoulder.

He stumbles sideways and barely escapes having his face smashed on the ground.

Ava is the one who notices me next, pauses her manic jumping, and nudges Annika.

The infuriating little minx is the only one who keeps swaying and wiggling her hips.

I grab her by the nape and pull her toward me in one swift go. Her back crashes against my chest with a thud and the scent of violets fills my nostrils.

A shudder slashes through her body and seeps into my system. No clue how I manage not to tighten my fingers around her neck and give her a red necklace.

Annika must feel the darkness radiating off me. Her pupils dilate and her fuckable lips part in clear invitation.

She goes still in my hold, and I'm addicted to the way her inner submissive knows when to lay low and not provoke me further.

It's probably her survival instinct, too, because she knows this won't end well for her.

I catch a glimpse of both Cecily and Brandon joining us, drinks in hand.

"Spawn!" Remi shouts over the music. "You made it! Wait, you willingly came here without me having to hound the fuck out of you? Who are you and what have you done with my favorite spawn?"

"OMG!" Ava holds her hands together, completely ignoring Remi's speech. "You're here because of Anni! This is too surreal to wrap my mind around. I can't believe the traitor was totally keeping us in the dark about your relationship. I'm so wounded."

"Yeah," Cecily supplies. "She's been ignoring us and changing the subject so we wouldn't bug her for answers."

"Right? I mean, what's there to hide? They already went on a date! He even called her his in front of He-Who-Shall-Not-Be-Named. Right, Bran?"

"Yeah," he agrees. "I was there at the fight club and personally heard it."

"Hold on. What in the actual fuck?" Remi gets in my face. "A *date*? You went on a date and didn't tell me? And what's with the ownership declaration when I wasn't there? How am I your mentor if you don't come to me in times like these? And I'm the last one to know? You bitches have conspired to kill me young, haven't you?"

"We haven't gone on a date," I say.

Annika flinches in my hold, but she forces one of her loathsome fake smiles. "Yeah, it's not what you guys think. No date."

"Not one date. *Dates*."

Everyone stares at me, dumbfounded, Annika included. The whole scene draws attention to us, considering we're the only unmoving ones in the midst of the unfolding chaos.

"Wait. *Dates*?" Ava all but shouts.

"Plural, yes." I stroke my fingers over Annika's heated skin and stare between Remi and Bran. "She's mine. If I find out either of you touched her, prepare to lose a limb."

Then I spin her around and my mouth claims hers in a savage kiss. My arms envelop her waist like a shackle, preventing her from escaping my possessive hold. All she can do is gasp, open up, and let me feast on her.

She sways on her feet when I release her lips and I drag her out of the club while the other four stand there in stunned silence.

Annika keeps up with my steps, her expression still caught in complete bewilderment.

"Uh, are you sure that was a good idea—"

"If you're in the mood to be able to sit at all tomorrow, shut the fuck up."

Her lips purse and a tinge of both fear and thrill seep into her eyes.

It should only be fear at this point, because my plans for her exceed anything I've done before.

EIGHTEEN

Annika

THIS NIGHT IS THE DEFINITION OF CHAOS.

It started with me being a little mad.

Well, not mad—upset. A little bit sad, too.

So I went to the club because I was trying my hardest to stop being so upset.

Did it work?

Partially. Okay, no, it didn't. Not really.

My mood became gloomier after the text exchange, but I danced and drank to forget about it. The icing on the cake was Creighton actually showing up to a club—shocker, I know—to stake a claim on me in public. *Again.*

My lips still tingle from his punishing kiss, from the way he devoured me whole and left me no room to breathe.

Or think straight.

Or remember that I'm actually slightly wounded by him.

After he gave me coffee to sober up, the car ride has been spent in utter silence. Every time I've tried to speak, he casts me a glare, and if I insist, he adds to the 'punishments' count.

He reached four before I gave up, crossed my arms, and stared out the window.

Because screw him.

He's the reason I've been in this mood and even needed a venting outlet. I'm simply not going to feel bad about that.

This isn't the first time I've been in Creigh's Range Rover. He used to drive a Porsche, but a week ago, I complained that it was too small when he told me to sit on his lap, so he changed it two days later.

When I asked him if he had anything to tell me, like maybe he did it for me, the heartless idiot only said, "It's nothing. This is an old gift from my favorite grandfather, Agnus."

On good days, Creighton is cold, but on bad days, like today, he's no different than the ice of the Arctic Ocean.

The car slows to a halt in front of a giant mansion's gate that resembles my brother's.

This is the first time I've been here, but I can already tell it's the Elites' compound.

The black metal gates open and Creighton drives inside, passing a well-manicured lawn until we reach the circular driveway.

The building is nothing short of a regal castle, definitely less gothic than the Heathens', and reeks of the powerful old money the entire REU is made of.

"Get out." Creighton's voice is deadpan, almost lifeless, and that causes my skin to crawl.

I'm probably sober if I can be assaulted by feelings this way.

As soon as he steps out of his car, I unbuckle my seatbelt and stumble outside. I only had like two drinks and I'm obviously a lightweight, because that was enough to get me tipsy.

But I'm not anymore and something else has been keeping me on edge.

Or, more specifically, someone.

"Follow me." Creighton starts in the direction of the huge front door.

"Can you stop dishing out orders?"

"Five, and no."

I clamp my lips shut and fall in step beside him, arms crossed, body rigid, and with frustration bubbling in my veins instead of blood.

Rather than focusing on the asshole, I choose to study my

surroundings. The interior is as elegant as the exterior, considering the marble flooring, baroque wallpaper, gold-trimmed railings, and classical furniture.

They could definitely invite the queen for tea if they felt like it.

Creighton leads me up the stairs, where we pass a few closed doors before he pushes one open and motions me inside.

I step in carefully, expecting to find some torture devices that suit his character.

My feet come to a stop right past the entryway. It's just a bedroom.

All gray like England's sky and could use a splash of color, but it's still a normal guy's bedroom.

A breath whooshes out of my lungs, but it catches when the distinctive click of a lock echoes in the air.

I spin around, but I'm not even fully facing him when his fingers wrap around my nape and he flings me against the wall.

My front slams on the hard surface and his collides with my back. Tall, muscular, imposing.

Threatening.

His hot breaths meet my ear and he whispers in dark words, "Mind telling me what you were thinking?"

I attempt to look behind me, meet his eyes, but his merciless grip forbids any movement.

"About?" I try to sound calm, even as my insides quiver and explode in a thousand colors all at the same time.

"Don't fuck with me, Annika. Did you go to that club with Remi and Bran to prove a point? Maybe to pick up your fake boyfriend plan where you left off?"

"It's not like that..."

"Then what is it like? What made you go out with them without asking me to come along?"

"You don't even like clubs."

"And I don't like dates or dancing, or the fucking cinema, but I've obviously been doing all of those. So why don't you tell me the reason behind tonight's little rebellion? Were you trying to be a brat?"

My lips press in a line and I stare at the wall, summoning patience that's nowhere to be found.

Creighton tightens his hold on my nape. "I'll take that as a yes."

"No," I murmur.

"Then what is it?"

I remain silent for a beat and his hand comes down on my ass, hard. I yelp as the sting spreads across my whole body and settles between my legs.

"For every second you stay silent, your arse is mine to punish."

Slap.

I get on my tiptoes, my heart hammering in an unnatural rhythm. I can feel the stiffness of his chest against my back, I can sense how much he's repressing and how far he wants to go with this particular punishment.

If it were up to him, he'd probably crush my limits and leave me with nothing.

Hell, maybe he'll leave me and I'll have nothing.

I've been trying so hard to understand him that I didn't stop and think to help him understand me, too. Mum said relationships can only be formed when there's a middle ground, and in order to find that, I have to communicate what I feel.

"I was upset," I admit in a low tone, hating how vulnerable I sound.

His hand squeezes my ass, but he doesn't spank me, even as his voice remains clipped. "About?"

"It's my birthday tomorrow and I was looking forward to this one in particular because I'm turning eighteen. So this morning, when I asked if you had plans tomorrow and you said yes, I was upset that you have other plans on my birthday. But it's not fair to be upset when you probably don't remember my birthday since I told you about it a few weeks ago. I realized I was being immature and I chose to vent that energy at the club."

I can feel the in-and-out of his breaths against my back. How it's slowed after quickening, matching the rhythm of his strokes against my ass.

Silence stretches between us, but I don't try to fill it. I wait for him to mull over his words before he speaks them.

"You should've told me that."

"Have you missed the part where I said I thought I was being immature? I'm embarrassed to even talk about it now, so can we drop it?"

"No."

"Creighton—"

"The plans I had were with you."

I pause the self-shaming display at the low tenor of his words. I heard that correctly, right? He had plans for *me*?

Every single one of our dates has been in one way or another planned by me and he's just come along for the ride. This is the first time he's planned something.

I attempt to look at him, but he still won't allow it, so I stare at the wall, relishing his authoritative touch. "What…what did you plan?"

"You have no right to know when you pissed me off."

"But I didn't mean to."

"Yes, you did. You were being a brat on purpose because you missed your punishments. You've been a bad girl, Annika, and do you know what happens to bad girls?"

My body presses back against his as that familiar tension builds in my core. He has a way of waking my most demented desires with a mere change of his inflection.

The moment his voice lowers, I know I'm in deep trouble.

"They get eaten out."

Slap.

I flinch at the hit, but his grip still forbids me from moving.

"Creigh…please."

"No amount of begging will save you tonight." His hand slides from my ass to my hip and to the curve of my waist before stroking the skin of my back. "You should've never been in that club dressed like a present waiting to be unwrapped. You should've never defied me."

He fists the fabric of my dress, then rips it in one savage go, and I gasp. It's not only due to his aggressiveness, but it's also because of the stimulations invading me all at once.

My breast slips from the built-in bra and the dress pools on the floor and I remain in nothing more than my panties.

Absolutely soaked panties.

How could a few spanks and the change of his tone be enough to turn me into this mess?

Creighton pushes off me, and my skin tingles where his hands touched me.

"Lie down on the bed."

His authoritative tone leaves no room for negotiation, and I stumble in the direction of the bed and then lie on the messy sheets.

They smell like him, all male and addictive. It takes everything in me not to hug his pillow to my chest or something.

Creighton reaches into his closet and I strain to see what he's up to.

He reappears again with a black leather bag. Usually, I would comment on its fashion and quality, but I don't get the chance to before he starts to retrieve ropes from it.

His low, rich, and absolutely collected voice rings through the room, then strikes my skin. "I planned to get you more immersed in pain, to train and discipline you better before bringing you to this point, but you had to go and provoke me, little purple."

Ropes.

Ropes.

More ropes.

I swallow the lump that's gathered in my throat, but it only grows in size.

Creighton drops the bag on the bed and climbs up. The mattress dips with his weight as he straddles my middle with his knees on either side and grabs both my wrists with one hand and shoves them above my head.

His jeans create a heated friction against my naked flesh, causing goosebumps to erupt and multiply at a scary speed.

"Creigh…"

"Shh." He wraps the rope around one wrist and secures it to the metal headboard and then does the same to the other.

I try to pull my hands, but the knots he's made get tighter with every attempt. Shit. He's an expert at this, isn't he?

Creighton pushes off me, appearing way bigger than I remember him as he stands opposite me.

I lift my head, watching him grab an ankle and tie it to the foot of the bed. Then he repeats the move with my other foot so that I'm completely stretched out on the mattress and only my panties offer any sort of barrier.

And I need that right now.

While he was tying me up, I was kind of hyperventilating. And although I enjoyed the foreplay of punishment and pleasure, this situation is different.

I'm completely at his mercy, where I wouldn't be able to escape even if I wanted to.

I'm trapped by a cold-blooded, ruthless monster who wants a pound of my flesh.

Literally.

Figuratively.

Creighton rummages in his bag that's on the floor and reemerges with a blindfold.

I shake my head frantically.

Yes, I'm agitated, but I would rather see what he has in store for me, even if it's too much to handle.

He lifts my jaw with two fingers, then skims his thumb over my parted lips. "You'll be my pretty little doll tonight, Annika. I'll use your pale flesh as my canvas and mold you into my plaything until you're all stuffed with my cock, sobbing and screaming my name. The only thing you'll have to stop me is that one word."

And then he straps the blindfold over my eyes, turning my world black.

My mind races the moment my vision is confiscated.

He's right. I have that word and I can stop this.

I *can*.

But for some reason, I don't want to. At least, not now.

So I breathe slowly, like whenever he had me on his lap or on a table. In a way, this isn't any different. I'm just tied to the bed.

Besides, it's not like he allowed me to move before, even if I wasn't bound.

This is exactly the same situation in a different setting.

Or I'm just deluding myself.

My senses heighten due to my loss of sight. My ears home in on the slightest sound, my nose gets permeated with Creighton's scent, and my skin becomes so sensitive that I can barely handle the soft sheets.

A sound comes from off to the side and I figure out he's rummaging through his bag of terror again.

Anticipation and thrill mix together, warring inside me until I think I'll throw up.

My breath catches when the noise stops and I feel him hovering over me, watching me silently, expectantly.

Then something cold touches my stomach and slides down to the waist of my panties.

"C-Creighton?"

"I love it when you call my name in that scared little voice. It turns me on."

A whole-body shiver slashes through me because I have no doubt that my fear is his catalyst and that he gets off on it and my pain.

Still sliding the cold—now warmer—thing over my stomach, he bunches my panties with his fist, pulling them against my clit.

My body arches off the bed as inexplicable pleasure washes through me. How could the helplessness and the darkness turn me on this much?

I'm so sensitive that a mere rub of my clothes is enough to send me into overstimulation.

A slitting sound brings me out of my reverie.

Air hits my core as my panties are removed. And then something plastic is placed at my mouth.

"Suck."

I part my lips at his command and wrap them around what feels like a ball.

"Good girl."

My movements become more enthusiastic at his praise, and I suck and lick as if it were his cock.

Too soon, Creighton pulls out whatever he put in my mouth and runs it down my clit, between my folds. He teases, rubbing and sliding it through my wetness until I'm writhing.

Then he thrusts it inside me. I jerk as the object—a sex toy, I assume—fills me. And then a slow humming starts in my core and against my clit.

A shiver goes through me at the tame stimulation, almost like a tender touch, which Creighton is too cold to ever offer.

"We'll play a game." He glides the tip of the object he first touched me with over the hard tips of my nipples. "If you don't come by the end of your five punishment strokes, I'll let you go. If you do come, however...you're mine to devour."

I gulp, but it turns to a full-on shriek when his first slap lands on my tender breasts.

Fire spreads across my skin and eats me up from the inside out. The place where he struck me burns and tingles in a chaotic mayhem.

It's a crop, I think. He's punishing me with a crop.

Holy shit. I didn't sign up for this.

Or did I?

Creighton has always been transparent about who he is and what his tendencies are. He's never once said he'd offer me normal or vanilla.

Hell, he even bluntly announced that he doesn't date, doesn't believe in the whole relationship charade, and has deviant tastes.

Singular cravings.

Violent tendencies.

With time, I've figured out he's a natural Dom and an unabashed sadist who's brought out the masochist in me.

In a way, I've been falling into that rhythm, into his abnormality. I like the freedom that loss of control offers.

I relish the feeling of not having to count my every step, be a perfect mafia princess and everyone's favorite person.

I crave the depravity and freedom he offers in a 'take it or leave it' deal.

But maybe I overestimated my pain tolerance abilities.

When the second slap comes, tears soak the blindfold and stream down my cheeks. The safe word is at the tip of my tongue.

I can end this.

If I choose to, I'll end this.

The third strike hits me with something completely different than excruciating pain. The vibration in my core and clit heightens until it's everything I feel.

By the fourth stroke, a moan and a sob tear from the back of my throat.

Pleasure pools between my legs and I try to clench them together, but that only tightens the binds around my ankles.

A foreign itch starts in my core, burning, waiting, throbbing for release.

I want to come.

I want to come.

I want to *come.*

I've never experienced this type of stimulation before and I think it'll be the death of me. That, somehow, I'll faint right here, right now with the need to just come.

"Creigh...p-please...please..." I don't recognize my voice or the lust in it.

I don't recognize the need rippling, aching, contracting in my core.

He runs his crop over my hard nipples and I shudder.

"This is supposed to be a punishment, little purple, remember? And yet your cunt is dripping a pool on the mattress. So messy."

"Please...please..."

"Please what?" He teases the tips of my excruciatingly painful and stimulated breasts. "Let you come?"

Unable to find words, I nod frantically.

"But that's a privilege exclusive to good girls, and you haven't been one tonight, Annika. Do *not* come."

The crop swishes in the air before it slaps my nipples again.

I'm a goner.

The wave that slashes through me is so different from any other orgasm I've experienced before. The power of it nearly blinds me.

It's a mixture of pain, pleasure, sobs, moans, and an unending throbbing ache.

It's a symphony of contracting muscles and a flooding arousal.

My nails dig into the rope for dear life as I fall on and on with no landing in sight.

A low, dark tutting sound surrounds me.

"I told you not to come, didn't I?" The rich darkness of his tone freezes me in place.

The mattress dips and soon after, he removes the blindfold.

I blink away the tears as light blinds my now sensitive eyes. That's when I see Creighton between my legs, his pants half down and his hard cock cradled in his hand.

He does a long jerk, handling himself with assertive roughness that dries my mouth. "I'm going to rip through your cunt and own you, Annika. I'll mark you so no one dares to come near you again."

Before I can say anything, he wrenches the sex toy away and thrusts inside me in one go.

His groan and my gasp mix and echo in the air. If I thought the toy filled me, then he's tearing me apart.

My whole body jolts and I hold on to the ropes for dear life.

Creighton stops, and his ocean eyes turn from dark lust to bewildered lust. "You're...a virgin?"

"It's okay," I breathe out, nails digging into the rope. "It's okay if it's you."

"Fuck," he curses low, so low that I hardly hear him.

Then he reaches to the side and retrieves a knife. Please don't tell me that's what he used to remove my panties earlier.

With expert moves, he cuts the rope around my wrists, pulls me against him, then reaches back to undo my ankles.

All while his cock fills me to the brim and the welts on my breasts throb, eliciting both pleasure and pain.

Creighton lies me back on the bed, his hands on either side of my face. His ocean eyes get lost in mine, dark and unyielding, as he slowly rocks his hips. "A fucking virgin. Why didn't you tell me you were a virgin, Annika, hmm?"

"I didn't think it mattered," I say between moans, falling into the rhythm of his cock.

"It matters if I was planning to fuck you like an animal."

I reach out both hands, ignoring the red marks on my wrists, and place my palms on his cheeks. "I like it when you're an animal."

"Fuck."

He says it in a voice that's barely audible before he crashes his lips to mine and thrusts into me. I can tell he's suppressing his true self in his attempts not to hurt me.

But when I dig my nails into his back and rock my hips, he ups his rhythm on and on until he's wrecking me from the inside out.

The ache from the welts adds to the friction and he pushes back to whisper, "Do you feel how your cunt strangles my cock, demanding more? It's my cunt, isn't it?"

I nod, letting the pleasure wash all over me.

"Say it."

"It's yours…"

"Tell me to fuck my pussy as I want."

"Fuck your pussy whichever and whatever way you want." I shudder.

"Fuck." *Thrust.* "Your cunt was made for me." *Thrust.* "*You* are made for me."

He slides all the way out, then slams back in. My vision whitens as the orgasm hits me with a strength I didn't think was possible after the pleasure from earlier.

This time, I call his name as he pounds and pounds until I'm driven to the edge, literally and figuratively.

"Creighton… Creigh…"

"I love it when you call my name with that erotic little voice of yours." He strokes my lips, my cheek, my nose, peppering hard kisses everywhere. "I love your face when you're being ripped apart by my cock." His rhythm goes up and up until the headboard bangs against the wall from the power behind his brutal fucking. "But most of all, I love how you take me like a good fucking girl."

I'm not sure if it's a continuation of the first orgasm or a new one, but his words coupled with his intense touch make me come again.

And *again*.

Creighton's lips meet the hollow of my throat before he bites down hard as he empties inside me with a grunt.

Pleasure with pain.

No pleasure without pain.

The stronger the pain, the greater the pleasure.

I think I start to understand that concept as I fall slack in his arms with a smile on my lips.

I'm not sure if it's a dream, but I can feel him cocooning me, touching my throat, then kissing my cheek and whispering, "Happy birthday, little purple."

NINETEEN

Creighton

I HAVE ALWAYS THRIVED ON CONTROL.

Not only is it safe, but it's also the only way I can express myself.

As a result, I've been too meticulous about it, too disciplined, too careful not to allow any chinks in my armor.

There hasn't been a day where I've given rein to petty, irrational emotions or even entertained them.

There hasn't been a day where I've let anyone close enough so they'd have the ability to peek inside me.

Peel my exterior open.

Smash my discipline to bits.

That is, until this fireball of a girl barged into my life uninvited, planted herself where no one has tread before, and has been detonating me from the inside out ever since.

Despite the streak of submissiveness that shone in her blue eyes, I chose to pay her no mind and ignored her as if she didn't exist.

She's too young, too different, too…full of life.

That's what Annika's image in my mind is. *Life.*

Bright, dazzling, full-of-purple-and-violet life.

And my pitch-blackness has no business tarnishing that light, slowly but surely devouring it.

Once I'm done with her, there will be nothing left for others to pick up.

She'll be too hollow. Too...lifeless.

The most logical choice is to let her go. I should've done that the first time I touched her. Preferably before. Because one taste is what started it all.

One taste is what tipped everything over the edge.

And yet, I fail to even contemplate the option where she's out of my life.

She came in like a wrecking ball and now there's a hole where the impact happened.

There'll be a day when I'll have to let her go. She's so beautiful and I'm destined to destroy anything of beauty.

But that day isn't today.

After turning on the faucet and letting water fill the tub, I grab a towel, wet it, and head back to the bedroom.

Annika passed out a while ago and is currently sleeping on her side, a slight crease furrowing her brow.

I push away the sheet that's covering her middle and she winces, probably due to the welts.

My cock strains against my boxers at the view of the angry red marks blotching her pale skin on her neck, tits, and her hard pink nipples.

I flick one nipple and she moans, burying her face in the pillow.

Only Annika would find this extreme pleasure in pain. She says she doesn't like it, but on the contrary, her body has become attuned to it.

The more I inflict pain, the harder she breaks apart.

She's a natural masochist. She just didn't know it.

Sitting on the mattress, I pull her legs apart and pause at the view of dried blood between her inner thighs.

She was a virgin.

A fucking *virgin*.

I should've suspected it, considering her sheltered upbringing, but on the other hand, she's resourceful and cunning enough to have had sex if she'd wanted to.

Maybe she didn't want to.

I reach a hand down to readjust my hard-on at the view of my cum that's mixed with her blood. Then I proceed to wipe it off with steady, unhurried fingers.

Low moans spill from her and it takes me more time than needed to clean her pink cunt.

I stall on and on, engraving this visual of her in the deepest, darkest corners of my memory.

Once I'm done, I throw down the towel, then open my side drawer and fetch a tube of ointment. I've never done any type of play at home, but I planned to bring Annika here all along—though not this soon—which is why I bought everything necessary.

From the ropes to the toys and finishing up with the ointment.

I slide it over the welts, my fingers lingering a bit too long on each angry mark.

My marks.

My bruises.

I marked her, so she's mine.

A sense of raging possessiveness grabs me in a chokehold as I inspect the map of welts I left. Or when I recall how she screamed and sobbed, then came apart while she took them.

Annika whimpers while I tend to her, but she shows no sign of waking up as she hides further in her pillow.

After finishing with the ointment, I carry her in my arms bridal style. Her head lolls and drops onto my chest, hair in disarray, lips parted, mascara running down her cheeks, but there's still no hint of consciousness.

The scent of violets mixes with the smell of sex and me, choking me and sending a redo signal to my half-erect cock.

Too soon.

If I follow that instinct, I'll just break her this time, and I don't want that. As much I get off on hurting her, I don't want to drive her to the point of no return.

I carry her to the bathroom, check the temperature of the water, and then I slowly lower her into it until her tits are partially covered.

If it were up to me, I'd keep her like this, with my dried cum between her legs and my scent on her skin.

But I'm not willing to sacrifice her discomfort for that.

If I expected her to wake up at the contact with the water, she doesn't. Her head angles to the side, letting her hair cascade down her shoulders and into the tub.

"Annika." I lift her chin. "Come on, wake up, little purple."

"Mmm."

Her tiny sounds of pleasure and her whines nearly have me coming in my boxers. Fuck. I feel her everywhere, in my bloodstream, on my flesh, and down to that forbidden nook in my heart.

I nudge her again, but an unintelligible sound is all I get. So I lean over and whisper in her ear, "What type of date do you want to go on next?"

That gets her attention, because her bright blue-gray eyes slowly open and she stares at the opposite wall, dumbfounded, almost without concentration. Then she focuses on her body that's entirely hidden by the water.

Her expressive blue-gray gaze slides to me and some of the confusion automatically withers away.

It's as if she...trusts me.

Big fucking mistake.

A sheep can never put its faith in the wolf. No matter what type of nice mask it wears.

Her fingers touch her neck, latching onto the necklace around her pale throat that I put there when she was asleep, and then she gathers the pendant in her palm, eyes growing in size.

"What is this...?" Her voice is a little bit hoarse, a little bit raw.

She's effortlessly the most erotic thing I've ever encountered.

And maybe, just maybe, that's not only due to her body that's made to be fucked and marked and tied up.

"Your birthday present. That's the closest thing to purple I could find."

"It's a diamond."

"So?"

"It's a pink-purple diamond. This is like so rare and expensive."

"Nothing's too rare when I ask my father for help. And thankfully, I'm rich."

She smiles softly, her fingers raking over the jewel. "This is so beautiful. I'll treat it like a treasure."

My breathing eases as she examines the necklace with awe. It makes all the effort I went through, having this specifically made for her, worth it.

After a full minute of admiration, she focuses on her body. "Wait. Did you run me a bath?"

"Obviously."

"But why?"

"Aren't you sore?"

She winces, then her lips push forward in a soft pout.

Adorable.

"Do you even have to ask? You kind of broke me with your monster cock. Literally and figuratively." She wiggles her toes beneath the water and sighs. "This is nice."

I retrieve my bottle of shampoo, sit on the edge of the tub, then lather her hair. "Monster cock?"

"Mmm." She leans into my hold, eyes closing. "Have you seen it lately? It belongs in porn."

My fingers thread in her hair and I tug it until her head clashes against my stomach. "You watch porn?"

Her eyes shoot open. "Everyone watches porn."

"I don't."

"You don't need to, considering your very *singular* tastes. Why watch fake scenarios when you can reenact them in real life? Check your privilege, not all of us could experience sex so young."

"One of these days, I'm going to fuck the sassiness out that mouth of yours."

"You're being impossible. Porn is normal, and it's not like I watch it all the time."

"What type of porn do you watch?"

Awkward laughter spills from her. "I thought you weren't a porn person. How did you know there are categories?"

I tug harder on her hair. "Answer the question, Annika."

"A little bit of everything. And, as I said, I only do it like maybe once a month."

"What terms do you search when you first open a porn site? When you're horny and your little pussy is throbbing, what do you look for?"

Her lips part and it takes everything in me not to stuff them with my fingers or my cock.

"Rough," she whispers, averting her gaze from me. "Hardcore. Amateur. I don't like the…uh, fake moans and orgasms, and I prefer seeing how it looks in real life."

"Don't watch it anymore."

"Why not?"

"I don't like it when you look at other men's dicks."

"Don't worry. Yours is much more brutal."

"I mean it."

"I can't believe you're being jealous of porn. You don't see me throwing a fit about all your *submissives*."

"You can."

She releases a sigh. "I won't. That would just be embarrassing. And, by the way, you didn't use a condom. I'm on birth control, so it's all good, but I don't want to catch anything your previous sex partners gave you."

"If they did, you already have it."

Annika pales to a deep shade of white and I laugh. "I was kidding."

Her lips part and she watches me closely, as if engraving every detail of my face to memory before she swallows. "Since when do you do that?"

"Since you."

"You also laughed."

"I only laugh around you." I stroke my fingers through her hair, massaging her scalp. "On a serious note, I'm clean. Not only do I always use a condom, but I haven't had penetrative sex in months."

"Why not?"

"Inflicting pain is usually enough stimulation."

"But not with me?"

"Not with you." I had to fuck her, own her, put my mark on her so no one dares to come close.

She nibbles on the corner of her lip. "If you've always used a condom, why didn't you with me?"

"I forgot, and when I remembered, you were soaking my cock with your blood. There was no way in fuck I would give up that feeling."

"You…don't have to be so detailed."

"You're the one who asked. Now, tell me…" I caress the long strands of her hair, pulling it to my face and being slightly disappointed that it smells like my shampoo and not her violet. "Why were you a virgin?"

She wiggles her toes in the water again. "It's kind of hard to lose it when I was surrounded by an overprotective family. But even when I had the opportunity, I didn't want to have sex in the back of a car or in a dark corner at a party where it'd just be underwhelming. This might sound clichéd, but I wanted it to be special."

"Was it special?"

"It was way more than that." She glances at me. "Definitely not what I expected."

"Despite all the porn?"

"Despite that. And stop being so judgy. At least porn taught me things."

"Such as?"

"That it's different from real life."

My fingers go back to the gentle rhythm of washing her hair. "How different?"

"Real life is more powerful, more intense, more…overwhelming." She glares at me. "And it hurts."

"Pain is a catalyst to pleasure." I grab the showerhead and start to rinse the shampoo off her hair. "You could've stopped it if it got to be too much."

"Nah." She leans against my hand, rubbing herself on me like a kitten. "I like the pain, but only if you give me baths like this afterward."

"Just so you know, I won't be going easy on you."

She blinks the water out of her eyes and rolls them. "Never expected you to, sadist."

A smile twitches my lips.

"Look. You're even being all happy about it." She glances at me over her shoulder. "Did you know that you're the most amicable after you inflict pain? Not sure if I should be glad or freaked out about that tidbit."

"I vote for the second."

"My Tchaikovsky. You're so cutthroat."

My good humor vanishes. "What the fuck did I say about worshiping that composer?"

Her eyes widen and she slams her fingers against her lips. "Sorry, I forgot."

"Next time, I'll put you on my lap."

"Yes, sir," she mocks.

"Don't call me that."

"Don't you guys like being called Sir or Master?"

"Not me, and not with you."

"Good, because I prefer Creigh." She grins, so widely, so happily, that I want to devour that smile.

And *her*.

I want to flog her, spank her, bend her on the edge and fuck her over and over until she's screaming my name.

It takes all my control to get up. "I'll leave you to it."

A small hand catches mine, pulling me to a stop.

Her innocent expression fills my vision as she murmurs, "Do you have to go?"

"I can't just stay and watch you."

"You totally can." She splashes the water in the opposite direction with her foot. "You can also join me."

I revel in the sight of her victorious grin when I turn around. Those inquisitive eyes of hers watch me openly as I slide down my boxers and kick them away.

She studies my every move, and it's no different than if she were digging her sharp nails and teeth into my flesh.

I've never been so proud of my physique as I am in this moment where Annika watches me as if I'm her custom-made god.

My cock hardens at her attention, demanding a second round of fucking her brains out.

I force myself to sit in the lukewarm water opposite her instead.

She stretches her legs so that they rest on my thighs. "I think the tub is too small for the two of us."

"And you only now thought of that?"

"It just came to my attention." She slides her foot up, stroking my side with her purple-polished toes.

The skin where she touches me sends an electric shock straight to my cock.

"Stop that unless you want to be fucked raw right here, right now."

She bites her bottom lip like the little brat she is, but she lowers her foot so it rests on my thigh. "What does the spider tattoo mean?"

"Does it need to have a meaning?"

"No, but it's unusual for someone to tattoo such a big spider on their skin, so I thought maybe there was a story behind it."

I let my arms hang over the edges of the bathtub and lean my head back. "More like a tragedy."

"A tragedy?" Her voice is barely a murmur.

Not sure if it's because of that or the peaceful atmosphere, but the words tumble out of me with ease I've never experienced before. "There was a three-year-old boy whose father was powerful enough that he and his mother were treated differently because they were his family. Though the boy always thought they weren't really a family. His parents fought daily, cheated on each other, and only acted like the perfect couple in public. But they both loved him, so he was okay with it. One day, he woke up to find his father had died after being caught in a scandal. One that shook their city. The boy and his mother were hounded by reporters, strangers, angry enemies, dissatisfied investors, powerful foes, and police. Lots of fucking police and other burly men. They all kept coming and coming and coming, like sewer rats. They questioned and demanded. They threatened and beat the boy and his mum's up. They seized almost all their property—his mum included. A three-year-old shouldn't have remembered it all, but he did. In vivid detail. He remembered hiding under the bed, behind the door, and in the wardrobe. Not only from the men, but also from his mother."

The drip, drip, drip from the open faucet is the only sound that fills the bathroom.

It clashes against my thoughts, turning them absolutely vile.

When I remain silent, Annika's low voice echoes around me. "Why did he have to hide from his mother?"

"Because she picked up drinking again and it was better if he didn't get in her way when she had a bottle of tequila in hand. At first, she'd start crying, then…she'd expel that energy onto the boy. It went on and on until she no longer let him go outside and he was caught in her self-pitying violent circle, where she didn't feed him, didn't care for him, and left him to rot. Until she had the urge to beat him up again. The boy thought that his reality would never end, but then a groomed man came to announce that the bank would seize the last thing they had—the house. That night, the mother didn't drink much. She even hugged the boy and said, 'Do you miss your dad, sweetie?' When he nodded, she smiled. 'Mom misses him, too. It's so hard without him. What do you say we go to him?' The boy thought his dad was in heaven. How could they go to someone in heaven? He was sleepy and dizzy, probably because he hadn't eaten in days. So he closed his eyes and listened to his mother tell him that everything was going to be okay. When he opened his eyes again, he saw a giant spider hanging from the ceiling. Or that's what he chose to think of the sight as he crawled and fell down, then crawled again until he collapsed. Turns out, the mother planned for them to both die that night, her by hanging, him by gas."

A splash of water echoes around me before a small figure presses into me.

I stare down to find Annika lying against my chest. Her trembling fingers stroke my clenched jaw and two streaks of tears stain her beautiful face.

My muscles slowly relax and I wipe her cheeks with my thumbs. "Why are you crying?"

"Because I want to reach out and hug that boy, but I can't." She wraps her arms around my waist in a tight, warm embrace. "I'm so sorry."

My fingers fist in her hair and I wrench her face away. "That boy is dead, along with those scum who called themselves parents. A completely different person resurrected from his ashes and the only parents I have are called Aiden and Elsa King. So why the fuck are you sorry? Did I not say not to pity me?"

"I'm not." Her lips quiver and she doesn't attempt to fight my grip on her hair. "I just want to share your pain."

"There's nothing to share. That chapter has ended."

"But—"

"Shut up." I release her hair. "And get out."

She's the reason I dug into a part of me I like to keep buried deep, with no one ever having a chance to uncover it.

Annika fucking Volkov just had to stuff her nose where it doesn't belong.

She meets my eyes. "If you keep pushing me away, you won't have anyone left."

"I can live with that."

"Well, I can't."

"Annika." I grind my jaw. "Either leave or I fuck you. Sore or not."

She doesn't make a move or even hesitate, her eyes never leaving mine.

"You should've run while I was being nice, little purple." I pull her by the waist. "Sit on my cock. This will be a long fucking night."

Then I fuck her, bite her, mark her, and make her completely regret ever choosing me.

Getting under my skin.

Being the person I didn't know I needed.

TWENTY

Annika

LICK, *LICK, LICK.*

I wince as the up and down of a harsh tongue continues. On my face.

I startle awake and my eyes nearly bug out at the tiny little face, ears, and whiskers.

"Tiger?" I all but shriek, and he jumps back on the bed, startled, then he slowly waltzes in my direction again.

He's grown since the last time I saw him at the shelter weeks ago, but I have no doubt that it's him. He even has the cute heart-shaped mole between his eyes.

I sit up and wince when my sore muscles cry out in pain. The bath barely did anything after Creighton fucked me on all fours on the tiles, then against the wall and on the bed.

It was so powerful and raw and he didn't hold back like the first time. He took and took and gave me blinding pleasure in return.

He was enraged, absolutely animalistic and unhinged.

To say I escaped with my life intact would be an understatement.

Well, I did enjoy it, but I don't like that he felt distant afterward. Even as he took me to the shower and cleaned us both. There wasn't that tender touch from when he ran me a bath and washed my hair.

For a moment, I thought maybe I'd taken down his walls, but he proved that was wishful thinking on my part.

But he gave me the most beautiful necklace ever as a birthday present. I glide my fingers over it to make sure it's still there.

Also, he had me sleep tucked into the crook of his body, so maybe it's not all hopeless?

Though he's nowhere to be seen now and I'm the only one in bed. With Tiger.

He jumps on my shoulder, reaching for my head like he used to, and I laugh, petting him. His purrs fill me with a much-needed dose of dopamine.

"Were you here all along, baby? You even have a collar, so cute." He bumps his head against my hand and purrs some more, then meows, probably for food.

Leaving him on the bed, I stand up with effort and search the room, but there's no food or any sign of my clothes.

So I throw on one of Creighton's hoodies that swallows me whole and step into the hall, carrying a fussy Tiger.

"All right, all right. I'll just find you some food."

That's easier said than done, because I soon get lost, not sure which direction I should go in.

It takes me a few moments to find the stairs and even longer to reach the base of them.

Then I walk through the living area, looking around and wondering if I'm somehow trapped in a ghost house.

The lack of noise in such a huge place raises the hairs on the back of my neck and I hold Tiger tighter.

Now would be a good time for Creighton to show himself.

Unless he disappeared before I woke up to save me the embarrassment of asking me to leave?

My heart squeezes at that thought and I promptly shove it back into the abyss of my soul.

"Who do we have here?"

I flinch and so does Tiger. He jumps from my hands and hisses at the newcomer, tail up, body curved, and ears back.

Eli stares down at him as if he were nothing more than dirt on his shoes, and then the strangest thing happens.

Tiger tucks his tail and runs to hide. Did he just scare him away with a look?

"I'm not that popular with animals." He smiles at me, but there's not an ounce of honesty or welcoming feeling behind it.

He leans against the wall, a slaughtered buffalo head hanging above him, giving him a gruesome edge. His expression and aura conflict with the classy way he's dressed. Pressed black pants, elegant button-down, and stylish Italian loafers.

He could walk into a shoot and the photographers would drop to their knees to have him in their lenses.

"Hi," I say, trying hard as hell to sound casual and not at all intimidated by him.

If only Creighton would show up right now. Not that he's any better than his brother, but the devil you know and all that.

"Annika. If I remember correctly, we have an unfinished conversation."

Right. Back at the fight club when Ava went for his throat and Creighton kidnapped me. I wish those two were around at this moment.

But since they're not, I'm about to force a smile but recall how Creighton told me I don't owe the world anything, so I ask in a calm tone, "What did you want to talk about?"

"One, your relationship with my brother. Two, your relationship with *your* brother. Three, how it'll be a bad idea if you one day have to choose and you pick your brother and leave my brother behind. I'll take it personally and do everything in my power to destroy both of you."

My spine jerks at the amicable way in which he issues threats. His voice sounded suave, absolutely eloquent, as if he were a BBC News anchor.

"I won't hurt Creighton," I manage to reply calmly, assertively. "And Jeremy isn't the monster you make him out to be. He won't brutalize Creighton just because I'm with him."

"Do all these delusional thoughts help you sleep better at night? We both know your dear Jeremy is capable of more than that. So how about you take the easy way out before the shit hits the fan?"

"With all due respect, you have no right to intervene between Creigh and me. And I'm not leaving."

I realize that Creighton and I have a long way to go and that the brutal fucking from last night after he revealed a bit of himself is only the beginning, but I don't mind.

I like myself with Creighton, I like the way I'm more outspoken and less of a people pleaser. And I want him to like himself when he's with me, too.

For that, I'm willing to do anything.

Eli watches me for a beat, his gray eyes looking almost black. And while I want to run and hide, I force myself to maintain eye contact, to meet his stare with one of my own.

"Very well." He pushes off the wall. "I'll keep my eye on you."

"I'll keep my eye on you, too."

"Oh?" He smiles like a wolf, head cocked to the side. "What for?"

"For whenever you think it's a good idea to intervene."

His smile widens. "No wonder Creigh chose you when he never had interest in anyone before."

Fire erupts in my belly, but it's the good type, the type that warms me from the inside out.

I flip my hair back and can't help but grin. "I'm special like that."

"Arrogant, too. I see why you're friends with her."

"Who's her?"

"Never mind."

He's about to leave, but I step in his way. "Can I ask you something?"

"I only take questions on Sundays. Like the church."

"Today is Sunday."

"Lucky you," he says with that permanent smirk and I pause, thinking maybe I'm missing something, but then I promptly let it go.

I inch closer to him. "Do you know when Creigh got his spider tattoo?"

This is my attempt to frame the time he realized he was still haunted by his childhood memories, despite having a family. No matter how much he denies it, I know what happened in his childhood has an effect on him one way or another. I didn't get the chance to ask him due to all the fucking that he must've used to shut me up, but I can fish for information from Eli.

"In secondary school. High school to you Americans. It's a memento to the younger version of him."

"You...knew."

"That he's adopted? Of course. Everyone knows."

Oh. How come no one told me? Maybe it's a close-circle thing and I don't belong there. Although I'm slightly hurt, I decide to focus on a much more pressing issue.

"Do you also know of his...past?"

"There's nothing I can tell you about it aside from what he divulged."

"I just want to know if he became the way he is due to that."

"The way he is?"

"I'm sure you know he's a...sadist."

He grins. "Proud of him."

Of course he is. Now, I'm starting to understand why Ava calls him He-Who-Shall-Not-Be-Named.

Eli is an anomaly.

But maybe he's the type of brother Creighton needed while growing up with that sort of baggage.

"So?" I press. "Is he that way because of his past?"

"Maybe. Probably."

It dawns on me then. Creighton once said that he eats too much because he was starving at a point in his life. And he probably sleeps whenever possible because of how he felt when suffocated by the gas.

When he was dizzy and crawled and crawled.

Goosebumps erupt on my skin with creepy speed, like when he was telling me the story last night.

To think that someone so young went through that makes me want to cry.

But I don't want him to take it as pity. I really do not pity him. I just want to be there for him.

I'm apparently shit at expressing that, though, because he was offended by my words last night and took it out on my poor body.

"My turn to ask questions." Eli's voice brings me back to the present. "How did you coerce him to talk?"

"I didn't."

"Try again. He went through intensive therapy when he was a kid and has long since gotten past that phase of his life. He wouldn't talk about it unless he was poked. So tell me, Annika. What type of poking method have you used?"

"I really didn't. I just asked about his tattoo."

He narrows his eyes for a beat, then schools his expression. "Huh."

We remain silent for a moment before I murmur, "Do you know where he is?"

He cocks his head to the left. "In the kitchen."

"Thanks." I start in that direction, only to find out that Eli is coming with me. I choose not to comment on that in order to avoid any type of unnecessary conflict.

If I want to be with Creighton, I need to get used to Eli since he's part of his life.

A commotion greets us as soon as we open the door.

Creighton is wearing an apron and scrolling through his phone while flour stains his hands, face, and even his pants.

Remi seems to be his coach, considering the matching aprons and his folded arms.

Across from them sits Brandon, seeming oblivious to the whole mess as he drinks his coffee and reads from a tablet.

"I'm telling you, spawn, all these recipes are stupid and wrong. How dare they compete with my lordship's opinion?"

Bran lifts a brow. "And you happen to be an expert?"

"Of course." Remi throws his hands in the air. "I'm always right."

"More like always wrong," Creigh mutters.

"What the fuck? What the actual fuck, spawn? I woke up early after my shagging session last night—make that sessions—to help you with your quest and you say I'm wrong? I'm reporting you to human rights associations for abuse."

"Here we go again." Bran sighs.

"You shut up. Don't go acting innocent after you started this irreparable rift between father and son. Spawn, how could you do this to me?"

"Focus," Creigh says, still looking at his phone. "How much butter should we heat?"

"Enough to drown Remi in." Eli strolls inside, grabs an apple from the table, and grins.

"Blimey, what's with all the violence directed at me this morning?" Remi pretends to hold up a phone. "Hello? Witness protection? Come pick me up."

Creighton lifts his head, his eyes meeting mine from across the kitchen before they slide to his brother and narrow. He tilts his phone away, finger pressing at the back of it as he sizes me up from head to toe and back again.

The air shifts with hungry, animalistic tension that I'm surprised no one in the room picks up on.

When he shows no intention of cutting eye contact, I swallow the lump in my throat. Focus on the others. "Hi, guys."

Bran nods in my direction. Remi basically runs toward me and grabs me by the shoulder. "Save me from these savages, Anni. I swear they're after my lordship's life."

Creigh basically tosses his phone down and reaches us in a few steps. I watch with bewilderment as he grabs Remi's hand that's around my shoulder, twists it until his friend groans, then throws him against the nearest wall.

"What the fuck was that for, spawn?"

"No touching."

"Someone's jealous." Eli leans against the counter and nudges Brandon beside him. "Did you ever think we would witness our Cray Cray's transformation into a caveman?"

"I predicted it since he wasn't happy at the prospect of me becoming her fake boyfriend." Bran takes a sip of his coffee.

"The fuck?" Remi stares between us, having completely forgotten about how Creighton pushed him. "That long? How come I'm only finding out now?"

"Because you're slow?" Eli pours himself a cup of coffee.

"Or just don't get it?" Bran clinks his cup with Eli's.

"Too caught up in your dick to see straight."

"Short attention span, too."

Remi goes full dramatic mode and starts calling them names. Brandon and especially Eli keep escalating.

In the middle of their arguments, Creigh removes his apron, tugs on my hand and pulls me out of the kitchen, then drags me up the stairs.

As soon as we're in his bedroom, he shuts the door.

I'm slammed by his darkened eyes, closed-off features, and blank expression. All three directed at me.

His low voice strikes my skin worse than his crops. "What were you doing down there dressed like this?"

"Like what?"

"Like you're naked beneath it."

"I couldn't find my clothes. Besides, this thing is super oversized."

He grunts. "I like you in my clothes, but you're never walking around like that in front of them again."

"Don't be a dictator. Besides, I had a reason why I wanted to find you."

"Which is?"

"Tiger! How could you not tell me you adopted him? You know how much I love that cat."

"He was supposed to be your second birthday present."

I grin. "You can be so sweet when you're not an asshole."

He narrows his eyes and I blurt, "I meant, thank you."

"Kneel in front of the bed, chest on the mattress and legs wide apart."

That familiar tingle erupts all over my body and ends at my core. I bite the corner of my lip. "Can I get a little break? I'm happy to go again, but I'm sore all over."

"I won't fuck you. Don't be a brat and do as you're told."

Every time he tells me not to be a brat, that's exactly what I want to be. But to prevent any unwanted punishments, I kneel in front of the bed and do as he said.

"Lift the sweatshirt up. Let me see my pussy."

My fingers tremble as I glide the hem of the hoodie to my middle.

"Mmm. Good girl." He gives my ass a slap that feels like a reward and I jerk, then suppress a moan.

With my ass in the air, both of my holes are his for the viewing and I have no idea why that's such a turn-on.

The sound of a drawer opening and closing nearly deafens my ears.

I swallow. "Hey...I didn't do anything to be punished for. I don't think? Can we talk about this?"

"Shut up or I will give you a reason to be punished."

My lips purse together when I feel him behind me. He places something violet on my lips.

"Suck."

A toy, I realize. No, a butt plug.

My eyes widen and I shake my head.

"You know what this is?"

"Duh. And we are not doing anal."

"Not yet, but I will eventually claim your arse like I claimed your pussy. Mark my words, you will milk my cock and beg me to decorate your skin with my cum. Now, open."

My core throbs when it has no business to.

"Violet is not purple, you know. You should've at least picked an aesthetic color—"

My words are interrupted when he shoves the plug in my mouth, glides it against my tongue as if it's his cock, and then wrenches it out.

I'm panting when he kneels behind me and grabs my ass cheek in a hand.

"Relax."

"Easier said than done," I mumble, but I try my best not to stiffen.

"Do you trust me?"

"Not all the time."

A dark chuckle surrounds me like a fucked-up symphony.

"Smart little brat." He pours something cold over my backside—probably lube—and slides the plug against my back hole.

I tense up no matter how much I convince myself not to.

"Don't." He spanks my ass and I yelp. "The more you fight this, the harder it'll be."

His fingers stroke my clit in that expert way only he is capable of. I tried to mimic it when I was on my own, but there's no way I'd be able to touch myself the way Creighton touches me.

My muscles relax as moans slip past my lips. My pussy apparently hasn't caught on to the fact that I'm sore.

Creighton uses the chance to push the plug in little by little. My heart hammers as I'm filled to the brim.

But I focus on the bursts of pleasure exploding in my core. By the time he shoves the plug all the way in, I'm coming.

My lips part and I let the wave wash over me.

"You're so sensitive, little purple." He spanks my ass for good measure. "I love how you're so attuned to my touch."

I love it, too. But damn. That was fast.

Please don't tell me I also need the pain to have strong releases.

Is he corrupting me?

Probably.

Definitely.

Creighton jostles the plug in my ass, making me whimper, then straps something from the plug against my clit.

"You'll wear this two hours a day."

"W-what? You expect me to wear this every day?"

"Yes, and I will check."

"How will you be able to do that?"

"You'll figure it out." He pulls me to a standing position and gives me a box, probably for housing his latest torture device. "If you don't wear it, you'll be punished."

I shift and release an erotic sound despite myself. "It feels weird."

"You'll get used to it."

"Is this another birthday present?"

A beautiful smile stretches his lips. "One of many."

"Any others I should know about?"

"The cake that Remi butchered."

I laugh. "Is that what you guys were doing? Baking?"

"Attempting to."

"Pretty sure I can salvage it."

"Doubt it."

"I'll show you."

We go downstairs after Creighton demands I put on a pair of his sweatpants that I have to roll several times before tying them against my waist.

I don't have to salvage the cake since Eli threw it away and Remi ordered one. The five of us sit for breakfast in the midst of Remi's antics and the others' sarcasm.

Creighton doesn't speak much, but he's attuned to each and every one of them.

He likes them, I realize. That's why he's willing to spend time with them. He even comes to Remi's defense whenever Eli goes too far.

He's loyal like that.

And he's mine.

This gorgeous, beautiful man is all mine.

Even if only temporarily.

TWENTY-ONE

Creighton

"**S**HOULD WE LEAVE?"

Annika lifts her head from my shoulder and whispers so the people surrounding us don't hear her.

Her voice is sheepish, reluctant. Two traits that I would've sworn she lacked.

But then again, Annika has always proved that she's the exception to every conclusion I've drawn about her.

In the beginning, I thought she was nothing more than a hyper, spoiled mafia princess who was too sheltered to understand how the world works.

And while some of that is true, I know for a fact that she's been trying her hardest to forge past the image her parents and upbringing have tailored for her.

The process is slow, but she's determined to gain back control of her life.

If her persistence in getting my attention at the beginning is any indication, then that determination will pay off.

I slide my fingers through her hair and lay her head back on my shoulder.

It's been a week since I fully claimed her as mine, and I've been having this urge to constantly touch her, her hair, beneath her jaw, over her shoulder.

Anywhere I can reach.

However, that proves to be a problem, considering we have different classes, don't share the same living space, and she still has to hide from her brother's watchful eye.

"Does that mean we can stay?" she murmurs, her voice hopeful and trusting.

"I didn't say we have to leave." Despite an annoying group at the back who's focusing on eating and being a loud nuisance instead of watching the film.

"I just thought all the noise would bother you." She stares up at me. "I want to go out with you all the time, but not if you're uncomfortable."

Would you look at that?

My Annika has been learning my patterns with a speed even I can't fathom.

She's considerate of my character, has developed a liking for dates in quiet places, and doesn't push when I refuse to comment further about my past.

Instead of antagonizing me, she understands.

Instead of pressuring me, she steps back.

And I know that must take effort, considering her persistence traits.

I stroke her hair and can't resist inhaling the scent of violets. It flows through my blood, slowly but surely becoming a part of me.

"I'm not uncomfortable when I'm with you, little purple."

I don't see her reaction to my words, but I feel it in the way she presses tighter into my side, wraps her arm around my middle, and even leans into my touch.

She's a myriad of colors and a splash of energy. A very expressive person, whether through her fluid body movements or her words.

If I was told I would be into someone like Annika a few months ago, I would've considered the possibility insane.

But while that was a blasphemous idea at the time, the thought of reverting to the life I had before her fills me with inexplicable rage.

And emptiness.

I've never minded that emotion before. The bursts of hollowness have been a constant since I crawled out of death's clutches.

However, it's not a welcome emotion now.

After the film ends, I wrap an arm around Annika's waist as she chatters on and on about the plot, the characters, the actors, and the special effects.

Everything.

I'm more interested in how her tulle skirt swishes up her pale thighs with every move. Or how her top molds against her tits and stops right at the waist of her skirt.

I stroke the visible skin at her stomach, up and down in a torturous rhythm that's affecting the state of my cock.

It doesn't matter how many times I bind, spank, flog, or fuck her. The moment I'm done, I need more.

More.

And fucking more.

The worst part is that it's not only about sex with Annika. It's about *her*. It's about the way she submits to my dominance, the way she's a masochist to my sadism.

The need to feast on her is constant, intense, and infinite.

"Did you like it?" she asks on the way to the car park.

I press my thumb against her skin, then continue my rhythm. "Very."

"And here I thought you weren't a fan of the movies."

"I wasn't talking about the movie."

Annika must notice the change in my inflection, because she pauses, her lips parting, and pink splashes across her cheeks and translucent neck.

"You…you…"

"Are you actually speechless?"

She releases a breath. "I swear I only become like this around you."

I smile and pull her further into me when some kids run by us to their parents' cars.

"What are you smiling about?" She pokes my side. "This isn't funny."

"It's entertaining."

"Happy to be of entertainment." She sulks, and it looks adorable as fuck.

So adorable that I teasingly flick her on the forehead.

She glares up at me. "No, nope, don't even try to flirt with me."

"Was that what I was doing?"

"Uh-huh. You're just thinking of ways to strap me to your bed and make me beg."

"Me?"

"Oh, please. I can see the sadism shining in your eyes, you know. Sigh. If someone says it's hard to be your plaything, I would totally believe them."

"You're not my plaything."

She freezes, that pink hue returning to her cheeks again. "Then what am I?"

"Mine."

"Is there a difference?"

"I never wanted to keep my playthings."

"Until me?"

"Until you."

She pokes me again while biting the corner of her lip. "You're saying and doing all the right things today. Not that you don't on other days, but you're not usually this...carefree."

"I'm not carefree."

"No one else would accuse you of that. But don't worry, I'll do the carefree part for both of us. I'll take care of the things you can't and vice versa."

"And what are those?"

She wrenches herself from my hold and stands in front of me, then starts counting on her fingers. "I'll plan all the dates and make sure there aren't a lot of people around. I'll plan birthday parties and invite our friends, but when I feel you're annoyed, I'll kindly kick them out. I'll also talk to all the people on your behalf since you don't like them. I'll take care of decorations and pretty aesthetics. Oh, I'll also dance for you, like a swan, though you'll probably shred my beautiful dresses afterward because you can be savage. But anyway, that's a breakdown of what I'll do."

I raise a brow. "What will I do then?"

"You can punch people if they annoy you. Though I prefer you don't, but you said you need to purge energy, so I guess it's fine once in a while or at the fight club. And oh, you can totally kidnap me out of any social situation if you feel I'm uncomfortable and have resorted to faking it. No one will mind if it's you, because everyone is used to your blunt personality."

I can't help the smile that lifts the corners of my lips. An occurrence that happens more often than not around Annika.

"More importantly, we should talk about stuff."

"What type of stuff?"

"Everything. I know you're used to keeping your emotions in a vault, and I respect that. But since we're in a relationship, you should tell me how you feel sometimes, so I can understand you better. Mom once told me that communication is the key that can make or break a couple and I don't want to break us, okay?"

"Okay."

"Really?"

"It doesn't come naturally, but I will try."

"Trying is a good start." She grins then lifts an index finger. "Oh, and I forgot something very important. I will do all the cooking since you don't know how."

I internally wince. "We should probably outsource that."

"But why? You like my food."

Because you put effort into it, not because it tastes good.

"Is there something wrong with my cooking? Ava calls it horrendous and Papa flat-out ordered me not to cook anymore back home and Jeremy barely touches the dishes I make for him. And now, you said we should outsource it."

I stroke her hair. "You can cook if you like. I just don't want you to exert yourself."

"Aw, really? I knew you were my favorite."

"Don't." My tone hardens.

"W-what? What have I done?"

"Don't say I'm your favorite when you tell everyone else that exact sentence."

Her lips part, then clamp shut before she clears her throat. "You're at the top of my favorite list, so don't be jealous."

"I'm not jealous. I'm territorial."

Her eyes widen and then she smiles a little. "Wow. That was intense."

I open the car door. "Let's go to my place and I'll show you what intense actually looks like."

"Uh, I'm supposed to spend the night with the girls at the apartment."

"No."

"But, Creigh…"

"Either you come amicably or I throw you over my shoulder."

"Territorial and a caveman. Don't you think that's a little over the top?"

"No."

"It was a rhetorical question." She releases a breath, then pauses when her phone beeps. Upon checking it, she scrunches her nose.

I step beside her to see what she received. It's a selfie Harry took with me earlier today at the shelter as I was about to wash up.

Harry: I'm stealing him from you, Anni. Muahaha.

"I'm going to mess up his pretty hair next time I see him and he's totally not getting any more skincare tips from me," she mutters, then basically punches the screen of her phone.

Annika: He's mine. Stay away from him.

"I thought being territorial was over the top," I whisper near her ear and she jumps, then hides her phone.

"Uh, Harry is an antagonistic little shit and I just had to make a statement. He's the admin of your fan club that keeps growing tremendously, and he kicked me out because of a 'conflict of interest.' It's not that I'm jealous or anything. Okay, maybe a little."

"Of a man?"

"He's gay."

"And I'm not." I slide my fingers into her hair. "You're the only one I want. Everyone else is just white noise."

"Oh." She blushes, then grins. "You're really saying all the right things today. Be easy on my heart, okay?"

"Not unless you come home with me."

She spreads her palms on my chest, touching, exploring, sinking her nails into a part a lot deeper than my skin. "And what do you have in mind for me?"

I grab her by the arse and slam her against my front, relishing the sound of her gasp. "I'm going to strip you until you're only wearing this skirt and then I'll shred it to play with your every hole. No, not play. Fuck. You'll be taking my cock like a good little girl, won't you?"

She nods frantically. "But are you going to hurt me?"

"Oh, I will." I kiss the top of her head. "But I promise you'll enjoy every second of it."

TWENTY-TWO

Annika

I THINK I'M IN TROUBLE.

When I first took interest in Creighton, I never thought things would get so…out of control.

In the best way.

Or maybe in the worst way.

It's been two weeks since he took my virginity and must've put some voodoo spell on me, because I haven't been able to stay away since.

It doesn't matter that the girls gave me shit about having gone on dates and not telling them—especially Ava.

I've even started to slack off on the excuses I offer my brother—that he somehow believes.

Or he's probably too busy with the clubs' war to pay me attention. An opportunity I've used to the fullest in order to spend as much time as possible with Creighton.

I don't have to bug him about dates anymore since he willingly takes me out like that time in the cinema a week ago. Otherwise, Creighton's idea of a fun date is going somewhere where we're secluded from the world so that he can have me all for himself. And fuck me whenever he wishes.

That man has the stamina of a porn star, I swear.

When I grumbled that he only takes me to secluded places because he wants to have access to my pussy, he merely said, "People have no place in what we have. I'm out for you, not for them."

And it's true. If it were up to Creighton, he wouldn't get out, but he does. For me. He even takes me to the movies because he knows how much I love them.

He steps out of his comfort zone for me.

He treats me like a princess in public and his custom-made whore in private. He fucks and punishes and pushes me to lengths I didn't realize were physically possible.

My favorite parts are right after he unties me, gathers me in his strong arms, and kisses me. It's the little things, like how he washes me, tends to the marks—that he left, but semantics—or how he cuddles me to sleep because he knows how much I need that connection after the intense sex.

Creighton gives the best aftercare in the world, and that alone makes me fall deeper into his web. I've never felt so safe, happy, and free as when I'm in his arms.

Sometimes, I feel so special but other times, I'm not actually sure if he's interested in me or in simply dominating me.

Maybe he likes my perseverance and my willingness to get immersed in his kinky, fetish-filled world?

When I asked him what he liked about me, he just flicked my forehead.

It wasn't antagonistic, but it wasn't an answer either.

So I will keep on asking until I get a reply.

Maybe after tonight ends.

We're at a pub with our friends to celebrate Remi's basketball team's accomplishment. They won against TKU, so it should be a conflict of interest to even be here, but anyway.

These people are the only real friends I've had in my eighteen years of life.

Ever since Jeremy gave me freedom, I've never gone back to the Heathens' compound. I do text back and forth with my brother, though.

As much as I love him, I realize how monstrous Jeremy can get under certain circumstances.

I'm lucky that he's too busy to focus on me much.

It's how I get to come to this pub.

It's cozy with wood-themed decor, not too big, not too small, and definitely the least rowdy compared to all the clubs I've gone to on the island. I used to call it a club, but I've been informed that everyone here calls it a pub, so who am I to go against the flow?

Soft indie rock music plays in the background and the smell of alcohol permeates the air. Our group is seated around a large table in the middle of the room.

Cecily and Ava keep whispering to each other. Bran is showing something to Glyn on his phone and she's laughing. This is one of the few times she hasn't ghosted us for Killian. Usually, he'd barge in uninvited, but apparently, the Heathens have a club event this evening.

Creighton and I are seated beside each other. I take a sip from my martini while he watches me openly.

Like, no kidding.

He leans his elbow on the table, supports his head on his palm, and never breaks eye contact or stops eating my face with his hungry gaze.

It's like I'm the only one he's interested in around here, and he's not the least bit discreet in showing it.

While I like his attention, it does put us in an awkward position whenever we're with people.

"Stop it," I whisper.

"I'm not doing anything," he murmurs back, voice rough.

"You're looking at me like…like *that*."

"That?"

"Like you want to punish and fuck me, probably in that order." My voice lowers further so no one hears.

"Then maybe we should've gone with my plan and stayed in my room."

"No," I whisper-yell. "You promised we could have this."

"Never promised."

I open my mouth to protest, but Remi stands at the head of the table and raises his glass. "This is a toast to the man of the hour, the basketball god, the unattainable star, Lord Remington Astor!"

I start to raise my glass but stop when Creighton gives me a look. Or more like a glare.

It's totally unfair that he gets to communicate so much with a mere glance.

"Hey, bitches, why aren't you raising your glasses for my lordship's toast?"

"We get it, Remi, you won." Cecily leans back against her chair. "You've been making a hundred and one speeches and toasts to inform us of the fact."

"You zip it, nerd. What do you know about winning highly competitive sports?"

"The fact that you act like a wanker after every win."

Ava laughs. "True that, Rems. We're starting to wish that you don't win anymore so we don't have to sit through these tedious speeches."

"What the actual fuck? You bitches are jealous of me and it totally shows on your snobbish faces. Anni, Glyn! Help me out here."

"I mean, it's not completely false," Glyn says with a raise of an eyebrow.

"You little—"

"You're really awesome, Remi," I cut off his rage-filled—or dramatic—comeback.

"Right? I knew you were my favorite." He takes a detour, comes to my side, and grabs my shoulder.

Or starts to.

The moment he touches me, Creigh slaps his hand away. "I said. No touching."

"Whoa." Remi laughs and puts both hands in the air. "Territorial much?"

"Tell me about it." Ava side-eyes Creighton. "He doesn't even let her spend time with us anymore."

"We went shopping yesterday," I offer with a smile.

"After, like, a whole week of no shopping. You're losing bestie privileges, Anni."

"You barely drop by the dorm anymore," Cecily supplies.

"Or spend girl time with us," Glyn says.

My smile becomes awkward at best. "It's not that I don't want to—"

"You spend more time with Killian than with us, Glyn." Creighton looks at her, then slides his attention to Ava. "And you ignore everyone when my brother is around." He stares at Cecily. "As for you, let's just say you've been sneaking out whenever everyone is asleep. So do not, under any circumstances, attempt to make Annika feel bad about choosing herself."

The table falls silent.

While Creighton has been slowly but surely becoming somewhat talkative with me—and by talkative, I mean his replies aren't monosyllables like in the past—he's still the silent presence at the table.

So the fact that he said all of that, and even attacked them during it, has driven everyone to the shock phase.

"Damn," Glyn breathes out. "Looks like you have one hell of a solicitor on your team, Anni."

"For the record, I don't ignore everyone whenever He-Who-Shall-Not-Be-Named is around." Ava points a finger at Creigh. "That's fake news!"

"You kind of do." Cecily coughs. "Constantly."

"You damn traitor!" Ava nudges her before a sly grin lifts her lips. "What's with sneaking out when everyone's asleep? I knew you were hiding something from me."

"T-that's not true."

"You just stammered, bitch!"

They start arguing, but when Remi joins in to egg them on, they give up on poking each other and gang up on him instead. Glyn and Bran try to mediate but are currently losing.

Creighton, however?

He has a pleased expression on his face, as if he did what he set out to do.

Everyone says Landon and Eli like to instigate chaos, but Creigh can reach their level if he puts his mind to it.

Or if he feels that I'm in a compromising position.

"Don't fake a smile when you're feeling uncomfortable. If you're in a bad mood, show it," is what he's been telling me again and again, trying to make me get rid of what he calls a nasty habit.

Being with Creighton is similar to being thrust into this country's weather. At times, he's amicable, allowing some sunlight to slip from between the clouds, but most of the time, he's rainy and miserable.

Well, he's not miserable, I am.

Because ever since he told me about his childhood and revealed the fact that he's adopted, he's shot down any of my attempts to re-open the subject.

No matter how much I talk about my family in an attempt to have him reciprocate, he just isn't having it.

His phone rings and I catch a glimpse of 'Landon' on the screen before he gets up and tucks a strand of brown hair behind my ear. "I'll be right back. Behave."

Then he's heading toward the hall to take the call.

I wonder what he and Landon talk so secretly about. The other day, I found them in the kitchen and Landon was whispering in his ear like the devil.

For some reason, that made me extremely uncomfortable. I'm aware he wouldn't really hurt his cousin, but I don't know why I have a bad feeling about whatever information they're exchanging.

Creighton told me it's nothing I should worry about, which made me more concerned.

While Landon and Eli might have similar traits, I know for a fact that Eli dotes on him and would never sabotage him. Landon, however, is a wild card.

Remi slides to my side, surprisingly interrupting his arguing session with the girls. I would've sworn that he enjoys that a bit too much to walk out on it.

He tips his glass against mine and grins, looking so aristocratically beautiful. "Now that the territorial little shit is out of the way, let me thank you, Anni."

"For…what?"

"Bringing him out of his shell. I was so sure the cheeky bastard would die alone and I'd have to worry about my spawn even as I was living my glamourous life. Don't you know just how pressing that is? The worst, I'm telling you. So thanks again. I'll be forever grateful and I'll sacrifice anything in your name except for virgin blood. Unless we go back several years in time?"

I can't help the chuckle that spills out of me. "Oh, don't be silly. Besides, I can't take all the credit. If you hadn't mentally prepared him before I came along, I wouldn't even have been able to crack the surface."

"True that! Damn, I feel like a proud papa." His expression turns serious as he grabs my hands in his. "But I'm still grateful as fuck. I thought his demons would devour him whole, but now, I'm sure you won't let them."

"You can totally count on...it."

My voice catches when a sudden vibration starts in my core.

Shit.

A burst of flames explodes all over my skin and my fingers turn clammy.

I glance around in search of the culprit, but there's no sign of him.

The vibration goes up in intensity and my legs clench as I resist the urge to topple over.

I swear to God, he's insane.

This isn't the first time he's turned on the toy since he made me wear it, but it's the first time he's done it in public. With so many people around.

The day after he inserted the plug, I tested the waters and took it out, but he found out because he has the remote control. After the punishment I got, I didn't attempt to remove it again and wore it for the duration he specified.

Two days ago, he switched to a bigger butt plug that's stretched me to lengths I didn't think possible. Though I did enjoy the way he played with it while he was fucking me raw in the shower last night.

I just never thought he'd turn it on in public.

"Anni, are you okay?" Remi watches me carefully. "You look all red."

I release a shaky breath as the vibration goes up a notch, causing me to flinch.

Dammit. Does he intend to make me come in front of everyone or something?

I stare down and find my fingers trembling in Remi's, then I swiftly remove them.

Creighton must be somewhere and have seen this. That's the only logical explanation for his craziness right now.

Damn the possessive asshole.

Despite the fact that I'm no longer touching Remi, the rhythm doesn't lessen, but it doesn't go up either.

"Anni?" Remi calls again. "You okay?"

"Y-yeah. Be…right back."

I don't know how I stand up, grab my phone, or walk. All I'm aware of is that I can't just orgasm in front of them. I'd rather die.

At first, I pick the bathroom, but the line in front of it makes me immediately change direction. I basically run outside to the parking lot, but before I can find a nook to dissolve in, someone grabs my wrist and drags me behind him.

"Do you need a hand, little purple?"

"Stop it…" My voice is too throaty, too turned on as I clench my thighs.

"I told you not to touch them. I specifically said no touching." His voice is calm, but anger flickers beneath the surface.

"I didn't mean to… *Oh*…"

The intensity goes up again as he opens his car door and slips into the backseat.

I remain outside, watching with bated breath, my legs shaking and sweat trickling down my spine.

Creighton unzips his jeans and pulls out his hard cock. "Sit on my lap."

My gaze strays sideways before I lick my lips. "We're in public—"

"When I'm done with you, the public will be the last thing on your mind."

You know what? Trying to please people never did me any good anyway.

Screw it.

I climb into the car and onto his lap, causing my dress to hike up to my waist. He closes the door, confining us in the narrow space. But it's still much more comfortable than his previous sports car.

"Can't you wait until later?" I whisper, but it ends on a moan when he slides his cock against my sensitive folds. The combination of that and the vibration sends my pulse flying.

"No underwear?" he whispers in dark words against my ear.

"I, umm, forgot?"

"Forgot or you were being a brat?"

He accentuates his statement with a flick against my overstimulated clit.

"Creigh, please…"

A pinch of his fingers against my clit, a slide of his cock near my entrance, but I'm not quite there.

He's torturing me on purpose, I realize. He wants to make me feel the pain yet deny me the orgasm.

It's a game he plays sometimes—driving me crazy for sport.

The rhythm goes on and on until I think I'll go mad from the friction.

"You're soaking wet, look at your cunt begging for me to fuck it. It's so ready for me, isn't it?"

I nod in quick succession, unable to say the words.

"But I'm tempted not to satisfy it tonight. You let another man touch what's mine, and I don't react well to that."

"Won't happen again, promise."

"You made the same promise the other day while you were falling apart around my cock, so maybe we don't believe you anymore. Maybe we'll keep you soaking wet and messy, but without any chance to come."

"No, please, Creigh." I grab his face and kiss him on the cheek. "You wouldn't do that to me, right?"

My lips move to his nose, then to his mouth. "You can punish me all you want after, but not like this."

He groans against my lips and we inhale and exhale each other's air.

Tension lingers between us, but he doesn't stop his rubbing.

Up.

Down.

Up.

Down.

His nostrils flare when I keep sliding my fingers in his hair. "Don't be a flirt."

"I'm only a flirt with you." I brush my lips against his cheek, knowing how much he loves it.

"Keep this up and you'll only get hurt."

"I don't mind if it's you."

A low grunt escapes his lips before he pushes the toy's extension away from my clit, lifts me up, then shoves me back down, burying himself inside me.

I cry out when he's fully sheathed, then takes a moment to adjust to his huge cock. But I don't have a moment.

Not even a fraction of a second.

Creighton jerks his hips and thrusts with rough strokes. I'm sure he can feel the thin skin between him and the plug. I sure as hell do, and it's so full, so absolutely full that it hurts.

The good hurt.

The type of pain I need with my pleasure.

Creighton fucks me with a brutality that leaves me gasping. I wrap my arms around his neck for balance.

With each thrust, a burst of pleasure washes over me. His hands grab my hips so possessively, so intensely, as I bounce off his cock and hit my head on the roof of the car.

He slows down when he notices. "Fuck, you make me an animal. Are you hurt?"

"No. Don't stop…" I murmur.

That's all the invitation he needs as he drives inside me with progressive intensity. This time with one of his hands on top of my head so it absorbs the shock of slamming against the roof.

The pleasure is overwhelming and the slap of flesh against flesh adds more to the erotic scene, but I'm not coming.

Something is missing.

Something…

My thoughts are scattered when he pulls my hair to the side and his teeth bite on the sensitive flesh of my neck. Then he releases my hip, yanks down the strap of my dress and bites my breast, adding more marks to the already fading ones.

When he traps my nipple between his teeth, I come. The blinding wave transports me to an alternate universe and I scream.

Creighton slaps a hand on my mouth. And even the muffled voice is so erotic that it adds to the consuming pleasure.

Pain with pleasure.

A combination only Creighton can give me.

He keeps ramming into me on and on until I'm almost out of it. When he shoots inside me, my eyes slowly close and I bury my face in his neck.

"I love you," I want to say, but I keep it hidden in that dark nook in my heart. The one that's too scared of letting people too close because I'd have to watch them leave.

The one that's scared my feelings would mean nothing to him and I'd be cruelly rejected.

We remain like that for a while, breathing each other in while he's inside me. Then we clean each other up with wet wipes.

It takes us more time than necessary, considering the stupidly narrow space. Cars aren't made for sex, seriously.

The chances of convincing him of that fact are close to zero.

I tell Creighton to take me to his place. I totally look like I just got laid, and if we go back inside the club, everyone will just give us shit.

Creighton is all for that idea since he didn't want to go out tonight anyway.

But instead of driving to the Elites' mansion, he stops at a grocery store.

On the way inside, I ask, "Why are we here?"

"I'm running out of ropes."

"Wow. Romantic."

"Only for you." He interlinks his fingers with mine.

I can't help grinning at that, because I know he's not the type to lie.

"I wonder what your parents would think if they knew about your tendencies," I say.

"Dad is all for exploring who we are, so he wouldn't mind. Mum… it's better that she doesn't know."

"I gather your dad is open-minded?"

"The best. Nothing is too wrong or too taboo. He encouraged me, Eli, and Landon to pursue what we wanted."

"He sounds badass. I wish Papa were the same. I mean, he's awesome, just too strict, I guess. Like Jeremy. It's why I wanted to have a fake boyfriend, you know. So my father doesn't marry me off to the first suitor."

"That won't be happening. You have me now."

My heart nearly explodes. "Does that mean you're my boyfriend?"

"If you want to put that label on it."

"What would you call me?"

"My girl."

"I like that." I beam. "You're like my man then."

"Your man, huh?"

"Yeah, sounds badass and suits your grumpy personality. I'll proudly introduce you to my family one day. Papa and Jer won't tell me what to do."

His lashes lower as he stares at me. "How about your mother? Is she like them?"

"Nope. Mom is the sweetest and constantly acts as my armor against both Papa and Jer. They can't defy her." I laugh. "Women rule."

"I like your mum. She sounds like mine."

I grin. "Yeah?"

"Mum managed to tame the lion, aka my father, and that's a

superpower. See, Dad is the most ruthless in our family aside from Grandpa Jonathan and Grandpa Agnus, but if Mum is unwell, Dad looks like he's ready to burn the world."

"Why would your mom be unwell?"

"She has a heart condition. Most of the time, she's this ball of energy who's capable of doing anything, but sometimes, her chronic disease acts up and Dad goes berserker. It's really nothing major, just some dizziness, and it's even confirmed by the million doctors he hired that it's not a threat to her life, but he doesn't understand that logic."

My heart warms. "That's because he loves her."

"It's more than love. Eli and I know that if she somehow dies, he'll join her, no questions asked."

"Honestly, I can't imagine Papa without Mom either. They had a dark past that Jer was a witness to—it happened way before I came along—but they've shared every sweet and bitter pill for as long as I've known them. I love how fiercely they love each other and us. Sometimes, I hate that I'm a mafia princess, for obvious reasons, but I wouldn't change my parents for the world."

"Such a good girl, my Annika."

I groan, feeling my body heating. "You can't just call me that in public. Now I want to kiss you."

"And why can't you?" He tugs on my hand that's in his, pulling me flush against his chest, and then his lips find mine.

I wrap my arms and legs around him, basically strangling him, to find balance more than anything.

The kiss steals my breath and all my thoughts. All I can do is fall harder and faster for this man.

More than I bargained for.

More than I thought was possible when I first met him.

He places me on my feet and pushes me against the nearest shelf to devour me.

Just when I think the kiss will never end, I'm jerked back by the elbow and I crash against none other than my brother.

Who's glaring.

TWENTY-THREE

Creighton

WHEN SOMEONE WRENCHES ANNIKA FROM MY ARMS, MY first thought is murder.

My second thought is to pound them until their features are unrecognizable and they're begging for death.

I come to a halt, clenched fist at my side, when I make out the person behind the interruption.

Jeremy.

Annika trembles slightly, the rosy blush in her skin slowly vanishing until her face is all white.

She looks so small beside her brother, and it's not only physically, but also in her aura. It's almost like his presence overshadows hers. Annika told me that she's always liked girly things and loved being a girl, because at least in that way, she's different from Jeremy.

And she desperately wants to be different from him, because even though she loves him, she realizes what type of path he has to take—becoming a mafia leader.

Annika has never liked that part of her family, which is proven time and again whenever she avoids the subject with every trick under the sun.

The manifestation of that life on the island is none other than her brother.

"Jer," she whispers, staring up at him with big, innocent eyes.

Despite his firm grip on her elbow, he doesn't look at her. His full cutthroat attention falls on me, dripping with every intention of causing pain. His face is closed off, his eyes unreadable.

I don't know Jeremy Volkov except for when I saved him from that fire, and only because his sister was ready to die for him. Obviously, that shit wasn't going to happen on my watch.

Before that, Jeremy and I had only crossed paths at the fight club, but not against each other.

He seldom participates, and when he does, it's only in fights leading to the championship.

This year, it'll be me against him in the finals since he eliminated Landon in the semifinals.

I watched it from the sidelines, and it was proper brutal. If I didn't know better, I would've sworn that Jeremy was taking it personally, and Landon was enjoying every second of antagonizing him.

My cousin ended up losing anyway, and now, everyone won't stop talking about the final that will take place in a few weeks.

And while I haven't thought about it much, maybe it's time to. My interactions with the Heathens have been through defeating both Killian and Nikolai in the ring, so Jeremy won't be any different.

"You have the audacity to touch my sister?" His inflection is flat, meant as a veiled threat.

"Jer...it's not what you think," Annika tries to explain in a soft voice with that infuriating fake smile of hers.

"It's exactly what you think," I interrupt her.

Annika is more readable than a book and if she thinks that I'll allow her to draw his attention away from me so that he'll direct his wrath at her, then she's sorely mistaken.

"What did you just say?" Jeremy enunciates.

"You heard me. Annika and I are together."

He starts toward me and Annika's eyes nearly bulge out of their sockets. Her polished nails dig into his leather jacket and her whole body jerks with his movement.

It's panic.

She's about to hyperventilate at the thought of a fight breaking out between us.

Always against conflicts, my Annika. Always so…elegant, even in her panic. That's what attracted me to her at first—her elegance and softness.

Her beauty and even her purply, violet-scented presence. I have no clue when it started, but at some point, I wanted to confiscate everything about her and keep it to myself.

"Jer…please. Let's go back to the mansion and I'll tell you all about it."

"Go back so he can lock you up again?" I take my own step forward so that I'm toe-to-toe with Jeremy.

She purses her lips and shakes her head at me. She might be a pacifist, but I'm most certainly not, and I will not, under any fucking circumstances, allow him to take her away from me.

"And what is it to you what I do with my sister?"

"She's not a kid anymore. She's eighteen and can and should have the freedom to make any decisions that concern her life."

"Tell you what, King. I'll give you leeway since you saved my and my sister's lives in that fire. Go find another girl to mess with, because she's off-limits."

"Thanks for the courtesy, but I'll have to decline."

He smiles, but it's cruel and holds no welcoming whatsoever. "You think I'll let you be with my sister?"

"You won't have a say in it. She's already mine. In every sense of the word."

"This fucking—" He lunges at me with his fist raised, and I do the same, ready to pummel the fucker to the ground.

"Stop!" Annika jumps between us, her petite frame trembling despite her upright posture. "Stop it, please."

"Consider yourself lucky." Jeremy grabs her by the arm and starts toward the exit.

"You will *not* take her away from me." I start toward them with every intention of spilling blood tonight.

Annika stares back, shakes her head frantically, and mouths, "Please. Trust me."

My feet come to a halt despite myself.

She played dirty and asked me to trust her, so I can't just pummel her brother and glue her to my side.

As much as I dislike letting her go, I choose to trust her.

Because, unlike her brother, I believe she's an adult with her own decisions and choice.

Still, I fetch my phone and type her a text.

Creighton: You only have a day to make him change his mind or we're doing it my way.

I'm unable to sleep.

An occurrence that's never happened in my life.

Ever since I was a child, sleeping has been the one activity I could effortlessly fall into.

Not tonight.

I stare at my phone long enough to drill holes in it. Annika hasn't replied, and I shouldn't really be bothering her in case she's busy talking with her fucker of a brother.

Or she's asleep.

A few notifications from the group chat appear at the top of the screen, and since I'm bored, I click on them.

Remington: If any of you bitches try to sabotage my orgy, I swear on my lordship's title that I will be coming after your balls.

Landon: I'll join.

Remington: Not a fucking chance. You'll just steal all the attention.

Landon: Don't be stingy, Rems. Bros before hoes, remember?

Remington: Go find your own orgy. You don't see me hijacking your fun. Besides, this is special since we're celebrating my win tonight.

Landon: Bran wins all the time. You don't see him flaunting his dick for anyone to see. Isn't that right @Brandon King?

Remington: Or that's what you think *laughing out loud emoji* *winking emoji* *side eye emoji*

Landon: Details?

Remington: Let's just say Bran surprised my lordship and it takes a lot to do that.

Brandon: Shut up, Remi.

Remington: Yes, sir. Off to go now. If I somehow die in the throes of pleasure, write 'He died doing what he loves the most' on my tombstone and tell my parents and grandparents that I love them. My spawn, too. You better miss me @Creighton King

Eli: Pretty sure he won't. In fact, he'll be happy to be rid of your bothersome clinginess.

Remington: Shut up, you unfeeling, antagonistic, crazy psycho.

Landon: It's true, though. Creigh couldn't care less about you, no matter how much you try. How does it feel to be unimportant?

Creighton: You are important to me, Remi.

There's a long pause, people typing at the same time. Then all the replies come at once.

Remington: Totally screenshotted that, will frame it and hang it in my room. You can't take it back, spawn.

Landon: Who are you and what have you done with our silent Creighton?

Brandon: Is it really you, Creigh?

Eli: Emergency state. He must've been kidnapped.

Remington: You guys are just jealous. Go die.

Then he sends a series of evil laughing GIFs.

I throw my phone aside, use my hand as a pillow, and stare at the ceiling.

A dark ball jumps onto my chest and I sigh as Tiger decorates my T-shirt with his hair.

This cat is another reminder of Annika. Of her sweet smiles when she sees him and the baby voice she uses to talk to him.

"Listen here, you little twat." I hold him up so I'm staring at him. "No more climbing onto her shoulder or head or I'll throw you out on the streets."

He merely glares at me with those hooded eyes the way snobbish cats do and attempts to scratch me.

Christ.

I can't believe I'm both talking to a cat and jealous of it.

My door slams against the wall as my brother strolls inside with the nonchalance of a jaded warrior.

Tiger jumps, then runs out, probably to find Brandon. He's his favorite after Annika.

Eli stops by the side of my bed, stares down at me with a critical gaze, and crosses his arms. "You're not kidnapped. Wait, have you lost your phone..." he trails off, a frown etching between his brows when he sees it on the side table.

Instead of buggering off and leaving me alone, Eli sits on the edge of the mattress and runs his fingers beneath my chin. "What's going on, baby bro? Is someone bothering you? Who should I maim to pieces, then dump their remains in the sea?"

"Forget it."

"Bullshit. If it's affecting you to the point that you're not only texting, but also defending Remi instead of drowning in sleep, I need to know about it."

I let out a long breath. Eli is no different than a dog with a bone, and he absolutely won't leave me alone until he gets what he wants.

And at the moment, maybe I can use his 'wisdom' to find a solution.

"Jeremy caught me with Annika in a grocery store and she went back with him."

Eli's movements halt beneath my chin, but he doesn't remove his hand. "And? Did you beat him to a pulp?"

"I wanted to. I still do, but Annika intervened."

"I see."

My eyes meet his muted ones, and it reminds me of those times we got in trouble—because of his anarchist plans—and he tried everything under the sun to come out unscathed.

Without implicating either of us.

Dad usually caught on to his schemes and punished him, though. But Eli didn't mind as long as I wasn't blamed for his actions.

The world might consider him abnormal, but he's been my role model ever since I figured out what a role model means.

I sit up in bed and he leans against the headboard beside me, stretching his legs out on the mattress.

"How can I get her back without antagonizing her brother?"

"Why can't you teach him a lesson or two? Maybe a few?"

"Because she loves him. She was ready to die in a fire with him, and while I'm game to beat him the fuck up for daring to come between us, I know I'll lose her if I do."

"Look at my little Creigh, all grown up and catching feelings." He reaches his hand beneath my jaw.

I slap it away, glaring. "Are you going to help or are you going to sod off?"

"Fine, fine. For your information, I feel used for my genius neurons right now, but I digress." He tilts his head in my direction. "What happened after she went with him?"

"She asked me to trust her. I told her I'll only give her a day before doing it my way."

"*Your* way? Pretty sure that entails violence and sending him to the hospital. I thought you didn't want her to hate you."

"I don't, but I'd rather have her hate me than not have her at all."

"Oh? That's interesting." He hums for a beat. "But for now, do as she asked."

"What?"

"Trust her. Let her deal with him. She's known him her whole life and, therefore, has the ability to convince him."

"You don't understand. She's anti-conflict and acts like Mum does whenever you and Dad verbally spar. She'll always, without a doubt, use herself as a sacrifice to bring peace to the situation. And that option is out of the question."

"You'll never really know until you let her do her thing. Trusting her as she asked will go a long way after this hurdle is cleared. Believe me when I say, women remember when you give them freedom. It doesn't have to be real, and you can always watch from the background, but the smokescreen of it is enough. So be patient. If that doesn't work, you can always do what you promised after the one-day deadline is over. We'll raid the Heathens' mansion together. Lan will take care of Kill—he can't stand him after the whole Glyn thing. I'll keep the crazy dog Nikolai down. Pretty sure Bran and Remi can hold off Gareth. And you'll have fucker Jeremy all for yourself."

I release a long breath, not wanting to agree with him but knowing it's the wisest, most logical thing to do.

Eli leans his head on his crossed hands. "I never thought our baby Creigh would be so bewitched by a girl."

"I'm not bewitched."

"You can't sleep because of her, have brought her here more times than I can count, mentioned her in a fleeting manner when talking to Mum—she won't stop asking me about her, by the way, so compensate me for all the hassle—and you even told her about your childhood when you've never seen the need to mention it before. Oh, and you act like an unhinged caveman with serial killer tendencies whenever anyone, us included, goes near her. Bewitched is me putting it mildly."

Well, fuck.

Am I that obvious?

"I like spending time with her. She's the light I never thought I needed and the one person who can fill up the hollowness."

"Ouch, I'm wounded. I thought filling up the hollowness was my role."

"You're empty yourself. How the fuck will you be able to fill up someone else?"

"By illusion?" He grins. "Jokes aside, you're not hollow. You just had shitty biological parents, who I'm sure are rotting in the devil's lair as we speak."

I snicker.

"I take it you're finally putting it behind you if you're talking about it to your girl?"

Your girl.

I like the sound of that. In fact, I like it so much that I wish I could have him say it again and record it this time.

"I'll never be over it," I tell him. "I'll have my revenge."

"What?"

"You heard me."

"You're avenging those useless parents?"

"I'm avenging the three-year-old version of myself who was driven to the gates of hell."

"And how the fuck do you intend to do that, genius? By taking a trip back in time? You can't ask Mum and Dad. Not only will they not answer, but the last time you asked, Mum was depressed for an entire month, thinking she was doing something wrong. In her mind, you being interested in your past is in direct correlation with your birth parents, and if you want to know about them, it means she failed as a mother."

"I won't get Mum and Dad involved and neither will you. I have other methods."

"Such as... Wait a fucking second, were you getting all mushy with Lan because of this?" His brow furrows. "You can't trust that snake. Any action he takes is purely for self-serving purposes."

"And you're different because..."

"I'm you brother. I wouldn't hurt you."

I release a sigh. "I know. But let me have this, Eli. If I don't, I'll never find the closure I need. I'll never be...whole."

"Bloody hell. Mum would undoubtedly cry if she heard that."

"Don't ever mention this to her." I stare at the wall. "I hate this part of me that's unable to move on from the past, despite having Mum, Dad, and our whole family. I tried to leave it behind, but the demons never disappear."

My brother remains silent, probably because he doesn't understand what the fuck I'm talking about, but he's still there for me, listening and offering a part of himself he never gives anyone.

And I'm grateful for that.

After a while, he inches closer. "What's the information you gathered from that slimy fucker Lan?"

"He said I was born in the United States, in New York City, to be more specific. He's currently searching for my birth last name and the circumstances that surrounded all that hell."

"You could've hired a PI instead of relying on that snake."

"I did, but all information about my past was wiped clean. Probably by Dad and our grandfathers."

"I wouldn't be surprised. They never liked to talk about your past. So in that case, how can Lan get his hands on the information concerning your past?"

"He said he had a hunch, that he won't reveal yet, and he figured out another way to get information."

"Sounds fishy."

"Lan's hunches are always right."

"And always get those involved in deep shit."

"I've come this far. It goes without saying that I'm ready to make some sacrifices."

"Some are more than you can pay."

"I'll deal with those when they happen."

He shakes his head, seeming absolutely displeased. Eli has always hated it whenever I put myself in an unfavorable position.

Always.

"Don't worry. I'll be fine," I say.

"Who's worried, you little shit? If you have the audacity to get hurt, I won't let you live it down."

A small smile grazes my lips.

He side-eyes me "Why are you smiling like a creep?"

"It's weird how you hate everyone but have always refused to leave me alone."

"Didn't have a choice. When Mum and Dad shoved you in my face, I had two options, like you or kill you. I would've gone for the second one, but I figured that would be frowned upon by our parents, so I had no choice but to like you."

"Must've been a struggle."

"I know, right? The worst of all. You're a lucky son of a bitch."

"Thanks, Eli."

He grabs me by the shoulder and runs his fingers under my chin. "There's no thanks between brothers, punk. Now, let's use the free time you have for something productive."

"Such as?"

A wolfish grin stretches his lips. "Landon is stalling and is probably gatekeeping information to keep a leash on you. I have the perfect solution to force his hand."

TWENTY-FOUR

Annika

"ANNIKA IS NOT ALLOWED TO LEAVE THE PERIMETER OF the property until further notice."

"Yes, sir."

Jeremy nods at his guards and strides inside the house.

I hop off his bike—that he never allows anyone to ride and only let me out of necessity—and run after him. His steps are so wide that it takes me a while to reach him and grab his arm, forcing him to come to a halt—or I think I do—in the entrance hall.

He faces me with drawn brows, a dark expression, and tense muscles. This has been his state ever since we left the grocery store.

I love my brother, I truly do, but I don't recognize him sometimes. Or more like, I don't recognize the darkness that flows inside him, barely tucked beneath the surface.

"Do you have an objection, Anoushka?"

"Of course I do. You can't just lock me up every time you decide to, Jer." My voice softens. "I'm not a dog."

"I wouldn't have had to do this if you weren't roaming around the Elites bastards."

"Creighton is not a member of the club."

"His cousin is."

"That doesn't mean anything. You're rivals with the Elites,

not with everyone at REU. Creighton has never taken part in their activities."

"Are you sure about that? Because no matter how much I go over it in my head, his sudden appearance during the fire is suspicious."

"I told you. It wasn't sudden—"

"Spare me the bullshit. You think I haven't figured out you were covering up for him?"

My spine jerks upright. "You knew?"

"Sure did."

"Then… Why did you let it slide?"

"Because he saved you and me. Not to mention that Gareth found evidence that the Serpents were behind that fire." He steps closer. "But that doesn't mean he wasn't aware of it. Perhaps he plotted it with that deranged cousin of his, then appeared at the right moment to be seen as a savior."

"That's not true."

Jeremy grabs me by the shoulder and shakes me. "Wake the fuck up, Annika. Do you really think it was a coincidence that he happened to be there at the right moment? Do you honestly believe there were no underhanded methods beneath it all?"

My throat dries and I stare into his dead eyes with my stinging ones. "I'm sure there's an explanation—"

"This is why Dad never wanted you away from home. You're so naive, it's fucking embarrassing." He releases me and I sway backward as if someone slapped me across the face.

No.

It wouldn't hurt this much if someone physically struck me.

"You won't be going out, and you'll be escorted in and out of REU." He heads to the stairs. "That's final."

Usually, I'd hide in my room, call Mom for emotional support, and maybe cry where no one can see me.

Usually, I wouldn't even attempt to go against my brother.

This time, however, I barge in front of him, shoulders pushed back, and I lift my chin as I speak in a calm though slightly trembling voice. "You call it naivety, but I call it giving people the chances they deserve. I refuse to see the world in black and white like you do, Jeremy. I want the gray, I want the purple, I want all the colors. And I won't allow you or anyone else to forbid me from seeing them. It's how I chose to love you despite your dark side. My affection for you isn't due to your rare warmth or, God forbid, your suffocating behavior, it's *my* choice. It is also *my* choice to trust Creighton. He's not the type to orchestrate such a fire just to play a savior, and he is *not*, under any circumstances, associated with the Elites. I know it as well as I know you. Don't insult me by insinuating that I would choose someone who's bent on hurting you. If you trusted me enough, you'd figure out that I would never do that."

My chest deflates from the overwhelming emotions I just unpacked in one go. It's been a long time coming, considering his asphyxiating overprotectiveness. Slandering Creighton is the straw that broke the camel's back.

At least Creigh trusted me to take this situation into my own hands. The same can't be said about Jeremy. I doubt he would trust me to even breathe on my own.

His brows dip in blatant confusion, but his voice softens. "It's not that I don't trust you, it's that I don't trust your trusting nature, Anoushka. That trait attracts all sorts of predators and invites them to hurt you. The entire King family is cutthroat and brutal. If they were to use you as a pawn, you wouldn't be able to survive."

"I've been surviving just fine with them, Jer. Hell, I like them better than your own unhinged friends."

"Will you still like them if they hurt you?"

"You see, that's your problem. You believe that either everyone is out to hurt me or I'm too fickle to handle myself. I'm eighteen years old, you know, and yes, I might have been a bit immature before, but I'm not anymore. I realize there's a whole world out there beyond the pretty little cage you and Papa built for me and I want that world, Jer. I want to live, make mistakes, and correct them on my own. I want to be *alive*."

Jeremy's hand clenches at his side, but he slowly relaxes it. "And all of that has to happen with Creighton?"

"Yeah." I bite the corner of my lower lip. "I love him."

"You can't be sure about that this early in the relationship."

"If I'm not with him, I think about him. Hell, I even think about him when he's there. He makes me feel happy and appreciated. When I'm with him, I'm just Annika and not Miss Volkov who's shackled by my family name and background. He's the place I go to when I want to feel safe, so yes, I love him, and I'm damn sure about it."

Jeremy tenses and I think he'll go down his dictatorial road with this, but then he sighs. "Why did it have to be Creighton?"

"Why can it not be Creighton?"

"If he has to choose, he'll go with his family."

"That's where you're wrong." I smile. "Creigh will always choose me. Just like I'll always choose him."

"You never know, Anoushka. All these rosy feelings you have for him might easily turn black."

"No, they won't."

"Are you up to proving that?"

I lift my chin further. "What do you have in mind?"

"In the morning, we'll go back home and you'll tell Dad all about these emotions. If he does his research on Creighton and ends up accepting him, I'll back off."

I swallow.

Talking to Jeremy is one thing, but Papa is an entirely different beast.

"What?" He smirks, knowing exactly which cord he hit. "Cold feet?"

"Of course not. You'll keep your word. If Papa agrees, you won't intervene."

"Cross my heart." He continues smirking.

Because he knows full well that Papa's approval is as impossible as seeing a unicorn.

But I have a secret weapon. *Mom.*

Seems like I'll have to fight a whole other battle back where I hate it.

Where I was nothing more than a sheltered princess.

Home.

Home and I share a love-hate relationship.

I cherish all the memories I have with Mom, Papa, and Jeremy growing up, but I dislike it for how helpless and suppressed I felt.

However, the moment we drive into the vast property that Mom has somehow changed from a gothic mansion to a homey one, the only thing I'm hit with are those precious memories.

Like when Papa taught me how to ride a bike. I ended up falling and hitting my knee, so Jeremy blew on it and Mom cleaned the wound as I cried a river. Then I was up and running again as if nothing had happened.

Or when Papa let me ride on his shoulders and I wouldn't stop grabbing onto his face and blocking his vision.

Or when Mom surprised Papa with a birthday party that he low-key hated because she invited all the guards.

It's the little things, minor things, that might seem unimportant, but they're what come to mind right now.

Maybe it's a psychological trick I'm playing on myself so that I'm mentally prepared for the upcoming battle.

The car comes to a halt in front of the imposing building that I call home. This is where I was born and lived for seventeen years, shielded from the outside world.

I never had friends, definitely couldn't invite anyone over or visit anyone else's home—unless they were willing to have their house flipped upside down for a security check and enjoyed the company of my guards.

I was supposed to be homeschooled, but after I begged and implored and was kind of depressed for a while, Papa allowed me to attend a private school. After he bought it and planted his people everywhere.

That's the type of person my father is. When it comes to our safety, no detail escapes him.

My brother steps out of the car and I open my door before the driver does, then I thank him with a smile.

"Jeremy!"

A tall middle-aged man gathers my brother in one of those side hugs men do and Jer grins. "Yan, how have you been?"

"Bored to fucking death from the lack of action."

They break apart and Yan nods at me. His long hair is gathered in a small ponytail and his face is as pretty as ever. He's one of my father's two most trusted guards and Mom's best friend.

Oh, and I totally used him as my makeup subject countless times because he's cool like that. Mom still has the pictures of my amateur creations as proof.

He smiles at me. "Princess."

"It's just Anni, Yan."

"Don't go using those tasteless American nicknames. Now, come. Your mother has been waiting for you."

We're barely two steps inside when Mom emerges from the kitchen, wiping her hands on her apron and smiling so big, I can't help but grin back.

She looks so radiant in the floral dress half hidden by her apron. Her hair is pulled up in a chignon with bangs escaping on either side. I've come to the conclusion that she's a vampire, because she hasn't changed a bit since I was young.

"Babies!" She opens her arms and I run straight into them, letting my bag fall to the floor.

When she embraces me and I drown in her rose scent, I feel like everything is going to be okay. She smells of warmth and unbounded affection. She smells of every beautiful memory and happy childhood dream.

"Let me look at you." She steps back to examine me closely. "You've gotten tall and more beautiful, my baby angel."

"I'm eighteen. Don't call me a baby."

"You'll always be my baby angel. I can't believe my youngest is already eighteen." She hugs me again. "I've missed you to death. I'm kind of regretting letting you go."

"Missed you, too, Mom."

"Can I say hi or should I come back in an hour, after you guys are finished?"

Mom steps back at Jeremy's voice and laughs, then pulls him down for his own hug. He's so tall compared to her that the angle looks comical at best.

"Come now, let's have dinner. I've prepared a lot of food for you two," she says once they release each other.

"You didn't have to. We could've eaten anything," I say.

"Nonsense. It's been months since you guys came home and there's no way you'll eat just anything." She ushers us into the kitchen with Yan's help. Ogla, our head maid, greets us and I give her a hug. Something she's found blasphemous for the past eighteen years, but I've slowly trained the stern Russian lady to accept them.

"Where's Papa?" I ask Mom while I help Ogla fill plates that look no different than a feast for an army.

"In his office with Kolya." Mom plants me on a seat and places my favorite salad in front of me. "You know how he gets with work."

"Let me go call them." Jeremy has barely finished his sentence when Papa strolls into the kitchen with Kolya—his second-in-command—in tow.

Papa has an imposing, intimidating presence that calls for everyone's attention whenever he walks into a room. I'm lucky enough to be his daughter, so I'm never the subject of his wrath, but I know that people tremble at the prospect of being in that position.

After he hugs Jeremy in greeting, he regards me with a soft smile. "Anoushka."

I run into his arms, and while they're not as soothing as Mom's, they're safe, like a fortress.

It's moments like these that make me glad to be home. Moments of normalcy, of warmth, and peace.

Of family.

Even if we'll never be the conventional type.

We all sit for dinner, Kolya, Yan, and Ogla included. Boris, another guard in the close circle, would've joined us, too, but he's apparently not in the house.

We've always considered these guys our extended family. The ones we go to whenever our parents are unreachable.

They're our godparents in a way.

Mom, who's beaming from ear to ear, doesn't stop pushing all sorts of food in our direction. Her happiness is contagious, to say the least, and so is her energy.

"How's everything at school?" Papa pours himself a glass of wine.

"The usual," Jeremy answers with a shrug. Needless to say, he made the guards report back that the fire that took place was minor and nothing to worry about. Otherwise, Papa and these ruthless guys would've come over and buried the Serpents with their own hands.

Especially if they'd found out my and Jeremy's lives were in danger.

I push my glass in front of Papa. "Me, too."

He levels me with a look that would bring a mountain to its knees. "You have your juice."

"But I'm already eighteen. People drink at this age in the UK."

"This is not the UK and you are not English."

"Well, I'm half Russian and people drink at eighteen in Russia."

Mom raises a brow. "She has a point."

Papa slides his attention to her and all I can do is watch as a different, cryptic emotion blossoms in his eyes. I've always loved the way he looks at her, like she's his world. How he searches for her when she's not there. It's like she's his air and he has to see her every moment.

My papa might be heartless, but he's the best husband and father alive.

"Don't feed her lies, Lenochka." He pins me with a stare. "I'm three-quarters Russian. That makes you about a quarter Russian."

"One-third at worst."

"Still a no."

"Let her have some, Boss. We need to prepare her for all the vodka." Yan fills my glass with wine and narrowly escapes having his head chopped off by Papa's glare.

Then he pretends not to have noticed the murder attempt and gets engrossed in his food.

"Didn't you have eat not two hours ago?" Kolya calls him out on his bullshit point-blank.

"So what? Food tastes so much better with the kids around."

"That's true." Mom sighs. "I'm so happy you guys came back, even if it's just for a few days. Apparently, you're all grown up and don't need to visit your mother anymore."

"Of course not." I side-hug her. "We're just too busy with school."

"And other things," Jeremy says casually while cutting his steak.

I make a face at him and he just remains in his blank mode.

We agreed that he'd let me talk to them on my own. Which I'll do in the morning because I'm too drained for that conversation tonight.

"Oh, I know." Mom rubs my hand that's on the table. "I'm glad you made friends. They looked nice."

"They're the best ever. We're having a lot of fun on campus."

"Not too much fun, though, right?" Papa levels me with one of his stern fatherly looks again.

"Oh, Adrian. Let her be," Mom chastises. "Tell me all about the fun you've had."

I chatter on and on, interrupted by Jeremy's semi-threatening objections whenever he feels like I've veered too close to the subject we're here for.

We stay around the table for a long time, even after we finish dinner. They fill us in on Yan's antics with Kolya, Boris, and Papa. Mom comes to his defense, which displeases Papa, judging by the subtle threats to Yan's life.

By the time we retreat to our rooms, it's super late.

That means it's early morning in the UK.

After taking a shower, I lie in bed and retrieve my phone. I send everyone a text that I'm visiting home for the weekend. I get replies from Cecily, Ava, Glyn, Bran, and Remi, but there's nothing from Creighton.

My heart sinks as I stare at the last text I sent him.

Annika: I'm going back home to convince Papa to accept our relationship. If I do, Jer will leave us alone. Wish me luck. I'll miss you.

It hasn't been read, so it's not like he's ignoring me. Maybe he's still asleep. After all, it's Saturday back on the island.

Rolling onto my stomach, I scroll through the album called 'My Purple.' It has all sorts of pictures of us, mostly selfies I've taken while he wasn't paying attention.

There's one picture that I love the most. It's when he was massaging my feet that were against his chest during a bath. It was right after he tied me up and brutally fucked me. Then he carried me to the bath and rubbed the red marks around my feet. He was so focused on his task that he didn't notice when I took the picture.

I zoom in on his face and sigh. Why do I suddenly miss him so much when it's barely been a few hours since I last saw him?

"Is this the reason you're having so much fun?" Mom sneaks up behind me, carrying a plate of pastries and it's too late to hide the picture from her.

Thank God it's only zoomed in on his face and not my feet on his naked chest with the bathroom as a background.

"Mom!"

Her smile immediately disappears. The tray shakes in her hand before it topples and falls to the ground with a haunting crash.

But I don't focus on that, because something worse happens.

Mom has paled, her lips are trembling, and her whole body has stiffened.

It's the first time I've ever seen her like this.

As if...she's seen a ghost.

TWENTY-FIVE

Annika

"**M**OM…?"

I slowly stand up, limbs shaking, and my heart thumping with the brutality of a torture device.

My mother remains frozen in place, her hands trembling at either side of her as she stares right through me.

It's like she's here but not really *here*.

And the sight scares the shit out of me.

Careful not to step on the broken glass and ruined snacks, I take my time approaching her until I'm toe-to-toe with her.

"Mom," I call again, louder this time. I wave my hand in front of her face.

She flinches.

I flinch.

That's the first time I've ever seen my mother flinch. Papa might be the bad mafia guy, but at home, they share everything. Just because she's soft doesn't mean she's weak. In fact, she can be extremely powerful if the circumstances call for it.

She's just not the type to flinch, period.

So why do her eyes look so…dead? They're usually the liveliest I know.

The warmest, too.

"Mom!" My voice translates all the panic that's spreading inside me.

She jerks, blinking slowly, before her attention zeroes in on me. And it's like she's seeing me for the first time. As if I haven't been her daughter, her baby angel, for the past eighteen years.

And this expression?

It terrorizes me.

This must be what amnesia patients' family and friends feel like when they realize they've been forgotten. That they're the only ones who recall every small memory, every little detail, every laugh, every smile, every precious conversation.

"Mom? Are you okay?" I speak in a brittle voice, my heart thudding against my chest.

"What... Oh, I'm good." She breathes heavily, her eyes flitting to my phone that I left on the bed.

"You look anything but good, Mom."

"It's probably exhaustion from working at the shelter. I just need a moment." She sits on the edge of the bed and pats the spot beside her. "Careful of the glass shards."

Relief zings through me, but the shadows of wariness linger in the room like a third presence.

An ominous sign.

The calm before the horror scare.

Still, I sit beside her and watch her carefully, so carefully that she smiles.

"I'm really all right, Anni."

"You didn't look all right a minute ago."

"It's just exhaustion. Happens all the time."

"That's the first time I've seen you like that, Mom."

"Guess I've done a good job hiding it from you guys." She smiles, ushers me to lie down, and leans my head on her lap so she can stroke my hair.

She used to do this a lot when I was a kid, but as I grew up, she did it less and less. Not that I'm complaining or anything. I'm the one who wants to be an adult sooner rather than later. But I miss her touch.

The in-and-out of her fingers in my hair is nothing short of a soothing lullaby. I close my eyes, picturing myself easily falling into peaceful sleep.

"Baby angel?"

"Yeah?"

"Tell me about the boy in the picture you were just staring at with a dreamy expression."

I wince, opening my eyes. "Was I that obvious?"

"Uh-huh. You were practically devouring him."

"I was *not*."

"Was too."

I sigh, turning onto my back so that I'm staring up at her. "His name is Creighton and we're…sort of going out."

"Sort of?"

"We haven't been together for a long time, but time is irrelevant because I share a special connection with him. The type I've never shared with anyone else."

Mom's fingers pause in my hair and I think her face pales a little, or maybe it's the lighting. After a moment, she goes back to her soothing rhythm. "Why haven't you told me about him before?"

"I wasn't confident that we had a relationship. He didn't really like me at the beginning, you know, so we had to get past that, and then, well, find compatibility. So I avoided telling you until I was sure about what we share."

"And you are now?"

I grin. "One hundred percent."

Her rhythm falters again, but only for a second. "Tell me all about him, his family, his personality. I want to know everything."

"Where do I even begin?" It takes me about fifteen minutes to introduce Creigh and his family to Mom.

She never interrupts and listens carefully, attentively. Because my mom cares.

"It sounds like you have a lot of fun with him," she says after I'm done.

"The best ever." I sigh. "I actually miss him."

"Can you tell me how the relationship started? Did he pursue you?"

I smile sheepishly. "It was actually the other way around. As I told you, he didn't really like me at the beginning and said I talked too much. My pride was bruised and brutally stomped upon, I tell you, but then he started to grow fond of me. He even listens to me talk on and on, and said he likes the sound of my voice. Guess that means I brought him around."

"He...really didn't pursue you?"

"No. And yeah, maybe a lady shouldn't chase after a man, but that's like a Middle Ages mentality. I say women should go after what we want. Also, he did warn me away, thinking we weren't...compatible, but I soon proved him wrong."

"Proved him wrong how?"

I chuckle awkwardly. "You don't need to know."

"Are you hiding things from me?"

"I just...would rather not talk about it. Everyone needs their own secrets."

"Since when do you keep secrets from me, baby?"

"Since I'm all grown up." I grin.

She sighs deeply, the sound slightly chopped off. Her gaze gets lost in the distance and I feel her escaping into another reality that I have no access to. Like earlier.

"Hey, Mom?"

She blinks, focusing back on me. "Hmm?"

"Remember when you told me that if I have someone I love, you wouldn't let Papa shove me into an arranged marriage? Creighton is that someone."

She pales, and this time, there's no mistaking it. But her voice is still composed and soothing. "You're still too young to know what love truly is."

"Would everyone stop saying that? I'm not that young, and there's no explanation for the feelings I have for Creigh besides love."

"Anni, honey, listen to me. Love isn't a crush or an infatuation. Love is when you go through life together, face your fears together, and at times, even hate each other in the process. It's not love if it hasn't been tested."

I get up, forcing her to release my hair, and face her. "That doesn't apply to everyone. And what are you insinuating, Mom? Does this mean you won't help me convince Papa? Jeremy said he'd leave me alone if Papa accepts Creighton, and I need your help to make him see reason."

She takes my hand in hers. "I think we should give it a bit more time before we bring it up to your father."

"I don't have more time. We're going back tomorrow, and I can't have Jeremy locking me up for sport. I'm so done with that."

"Honey…"

"You said you'd help me." My chin quivers. "You promised to be on my side in this world that treats women like second-rate citizens. I knew I could do it, because I have you. How could you turn your back on me?"

"It's not that I'm turning my back…we just can't be rash."

A tear slides down my cheek and I wipe it away. "I wouldn't be surprised if Papa or Jeremy said those words, because I know they don't really trust me to be responsible for my own life, but it kills me that you don't trust me either. I never expected this from you."

"Anni…there's so much you don't know."

"Then tell me. Don't just keep me in the dark and ask me to accept situations I don't understand."

"I will, but as I said, I need time, baby. I'm just asking you—imploring you, begging you—to cut off ties with this Creighton."

"Mom!"

"I've never asked anything of you, Anni. I only wanted you to grow up into the bright, cheerful, and absolutely beautiful young lady you are. I didn't stop you from ballet even though I'm uncomfortable with it, I didn't stop you from traveling to the other side of the world, although I was scared for your safety, but I'm begging you to let him go."

"I can't…do that. I love him."

"You haven't been together for long. Those feelings will eventually disappear."

"You can't possibly be serious?"

She stands up, releases a long breath, and whispers, "I'm trying to protect you."

"By hurting me? You're cutting me open by demanding I stop seeing the only person who's not only embraced me for who I am but who's also encouraged me to grow into myself."

She strokes my hair back, a sad expression covering her face. "It'll all get better with time. I promise."

Then she steps out the door, leaving me with pain, sadness, and, most importantly, confusion.

What the hell just happened?

When I wake up after a restless sleep, the first thing I do is check my messages.

My chest immediately deflates when I find no text from Creighton.

Maybe he's mad that the one-day deadline is over and I still haven't made good on my promise to fix things.

So I type another one.

Annika: Morning! It's morning here, so it must be around mid-day there? I'm going to find an opportunity to talk to Papa about us. I was hoping Mom would be my ally, but I guess that's out after she was weirdly opposed to our relationship last night. This will be the first time I've gone up against Papa head-to-head. Wish me luck! I miss you. I want to kiss you.

I wait for a few minutes in case he reads both my texts and finally replies, but there's nothing.

Maybe he lost his phone.

I stroke the necklace he gave me, then text the girls' group chat.

Annika: Morning! Did you get together with the guys this weekend?

Cecily: With Remi and Bran, yeah.

Annika: How about the others?

Cecily: What others? Eli and Lan don't hang out with us.

Glyndon: She means Creigh, silly. And no, Anni. He didn't come along.

My fingers tighten around the phone and I frown.

Honestly, I wouldn't be surprised if he's spent all his time sleeping, but ever since we got together, he doesn't sleep as much.

I was hopeful—and probably delusional—enough to think he probably preferred my company over sleep.

My screen lights up with another text.

Ava: Creigh was inseparable from He-Who-Shall-Not-Be-Named. Looked like they were up to no good.

Cecily: And how do you know that? Have you developed stalker tendencies?

Ava: Bitch, please. I only caught a glimpse of it when I was borrowing something from Bran.

Glyndon: Borrowing something from Bran, huh? *giggling GIF*

Cecily: Leave her be. She said she caught a glimpse. More like glimpses.

Glyndon: Maybe in compromising positions.

Ava: I'm blocking you two.

Ava: Not really, but I might.

My frown deepens, but I choose to remain calm as I change my clothes and then go down the stairs. I keep obsessing over my phone, checking the unread texts over and over.

Just because Creighton is spending time with Eli doesn't mean he wouldn't reply.

The more I think about it, the less it makes sense.

I find Mom and Jeremy having breakfast in the garden and whispering among each other.

The moment I approach them, they swiftly push back in their seats, putting an abrupt end to their secret conversation.

I've always envied the relationship Jer has with both our parents. Papa sees himself in him and Mom dotes on him as the firstborn. Her angel, as she calls him. She sometimes treats him like her best friend and her confidant.

Apparently, he's the one who brought my parents together. Something I can never measure up to.

So whenever they're having their moments like these, I feel left out.

"Morning," I mutter as I fall onto a chair and pour myself a coffee.

"Morning, baby. Did you sleep well?"

I make an affirmative sound. "Where's Papa and the others?"

"They went out late last night for some errands."

Errands? More like to kill people. I shake my head, not wanting to picture that.

Mom fixes me some toast. "Jeremy was just telling me about the rivalry between The King's U and Royal Elite University. It seems intense."

"So what of it?" I lose my cool. "Is this another way to convince me to stay away from Creighton for reasons you refuse to divulge? If that's the case, save it, Mom. I happen to be an REU student, and not once have the people there treated me differently just because I'm an American or a Volkov."

Jeremy glares at me over the rim of his cup. "Don't speak to Mom in that tone."

"You guys are obviously ganging up on me. Did you expect me to lower my head, follow your orders, and just go with it?"

"You have no choice, Anoushka. I spoke to Dad last night and he agrees that you are not allowed to see Creighton King anymore."

The cup of coffee shakes in my hand and I place it on the table before it falls and shatters. "We agreed that I would talk to him."

"We only agreed that he'd be informed of the situation, not that either of us would talk to him. Upon returning to Brighton Island, you'll break up with him or Dad will find you a suitor for marriage."

I stare at Mom as if I've been stabbed in the chest and she's holding the knife. "You said you wouldn't let this happen."

"Anni…"

"Forget it. I'm going to speak with Papa myself when he gets back."

"Don't, Anni," Mom says in a soft voice. "You'll only anger him and get yourself hurt. This is for the best."

"Whose best? Yours? Papa's? Jeremy's? It's certainly not for mine." Frustration bubbles in my veins. It keeps mounting until it's bursting at the seams.

And the worst part is that I have no clue how to placate it.

Make it better.

I'm so disappointed in Mom and angry at myself for being so trusting. For getting trapped in a situation where the only way out is to lose.

All doors are closing in my face and Creighton still isn't answering my texts.

Will he say it's for my sake, too?

Jeremy's phone vibrates on the table and when he checks it out, a crease appears between his brows.

"We're leaving," he announces, abruptly standing up.

"But you just got here," Mom protests.

"There's an emergency back at the island."

"What type of emergency?" I ask in a haunted voice.

"The bad type."

He storms in the direction of the house and I jog to keep up with him. "What happened?"

"Nikolai was kidnapped and the kidnapper is asking for me."

TWENTY-SIX

Creighton

"ARE YOU SURE THIS PLAN WILL WORK?"

Eli's body remains completely still while he tilts his head to the side, biding his time.

Waiting.

We've been hiding behind the bushes in the corner of the Heathens' back entrance for an hour now and there's still no sign of the 'prey' my brother said we're hunting tonight.

"Patience, baby bro. We have to let the prey come out of its own accord."

"Why can't we just weed it out?"

He gives me a sideways glance, one full of sadism. "Now, where's the fun in that?"

We're both dressed in jeans and hoodies and probably look like serial creeps with depraved tendencies. Which is true, to an extent.

It doesn't help that it's late, about two in the morning late, and the streets are practically empty.

Ever since I saw the text Annika sent me, the one where she announced going back to the States, I've been restless. Those black shadows lined my vision and I couldn't stay still.

The first thought that came to mind was that her father wouldn't allow her to come back here. She was always proud of how she convinced him to let her attend REU, but the fact remains that he was opposed to the idea.

Considering her mafia background, she's prone to lose whatever freedom she's enjoyed for the last couple of months. Especially if Jeremy has any say in it.

Which he wouldn't have had if she'd let me deal with him earlier.

Since that option is now out of the question, and I had nothing to say that wouldn't have come out sounding petty, I marked the conversation as Not Read until I could think of a better reply.

And that brings us to the now where I followed Eli in his nightly endeavors. Which is still better than tossing and turning in bed, being scratched by Tiger for sport, or entertaining Remi's drunk ramblings—that usually include revealing any secrets he's come across.

"There he is." Eli's lips pull in a smirk as he jerks his head in the direction of a buff man slipping out the back entrance.

"How can you tell it's him? He could be going out for a smoke."

"One, he could've had the smoke inside the property. Two, he's grabbing a blunt but not lighting it in order not to draw attention. Three, and most importantly, he's walking in strategic lines that I'm sure are the cameras' blind spots. Guess who goes to these lengths to leave a property they're supposed to be guarding?"

"Someone who has something to hide."

"Bingo." He grabs me by the shoulder. "Remember when we used to release those worms and cockroaches in the garden to watch them wiggle and struggle away only so we could catch them? Time to repeat the process."

"Dad aborted our plan every time, remember?"

His smirk widens in pure imitation of what I assume Lucifer looks like on his throne in hell. "Lucky for us, Dad isn't here."

It's useless to remind him that Dad eventually finds out about everything. But even I am willing to forgo that possibility if it means I'll get closer to my goal.

We follow the guard, keeping a safe distance away until he's off TKU's soil.

His hands are in his pockets and his steps are measured,

unhurried, and have a careless rhythm to them. He's used to this street, despite the fact that it's hidden.

Considering he's not a native to the island, like all of TKU's students and guards, this can only be a learned behavior he's acquired with time.

"He's off to meet someone," Eli voices my thoughts, then grins. "Want to guess who?"

Sure enough, the guard reaches a secluded area on the beach. We hide behind the corner of a building as he does a full sweep of the area before he opens the door of a high-end, and very familiar, black Tesla.

We expected the loud McLaren that Landon treats like a lover instead of a car. He absolutely loathes electric cars, so he would never switch to a Tesla.

"Brandon…?" I voice as the guard disappears inside.

"Brandon's *car*," Eli tells me with a raise of an eyebrow. "That Landon could've easily taken for a ride. It goes without saying that he wouldn't have used his own for this mission. He's probably used Remi's and yours before."

Now that I think about it, Landon did take my car for a spin in the past. He could've easily borrowed any of our keys to conduct this operation.

We wait for a few minutes, watching the black car with tinted windows. Then, finally, the guard steps out and starts walking away from us.

The Tesla revs, something Bran would never do, before it speeds down the street.

"We're getting that guard," I say.

"My thoughts exactly, baby bro."

We take our time following the man through all the twists and turns he takes.

When he reaches a secluded alley, Eli and I share a look, then we diverge in opposite directions.

I stand in front of the guard, hands in my pockets, with every intention of blocking his path.

He stops, narrows his mean eyes, and then reaches into his jacket.

Before he can pull out whatever weapon he has hidden, Eli smacks him from behind with a rock.

The guard falls to his knees on the dirty ground, revealing the manic smile on my brother's face.

"Improvising." My brother throws the rock in the air and catches it. "Can't say I hate it."

The man appears to be in his late thirties, has small eyes, thin lips, and white-blond hair cut military style. He slaps a hand on the back of his head where a small wound gushes with blood. I wouldn't call it fatal, but it definitely needs stitches.

"What the fuck...?" He stares between the two of us. "Who the fuck are you?"

"Judging by the Russian accent, you're part of the mafia. Check," Eli muses, appearing to enjoy this a bit too much. "I'm also going to guess you're on Jeremy's side, not Nikolai's. Or more accurately, you're a double agent who's crossing Jeremy?"

The guard's eyes turn bloodshot, narrower, which means we're getting close. He starts to stand, but I kick him back down with a foot and keep my leg on his chest.

He releases his nape and wiggles, just like those worms back when we were kids. But this time, he manages to get his gun and jumps up. I kick his hand, and it clinks to the ground.

Eli kicks it away, grabs the man's arms and hauls them behind his back, then shoves him to his knees again. "Now, now, let us not use weapons in this. They're illegal on UK soil anyway."

"We're going to ask you a few questions." I push the sleeves of my hoodie up. "You'll either answer them nicely or we can turn your face into a map of destruction first."

He spits at me and I smile. "A map of destruction, it is."

I use him as my punching bag, driving my fist into his face, chest, and stomach over and over as Eli holds him back.

My brother gets bored halfway through, suppresses a yawn, and chooses to scroll through his phone. While still grabbing him in a deadly clutch.

I slam my fist underneath the man's jaw, sending it flying sideways, and ask for the dozenth time. "What are you telling Landon?"

I expect the guard to remain silent like before, but he breathes harshly as blood pours from his mouth. "Are you going to take his place in clearing my debts?"

"We might." Eli's manic attention slides to the guard and he tucks his phone in his pocket. "But if you don't tell us what we want to know, not only will you lose us as sponsors, but we'll also make sure you lose Landon. King money might be infinite, but it's hard to come by for peasants like you."

"You don't even care to hide your identities," the guard pants out, sounding barely coherent with all the blood that's gushing from his lips and nose.

"Does it make a difference?" Eli releases the man's wrists, strolls in front of him, and cocks his head to the side. "Who would believe a traitor cockroach like you anyway? Definitely not Jeremy. And if you think Lan has your back, then you're in for a life lesson. My cousin has absolutely no fucks to give about anyone who's not himself and his dick. The moment he realizes you're no longer a useful pawn in his alleged grand schemes, he'll discard you."

"You'll pay the debts?" He's speaking to me, probably having figured out I'm the least unhinged, despite the galaxy of bruises I left on his face.

Poor cunt.

There's no such thing as a sane King.

Still, I nod and step back.

The guard takes a few moments to rise to his feet, then lets his weight fall against the dirty stone wall and taps his pockets before he fetches a blunt.

It takes a few more moments for him to light it. We don't interrupt, patiently waiting for him to divulge what he knows. As Eli said, it's better to allow the prey to come out on its own since any form of coercion might have the exact opposite effect.

And from what I gather, this man holds no loyalty to anyone. Except for his debts. Probably due to gambling.

"Landon wanted to know about the Volkov family secrets, but he was particularly interested in one that reached the media but remained a cold case." He releases a cloud of smoke. "This happened a long time ago, when I was twenty and had just recently left Russia to join the New York Bratva. I saved one of the leaders by putting my life in jeopardy and soon after, I was recruited by Adrian Volkov's men. Back then, he had this pesky problem that scattered his attention from his duties as the strategist of the New York City branch."

"Oh?" Eli leans against the wall, mirroring his stance, and even retrieves a cigarette, then shoves it at the corner of his lips but doesn't light it. "And pray tell, what might that be?"

"His wife went"—the man circles his finger near his temple—"crazy."

"Crazy?" I echo.

Is that what Annika meant when she said her parents had a dark start that she wasn't a part of?

"The type of crazy that was kept under wraps even within Boss's inner circle. We weren't allowed to utter her name unless we wished for a one-way ticket to the Spetsnaz, or worse, a grave."

"That's an interesting story, really. I'm all for craziness." Eli pulls his unlit cigarette from between his lips as if he's smoking. "But I don't see why that's of importance in the current circumstances."

"Her craziness drove her to commit murder."

"Now, that's a much better tidbit for drawing suspense. And?"

"The man she killed was a public figure. A mayoral candidate, in fact. The one who would've for sure won that year's election, considering he was the people's favorite. She stabbed him thirty-four times, repeatedly, long after he was dead."

My ears buzz with a grating ringing sound and the walls start closing in around me. The onslaught is so sudden that I have trouble breathing. The collar of my hoodie scratches against my skin and my side where my tattoo tingles and burns.

"Sounds bloody brutal," Eli says.

"Looked gruesome, too. I was sent with a few others to the murder scene to remove any incriminating evidence before the authorities came along. The man had an absolutely horrified expression, as if his soul had been extracted by the devil himself."

"And?" Eli asks.

"There's no and. That's the incident Landon wanted details about. I told him that the murder of the mayoral candidate was swept under the rug and no one was convicted for it. In fact, his mask was ripped off in public. Turns out, he was never the righteous man the media had portrayed him to be. Many women came forward confessing that he'd sexually assaulted them, including the homeless he was supposed to be taking care of as the shelter's director. He also kept a file full of videos and pictures of them that he held over their heads as a form of blackmail. His wife was also accused of recruiting suitable candidates for his sick tastes. It was the ultimate shaming event for him and his family, and all the vapid mouths turned to his wife. She lost everything her husband left her to loan sharks and was about to be prosecuted for abetting sexual assault. So she committed double suicide with her son. I heard he was just a toddler."

I pull on the collar of my hoodie with jerky fingers, my breathing so heavy, I'm surprised they don't hear it. When I speak, I don't recognize the raw quality of my voice. "Name."

The guard raises a brow. "What?"

"Name. The dead man's fucking name."

A cloud of smoke reaches me first, clogging my already closed throat, before his calm words cut me in half. "Green. Richard Green."

I drive my fist against the wall so hard, pain and blood explode from my knuckles.

Eli casts a glance at me, brows knitting before his face goes back to a blank slate. "I assume your boss is the one who encouraged those girls to come forward and pulled strings to destroy the Green family?"

"You assume correctly. I don't know how true those accusations were, but I'm certain that Boss made sure to ruin Richard's reputation so thoroughly that no one considered him a hero anymore. In fact, people started expressing relief that such vermin had been killed."

"And that's all you told Landon?" Eli asks.

"That's all I know." He throws his blunt down and steps on it with his shoe. "I'll be in touch for my money."

"I suggest you run as far as you can go." Eli squeezes his shoulder. "Debts will be the least of your worries if your dear boss or his son finds out there's a traitor in their ranks."

"You fucking—"

Eli squeezes tighter, then whispers, "You aren't running."

The guard glances at the ground, but before he can reach for the gun, Eli picks it up and releases a displeased sound, then points it at him. "No guns on UK soil, remember? But maybe I can change the rules just this once?"

The guard spits at him before he hobbles out of the alley.

I'm only half focused, half conscious about what's happening around me. Then the pieces of the puzzle start to fit together.

The clearer the image, the bloodier it gets.

The muddier my head turns.

The heavier my breathing becomes.

I pull my fist from the wall—my good one, the one I use to fight with—then slam it against the wall again. Stronger this time so that a splash of blood decorates the dirty surface.

Not enough.

This pain isn't enough to drown the chaos that's nearly splitting my brain open. Or the facts that come with it.

Such as Lia and Adrian Volkov being the villains of my childhood.

Annika's parents are the reason I grew up into this hollow person with no core whatsoever.

I'm on that floor again. My face tight, my lungs burning, and I'm crawling on the hard wood.

Like those worms, I'm struggling, wiggling, biting my lips, fighting. That's why I loved hunting them. I always liked squashing them.

It was better if they died fast instead of opening their mouths and being strangled further.

Instead of having white foam on the side of their mouths that wouldn't go away no matter how much they spat. Or gagging on their own vomit.

My heart burns to the point of self-destruction. This must be what happens to machines when they reach the end of their lifetime.

They need to be destroyed.

I punch again, but this time, I meet a softer surface.

"Ow." Eli uses his hand that he let me punch to shove me back. "Instead of hurting yourself, how about you use this destructive energy to hit someone who actually deserves your wrath?"

And then, like an unconventional older brother, he forbids my self-ruination and drags me to our next hunt.

The subject of the hunt happens to be back at the mansion.

The moment we walk through the front door, we find Landon lounging on a chair, a phone in hand.

"What took you so bloody long? I finished my pending business, paid a visit to a completely drunk Remi, played a game, and was just about to call it a night." He finally lifts his head. "I figured Eli would make you hasten the process if you confided in him. I must say, I'm wounded, right in the middle of my nonexistent heart. I thought we shared a connection, Cray Cray. Judging by your expression, the cunt spilt it all?"

I storm in his direction, pull him up by the collar of his T-shirt, and punch him with the same hand I nearly broke against the wall.

Landon falls sideways on the chair and his phone clatters to the ground. He smiles as I grab him again, my fingers digging into his skin.

"You saw me with her. You fucking witnessed it all, every single part of it, so why the fuck—" I cut myself off because my voice is too scratchy to be heard. I swallow hard. "Why didn't you tell me?"

"I didn't know it was her family for sure until recently. I'm superhuman, but not enough to locate the right guard who'll sing when his mouth is shoved full of money. I did try to warn you. Not my fault nobody listens to Lan, even when he's always right."

I drive my fist into his face again. "You should've told me." *Punch.* "You chose to use me instead." *Punch.* "I'm going to fucking kill you."

Blood explodes from his nose and the corner of his lip and he spits it on the carpet, but he doesn't attempt to fight me. He's letting me use him as my relief outlet.

"Would it have changed anything?" He grins, revealing blood-stained teeth. "You're so into that mafia princess that you can't see straight anymore, Cray Cray. I bet you're more upset about your relationship with her than about the truth you so earnestly searched for all these years. I must admit, I liked you better when you were an emotionless little heathen."

"Shut the fuck up or I'll turn you into one of your stones and no one will be the wiser." Eli comes to my side, glaring down at him. "I'm letting Creigh vent his rage or else he'll explode, but don't mistake my tolerance for forgiveness, Lan. I'll fucking end you for stabbing him in the back. So how about you take his punishment silently, because no matter how hard it gets, it'll be way more lenient than my outrage."

Landon flips my brother the middle finger, then smiles at me. "Everything I did was for the greater good, including yours. I know that's uncommon, but you have my word. I did prepare a peace offering if you're interested—"

I send him flying with another punch, and he grunts, wiping the corner of his mouth and flexing his jaw. "I'll take that as a no?"

My steps are sure and determined as I reach for him, haul him up by my grip on his shirt, then hit him again.

And again.

And fucking again.

But no matter how many punches I throw, it isn't enough to douse the fire inside me. If anything, it's transforming into a wildfire that's getting out of control.

"What's with all the commotion—what the…" Brandon's voice reaches me first and I can tell he's coming our way, but Eli grabs him by the nape.

"This isn't your place."

"What the actual hell? Lan's bleeding."

"Aw. You worried about me? I should've asked Creigh to beat me up earlier." Landon strains to place a hand on his chest. "So touched, I could cry."

Bran glares at him, but he still tries to escape Eli's hold. Me, on the other hand? I'm ready to rip my cousin a new one.

In the middle of me punching Lan, who's still not resisting, and Bran arguing with Eli but still no match to escape him, a fifth presence strolls in.

Remi stares at us with dilated pupils, then blinks slowly. "Not sure what type of freak show—or kink, not shaming—you King men are into, but I have a serious question. Am I too drunk or is there actually a guy tied up in our basement?"

Bran quits struggling against my brother. "A guy is tied up in our basement?"

"Sure as fuck, and if I'm not too drunk, then I'm pretty sure it's Nikolai Sokolov."

"That's the surprise I kept for you, Cray Cray." Landon grins, all bloodied teeth, lips, and chin. "He's your path to vengeance. Told you I had everything figured out."

TWENTY-SEVEN

Lia

THE THING ABOUT DEMONS IS THAT THEY'RE THERE FOR LIFE. Every time I think I've left them in the twisted past where they belong, they rear their ugly heads, bent on reminding me that they exist.

That they're here to stay.

That no matter how much I attempt to focus on my hard-earned happiness, it might be just a phase.

It's been so many years, but the memories are as vivid as if it were last night's dinner.

They creak and roar and splash my mind with images of pain, weakness, and shame.

Lots of shame and regrets that I can't contain.

I pace the length of the entrance, back and forth, back and forth, like a headless chicken.

I can hear the low sound of my snapping nerves, can feel the tightness in my stomach and the chaos bashing against my skull.

On and on, it mounts and shifts until I want to scream.

It doesn't help that Adrian had an urgent meeting and has been gone with Kolya for most of the night and morning.

Thankfully, Yan has returned. He's currently leaning back in a chair, sipping on a glass of vodka, and watching me with an unchanged expression.

"You're going to give yourself vertigo if you keep going at that pace," he comments dryly.

"I shouldn't have let her go back. Maybe we can catch them if we follow them now, and I can bring her home and tuck her close to my chest where no one can find her?"

"You're being paranoid."

"That's what you said when she was kidnapped as a child."

"She wasn't kidnapped, since we saved her before they could get her."

"But she was almost kidnapped."

"You sound like Boss when he excuses his overbearing behavior. 'I'm shielding her too much because they'd use her against me,'" he mimics Adrian's tone.

"It's true, though."

"Maybe, but you two need to know that she's no longer a little kid. Besides, she's with Jer. No way will he let anyone hurt her."

"What if he's also hurt?" I come to a stop, my breathing becoming so heavy, it echoes around us. "What if I lose both of them?"

He stands up and clutches me by the shoulders. "You're overthinking. That's paranoia and anxiety speaking, and those two are irrational fuckers that we hate. Would definitely murder the fuck out of them, decapitation style, if we met them in an alley... Now, inhale. Exhale."

I release a long whoosh, sensing the dissipation of the black cloud that's been swirling around my head.

A small smile pulls on my lips. "Thanks, Yan. I don't know what I would've done without you."

"Probably driven yourself to the point of no return." He lowers his head to stare me in the eyes. "Do you feel better?"

"A little."

"A little is a start."

We remain like that for a short moment as I attempt and partially fail to regulate my breathing. I honestly don't know what would've become of me if I didn't have a friend like Yan by my side.

He was the one who also convinced me that my fears about Annika sharing my fate with ballet are paranoia. That my daughter isn't me and we won't actually suffer the same things.

"You have exactly one second to remove your hands from my wife's shoulders before I break them."

Adrian's closed-off voice reaches us first, then his larger-than-life presence follows.

I've known this man for over twenty-five years and I still crane my head to get a better look at him. I still go the extra mile to engrave every inch of him to memory.

It's probably because of all the times I thought he was no longer part of my life.

His dark gaze falls on Yan, who has stepped back but still meets Adrian's solemn expression with a smile.

"Don't be jealous, Boss. It's not my fault that I'm charming."

"We'll see how charming you actually are when you're buried facedown six feet under."

Yan pats his shoulder. "You and I both know that won't be happening as long as Lia is alive. See you later, Boss."

He leaves the house with a nonchalant stride, completely oblivious to Adrian's deadly glare. I can't help the smile that appears on my lips. Adrian and Yan's relationship will never change.

I've got to admit that it's entertaining. Yan can't help provoking him, and Adrian is closed-minded enough to willingly fall for it every time.

"That fucker will meet his maker tonight. And stop smiling, Lenochka."

My heart races like it does every time he calls me by that nickname. My fingers smooth the wrinkle on his black shirt and I flatten my palm against the rippling muscles of his hard chest.

The chest that serves as both my pillow and my anchor. The chest through which I can listen to his heartbeat.

I've known him for so long and he still causes my stomach to flutter upon seeing him. He's still the most dangerously beautiful man alive.

I shake my head. "You're being irrational."

"Were you smiling at Yan in this way? With your eyes shining and your face brightening?"

"Adrian!"

"Were you?"

I release a sigh. "You're seriously impossible sometimes."

"Only sometimes?"

"I suppose." I stare up at his unfairly handsome face—at the sharp features, hard lines, thick brows, and dark gray eyes.

A face so closed off that it used to frighten me but soon became my haven.

This man is both my calamity and my salvation.

His brows dip as he cups my face with his large palm. It always amazes me how a hard man like him only softens around me—and our children.

If anyone had come to the younger me and told her Adrian would be a family man, I would've laughed in their face.

But I've witnessed firsthand just how absolutely devoted he can be. Yes, he's an important man in his organization, but nothing and no one comes before us for him.

"Is something the matter, Lenochka?"

It takes everything in me not to break down here and now. Just how can he be this attuned to my state of mind? Sometimes, more than I am.

"The kids left," I choke out.

"Kolya told me. Want me to order the pilot to bring them back?"

That's exactly what I want, but I'd be acting on paranoia as Yan said, so I shake my head. "I think we have a bigger problem."

"Such as?"

"Anni...our daughter has a boyfriend."

His expression darkens. "Jeremy informed me of that and mentioned he's not to be trusted. I told him to keep them apart until I investigate the fucker who thinks he can have a relationship with my daughter."

"You don't have to. I saw his picture on her phone and he…he has familiar eyes."

"Familiar eyes?"

"Richard Green's eyes. Not the color, the look."

He goes still, his muscles tightening against my hold. "What did you just say?"

"Richard, Adrian. I think…no, I'm sure he's related to him some-how, probably his son. I thought we were done with that nightmare, but how come…how come it's here again? How can that nightmare be unleashed on Anni this time? She's so sweet and innocent and doesn't deserve to suffer for any of our sins. She was devastated and absolutely disappointed in me when I told her to stop seeing him. What if…what if it's too late to stop this?"

Adrian wraps an arm around my shoulder and half carries me to the sofa, where we sit down.

His hand strokes my shoulder slowly, soothingly, while his other hand wipes away the tears on my face. "Breathe, Lenochka, breathe…"

I dig my fingers into his shirt and stare up at him with blurry eyes. "Are we being punished? Is that why Anni fell for him of all people?"

"There's nothing to be punished for. Richard was scum who de-served death, and we will not, under any circumstances, diverge the blame toward us."

"How about Anni? I told her I'd cheer her on and back up any relationship she has, but I pulled the rug from beneath her feet at the first test."

"I will talk to her. She'll understand."

"No." I pull away from him. "You'll just tell her that if she doesn't stay away from him, you'll hurt him."

"Which is the right thing to do."

"No, Adrian. She'll just fall in love with him more. At this point, any coercion from our side will only push her in his arms and muddy our relationship with her." I sigh. "I don't know when she grew up enough to even know the meaning of love."

"Let me have a talk with the bastard who dared to touch my baby daughter and we'll find out."

"You mean, let your fists talk to his face?"

"The only appropriate language under the circumstances."

"Adrian, no. I'll speak with her. We'll have the talk we should've had last night when I saw that picture. She deserves the truth."

His dark eyes watch me with so much care that I drown in it. "Will you be okay?"

"No, but I'll do this for Anni."

"Don't have any misconceptions about the results. She won't be happy."

"But she'll understand. Our daughter has grown up so much. She's no longer that sheltered child who followed your and Jeremy's orders like they were the holy scripts. She's matured and become a little spitfire."

"I don't like that," my husband grumbles.

Of course he doesn't. Adrian has always been overprotective, so he doesn't like knowing that his baby girl is growing wings that she'll use to leave him.

But I'm proud of how far she's come, and how she's turned into her own person. Something tells me the change in her personality happened because of this Creighton.

Annika always wanted to spread her wings, but something held her back; whether it was apprehension or fear, I'm not sure. What I am certain about, however, is that she's finally managed to live as her own person instead of what her last name suggests.

Adrian interlinks my fingers with his. "I'll be right here."

My heartbeat slows to a peaceful rhythm as I pull out my phone and FaceTime my daughter.

She picks up after a few beats, snuggling into what appears to be the plane's seat with the face mask pushed up on her hair.

Annika has always been the life of the house. The sunshine, the joker, the bright light all of us looked forward to.

She's Adrian's little girl, which is why he vehemently refuses to admit she's all grown up, the light to Jeremy's shadows, and the girl after Ogla's carefully-hidden heart.

This baby, who's not a baby anymore, has had us all in a choke-hold since the moment she was born.

So to see her downward expression and worn-out face squeezes my heart. She's not even wearing one of her pretty purple dresses and has settled for an oversized hoodie and jeans instead.

"We still didn't arrive yet, Mom. I'll text when we do."

"Anni, wait." I swallow. "I wanted to talk to you."

"If it's about staying away from Creigh, then you can just forget about it. I already turned eighteen and I don't need anyone's approval to date whoever I like. I love you and Papa, but I won't let you take the one thing I have of my own."

Adrian tries to take the phone, but I keep it out of reach so that I'm the only one in the frame, then smooth my voice. "Can I tell you a story?"

She shrugs her shoulder. "If you want."

"Remember when I used to tell you that a long time ago, I suffered mentally?" My voice chokes and Adrian squeezes my fingers.

The knowledge that he's here gives me the courage to poke the demons from my past.

At Anni's careful nod, I continue, "It was a lot worse than you could imagine. I was aimless, created a rift between me, your father, and your brother, and had the most hellish time in my life. Everyone has moments where they hit rock bottom, and that time was mine. As if that wasn't enough, one of the power figures who was supposed to protect me—and people like me—used my circumstances to... try to sexually assault me as he'd done to several others before me."

Annika gasps, her eyes shining with unshed tears.

"It didn't happen," I blurt. "I didn't let him."

"Oh. Thank God." She releases a breath. "Where was Papa at the time?"

"He...killed him."

"Phew. Good riddance."

"You're okay with that? I thought you didn't like it when your papa hurt people."

"It's okay if he's cleaning the world of scum like the one who tried to assault you and others."

Adrian smirks, looking so proud of himself.

"That man was a mayoral candidate, Anni."

"So what? That doesn't give him the right to go assaulting people. In fact, he should be held more accountable."

"True. But he had a family. A wife and a son."

"Oh." She purses her lips. "I feel sorry for them, but they're probably better off without a bastard like that in their lives."

"The wife attempted double suicide soon after the police started investigating her for abetting her husband's serial rape crimes. She was found hanging from the ceiling in their home, but her boy barely escaped being asphyxiated to death by gas."

It happens gradually, almost unnoticeably, but Annika's face blanches and her eyes widen as recognition slowly sets in.

That means he probably mentioned the incident to her. Damn it. I'm pretty sure the doctor said he wouldn't remember much of it.

He was so young back then.

I exchange a look with Adrian, whose face is closed off, probably thinking that this goes a lot deeper than any of us thought.

That maybe he approached her on purpose, after all.

"What…what are you saying, Mom? Are you trying to tell me that the man who hurt you, whom Papa killed, is Creighton's biological father?"

"Unfortunately, yes."

"But that can't be… It just…can't… Oh my God, is that why you acted strangely when you saw his picture? Does he look like his biological father?"

"Not really, but he has the same look in his eyes. I will never forget those eyes."

"No, no, no…" Tears stream down her cheeks with the persistence of an overflowing river.

"Anni?"

"No, Mom. No!" She sobs. "This…this just can't be true."

"I'm sorry, baby angel. I'm *so* sorry." It takes everything in me not to break down and cry with her. I wish she were here so I could hug her, try to make it better, but all I can do is be strong for her.

Her image shakes, probably from the way she's grabbing her phone. She brings it impossibly close until I can see every streak of tears, every wretched emotion pouring out of her.

"M-Mom…you don't understand… He thinks that time shaped who he is, and he wants revenge. No…this can't be true. If it is, if it is, he…he…he'll hate me. I can't… How will I live if he hates me, Mom? How can I face him, knowing Papa is the reason behind the darkest moment of his life?"

"You don't." Adrian slides my hand over so that we're both in the frame. "You stay away from him and move on."

"I can't just do that." She glares at him. "I'm not a robot, Papa. I can't simply erase him from my memories."

"You'll learn to. He'll never have affection for you anyway, considering his past. Since you already know he's so attuned to it, then you should also know that he'll only use you to hurt me and your mother. Maybe even your brother. Needless to say, I will not allow it. I'll give you a few days to pack your stuff, say your goodbyes, and return to the States."

"Papa!" She cries harder.

I snatch the phone from Adrian's hand so that it's only me again. "Don't cry, baby. I hate it when you do. We'll do our best to make everything all right."

"How can it be when it's all…wrong?"

My heart splinters along with hers, and her pain streams through my veins as if it's my own. It takes all my strength to remain calm. "Let me ask you this. How does Creighton remember? He was adopted soon after his mother's death, so he can't possibly recall all the details from such a young age."

"You know about his adoption?" Her lips part, letting the tears stream inside her mouth. "Don't tell me you shadowed his life all this time?"

"No, of course not. I've never met him, but after I heard about the incident, your father and I asked Rai to find him a better home. Her sister does a lot of social work and she agreed to sponsor him. He was soon adopted by European parents and left the States."

I was glad the innocent boy would have a better life and that the nightmare was finally out of our lives. I never liked the media play I later found out that Adrian had conducted, or the way he dragged Richard and his family through the mud because he considered death by so many stabs was too little of a punishment.

I just never thought those European parents were actually English and that we'd send our daughter straight into the boy's path.

"He must've found out the truth," Anni whispers, her voice spooked. "That's why he's been ignoring my texts."

"There's no way for him to know," I soothe. "This event is a mystery to everyone except for our family. Even his adoptive parents weren't given the full recounting of events, and from what Rai disclosed about them, they're people of great status and wanted to erase that part of his origin. I doubt they would tell him anything."

"But he has to know. He's been searching for the truth for so long."

"You will not meet with him, Annika." Adrian slides into the frame again. "It's dangerous."

"But—"

"No buts. We'll see you back home in a few days."

And then he ends the call.

"I didn't finish talking with her," I protest, dabbing at my eyes with the back of my hand.

"Anything you offer her would be an excuse that she won't understand in her current state. She needs time to process what she's learned, and hopefully, she'll come to the logical conclusion that whatever she had with the boy is ill-fated."

"The boy had nothing to do with what his father did. He was only a toddler back then."

"No, he didn't, but the truth remains that I was the one behind his parents' deaths and his family's demise. He'll only look at Annika as my daughter, and I will not allow him to put her through such torture."

"She'll hate us…"

My husband's large hand cradles my cheek and he strokes gently, causing tiny shock waves to erupt on my skin. "A few years down the line, she'll know we did this to protect her."

But at what price?

Adrian has always been methodical and solution-oriented, so he doesn't care much about feelings, but I do.

And I know, I just know that we might have accidentally killed a part of Anni that we'll never be able to get back.

TWENTY-EIGHT

Creighton

THERE WAS A PLAN ALL ALONG.
The universe's.
My parents'.
Landon's.

Everyone had a course of life and a path to follow from the beginning.

The universe decided my biological parents didn't deserve to live and destroyed my life in retrospect.

Mum and Dad thought any information about my past was unnecessary so they went to immaculate lengths to hide it from me.

Landon needed me as his instigator of chaos, the variable that he used to have the Heathens and Serpents clash without getting the Elites involved, so he withheld information.

But he had my revenge in mind.

That's what he called it earlier, after he casually mentioned that he kidnapped Nikolai because we can use him to draw out Jeremy.

"Once the Heathens' leader is here, you can punch him, kill him. Get your long-awaited revenge. What's better than punishing the parents' sin by taking away their only heir?"

Eli thinks Landon said that so I would let him go, but his words aren't far from the truth.

I've stayed locked up in my room since, sitting in the dark for hours, a whole day even, staring at my bloodied hands.

It's not enough.

This amount of blood is simply not enough.

There needs to be payback. Eye for an eye. Life for a life.

And since the parents are untouchable, the children will pay on their behalf.

Just like I did over seventeen years ago.

That would hurt them much more anyway, considering they poured all their lives into raising them to be the future leaders of the Volkovs.

A tinge of pain explodes behind my rib cage, achy at first but soon becoming absolutely unbearable.

The thought of *her* slashes through my bruised chest and brutally confiscates my air.

I always considered myself a little bit heartless, but it was Annika who proved that I actually do have a heart.

Only, it's reserved for a select few, an exclusive list that she somehow found her way onto.

A closed door that she barged right through.

A tall wall that she crumbled to the ground.

But for what purpose?

We've come to this point where I won't only break her heart, but I'll also ruin her until there's nothing left to pick up.

Annika has always looked at me as a god. Little did she know that the altar she worshiped at belongs to a tyrant god.

In the darkness of my room, I can barely see my hands. I barely exist.

It's like I'm floating out of my body in a parallel world.

Tiger mewls from his position by my foot. He hasn't left my side since I locked myself up in here. He's just rubbed himself all over me.

I pat his head and then I grab him and place him outside my door so that he can find Bran or Remi.

After locking myself in my room again, I fish out my phone to read and re-read the last text she sent.

Particularly the last part.

I miss you. I want to kiss you.

My fingers tighten around the phone, then I throw it against the wall with enough force that it shatters and clatters on the ground.

The room becomes suffocating with my heavy breathing and her fucking violet scent. It's all over my sheets, my bathroom, my wardrobe.

I might have been the one who dominated her, but she's the one who's left her mark everywhere.

In my air, on my skin, and down to the marrow of my fucking bones.

Standing up, I pull on the sheet covering the mattress and throw it to the ground. I smash a lamp and then use it to wreak havoc on everything in the bathroom.

Her shampoo, her perfume, her toothbrush, her fluffy towels. I accidentally cut my hand and smear them with blood.

By the time I'm done, I'm breathing heavily and everything is as broken as I am.

But it's still not fucking enough.

Rage bubbles in my veins, flowing with blood and demanding more.

Time to take this to the next level.

Landon already said he'd bring Jeremy to my door by threatening Nikolai's life.

It's been long enough for him to fulfill that promise.

I leave my room and head to the basement. Eli said he'd keep an eye on surveillance—and Lan as he nurses his wounds.

Remi passed out soon after Bran took him back to his room, too drunk to care about anything.

I expect to find Nikolai still drugged up. He woke up early this morning and nearly broke his arm trying to escape his bindings, so Landon had to drug 'the crazy bloody bastard' again.

My feet come to a halt near the basement when the automatic light doesn't come on.

There's no shortage of power to cause this, so the only explanation is that someone purposefully cut it off.

Sure enough, I make out a shadow moving swiftly along the hall. Strategically.

I track their movements until they reach their destination.

The basement door.

When they insert the key and unlock it, I catch a glimpse of none other than my cousin.

Surprisingly, it's not Landon, though.

Bran slips inside with swift agility that I'm witnessing for the first time.

I wait a few moments before I follow behind.

Through the ajar door, I can make out Nikolai's huge body slumped over in the chair he's bound to. His head has fallen to his chest and his long hair is loose, forming a curtain over his face.

Brandon remains a safe distance away, watching him with a blank expression.

He's always been the most even-tempered out of the four of us. He's never indulged in hunting, manipulations, pranks, fighting, or anything monstrous.

Brandon King is the only good boy among us.

Where his twin brother is a volcano, Bran is the earth—silent, deep, and actually has a core.

Morals.

Which is why I have no doubt he'll let Nikolai go. He's just not the type who'll sit by while someone else gets hurt.

A trait that will probably get him killed one day.

I'm about to barge inside and abort his plan, but I stop when Bran reaches a hesitant hand to Nikolai's...hair.

He slowly, gently slides it back, revealing his unconscious face. A groan spills out of Nikolai's lips and Brandon jerkily releases him. His hand finds the back of his neck and he pulls on the short hairs there.

Nikolai's eyes blink open, his pupils dilated, and he appears to be as high as a kite.

"Lotus flower…? What are you doing here?" His voice is craggy, a bit slurred, barely understandable.

Bran reluctantly releases his hair. Then he pulls out a knife from his waistband and starts cutting at Nikolai's bindings. "You're the one who came into my house. You just couldn't stay away?"

A lopsided grin lifts Nikolai's lips. "How else would I see you so adorably worried about me?"

"I am not worried about you and don't fucking call me adorable again."

"Wow. The posh boy can curse."

"Shut it or I'll leave you to my brother's and cousins' nonexistent mercy."

"If I'd known I'd see this side of you, I would've gotten myself kidnapped long ago."

"Are you insane?"

Nikolai lifts a shoulder. "Probably."

Brandon shakes his head and releases a long sigh. "I'll release you and leave the back door open, and you'll have to find your own way out."

"No." I stroll inside and Bran freezes, then slowly faces me.

"Creigh."

"Step back," I order when he continues trying to cut the ropes.

"This isn't right and you know it—"

"Step the fuck back, Bran. I won't repeat myself another time."

He complies, but he doesn't put away his knife and lets it hang at his side. When I went to my room earlier, Lan and Eli filled him in about the situation, so he knows exactly why I'm doing this.

"Get out."

"Listen…" He steps toward me. "I know you feel the need for revenge, but this whole thing is wrong."

"No one asked for your opinion. Stay out of this."

"I won't allow you to throw your life away for parents you've never known and a past you're better off without, Creighton." His voice hardens. "I'm letting Nikolai go and then we'll talk about this. *Rationally.*"

He turns around to our prisoner, but before he starts trying to free him again, I punch him on the back of his head.

A groan spills from his lips as his unconscious body falls on top of Nikolai. I pull him back, then lower him to the floor against the wall.

Sorry, Bran, but your morals have no place in this situation.

"That was unnecessary," Nikolai says in a deadpan voice.

I face him, both hands in my pockets. "Attempting to save you is what's unnecessary."

He's about to say something when the door opens again and Landon strolls inside dressed in new clothes and sporting a galaxy of bruises.

His gaze roams over the room and pauses at the sight of his brother, but he doesn't appear surprised in the least. "And what is he doing here?"

"He was trying to rescue Nikolai," I say.

"Should've known since the little fuck was acting suspicious." Landon's gaze is disapproving but he picks Bran up and half carries him, stops at the door, and says, "Oh, by the way, Jeremy's here. I'll let him in once I lock the king of morals up." With one last glance at Nikolai, he leaves, taking Bran with him.

I lean against the wall and cross my arms, summoning the calm I don't have.

Nikolai glares up at me from beneath strands of his wild hair. "What are you up to, King? What's the revenge lotus flower was talking about?"

I say nothing, meeting his glare with my signature blank stare.

"Shouldn't you be bribing Jer so he'll let you be with his sister instead of encouraging him to rip your balls out?"

My jaw clenches, but I neutralize my expression.

"The fuck? Say something. Wait a fucking minute. I say, were you playing Anni? If that's the case, I'll help Jeremy tear your head off and throw your body in the ocean as food for the fish."

When I continue my silence, he releases a long sigh. "You think Jeremy wasn't aware of your relationship? He's had an idea ever since that fire, but the reason he let you get away with it is because he knew his sister felt suffocated by all the security and guards, so he gave her some leeway. He kept watching you and knew you were treating her well and she was happy. The only fucking reason he started suspecting your intentions again is due to your intimate relations with that fucker Landon. He was leading you astray and Jeremy questioned whether or not he should've trusted you with his sister in the first place. Was he right?"

I walk toward him and pick up the knife Brandon dropped on Nikolai's lap when he fell. The same knife that this fucker has been trying to hide between his thighs while distracting me with his word vomit.

No clue if Bran left him the knife on purpose or not, but the intent is obviously there.

The door opens again and I slip behind Nikolai, holding the knife to his throat.

Landon and Eli lead Jeremy inside. He looks ragged and probably came here right after he landed.

Does that mean Annika came with him? Or did he leave her in the States?

I mentally shake the thought of her out of my head.

This is the worst time to be distracted by Annika Volkov.

Jeremy is forced to a halt in the middle of the room by a squeeze from Landon's hand. He slides his dark gaze from Nikolai's face to the knife I hold to his throat. "Anyone care to explain the meaning of this?"

"Old-fashioned revenge?" Landon says with a grin.

"That's right. Revenge." Eli circles him. "See. Your mummy killed Creigh's biological father and your daddy covered it up, ruined his reputation, and drove his wife to commit suicide. And the bitch attempted to drag Creigh with her to hell. He barely escaped the clutches of death when he was three years old. So...he kind of holds a grudge."

"A big one," Lan supplies.

"My mother did not kill anyone," Jeremy says. Point-blank. Matter-of-factly.

"Even when she was *crazy*?" Lan whispers the last word with a mocking edge.

Jeremy swings around and punches him across the face. "Call her crazy again and it'll be your funeral."

"Ouch. It's 'we're jealous of Landon's face' day." He still smiles. "Hit a nerve, mafia prince?"

I can tell he wants to send Lan to oblivion, but he schools his expression and stares at me. "Mom said she saw your picture on Annika's phone and recognized you because you have your father's eyes. Eyes she'll never forget."

"Because she killed him?" I don't know how I speak so calmly.

"Because he wronged her. She didn't disclose any details other than that, but I know my mother is not a killer. She'd never willingly orphan a child or be the reason for his demise."

"Then you obviously don't know your mother. Or you're too blind to it."

He grinds his jaw. "Dad told me to keep you away from Annika in any way possible, but I'm willing to listen. I'm willing to see the end of this bad blood."

"That makes one of us." My tone is dead with no inflection whatsoever. "There's nothing to listen to, Jeremy. My only goal is to wipe your family off the face of the earth. I'll start with you."

"Then I will kill you."

"If you can, by all means. That's the only way you'll be able to stop me."

"Hey, motherfucker." Nikolai grins up at me with manic eyes that resemble Landon's when he's on a high. "You're not using me for this."

And just like that, the crazy bastard shoves his neck against the blade. A deep gash opens on his skin, causing blood to pour out.

"Nikolai!" Jeremy roars and starts to run toward us, but Landon keeps him back.

I step away, still holding the bloodied knife in my hand.

"I...won't be your...downfall...Jer..." Nikolai gurgles, the sound vibrating off his throat.

"This crazy bitch." Eli starts toward us, removes his jacket and methodically presses it against Nikolai's bleeding throat. "Oi. Don't die, little fuck. You're not making my brother a killer when he didn't sign up for it."

"Nikolai!" Jeremy struggles against Lan and tries to punch him, but this time, my cousin ducks and even drives his fist in his face.

Me? I stare at the blood dripping from the knife. So taking a life is this easy and quick.

A nanosecond of slicing a throat is enough to end it all.

Why the fuck did I struggle so much back then? Why didn't I let it end so...easily?

"Creighton!"

My red vision shifts focus to my brother, who still has the jacket against Nikolai's neck as his head drops sideways, eyes barely open.

"Release him. He needs to go to the hospital." He glares at Lan. "Couldn't you bring Gareth? Why did you have to take this crazy prick?'

My cousin lifts a shoulder. "He insulted me."

My movements are sure and detached as I cut the ropes. Eli knots the jacket around Nikolai's neck for the time being. Once the bindings are gone, he carries him outside.

Jeremy tries to follow, but Lan shoves him against the wall. "We're not done with you yet, Heathen."

"The fuck are you waiting for?" He glares at me instead of my cousin. "Want to kill me? Want to avenge your pathetic family? Your weak father who couldn't protect you? Your criminal mother who wanted to kill you? Do it. I'm right here, so fucking do it."

I storm toward him, wrench him from Lan's grip and shove him against the wall, my elbow and the knife at his throat. "You think I'm avenging those fucking losers? I couldn't give a fuck about them, their makeshift family, or their rotten world. This vengeance isn't about them, it's about *me*. I was the fallout of the whole situation that no one thought about. I was the one who was left starving, thirsty, and with no destiny but to die. I didn't crawl out of that hellhole to let bygones be bygones."

"If you don't let go of that grudge, you're going to die at the end of this," Jeremy says calmly, assertively. "One way or another, whether it's at the hand of my father, his guards, or his friends. You'll be killed in the most brutal way possible and lose the life you fought so hard for."

"At least I'd get closure."

Lan raises a hand from his position against the wall. "I vote for closure."

My knife presses closer to Jeremy's neck. He attempts to kick me but misses when I tighten my grip.

"Anoushka will hate you," he murmurs.

"Not more than I already hate her."

And myself for allowing her to have this hold on me.

I hate her for coming into my life, destroying my plans, and somehow still tugging at a strange part of me.

Even now. As I threaten Jeremy, I can't forget that he's her fucking brother.

"What the fuck? What the actual fuck?" Remi's bewildered voice comes from the entrance. "Is that blood? Like real blood? Is this what you meant by an emergency, Anni? What—"

I throw a glance over my shoulder to tell Remi to fuck off but freeze when my eyes meet Annika's.

Hers are glittery, rounded, and caught in a stupefied faze.

For the first time since I've known her, she's not in one of her purple dresses and is sporting jeans and an oversized hoodie instead.

Her hair is covered by the hood and she's shaking from head to toe.

"The fuck are you doing here?" Jeremy yells. "Leave!"

She purses her lips and still manages to maintain eye contact with me. It's steady, like when it gets to be too much during sex, but I tell her to keep her eyes on me and it instantly calms her down.

Why the fuck am I thinking about that?

"Creighton…please stop. We can talk about this whole thing."

"You're aware of this?" I ask, unable to hide the bewilderment from my tone.

"M-Mom…just told me." Her lips quiver. "I'm so sorry for all of it. Mom is, too. I swear. So please don't hurt Jeremy. He has nothing to do with the past."

My insides coil with nefarious disgust.

At her.

At myself.

At every fucking thing.

"Your parents do. The best way to hurt them is to take away their precious firstborn. You said it yourself, that your parents have a special spot for him."

"No, please…" A tear slides down her cheek as she steps forward.

"*Don't.*" I push the knife farther into her brother's neck.

If she gets too close, I might pull a Nikolai and extinguish this fire once and for all.

Annika comes to a halt, more tears streaming down her cheeks.

More anguish.

More sadness.

I've always hated her tears outside of sex, and now that they're there because of me, it's nothing short of ripping my guts out.

"Annika." Jeremy's chest rumbles against mine. "Get out of here."

"I'm not leaving you, Jer." She stares at me and says with confidence, "Take me on his behalf."

"Annika!" Jeremy all but roars.

"I'm begging you, Creighton. If I ever meant anything to you, if you had even a sliver of affection toward me, don't do this to me. Don't take away my brother, don't make me hate you. Don't…make me choose."

My chest burns so bright, so hot that I'm sure it'll explode into tiny gory pieces.

"Creigh…" Remi calls softly. He's been watching the whole show from the sidelines, probably trying to figure out if he's still drunk. "Stop this. Let's talk."

"There's nothing to talk about." I stare at Annika. "I will not stop until your entire family is wrecked like I once was."

"I told you not to make me choose," she says in a brittle voice as she reaches underneath her hoodie and brings out a gun, then points it at me.

Her whole body trembles, except for her arm that holds the weapon.

"Anni." Remi comes to her side. "Drop that."

"Annika, fucking leave," Jeremy mutters with an edge to his voice.

Her gaze never breaks from mine. "Let him go."

"No."

"I'm an excellent shot. I told you I don't miss, remember?"

"I do."

"Then release my brother." She's ordering me, but she's crying, her voice choking.

"No."

It's a death wish, I think. For a moment, thoughts like 'I should've died with my mother' invade my mind.

What's the point of living if I'm too attached to the past?

What's the point of living if I'm tearing the one person who made me feel alive to pieces?

Even if I somehow get past the burning rage and put a stop to this, I'll never be with her again.

It's the end.

I turn around and stab Jeremy in the arm.

A shot rings in the air, coupled with an equally loud sob.

A sound I'll never forget for as long as I live.

A sound that will haunt me to my grave.

Pain explodes in my chest and a smile curves my lips as I sway and fall toward the ground.

She said she didn't miss and she meant it.

But I don't hit the ground. Instead, I'm held by Landon.

He stares at me with his soulless eyes and it's fucking sad that he's the one I see last.

It could've at least been Eli.

But I guess someone like me doesn't get to choose.

"Creigh! Can you hear me?"

I grab him by the collar and use the last breaths in my lungs to choke out, "T-tell…Mum and…Dad…t-that I-I'm sorry…"

The last sight I catch is blurred blue-gray eyes and the last thing I hear is my custom-made Grim Reaper calling my name.

But I'm already gone.

The rage dulls to nothingness and I close my eyes.

It's finally...over.

TWENTY-NINE

Annika

No. No.

Just *no.*

This must be a nightmare. If I wake up, I'll find myself back to two days ago. In the grocery store, holding Creighton's hand and talking about everything and nothing.

This time, I won't let Jeremy find us, and if he does, I won't leave with him. I'll grab Creigh's hand and stay.

I'll take him with me and run.

That way, everything will be okay. Everything will go back to normal, and I won't be trapped in this nightmare.

It's strange, the type of thoughts that run through your head when everything else cancels itself out. When it's white noise, bleak silence, and red.

Lots of red.

Blood red.

Red. Red. *Red.*

I don't know how I end up on my knees. I don't walk to where he fell. I crawl on the rough surface with the uncoordinated speed of an injured animal.

My vision is blind to all the people surrounding us and my ears are deaf to the shouts and chaotic noise.

The only sound I hear is a long buzz and the only thing I see is him and red.

He's all red.

Because of my gun. The one I shouldn't have brought with me when I found out Jeremy was in danger. The one I should've kept in the car and not slipped beneath my hoodie.

My body rolls or maybe it's the room that's spinning in an irregular rhythm. Maybe my prayers will be answered and I will wake up from this nightmare.

Now, please.

Someone wake me up.

Instead of opening my eyes, I sink my hands into that red, all dark and sticky and not where it's supposed to. It should be inside him, not outside.

Through a blur, I lift my hand to stare at the blood that's coating my fingers and then at the body it's left.

Someone, Landon, presses both his hands on the gash in Creigh's back harshly, where more of his life essence escapes.

On and on, it keeps flowing, forming a pool beneath his body.

Creighton's face is pale, lacks expression, and his eyes are closed, causing his lashes to flutter on his cheeks.

His massive build is unmoving, lifeless.

He…looks nothing like the Creighton I know.

People might see him as gloomy, too silent, or too cold, but he's the one who made me feel alive.

The one who changed everything.

And I took it away.

Everything.

All of it.

I think I'm going to throw up.

Just when nausea clogs my throat, a strong hand pulls me by the arm. For a moment, I think it's that wake-up call I've been praying for.

Maybe it's Creigh, who's calling me a sleepyhead—when he's way worse—and he's surprising me with a date.

Maybe he'll watch *Pride and Prejudice* with me again, call me a hopeless romantic, then fuck me.

Maybe Tiger will have a Peeping Tom session and he'll be irrationally jealous about it.

So I let it happen. Closing my eyes, I chalk the whole scene up to a horrible nightmare.

The nightmare of all nightmares.

I wait for the ball that's clogging my throat to disappear. I wait for the trembling in my limbs to subside and the stickiness to vanish from my fingers.

It gets worse.

Seeps deeper.

Closes my throat further.

When I open my eyes, I'm being shoved in the direction of a car, fresh tears streaming down my cheeks as I catch a glimpse of Jeremy.

His brow is furrowed as he studies the Elites' circular driveway.

"No," I murmur, clutching my head with my bloodied hands. "No, no, no, no…a nightmare, a nightmare, this is only a nightmare…"

"Anoushka…stop fighting me and get in the car."

It's then I realize I've been wiggling, struggling, and jerking, preventing my brother from pushing me into the passenger seat.

I come to a halt, pull my hands from my temples, and drown in the red.

All red.

Blood red.

His red.

"Anoushka…"

I stare at my brother and the cut on his shoulder through my blurred vision. "Tell me this is a nightmare. Tell me you're not real, Jer. This…this is just in my head. I didn't… I didn't…shoot him."

"You did, and we need to get the fuck out of here while they're distracted."

I shake my head continuously, with enough force that I'm surprised it doesn't fall off. "I-I'm…going to go back in there and make sure this is a nightmare…it has to be…"

My brother grabs me by the shoulders and slams me against the car. "Wake the fuck up, Annika. You shot him in the fucking chest. He's probably dead, and if you go in there, they'll only kill you, do you understand?"

"No…no…no…" My murmurs grow in intensity and so do my wiggling and distressed attempts to escape his hold.

This time, Jeremy throws me inside, uses the seatbelt to strap me in, and then he runs to the driver's side.

I try to free myself, desperately, manically. But my involuntary tears and trembling bloodied hands make it impossible.

My brother's car raves down the driveway and he nearly breaks the gate on his way out.

He's speeding, and I'm wailing, looking behind me, through the mirror, through the gaps. Anywhere that I can catch a glimpse of him.

It doesn't take us long to reach the Heathens' compound. The moment Jeremy undoes the seatbelt, I run back toward the entrance.

No clue where I'm going on foot, but I can find a solution as long as I'm out of here. I can—

Merciless arms wrap around my middle and Jeremy all but lifts me off the ground. "The fuck you think you're going?"

"To make sure it's a nightmare."

"It's *not*." His voice is harsh, all dark and businesslike. Usually, that would send me running. Now, it does nothing compared to the horror invading my bones.

He puts me down, grabs my elbow, and drags me with him inside the mansion. I try to free myself, but there's no reasoning with my buffalo of a brother.

"What's going—well, fuck." Gareth stops near the entrance and studies all the blood decorating us. "Are you okay?"

"Nikolai," Jeremy lets out through gritted teeth. "We have to make sure he's okay. The crazy fucker had his throat sliced to keep from becoming my weakness."

"Holy fuck." Gareth retrieves his phone and storms toward the door. "I'm on it."

"Where's Kill?" Jeremy shouts, but Gareth has already left.

"A nightmare," I murmur, half conscious, half trapped in a loop. "It's just a nightmare. It can only be a nightmare."

"Looking for me?" Killian appears at the top of the stairs, tilting his head to the side, narrowing his eyes on me. "Did you really shoot Creighton?"

My murmurs come to a halt and I stare, dumbfounded. Could Killian also have been in my nightmare?

"How did you know so fast?" Jeremy asks.

"Glyndon just called me, crying because her cousin is about to die. I don't really appreciate it when someone makes my little rabbit cry, Annika."

"I didn't." I shake my head frantically. "It's only a nightmare. Jer was stabbed and it was also a nightmare."

My brother releases a long breath. "She's not herself. You go strengthen security. I'll take care of her and join you."

"I'm fine. Totally fine, and it was only a nightmare."

Jeremy practically drags me up the stairs and into my room. The room Creighton came into that first night.

The night after which we got close.

The night I recognized him by the look in his eyes only because he was a god. *My* god. And I reached for him anyway.

I knew it was forbidden, but I touched that god, and now I'm being punished for it.

"Annika...Annika? Annika!"

I jerk out of my daze at my brother's harsh voice, and the nightmare that just refuses to end filters back into the immediate reality.

Jeremy's grabbing my shoulders, his eyes searching mine. "Will you be okay?"

My gaze flits to the blood on his T-shirt. It's not as red as the pool from earlier, but it's there. I touch it with my dirty hand, my fingers clenching and unclenching.

"This is a nightmare, too. You're not bleeding, Jer."

He winces, and then removes my hold. "I'll survive. I don't think he really wanted to hurt me."

A sob tears from my throat as reality comes crashing down on me in all vivid red.

"He…he didn't?" My voice breaks as wetness soaks my cheeks and neck.

Jer shakes his head.

"Then…then…then why…why did I pull that trigger? Tell me, Jer! If I wasn't going to save you, if I didn't have to, why did I pull it?"

"Because he wanted you to, Anoushka." Jeremy's voice softens, and my brother's voice doesn't soften. "He looked to be in pain and resolved to see it all…end."

"No…" I sob, hitting my brother's chest. "Ah…ah… This…hurts. Why does it hurt? Ah…make it stop hurting. There was a lot of blood, Jer. What if he…? What if… What…"

The word knots and chokes me, refusing to be said out loud.

My brother pulls me close to his chest with his good arm and I cry.

I just cry and cry until I think I have no tears left. Until I think I'm going to faint from the amount of pain that's wrecking my chest.

The image of red and his pale face haunts me.

The face that might never get life back because I ended it.

With my own hands, I fucking ended it.

When my tears turn into hiccups, Jer takes me to the bathroom, by my hand, like when I was a toddler and fell down and dirtied myself.

He turns on the faucet and patiently scrubs my hands of all the blood.

Scrub.

Scrub.

Scrub.

All the red washes down the drain in a haunting symphony of crimson against white. But the evidence remains beneath my nails, clinging to my fingers, refusing to vanish.

Then Jeremy washes my face and combs his fingers through my tangled, dirty hair. After he's done, he leads me back to my room.

I'm lifeless, half moving, half dead. I don't protest as he sits me on the foot of the bed and brings out my first aid kit.

He starts to clean the cuts on my fingers, on my palms.

I touch his shoulder and the tears I thought were no longer there gather in my lids and stream down my cheek.

My voice comes out too hoarse, too raw. "He stabbed you... I thought...I thought he was going to kill you... I couldn't...I couldn't let him do that. I couldn't lose you. I didn't think when I pulled the trigger. Why did I go for his chest? I tried to miss, but it was too late. It's too late."

Jeremy strokes my arm. "It's okay, Anoushka."

"It's not! It's not okay! He wasn't going to kill you, but I killed him... I killed the man I love, Jer. I k-killed him... I...I..."

"He's not dead," he speaks slowly, patiently. "You're not a killer. You just love me, and that's okay, Anoushka. Choosing is okay."

That only makes me cry harder even as I try to clean his wound. I end up hurting him more and he says he'll just have Kill stitch him up.

Jeremy doesn't leave my side. Not when I finally pass out.

Not when I wake up crying.

Not even when I hit him and blame him for interrupting us that night in the grocery store.

For taking me back home.

I blame him for being the reason I found out the truth about my ill-fated relationship.

I blame him for blindly going to Nikolai's aid when he didn't have to.

I'm illogical and emotional, and a mess of epic proportions.

But my brother stays by my side the whole time, offering his support silently, taking the lash of my words with understanding.

Killian comes and stitches him up in my room. When I ask him if he's heard any news, he glares at me and then leaves without a word.

So imagine my surprise when I wake up early the next morning after a restless sleep and Jeremy says, "Do you want to go to the hospital?"

"You...you'll really let me?"

"If I don't, you'll sneak out behind my back and get yourself in trouble. I'm going to see Nikolai anyway, so you can look from afar."

"Is he...okay?"

"Nikolai or Creighton?"

I swallow. "Both?"

"Thankfully, Nikolai didn't slice his throat too deeply. Creighton, however, is in the ICU. He has an extensive hemorrhage and is in a coma. The next two days will be important to decide whether he lives or dies."

I slap my palm to my mouth and shake my head frantically.

No. This can't be true.

Jeremy wrenches my hand away. "Snap the fuck out of it, Annika. Either you crumble and wither away, and mark my words, if you do, I will lock you the hell up here with no way out. Or you take a shower, change your clothes, and meet me downstairs so we can go to the hospital together. There will be no third option." Then he heads to the door. "You have fifteen minutes."

I'm on autopilot as I take the quickest shower in history and blank out all my thoughts.

By the time I change my clothes and go downstairs, I find Jeremy waiting for me with one hand in his pocket and the other scrolling through his phone.

He nods in approval and then we get into the car.

I'm better and worse during this car ride. Better, because I'm not crying like a baby, even though I want to.

Worse, because at least I was numb last night.

Now, I can feel every prick of emotion. Every heartbeat and every screwed-up memory.

I can recall in vivid detail the way I held that gun, the way I pressed the trigger. I can feel the doomsday sensation that overtook my head.

It all happened too fast and yet too slow.

Jeremy keeps driving in silence, giving me all the space I need. Even if the sound of the engine becomes suffocating and the roads blur into one.

I lean my head against the window and breathe so heavily that the glass fogs up.

"If we see any police, we're getting you the hell out of there,"

Jeremy tells me, eyes on the road. "I don't have a good feeling about the fact that they're not involved yet. Landon and Remington were there. Surely, they would've testified against you. Good thing I took your gun when we left, so there's no incriminating evidence."

"But I did it," I murmur. "I shot him."

"Listen to me and listen to me well, Anoushka." He tilts his head to the side. "You are not throwing your life away for this. You thought you had no choice, which is why you shot him. That's the only version we'll go with."

"But—"

"No buts. This is the only hospital visit you'll have, so make good use of it."

"What? Why?"

He gives me a blank look as he parks the car in front of the hospital. "Dad is on his way here. He's personally taking you back to the States. Indefinitely."

Anything I have to say on the issue is unheard as Jeremy steps out of the car.

My opinion wouldn't matter anyway. Papa, Jer, and even Mom think I'm in danger here.

The plot twist is that I'm the one who hurt Creighton instead.

I'm the one who—

A bang sounds on the window and I flinch as Jeremy stares down at me. Then I step out of the car and follow him inside.

"You can visit Nikolai," I say, my voice sounding a bit scratchy. "I'll go to the ICU and join you in a bit."

"I'm coming with you."

"You don't have to..." I trail off when he matches my steps.

Soon after, we get to the ICU, and I stop at the corner when I catch a glimpse of a blonde woman with bloodshot eyes and a tear-streaked face sitting beside a stiff Eli and leaning her head on his shoulder.

Her hand is in a man's hold, or more like her wrist is. He keeps watching her face with a furrow in his brow.

He has a striking resemblance to Eli, looking like an older version of him.

Aiden and Elsa King. Their parents.

This is the first time I've seen them in person. Creighton often talked about them with adoration and almost reverence.

For someone who thought himself unfeeling, he loved his parents, and even Eli, unconditionally. Deep inside, he considered them his family and he hated himself for being hung up on the past version of himself.

A version that my family created, even unknowingly.

Glyndon strolls to the scene with Brandon. His face is tight while hers is all red and as much of a mess as Creighton's mom's. The siblings carry coffee that everyone but Creighton's dad refuses.

I want to step forward, to see him even once, but I don't dare to.

Creighton said his mom has a fragile heart, which is why I assume Eli's remaining by her side and his dad is probably monitoring her pulse.

I'll never forgive myself if something happens to her because of me.

Swallowing down a choke, I turn around. "Let's go."

Jeremy watches me for a beat. "Are you sure?"

No. But I nod, letting my feet carry me down the stairs. Maybe I can get information about Creighton from the hospital staff or I can just snoop from afar.

Or maybe, just maybe, this whole nightmare will end soon.

"What are you doing here?" The familiar voice, now vicious, reaches me before I'm flung back and slapped across the face so hard that my vision burns.

Jeremy grabs the assailant, Ava, and bangs her whole body against the wall. Her face is red, probably from having the breath knocked out of her lungs, but she glares at me anyway.

Cecily catches up to her and only stares at the scene for a second before she comes running to pull Jeremy off her.

"Let her go!" She scratches at his hand, her voice raw.

I touch his arm and shake my head. As much as I feel hurt and want to cry, I don't.

Jeremy reluctantly releases her, but Ava doesn't pause before coming at me again.

This time, with tears in her eyes. "We trusted you! We let you become our sister from another mister, but you...you dare to shoot Creigh... How could you do that when he cared about you so much? Who the fuck are you to steal him from us?"

My brother tries to shield me, but I step forward and let her hit me. I don't try to remain strong. I *can't*. The harder she cries and hits, the more I let the tears loose.

"Ava..." Cecily tries to pull her off me. "If Aunt Elsa or Uncle Aiden sees, we'll be in deep shit."

"I don't care!" she screams. "I thought this bitch would make Creigh happy and God knows he needed that, but she's sending him to his grave!"

"I didn't want... I'm so sorry..." I whisper between sobs. "I only...I only thought about saving my brother. I swear I didn't want to hurt him. I swear..."

"Leave," Ava all but growls, her face flushed, her cheeks tear-streaked. "The only reason we haven't reported this to the police is because Landon is leaving the ball in Creighton's court for when he wakes up, and none of us want to upset Aunt Elsa any further, so we said it was a robbery. But I swear to fuck, Annika, if something happens to Creigh, I'm gonna fly to the States and personally kill you."

"Not if you end up dead on the way," Jeremy says in a deadpan voice.

Ava continues glaring at me, but it's Cecily who glares at my brother. "I suggest you take her and go."

"And I suggest you shut the fuck up," he says with chill-inducing calm.

Cecily meets his harsh eyes for one more beat, then drags Ava away. "Let's go."

"Don't ever show your face around us again," Ava whisper-yells. "*Murderer.*"

And then they disappear, leaving me with a choked sob and a pain so deep, I just want to...end it all.

THIRTY

Aiden

"**S**WEETHEART?"

Elsa doesn't hear me. Her gaze is glued to our youngest son's unmoving body through the window.

He's been hooked to those machines for two days now, and there's still no sign of him coming back to life.

To us.

A fact that's been stressing Elsa and slowly robbing her of the light that I've always loved about her.

The same light that Creighton put there the moment he came into our lives.

Now, he's slowly but surely sucking it away.

"Elsa," I call again, more firmly this time.

My wife finally slides her attention from the window to me. Her beautiful long hair has lost its shine in the span of forty-eight hours, her face is pale, and dark circles dim her usually electric-blue eyes.

They're lifeless now, like the rest of her.

I'll commit murder before I let anything rob away my wife's life source.

At this very moment, that happens to be Creighton.

"You should go back to the hotel and rest." It's surprising how calm and collected I sound, considering the circumstances.

"No, I'm fine."

"You look positively exhausted." I grab her wrist and clench my jaw. "And your pulse has weakened."

She pulls her hand from mine subtly but with enough force to have my entire body tensing. "Our son has been shot and he's refusing to wake up. My whole life is in proper chaos right now, so my pulse is the last thing on my mind."

"It's the first thing on mine." I wrap my hand around her waist and slam her to my side. "And what did I say about pulling away from me, sweetheart, hmm?"

Her worn-out face creases. "Aiden…"

"What the fuck did I say?"

She releases a long sigh. "That we can be mad at each other while you touch me."

"That's right. So don't attempt that stunt again or we're going to have a problem."

"We already do have a problem." Her voice becomes brittle and she trembles in my arms as she stares through the window again. "What are we going to do if he doesn't wake up?"

"He's Creighton, sweetheart. The same Creighton who crawled out of that gas-infested house because he refused the ending his monster of a birth mother chose for him. He's the boy who accepted us wholeheartedly and called us Mum and Dad within the first month of coming to live with us. He chose us as a family, and we'll have to believe that he'll keep choosing us."

A tear rolls down my wife's cheek and I want to massacre that fucking tear to pieces. I want to stab the pain that's haunting her and choke it to fucking death.

"But what if he doesn't? What if he…went back to asking questions about who he is and where he came from and why he had to crawl out as a little boy? What if he stopped asking those questions out loud and started to answer them privately? Maybe…maybe that's why he got shot."

Her heartbeat quickens against mine, and I want to shake the fuck out of her for it. The doctor said that it's recommended to not expose her to extremely stressful or emotional situations.

Which is why she works less now and spends most of her time talking to our kids and having girl time with her friends—that I absolutely loathe, by the way, because that means less time for me.

Or more like she talks with one demon spawn—Eli. It's a known fact that Creighton would rather sleep than indulge in small talk. We've always respected his nature and his constant need for space.

But what we've been afraid of all along seems to have become a reality. It's been some time since I suspected that his need for space is actually him withdrawing into himself to plot self-annihilation.

Still, I force myself to keep calm and stroke her waist in a soothing rhythm. "Breathe, Elsa, and while you're at it, purge those cancerous thoughts from your head."

"But—"

"*Now.*"

She goes still at my harsh command, then she glares at me. Good. Glaring means she's distracted and won't allow that poison to consume her. Little by little, her pulse returns to normal and she releases a long breath.

"You and your orders are too much," she mutters under her breath.

"You letting dark thoughts consume you is the actual definition of too much." I soften my voice. "Go rest, even for a few hours, then come back."

"I don't want to leave him. What if something happens when I'm not here?"

"I'll be here. So will all the kids that alternate visitation time."

"Still…"

"Elsa. Don't make me throw you over my shoulder and personally drag your tight little arse to the hotel. You know I'm fully capable of that."

She lets out a resigned breath. Though it doesn't really matter whether we do it the nice way or the rough way. My wife knows full well that I would act on my every promise.

"I'll take you back, Mum." Eli appears from around the corner like a shadow, probably having eavesdropped on the whole conversation.

He has that loathsome habit that I tried to get him to drop when he was a kid, then soon gave up when he escalated. Eli understood early on that information is power, so he made it his mission to get his hands on any valuable tidbits.

That includes his own parents.

He wraps his hand around Elsa's shoulder and gives me one of his fake smiles.

I don't release her.

He doesn't release her.

Elsa sighs. "You guys know that I can actually go back on my own, right?"

"Nonsense," I say.

"No way," Eli says at the same time. "I'm sure Dad will keep an eye on Creigh just fine as I'll make sure you're all comfy, Mum."

"Aw, baby. What would I do without you?" She smiles at him, and although she still looks exhausted, some of that light returns.

"Live a boring life with Dad, probably. Sounds tedious even thinking about it."

"I will kill you," I mouth so his mother doesn't see.

"Mum." He puts on his acting cap, which he most definitely learned from that fucker Ronan.

Note to self: make him pay next time I see him and promptly think of a way to escape my wife's wrath.

"What is it, hon?"

"Dad just threatened to kill me."

"Aiden!" She furrows her brow and Eli grins in the background like a little devil. When Elsa focuses on him again, he switches back to the hurt expression. "You know how your father likes to threaten for sport. He doesn't mean it."

"I'll take your word for it, Mum. Now, let's go. I'll escort you safely to the hotel. No one can protect you better than I can."

"Like the way you protected your younger brother?"

Elsa pales and Eli freezes. His face gradually loses all humor and his posture stiffens.

"Aiden," my wife whispers. "How can you say that?"

"Isn't it the truth?" I don't break eye contact with my son, the one who resembles me so much that it feels as if I'm staring at a younger version of myself. "You had one mission. To keep an eye on your brother and not let him spiral down any destructive paths and to inform me or your grandfather if anything were to go awry, but you've failed that with flying colors."

"I had it under control." His voice hardens, all attempts to rile me up gone now that he's the one under attack.

I point at Creighton through the window. "Does that look under control to you? He's fucking dying."

"He is not dead." Eli's jaw clenches. "I left for a minute, to fix another situation, and when I came back—"

"All I hear are excuses." I tower over him. "Admit that the situation got out of your control."

His lips purse.

"Say it, Eli. Say that I'm right and Creighton should've stayed in London, where I could've monitored him better."

"And you think that wouldn't have cost him his life, Dad?"

"Stop this, please." Elsa places a palm on each of our chests. "This isn't the time to throw blame. We're a family and we're supposed to stand together at times like these.

"It was under control," my son repeats.

I step toward him. "If you don't admit you're wrong, you'll never win, punk."

He glares at me and I stare back, not backing down.

Eli and I share the richest yet most complicated relationship any father and son could have. Ever since he realized what a challenge is and that I'm the best opponent he can have, he's been actively trying to get on my nerves.

I gave him leeway when he was young since I understood him the best. If there was anyone who knew what it meant to try everything under the sun just to stop being so fucking bored with life, it was me.

Since I didn't want to recreate the strained relationship I once had with my own father, I gave him green light to do everything he wished. Even supported his methods that are socially frowned upon. Where Elsa tried to shackle his nature by teaching him about love and sunshine, I let it loose. When she wanted to take him to a therapist, I vehemently refused.

Just because we're different, that doesn't mean there's anything wrong with people like us.

It's not our fault we were born superior. The world needed to learn how to accept us like Elsa did.

However, Eli never, and I mean *never*, saw any attempts I made to understand him as support. He had this weird fixation about winning against me. In everything.

He's competitive to a fault, and goes against me in whatever he finds worthy of his time. Including gaining the affection of his mother and brother.

Which is why I went off on him just now. He needs to learn that Creigh's life isn't a fucking game that he can use in his plans.

"Um, hi." A small feminine voice breaks the tension.

Elsa smiles, completely ignoring us, and goes to hug the newcomer. After they break apart, she strokes her hair like a loving mother.

My son watches the entire exchange with a stiffer posture, his eyes darkening until they're almost black.

"Ava, honey. What are you doing here?" Elsa continues patting her hair and clothes, not leaving a single imaginary wrinkle alone.

My wife always wanted a little girl, and since she didn't get one, Ava kind of volunteered to act as her surrogate daughter.

Sometimes, Eli used to grumble, like a sorry sod, that Elsa loved her more than she loved him and Creigh.

A fact that my youngest smiled at and teased his brother about.

As much as Eli can be difficult, he's still the best brother Creighton could've had. Which is why I'm pissed off that he failed to protect him.

Ava keeps her full attention on my wife. "Uncle Aiden texted me."

"You did?" Elsa asks me. "You should've let her rest and go to school. She was here last night."

"I thought you'd be more at ease if Ava took you back and stayed with you. She already agreed. Isn't that right, Ava?"

"Yeah, sure!" She interlinks her arm with Elsa's and smiles. "Anything to help and spend more time with you, Auntie."

"I'll be the one to take Mum back. *You.* Leave." Eli steps toward them, having completely forgotten about the topic of discussion from earlier.

"Eli! Don't talk to Ava that way," Elsa scolds.

"Never mind him. Uncle Aiden invited me over, so his opinion doesn't matter." Ava's smile falters before she forces it back in place. "Let's go."

My wife gives me a warm look and doesn't protest as Ava leads her down the hall. Eli follows after.

Silently.

If I had known Ava's presence would have Elsa finally listening and actually relaxing, I would've had her come a long time ago.

I slide a hand in my pocket as I stare at my son's unmoving form. The doctor said it's entirely up to him now, and while I threatened to kill all the doctors and sue the hospital if something happens to him, I know the current situation is all on Creigh.

There's a hurdle that's stopping him from opening his eyes.

What, I don't know. But I'm sure it has to do with what the kids have been whispering about in the corner and refusing to tell us.

Needless to say, I know this isn't some robbery like the shit actors, except for Landon, tried to convince us of. They got their stories straight, but it was all too perfect and had Lan's scheming stench all over it.

I'm curious to know what drove them to go to such lengths.

The only one who can answer my question is none other than my nephew, Landon. The others are easier nuts to crack and would bring me faster results under duress, but he's the mastermind behind this and, therefore, he's hiding the true reason.

One problem, though. He's been methodically avoiding being cornered by me.

An issue that I'm currently finding a way around. Just like I found a way to have Elsa actually rest instead of straining herself.

My gaze flits to Creighton and helplessness bangs against my rib cage. The fact that I can't do anything to get him out of this state, short of inventing a time machine, wraps around my neck like a noose.

Eli is my biological son, my flesh and blood, and the only son I thought I could father, but it's Creighton who's has been the son I didn't know I needed.

He's the one who randomly texts me a new fact he's learned or makes sure I'm included whenever that punk Eli tries to antagonize me for sport.

He plays the mediator between us, the link that keeps our father-son relationship functioning. Without him, we'd probably fall apart.

Not once have I considered him any less just because we don't share DNA. Creighton is proof that family doesn't depend on blood, and I considered him a miracle, just like Elsa did.

"Wake up, son," I whisper, my voice gaining a haunting quality in the silence.

I know he can't hear me, but I'm ready to try any method, including satanic rituals, if it means we can get him back.

Which could start with pestering the doctor. So I do just that, barge into the chief doctor's office while he's in a meeting.

He and his associates gape at me as if I'm the devil fresh out of hell.

"Mr. King…is there anything I can do for you?"

"Besides actually being competent and bringing my son back to consciousness?"

Dr. Strauss, a bald old man with bulging brown eyes and a pointy nose, appears flustered. "As I told you, we've done everything we could."

"Not enough to make me pour more donations into this establishment and satisfy your research kinks."

"Mr. King—"

"If he doesn't wake up in the next twenty-four hours, I'm transferring him back to London and cutting off my checks."

I don't wait for his reply as I stride out of the room, not feeling even the slightest bit relieved.

Stopping by the vending machine, I pause when a finger comes from behind me and hits Water.

"Only mineral water is good from these waste-of-space machines, right?"

I grab the bottle and turn to face my nephew.

Lan leans back against the wall, arms and ankles crossed as a shadow of a smile tilts his lips. "Hi, Uncle."

"That didn't take long."

"You can't just text me that you can hand me information and not expect me to show up. Though it's a low blow, Uncle. You all but dug a hole in the place where my heart used to be."

"Quit the dramatics, and stop hanging out with Remi and picking up his nasty habits. Now, tell me."

"Tell you what?"

"The truth about what happened to Creighton. Who did that to him?"

"Nah, I planned that whole thing all too carefully, I can't just tell you my secrets."

"Either you tell me or there will be no deal."

"Jesus. You sure we're actually family?"

"Probably a mess-up in genetics."

He chuckles, the sound easy. "Well, I'm not that opposed to spilling the truth, but it depends on whether or not you'll hate me if you know I was the one who dug up and shed light on Creighton's past."

My jaw clenches, but I force the discomfort down. Deep down, I knew there would be a day when Creighton would get in touch with his past, no matter how much my father and I tried to block it.

"You're not mad?" Lan asks slowly.

"I'll beat you the fuck up later, but that doesn't answer why he's in this state."

"Thing is, Creigh always wanted revenge, so when he found out the name of the couple who caused the demise of his family, he went after their son."

"Is he the one who shot him?"

"Nope, his sister did. I swear to fuck, I didn't think that Barbie doll had it in her, but then again, maybe I underestimated her, considering she's a mafia princess."

"A mafia princess," I repeat, not asking a question.

Of course.

Elsa and I first met Creighton in the States when we were visiting my friend, Asher Carson. Back then, his wife, Reina, was sponsoring a three-year-old orphan in one of the organizations she runs.

He looked lifeless and scrawny and apparently escaped death by an inch.

My wife fell in love with him immediately. Up until that point, she was having these sad episodes whenever she saw children. She always wanted to give Eli a sibling, preferably a sister, but since the doctors said that her first pregnancy was a miracle and any additional pregnancies would bring certain risk to her life, I had a vasectomy.

Because there was no way in fuck I'd put her life in danger.

She understood that decision, but she cried anyway. She was depressed for a whole month after I killed her hopes for another child of our own, and while I hated seeing her like that, I never regretted the procedure.

We'd never thought about adoption prior to hearing about Creighton, partly because the topic of children made Elsa depressed, and I honestly didn't think I could care for someone who wasn't my flesh and blood.

But that was before we met Creighton.

When Elsa looked at him with those motherly eyes, I didn't think twice before asking her if she wanted the child to be her own.

I've never seen my wife so irrevocably happy than in that moment. The look in her eyes rivaled with the way she looked at me on our wedding day and when Eli was born.

But we understood that Creighton came with baggage. Reina told us that her sister, who was tied to the Russian mafia, was the one who'd entrusted him to her, and he had an ambiguous past that they weren't willing to divulge.

I figured the reason his parents had died was because they'd pissed off the mafia, but Reina assured us that the boy had no ties whatsoever to the mob.

And I assured her that he'd only be a King going forward. No longer American, no longer alone.

He'd become my son.

"That's not the worst of it." Landon's voice brings me back to the present.

"What is then?"

"She's Creighton's girlfriend. Or was, considering the circumstances."

"*What?*"

"The one who shot him is his girl," Lan repeats. "So the thing is, I've been looking into his past for some time, but I only managed to corner the guard with the right information recently. Once all the pieces of the puzzle were in place, I tried to warn Creigh away from Annika, but he was too pussy-whipped to listen. Now that I think about it, he looked more devastated finding out she's the daughter of the people who wronged him than he was about his origins. Do you think that's why he provoked her so she'd shoot him?"

"Tell me more."

I listen carefully to Lan's recounting of events. By the time he's done, I've already formed an image in my head regarding what seems to be the issue.

Landon gets his prize and says he's going to find his brother, who's in a place he's not supposed to be.

I'm still thinking about my nephew's words when I arrive in front of Creighton's room.

My feet come to a halt when I catch a glimpse of a petite girl in sweatpants and a hoodie, her hair falling on either side of her face, and she's crying. Silently. As she glues her face to the glass. Both her palms are on the surface, her lips trembling as she murmurs something I can't hear.

That must be Annika Volkov.

The girl Eli was giving Creighton shit about when they talked to Elsa once.

My wife wouldn't shut up about it that night, retelling me every word with her bright expression and smiley face. She was so happy that her youngest was finally finding love.

She'd assumed both our boys would die alone and she wouldn't have any grandchildren but was happy to be proved wrong.

Annika is also apparently the girl who shot my son.

The one who stabbed him in the back when it mattered the most.

I approach her with powerful strides. She doesn't sense me, seeming too focused on the other side to notice her surroundings.

When I stop behind her, I can hear what she's whispering in a brittle voice.

"I'm sorry…so sorry… Please wake up… If you do…if you do, I don't mind if you kill me. I'm so sorry, Creigh…so sorry."

"Is that all you have to say after what you've done?"

She flinches, and slowly turns around to face me, her eyes wide, her cheeks tear-streaked, and I realize exactly what she is.

Annika Volkov is the missing piece that's forbidding Creighton from waking up, and I'll do anything to get my son back.

THIRTY-ONE

Annika

I SHOULDN'T BE HERE.

If Papa finds out I've come to the hospital, which I'm sure he will, considering the thousand and one guards he brought with him—Kolya included—I'm done for.

But I managed to sneak out in disguise while everyone was busy.

I had to see Creighton one final time before I'm dragged back to the US.

I had to hear the machines beeping, signaling that he's alive.

But he's not awake.

From what little info Remi fed me, his condition gets more complicated the longer he stays in a vegetative state.

Remi is the only one who talks to me, secretly, monotonically, even. Like everyone else, he hates me for putting his friend and cousin in this state, but he also said, "I understand that you did it to save your brother, but I still don't like you right now."

That's okay.

As long as I'm updated about Creighton, I don't care if I'm disliked, hated, or downright tortured for what I've done.

And I think that's exactly what will happen as I stare into Aiden King's soulless gray eyes. They're so much like Eli's, both in their terrifying edge and in color, that it's absolutely horrifying.

Actually, no. Eli's are probably tamer in comparison.

After all, Aiden is the father, and he seems to have seen the world with those merciless eyes.

"I asked you a question, Miss Volkov. Do you believe apologizing is what you're supposed to be doing after you shot my son?"

My spine jerks upright, half due to the shock of hearing his ruthless, deep voice and half due to the information he just divulged.

He knows.

I thought Ava said they weren't going to tell Creighton's parents the truth. Or maybe they just meant his mom.

Not that I mind. If paying the price for what I've done will bring Creighton back, I'll turn myself in. Hell, I'll do it even if he doesn't wake up.

I made a mistake and I'll own up to it.

But my family, namely Papa and Jeremy, would never allow me to do that.

"I..." No other words come out. It's as if my tongue is tied.

"You're what?" Aiden closes in on me, and even though he doesn't invade my personal space, my heart flounders to the ground under the force of his intimidation.

Now, I can see how Eli and Creighton became who they are. It's a given with a father like this man.

He appears elegant and has the poshest British accent, but deep down, he's cutthroat and utterly scary. A little like my father and all the other members of the Bratva.

Only, he isn't a mafia man, which makes his personality downright scary.

"You have the nerve to show your face here after what you've done?"

I shake my head, try but fail to keep my posture upright. "He stabbed my brother and I thought he was going to kill him, so I... couldn't... I just couldn't watch without doing something."

"All I hear are excuses." He glares down his nose at me. "You could've done any number of things instead of shooting, such as physically stopping him or asking Landon and Remington, who were both present, to subdue him, but you chose to take away his life. You chose the easiest and bloodiest option."

"No…" My lips tremble and moisture stings my eyes. "I didn't have time. Jeremy could've died."

"And what's so important about your brother? Does his life have more value than my son's?"

"I didn't say that…"

"You obviously thought it when you pulled that trigger." His voice becomes blank, so emotionless that I shudder. "Is it not enough that your parents traumatized him as a child? Are you picking up where they left off and ending the life he fought so hard for?"

"Please…stop…" My voice chokes. "Please…"

"Why should I? So you'll feel better about what you've done? So you'll get rid of the guilt and live your life as if my son never existed?"

I release a long breath and let my lips pull in a bitter smile. "I could never feel better about all of this or forget Creighton. You might not believe this, but that bullet killed a part of me as well. The part who thought Creighton was meant for me and that we were destined to be together. I learned the hard way that he isn't, and I haven't been able to live with myself since."

He narrows his eyes, watching me closely as if he's peeling off my skin and inspecting what lurks beneath it.

Determining if what I'm saying is the truth or just a mash of half-truths and well-crafted lies.

When he speaks, the timbre of his voice has turned eerily calm, the deceptive, haunting type. "Know this, Annika. If my son dies, I'll haunt the fuck out of you and your family."

A chill splashes down my spine, but it's not due to his words.

It's because of the shadow that appears behind Aiden and clicks a gun to the back of his head.

"Step the fuck away from my daughter before I spill your brains on the floor."

Aiden's posture and expression remain the same, absolutely un-fazed by the threat Papa not-so-subtly poses.

As if that's not enough, he turns around, letting Papa hold the gun to his forehead. "Go ahead, shoot. This is the only chance you'll have to get me in a position like this. Use it well."

Shit.

Shit.

Is he crazy? How can he provoke my father like that when he's holding a literal gun to his head?

He must know the type of man Papa is. He must've heard about it if he's already aware of his implication in Creighton's life, so why the hell isn't he backing off as any sane person would?

Is he that fearless?

Because I have no doubt that Papa would pull the trigger and make good on his promise.

Before he can actually do that, I jump to his side, "Papa, no."

My father's face could compete with a statue—cold and unmoving. This is the type of person he turns into when he feels any of us is in danger.

When the great Adrian Volkov personally steps in and chooses to inflict violence.

"This man thinks it's a good idea to threaten my daughter and I'm here to prove him wrong. Step back, Anoushka."

"No! He's in pain because his son is hurt." I touch his arm, grabbing onto it for dear life. "Papa, please. Take it as if I'm begging you."

I think he'll shoot him anyway since he doesn't take anyone threatening his family lightly.

He takes it seriously, mercilessly, and remorselessly.

But after a beat, he lets his hand with the gun drop to his side. However, instead of tucking away his weapon, he leaves it there, as a form of both intimidation and threat.

Both men stare at each other, or more like glare, in a war of unbound power.

"Talk to my daughter in that manner again and you'll disappear as if you never existed."

"Papa!" I shake my head at him. "I'm the one in the wrong, I'm the one who did this."

"If there's anyone who started this, it's me," he speaks to Aiden. "I killed Creighton's father because he dared to touch my wife. I slaughtered him like a pig while he wailed and begged. I stabbed that scum and watched as blood poured out of his orifices, then I did it again and again, long after his body turned lifeless. And I would do it again in a heartbeat, with more stabs this time to make his face unrecognizable. I would bring him out of the grave he's rotting in and display his head on a stick so the world would realize that my wife and my children are off-fucking-limits. I never wished for things to come this far, but I will not, under any fucking circumstances, apologize for protecting my family."

"Neither will I," Aiden says calmly, assertively. "I don't give a fuck who you are and what type of demons you worship. If my son doesn't wake up, I'll end you and every last member of your dear family."

I'm trembling like a leaf, not only at the escalation and subtle threats they're exchanging but also at the fact that this situation could become so much worse.

Aiden is powerful, yes, but Papa is more violent, and I believe every word he says. My father is prone to become a monster if he feels that we're in jeopardy. I witnessed that firsthand during my kidnapping attempt.

Judging by his stiffened posture and harsh eyes, he definitely thinks I'm under attack and won't stop until that threat is out of the way.

And that threat is Aiden.

I've already hurt Creighton enough, I can't be the reason behind his father's death, too.

Think, Annika. Think.

I need to somehow dissipate this tension, but how?

Closing my eyes, I sway and let myself fall forward. Papa catches me before I hit the ground.

"Annika," his low voice calls. "Annika?"

I force myself to remain slack against him. Through the small slit in my eyes, I catch a glimpse of him finally tucking away his gun before he picks me up and carries me in his arms.

Like when I was a baby and I thought it was a good idea to take his place and sleep beside Mom. He always, without exception, carried me back to my room. I still snuck to their bedroom first thing in the morning and when they locked the door? I would bang on it until they opened it.

Like all those times, Papa's arms feel safe. Overly protective, yes, but still safe.

"My son will wake up, and when he does, I'll keep him the hell away from your daughter and your destructive family. I suggest you do the same."

"Annika is leaving UK soil effective immediately and I will make sure your son is erased from her life. Do not try to legally pursue her, for it won't have any result."

"If Creighton chooses to do so, nothing will stop me. Not even you."

"Let's hope we never meet again, Mr. King."

"I suggest you pray for it, Mr. Volkov."

And then Papa is carrying me out of the hospital, his steps steady, his hold firm, as if I'm weightless.

I feel him putting me in the backseat of the car and sliding in beside me.

"Where to, Boss?" Kolya's voice comes from the driver's seat as he reverses out of the parking lot.

"The airport," Papa says calmly before he whispers, "We're out of the hospital. You can wake up, Anoushka."

I bite my lower lip as I slowly open my eyes and stare at Papa sheepishly. "You knew?"

"You're good, but not that good. Besides, you used to pretend to be asleep whenever you wanted to spend the night in our bedroom."

"It's different this time."

"You didn't want me to hurt him. I know."

"And I don't want him to hurt *you*, Papa."

"He won't be able to." A small smile grazes his lips as he ruffles my hair. "Didn't know you were so grown up that you could single-handedly protect your brother and even me."

"I'm a Volkov, too."

"Yes, you are. That means, next time someone threatens you, you beat them the fuck up."

I shake my head. "I wouldn't be able to live with myself if I were to hurt the man Creighton considers a father and a role model."

"That still doesn't excuse the way he talked to you."

"Listen, Papa…"

"No, you listen to me. I know you like that boy, and you're in pain because you had to shoot him. But that's the keyword, Anoushka. You *had* to shoot him. By threatening Jeremy's life, he gave you no choice but to pull the trigger. He knows how much your brother means to you, he knows you won't hesitate to protect him, but he still stabbed him anyway. He's the one who forced your hand, he's the one who didn't consider your feelings or the circumstances when he made that choice. So don't beat yourself up for choosing your family or for making a decision you were forced to make. If he loved you, if he cared about you instead of vengeance and a past vendetta, he wouldn't have put you in that position."

A tear slides down my cheek, then more follow.

I see the reasoning behind Papa's words, I do, but the only scene in my head is that of red.

Deep red.

A lot of red.

The only scene that plays in the back of my head is that of a pale Creighton hooked to machines, unable to open his eyes.

A ghost of his former self.

He seems like such a distant memory now.

The last day we spent together was a few days ago, but it feels like it's been a century.

So much has happened between that sweet honeymoon phase and this nightmare that I can't keep up with it anymore.

"It still hurts, Papa." I grab a fistful of my hoodie. "Right here, it hurts so much."

"It'll hurt less with time."

"You don't even believe that."

"It has to. You need to get over him, Annika. If he's bent on revenge, then he won't stop until he destroys you, even if it also means destroying himself in the process. Do you understand?"

My lips purse, but I nod.

"I need you to promise me that you won't seek him out. In return, I'll let you study ballet, give you the freedom you've always yearned for, and I will fight the entire brotherhood so you won't be shoved into an arranged marriage."

I can't believe my ears.

That's what I always wanted from my family—freedom to decide my own destiny.

I just never thought I would get them at this price.

"Promise me, Anoushka."

"I promise," I murmur.

Deep inside, I pray.

I promise to let everything between me and Creighton come to an end, but only if he wakes up.

Only if I'm sure he's all right.

After that, I don't care about my life.

"Good." Papa nods. "Now, let's go home. Your mother is worried about you."

I nod soundlessly. There are no other words spoken as we board the private jet.

It's not out of awkwardness or anything. Papa isn't talkative by nature, and he's probably giving me the space he thinks I need.

He and Kolya sit opposite me, discussing business.

A tear rolls down my cheek when I catch my very last glimpse of the island.

I've only been here for a few months, but I had friends, a nail-biting experience, and a man who gave me the world.

Right before I ruined everything.

Maybe it's better that I leave, after all.

This island might have made me feel alive for the first time since I was born, but it also ripped my heart to shreds.

Papa's and Kolya's voices filter in the background as I force myself to drift to sleep.

As soon as we land, I'm ready to go home and cry into Mom's chest. I'm ready to let her console me, even if I blame her and Papa a little for this.

I don't blame Papa for protecting her, but maybe I blame them for giving birth to me, for letting me be in this world where the only person I wanted with my heart and soul is impossible to have.

And is fighting for his life because of me.

Once we're in the car, I check my messages and choke on my sobs when I read a text I got while I was on the flight.

Remington: I thought you should know that Creighton woke up. He's disoriented, but the doctors said he'll get better with time :)

THIRTY-TWO

Creighton

I T'S BEEN TWO WEEKS SINCE I WOKE UP FROM THE COMA.

The first week was spent in the hospital and passed in a blur of tests, rehab, and a lot of fucking noise.

It was filled with pitiful looks from the friends I grew up with all my life and with meaningless, needless sympathy.

There was a jumble of motion, words, and sensations. I barely remember anything aside from Mum's tears and the innate need to put a stop to them.

She was both happy and sad, and I still have no clue why she was sad.

Was it the fact that I was hurt or did she see the look in my eyes?

Did she peek beneath the surface and uncover the façade I used as camouflage?

I didn't get to ask that question after I was discharged a few days ago. My parents brought me home with them and I didn't protest. At least this way, I can escape the faces dripping with pity.

I can stay away from their mine-filled conversations that always somehow lead back to how I got shot.

Or more like the person who shot me.

Her.

My nemesis and my damnation.

I've successfully avoided the subject by pretending to be tired or sleepy. A privilege I'll soon lose since my wound is healing—the stitches have almost all dissolved into my skin, leaving a hole near my upper chest.

"A few centimeters to the right and the bullet would've gotten his heart," is what I heard the doctor tell my father.

And I'm left here wondering why those centimeters didn't happen.

I wanted to die.

I should've fucking died, so how come I'm still breathing?

That question has been living in my head rent-free ever since I woke up and I still can't find an answer.

Which is why I'm 'recuperating.' Though I'm not sure that's the right word with the world war atmosphere I find myself in.

As the rain hammers down outside, I sit in the playroom downstairs, my fingers patting a surprisingly docile Tiger. I brought him with me from the island, despite Brandon's protests.

He FaceTimes me every day and I just show him the cat because that's what he's interested in.

It's mind-boggling how Tiger remains soundlessly asleep in the current situation.

My grandparents from my mother's and father's sides have come to visit. At the same time.

And to make things worse, Grandpa Jonathan, Dad's father, thought it was a marvelous idea to play a game of chess against Grandpa Ethan, Mum's father.

They're supposed to be friends, or were some sort of friends, but that's not the current atmosphere. Probably because Grandpa Agnus, Grandpa Ethan's husband, can't and won't stand Grandpa Jonathan. A known fact since I was a kid.

I sit across from them, sipping some herbal drink Mum gave me and choosing to be engrossed in the scene in front of me instead of getting lost in my fucked-up head.

Grandpa Jonathan pushes his rook a few rows forward. He's an older version of Dad and Eli with his black hair that's streaked with white and his merciless gray eyes. "You were never able to win against me, Ethan. Give it up."

"At your funeral." Grandpa Ethan blocks his move with his rook and grins. He looks the youngest of the three, despite being the same age as them.

It's probably due to his blond hair, which he passed down to Mum, and the generally pleasant expression he wears at all times.

Grandpa Agnus is the most silent and absolutely unapproachable out of the three. He has a generally grim expression, never smiles, jokes around, or allows anyone to get close to his husband unless they're ready to suffer a severed limb.

He's always been my favorite. Probably because we silently understand one another.

While everyone was fawning over me, he methodically kicked them out so I could rest. Grandpa Ethan still manipulated him to let him and Mum come see me, though.

"That was a rookie mistake." Grandpa Jonathan grins with pure mischief as he eats the white knight.

Grandpa Agnus, who's sitting on the armrest of Grandpa Ethan's chair, leans over and whispers something in his ear.

"No cheating, Agnus," Grandpa Jonathan says. "Two to one is not happening."

"Who says it's two?" Grandpa Ethan interlinks his fingers with his husband's and smiles with mischief. "We're one."

A rare smile twitches Grandpa Agnus's lips and Grandpa Jonathan's expression pulls downward. "Such a revolting sight."

"Someone is jealous. Maybe you should join your wife outside."

"You might want to wipe that, Jonathan," Grandpa Agnus says with a neutral expression. "It's dripping all over the floor."

"Are you sure it's not *your* jealousy that's messing up the floor, Agnus?"

"Mine?"

"If I remember correctly, I received a bunch of drunken texts from you not too long ago."

"Texts?" Grandpa Ethan stares between them. "What type of texts?"

"Since when do you even check your texts?" Grandpa Agnus asks with a tight voice.

"Since they're from you. I admit, I was thoroughly entertained and even learned them by heart for a moment like this."

"Don't you dare—"

"They said, and I quote, 'Fuck you, Jonathan, for being able to share all those threesomes with Ethan. I'm surprised I didn't kill you.' Another one went on like this, 'You knew my feelings very well and still provoked me. Rot in hell. I know I'm going there, too, but I'll make sure I have a room opposite yours so I can watch you burn for eternity.' My personal favorite, however, is 'Bet you thought I would never make him mine, you bloody sod. Touch him again and I will kill you.' I must say, I fancy drunk Agnus. He's much less dull than the one in front of me."

"I'm going to kill you," Grandpa Agnus deadpans, then stares down at his husband. "And stop smiling."

"Come now, this is amusing." Grandpa Ethan strokes his hand. "If I'd known you held this type of jealousy all these years, I would've done something about it."

Grandpa Agnus doesn't appear amused as he stands, throws one last glare at Grandpa Jonathan, and leaves after a nod in my direction.

Grandpa Ethan hits Grandpa Jonathan on the shoulder. "I owe you one, Jonny." Then he follows after his husband.

He stops at the entrance, pats my arm, and leaves.

"Bunch of little fuckers," Grandpa mutters under his breath as he stands up.

"Did you have to do that?" I ask.

"How else will I get a reaction out of Agnus? Though I believe I might have unintentionally done him a favor and brought them closer. It's unfortunate how Ethan never understood how to go with the flow." He halts in front of me. "Do you need anything?"

Aside from going back into a coma and never waking up? I shake my head.

"If you want to escape your parents, come to my house." Grandpa ruffles my hair as if I were still a child. "Get well soon, kid. I mean it."

And then he's out the door, probably to get my nan and leave. She's been there with Mum every step of the way, fawning over me, and making sure I'm comfortable.

That means she's given less attention to Grandpa.

He's never liked sharing Nana's time with anyone, including his grandkids. Except for Glyn. She's always had an all-access card to Grandpa's mansion.

Now, apparently, I do, too, since he invited me over.

I'm staring at the rain, absentmindedly patting Tiger's head when Mum comes in carrying a plate full of all sorts of food.

She's wearing a beautiful white dress that makes her look younger. The dark circles and bloodshot eyes eventually disappeared as I was getting better, and she's been dedicating her life to becoming my personal chef.

Something she really sucks at—cooking, I mean—but Dad, Eli, and I choose not to tell her that fact.

It's how I managed to eat all of Annika's horrible dishes when everyone else avoided them like the plague.

My wound itches at those memories, tingling and burning, and it takes everything in me not to rip the stitches open.

As if feeling my distress, Tiger jumps from my lap and chooses the chesterfield sofa as his next sleeping spot.

Mum places the tray on the small table in front of me and stares at the door. "What happened? Why did Agnus look mad and Dad actually seem happy about it? And does it have to do with Jonathan's smug expression?"

"Definitely. But you don't want to know about it."

"You're probably right." She strokes my hair away from my face. "You need a cut. Or not. I like the new look, actually. What do you think?"

"I don't have a preference."

"Why, of course you do."

"I don't, Mum."

"Okay," she says slowly. "Do you want to go back to school?"

I stare at the tiny droplets of rain that dust the tall windows. "Don't care either way."

"Are you mad at me, Creigh?"

My gaze slides to her wretched-looking expression and I frown. "No. Why would I be?"

"Because we hid the truth and ever since you found out about it, nothing good has happened."

Thanks to Landon's big mouth, Dad found out everything that went down, but Mum still believed it was a robbery gone wrong. But she had a hunch that no one was telling her the whole truth, so Eli gave her a recounting of events.

Like me, he hates to put her health in jeopardy, but we don't like hiding the truth from her either.

After all, she's the woman who gave me unconditional love when she didn't have to.

"I'm not mad at you, Mum. I'm mad at myself for digging deeper, for not respecting your wishes and keeping the past where it belonged. If I had, if I'd given up after you told me to, I wouldn't have been standing at this edge of in-between. I wouldn't have lost…everything."

"Oh, Creigh. You didn't lose everything." She grabs my hands in hers. "You have us. No matter what happens, no matter what the world, nature, or science says, you're my son. You became my son the first day I met you in that room at the shelter. You were so scrawny and small, but you didn't hide. You stood up from that bed on your tiny feet and stared at us with these beautiful inquisitive eyes. They held so much pain, so much torture, but they had a lot of hope, too. Hope for a different life, hope to move past your trauma, and hope to actually find a family again. You looked at us like we were already your parents, and I fell in love at first sight. And believe me, I've never fallen in love at first sight, not even with your father, not even with your brother—since I gradually fell in love with him during the nine months of pregnancy, but you, you're different, baby. You're the one I'd fall in love with over and over again if I had to. I'd kill your demons for you. If I'm ever reborn, I'd sacrifice myself if it meant I'd get to have you as my son again. So please, if you have any issues, talk to me, or your father, or Eli. Don't just battle your demons on your own. Don't just…leave us."

She's flat-out crying, my mum. Her tears cling to her chin, and that wretchedness fills her once bright blue eyes again.

Is this what I do? Put darkness in the place of light?

Destroy everything I touch?

These are the thoughts she must've had ever since I woke up in the hospital, or maybe since she found out that I'd been shot and the reason behind it.

She probably thinks she's not enough, which is why I wanted to die.

"I know I didn't give birth to you, but I felt like your mother since the moment I met you. The first time you called me Mum was one of the happiest moments of my life, and I'll always, *always* consider you my flesh and blood."

"I never considered you any less. That woman who gave birth to me was never my mother, *you* are. And that scum who donated the sperm isn't my father, Dad is."

A soft frown etches across her features. "Then why were you so bent on avenging them?"

"I wasn't avenging them, I was avenging myself. I wanted closure for the weak three-year-old version of me." I hold my head between my hands. "But I ended up fucking it all up."

"Oh, baby." Mum leans my head against her chest and strokes my hair, silently offering me her support.

No clue if it's due to that or the weight of all the events catching up to me, but I confess it all.

"I wanted her to kill me, Mum. I wanted the one person who made me feel alive to shoot me. I would've died and ended it all and she'd never forget about me. I wanted her to not be able to move past me. I wanted to be a stain on her life forever so whenever she looked in the mirror, she saw my shadow. I wanted to haunt her, to prevent her from being with anyone else after me. How fucked up is that?"

"You were just on a high of emotions." Her voice is soft, soothing, and holds not an ounce of judgement.

Because that's how mothers are.

"No." I pull back and tap my chest, where the wound is. "I still wish I could go back in time and make her kill me properly. That way, I wouldn't feel so fucking empty knowing I lost her for good."

"Nonsense." Dad leans against the doorway, arms crossed, probably having listened to the whole conversation. "There's no such thing as losing someone for good if you put your head into it. I admit that I wanted that bloody mafia miss out of your life for daring to hurt you, and I threatened her to stay the hell away from you, by the way. But if you want her, go for it. I'll back you up."

"Aiden." Mum wipes her eyes with the back of her hand. "How can you say that? If he goes to the States, her father will kill him."

"Not if I have a say in it." Dad raises a brow. "Let me ask you, Creigh. Do *you* want to go after her?"

I shake my head. "I can't."

"Why not?"

"We're ill-fated."

"Bullshit. You're just letting fear of rejection get the better of you. I didn't know I had a coward of a son."

"Aiden!" Mum reprimands again.

"It's not that—"

"Then what is it?" he cuts me off. "You expect me to believe you're over her when you vehemently refused to press charges against her? You were barely speaking at the time, but you begged me not to bring her name up to the police. I won't tell you what to do, but I'll tell you this, son. If you let her go, someone else will swoop in and take her."

Hot fire spreads in my chest with the lethality of an erupting volcano. That thought has been plaguing my waking and sleeping moments. Images of Annika with another man have left me mad and with a sense of trepidation. Especially since I overheard Cecily and Glyn say that she might be arranged to marry some mafia man, after all.

"I just…can't forgive her parents. I won't. I *can't*. And I know how much she loves them."

"And you're scared she'll choose them like she chose her brother?" Mum asks in a soft voice. At my nod, she strokes my cheek. "If that's the choice she makes, then she doesn't deserve you, baby."

"What your mother said," Dad agrees. "If she doesn't recognize your worth or hurts you again, you'll know her nature and that way, you'll be able to move on. For good."

I mull their words over in my head as a crazy and utterly twisted idea forms. One that I'm sure Dad will help with.

Because he cares about me.

And so does Mum.

"Thank you," I whisper. "And I'm sorry if I made you doubt how important you are to me. I'm lucky to be your son."

Mum holds both hands to her chest, tears glistening in her eyes. "Now you went and made me emotional. Be right back. I'll bring biscuits; they must be ready."

She passes by Dad, kisses him on the cheek, then disappears to get more of her creations.

Dad takes her place and grabs one of the weird-looking things she brought earlier.

"Mum made those," I warn.

"And some of them have to be eaten or she'll be sad." He doesn't even wince as he crunches on what should be a muffin. "She never wanted to learn to cook until she found out you love food so much. She tried hard to be accepted by you." I grab a muffin, but Dad shakes his head. "You're sick. I'll eat them."

"Don't even try to be cool. I'm not that sick and I can handle these. After all, she made them for me." I wince at the overly-cooked thing. "Have you heard the part where she fell in love with me at first sight? Something that didn't happen with you or Eli?"

He narrows his eyes. "You get a pass for being sick."

"That means I'm more important than you two."

"Don't push it. And quit channeling Eli or I'll smack you. Sick or not."

"I brought biscuits." Mum rushes back in with half-burnt biscuits that look like murdered Smurfs.

Dad and I groan, but we eat every last bite.

And that idea from earlier? It's becoming more of a reality with every passing second.

THIRTY-THREE

Annika

I T'S WEIRD HOW TIME CAN GO ON WHILE SIMULTANEOUSLY remaining stuck in the same place.

That's exactly how it's felt ever since I was hauled back to the States.

It's been a whole month.

A month of convincing myself to get out of bed every day. I push myself, speak to my reflection in the mirror and try so hard not to wallow in the darkest parts of me.

I'd try so hard not to think about what I left on Brighton Island and how desperately I've been yearning to go back.

Even if it's impossible. Even if I'll get hurt.

Creighton and I are meant to be dots that never overlapped. We wouldn't have if it weren't for my loathsome character.

If it weren't for my persistence, chattering, and attempting to be liked by everyone.

If it weren't for my toxic curiosity and stupid determination.

It's all on me, myself, and I.

Which is why I have to be the one who fixes it and moves on.

I wouldn't say I've succeeded, but being here with my parents, Yan, and the others certainly helps. I picked up ballet again and religiously go to practice, then I volunteered at the shelter Mom supervises.

That way I'll be too beat when I come home and I'll have no choice but to sleep, right?

Wrong.

Nighttime is the worst. That's when my demons come out and I turn into a ball of jagged edges and suppressed emotions.

When the longing and impossible feelings I successfully manage to keep under wraps all day long transform into bats and explode in the cave of my chest.

Like right now.

Usually, I'd take a pill and force myself to sleep. Not tonight.

Tonight I want to let the pain seep inside me so that I can feel every lash, every whip, and every strike.

It's only fair after what I've done.

I roll onto my back and stare at the glittery ceiling, and it takes everything in me to keep the tears at bay.

Sleeping alone never gets easier or feels normal, no matter how much time passes. I don't recall how I used to sleep before Creighton came along, but now?

All I can picture is his muscular arms cocooning me in his tight embrace and shielding me from the world. He'd bury his nose in my hair and inhale deeply, and his strong hands would be on my hip, my waist, my breasts, my ass, my neck.

Everywhere.

Now they're nowhere. Only a cold chill rips through my body, hooking against what remains of my soul to freeze it to death.

Instead of focusing on that and driving myself crazy, I grab my phone and open Instagram. During the first week home, I actually deleted all my social media apps.

The pain was too raw, so much so that not even my obsession with biographing my life could've lessened the blow.

But then I became greedy for any sliver of an update about him.

Remi texted me back and forth, though secretly, as he told me. He's the only one I offered excuses to. The only one who knows I couldn't just let my brother die and that pulling that trigger killed me inside.

He still hated me at the beginning for hurting his cousin, but I think he soon forgot about it.

Though we don't really talk about Creighton anymore. It feels weird to ask about him, knowing full well he and his entire entourage hate me.

I expected him to come after me for shooting him. Hell, reporting me to the police would be his perfect revenge against my family. Sure, Papa wouldn't allow anyone to arrest me, but that was a valid option he could've gone for.

So imagine my surprise when Remi said that Creighton told the police it was an anonymous man who robbed and shot him.

I couldn't stop crying that night. Half because he actually protected me after I nearly killed him. Half because of the reality that he wants nothing to do with me anymore.

That we're really over.

Sometimes, I think it's for the best. Oftentimes, I get stuck in a loop of my own making and can't find a way out.

The first picture that appears on my feed is of Remi shoulder-hugging a blank-faced Creighton.

Cousin, best friend, spawn, you name it. This cheeky bastard is stuck with me for life.

My fingers tremble as I zoom in on Creighton. He looks good—his face is eternally beautiful, silently dashing. His eyes remain unfazed though a little lifeless, and strands of his now longer hair kiss his forehead.

Sometimes, I can't believe he's recuperated and is doing well. I can't believe that life has found its way back to his face, wiping away the paleness.

Sometimes, I recall that version of him I saw in the hospital or all the red that he drowned in and I choke on my own breaths.

But he's safe now.

All safe.

That's the only thing I wished for from the beginning, so why can't I simply let go?

Why am I thirsting after the tiniest update or the smallest glimpse of him?

I'm supposed to be moving on by now. Time should've made me forget as Papa said, so why is the exact opposite happening?

There are no answers to my questions no matter how much I ask them. In fact, they become more complicated the more I do.

I click on Remi's profile and scroll through the other posts.

Creighton recently went back to school, as in, about a week ago, and Remi has been posting a selfie with him or catching him in the background daily.

I tap on a group picture and then go to Eli's profile through it.

He unfollowed me and removed me as a follower, but at least he didn't block me.

A jolt goes through me when I see the last picture he posted. Both Eli and Creighton stand half naked, the planes of their chests glistening with moisture and their hair damp.

A bandage covers a part of Creighton's chest, where the bullet went in, and it takes everything in me not to choke on my sob.

Sauna day, sponsored by yours truly since I heard it's good for recuperation. Welcome back, baby bro #BrothersTime #SleepingBeautyChroniclesResumingSoon

I take a screenshot of the picture, crop Eli out, and add it to the collection I've been keeping on my phone.

Then I fall asleep staring at them with tears in my eyes.

The next day, I'm ready to volunteer at the shelter.

"You don't have to go all the time, Anni," Mom tells me when we're stepping out of the house.

"I don't mind." I check my bag and make sure my phone is in there.

She clutches me by the shoulder and kind of forces me to stare up at her. "Do you need anything?"

"Nope, I'm cool."

"Are you sure?"

"Yeah."

"All right. How about we have girls' night later and then I'll sleep beside you?"

Mom hugged me to sleep the first few nights after I came home. She didn't tell me this, but she I figured she was scared shitless that I would do something to hurt myself.

Not going to lie, I did have those thoughts, especially after I kept having nightmares about all the red that surrounded Creighton. But that edge lessened as I received more updates about how well he was doing.

"Please don't or Papa will hate me for daring to take his place."

She beams and strokes my hair back. "Let me worry about your father. If you want me to keep you company, let me know."

"Nah, I'm not a little girl anymore." I can and will find a solution for my own problems.

My phone vibrates and I pull it out fast, thinking it's a text from Remi. The name that appears on the screen makes me pause.

Cecily: How have you been, Anni?

My chest aches and a sudden influx of tears blurs my eyes.

After everything went down, I didn't only lose Creighton, but I also had to let go of the friendships I thought I'd formed with Ava, Cecily, Glyndon, and Brandon.

They stopped talking to me, and rightfully so, considering they've known Creighton way longer than me.

So to see Cecily texting me after I thought I'd lost her for good wrenches those buried emotions to the surface.

Annika: I'm doing okay. How about you?

Cecily: Same old. We miss you.

I choke on my own breaths as that familiar sting burns my eyes.

Annika: I miss you guys, too. So much.

Cecily: Can we meet?

Annika: I don't think that's possible. Not sure if you heard, but I'm no longer on Brighton Island.

Cecily: Oh, I know. I'm in New York City.

Annika: What? You are?

Cecily: Currently roaming in Central Park in pure touristy fashion, haha.

Annika: Send me a location. I'm coming right over.

It isn't until I slide my phone into my pocket that I find both Mom and Yan watching me expectantly.

Mom's expression softens. "Good news?"

"Uh, yeah. Remember my friend, Ces? Cecily? She's come to visit."

"Invite her over," Mom suggests. "I'll make us lunch and she can stay with you."

"I don't think it's a good idea to bring her into our house that's so full of guards and security. She wouldn't be able to handle this whole atmosphere and would be super uncomfortable. It's better that I go meet her."

"I'm coming with you," Yan announces.

"No, Yan. I'm just meeting my friend and you'll intimidate her."

"Boss will have my balls on a stick if I let you go alone."

"Please, Yan." I grab his arm and bat my lashes. "I just want to feel normal for a little while. Besides, Papa has been giving me more freedom."

"Not when it comes to those fucking English kids," Yan says, revealing his extreme distaste for the way they all cut me out of their lives.

He knows how ecstatic I was to have friends, so he's mad that I lost them so easily.

I tried to tell him that Creighton is their family and childhood friend and they wouldn't forgive me for shooting him, but he said that if they were true friends, they would've at least tried to understand me.

"Everything's going to be okay." I smile. "Besides, Papa doesn't need to know, right, Mom?"

"Right." Mom catches his other arm. "Let her go, Yan. She deserves this."

"You two will get me killed one day," he grumbles, but he allows me to go unescorted after reminding me to call him at the first inconvenience.

And to keep my phone close—since they can track me through it.

Truth is, I don't always have security with me. Papa was a pain in the ass at the beginning, but he soon allowed me the freedom he promised me and I no longer had to fight for it.

For some reason, that has felt like a tasteless victory.

What's the point of freedom if I can't use it to be with who I want?

After a long drive, I find Cecily sitting on one of the benches in the park, reading from some psychology book and giving zero fucks about the attention her silver hair gets.

She's wearing a shirt that says, *Wait…you can see me?*

The moment my shadow falls on her, she lifts her head from her book and stares up at me.

"Hi," I try but fail not to choke on the word.

"Hi," she says slowly, carefully.

An awkward silence permeates the air, then I fall in beside her. "I can't believe you've come to the States on your own."

"Yeah, me neither." She closes her book, slips it into her backpack, and faces me. "Is, eh…are you okay?"

I place both my palms on the bench and stare at the sky. People, movement, and noise swirl around us like the buzzing of bees, but they soon disappear. Unlike my wishes, time doesn't stop, it keeps flowing on and on in an endless circle.

"I guess."

"You don't look okay." Cecily's voice softens.

"No?"

"Not really. You're kind of pale and you've lost weight."

"I'm on a diet for the ballet."

"Does that mean you're permanently relocating here?"

"I don't really have a choice. It's for the best anyway."

"The Annika I know wouldn't give up that easily just because the circumstances stole her choice. She'd fight to get it back, and if that didn't work, she'd find another solution to get what she wants."

I release a long sigh. "What I want is impossible."

"Says who?"

"The one I want." An onslaught of tears sting my eyelids, but I push them back down. "Enough about me. Tell me about you."

"The usual." She sounds sad, like someone who was beaten down. I thought she was mirroring my tone earlier, but she genuinely sounds a little bit broken. "Listen, Anni."

"What?"

"I'm sorry."

"For what?"

"For cutting you off after what happened. I shouldn't have and I'm so sorry."

"You guys were hurt on your childhood friend's behalf. It's okay. I understand."

"It is not okay." Tears gather in her eyes as she grabs my hands in hers. "We were your only friends, but when it mattered the most, we let you down. I'm so sorry you had to deal with this whole mess on your own."

I choke on my tears and squeeze her fingers in mine. "Thank you, Ces. You have no idea how much your words mean to me."

"Whatever happens, I'll always be here for you."

"Does that mean I can text you sometimes?"

"Of course. Any time."

I grin and remove my hand to dab at my cheeks. "How's everyone back at REU?"

"Back to normal, I guess. Glyn is constantly being kidnapped by Kill as usual. Bran has been disappearing on us more often than not. Lan is Lan, always scheming some trouble. Eli is MIA. Remi keeps pestering Creigh to join his satanic endeavors. And Ava is miserable because she has no one who listens to her fashion talks anymore. She got drunk the other night and said she misses you."

"I miss her, too."

"Despite the show she put on at the hospital?"

"Yeah. I know she didn't mean to. She was hurt and upset and she had every right to be. She's always been close to Creighton's mum, and Eli means something to her, despite her attempts to deny it. So her strong reaction makes sense and I don't fault her for it. Tell her I'm sorry."

"Don't you think there's someone else you should apologize to? Such as the person who actually got shot?"

My heart jolts at the mere mention of him and it takes me a few moments to compose myself. "And what good would that do?"

"You never know until you try."

"It's over, Ces."

"But—"

"I'm simply not dragging my family through the mud for this. My mom has been worried sick since this whole ordeal started and her insomnia kicked in again. I won't be the reason behind the relapse of her mental health issues. I'd never forgive myself."

"So you'll just sacrifice yourself?"

"I'll just do what I was supposed to all along. Marry into the mafia, make my parents happy, and that's it."

"What about you then?"

"Nothing good happened when I chose me."

"Anni…"

"I'm barely hanging in there. I'm doing my best, okay? I'm trying to convince myself to keep going no matter how much I want to stop and let my head get the better of me. I'm really, *really* trying, so please don't push me, Ces."

"Okay." She strokes my shoulder.

"Okay?"

"Yeah, okay. I won't pretend to know what it feels like to be in your shoes right now."

"Thanks." I release a long breath, but it does nothing for the knots inside me. "Should we get something to eat?"

Cecily agrees and opts to try the street food experience. We have hot dogs and lots of unhealthy soda and then I drive her to the airport.

Despite my attempts to invite her to stay, she's bent on leaving and says this was an impromptu visit anyway.

She came in a private jet, so I escort her all the way to the plane.

"Don't they have a car that goes with one of these planes?" I ask as we walk to the stairs. "Not that I mind driving you."

"Uh, I didn't think to ask. First time flying solo, remember?" She smiles forcibly and I stop pushing.

She's probably embarrassed or she could have a fear of flying.

"I guess this is me." I stop at the foot of the stairs.

"No, come up with me. I still have time until departure." She grins. "We can have a drink."

"Papa won't like that, despite my attempts to prove my Russian ancestry."

"Oh, come on." She grabs me by the elbow. "I'm sure he won't find out about one drink."

"You say that because you don't know my father." I let her lead me up the stairs anyway. "He could find a fly in the Atlantic Ocean if he puts his mind to it. Jer inherited that trait, you know, and sometimes, I feel left out of the cool Volkov club."

Cecily stiffens and I pause in the middle of the stairs. "What's up?"

"Uh, nothing."

"You went all rigid at the mention of my father and brother. Considering you never met Papa, and all the strategic disappearing you do when my brother is around, I guess this is about Jer?"

"Nooo." She laughs awkwardly.

"That didn't sound convincing."

"You know your brother is scary."

"Didn't scare you that time you defended me at the fight club."

"Maybe I should've been scared," she mutters under her breath.

"What is that supposed to mean?"

"Nothing, nothing." She leads me up the stairs and we sit down opposite each other on the luxurious velvet seats.

A flight attendant brings us two flutes of champagne and we make a toast before we drink.

Or I drink.

Cecily watches me the whole time with a downward expression.

"This looks oddly familiar, as if I'm the one who's going on a flight." I grin, then pause. "Is it just me or do I sound drunk after just one glass of champagne?"

Cecily stands up. "I'll be right back."

I try to follow her with my gaze but even my body feels drunk.

Papa will kill me.

Unless I convince Mom and Yan to smuggle me inside.

I stand up and the plane sways off its axis.

Shit.

I'm thrown backward and I hit a wall.

No. Not a wall. *Muscles.*

A very familiar scent fills my nostrils, confiscates my breathing, and leaves me floundering and gasping for air. My body heats and my heartbeat picks up in recognition of this touch.

The same touch I fell asleep with countless of times.

I think I'm dreaming. Again.

Like those tortuous nights where I imagine myself snuggled in these solid arms. Where everything is back to before my world was ruined.

But his deep, rich voice sounds absolutely real when he whispers, "Did you think it was over, little purple?"

Yes, I want to say, but my tongue is too heavy. Too big. Too *unnatural.*

My words die in my throat as my vision goes black.

THIRTY-FOUR

Annika

I BLINK AND PAUSE AS THE WORLD COMES INTO A BLURRED focus.

I expect to find myself in my room, but the walls that greet me are entirely different.

Elegant modern wallpaper, a sophisticated sofa, a nightstand, an extravagant lamp.

What the…

All sleep vanishes from my eyes as I jump up in bed and pull the sheet to my neck, flinching at the sound of rustling clothes.

Where am I?

The last thing I remember is having that glass of champagne with Cecily and then falling…

Falling…

Into Creighton's arms.

No. Nope.

That one was a cruel dream.

Slowly, too slowly, I let go of the sheet and swing my feet onto the plush carpet.

I'm still in my dress, so that should be a good sign.

My gaze roams around the hotel-like room for some sort of a

clue, but I still come up empty. No idea what this place is, but it reeks of money and an ominous feeling.

I search for my bag, my phone, but they're nowhere to be seen. Even my smartwatch is gone.

Okay, don't panic.

Don't. Panic.

I open the door and step into an equally elegant hall filled with modern paintings. After walking a while, I reach a patio that overlooks a cozy living room downstairs.

My fingers latch onto the railing, using it as an anchor while I descend the glass stairs.

I don't think twice as I head to the entrance. To my surprise, the double doors aren't locked. When I open them, I slam into a hard chest.

For a moment, I think this is a continuation of the dream from earlier.

For a moment, I stop and stare as if I'm caught in a trance.

Gorgeous, absolutely haunting ocean eyes swallow me in their dark depths with a promise of complete destruction.

It's been a long time since I last saw Creighton in person, and being in his presence right now is nothing short of being shoved down from a height that's meant to kill.

It's being thrust into the fog and having no hope of finding a way out.

It's breathing but getting no air.

It's crazy how everything can change in the span of a month. There were times when I found Creighton overbearing, a little bit frightening, a little bit assholish, but this is the first time he feels... intimidating.

Like the type you'd deliberately change paths upon seeing to avoid being smashed by his disastrous energy.

He's in his usual jeans and hoodie. His now longer hair flops to one side, kissing his forehead.

I almost forgot just how tall Creighton is and how small I feel in comparison. How his broad shoulders block the sun and he becomes everything I see. Unlike the past, though, right now, the difference in height and physique feels downright threatening.

It's in the aura. In the way he stares at me with enough dispassion to dry up the blood in my veins and watch me as I shrivel and die.

I blink twice, but he's not disappearing. If anything, he gains more presence.

A *real* presence.

My heart beats wildly in my rib cage and I could swear he feels it through my skin and my clothes.

It dawns on me then.

At this moment where my breasts are crushed against his chest and my space is filled with his cologne.

This is *not* a dream.

It's more real than the breaths I'm inhaling and the air that's mixed with his distinctive clean scent.

I step back, not-so-subtly forcing some distance between us.

Creighton's brow dips from my breasts to my waist and down to where the dress stops above my knees.

It's a miracle I don't catch fire under his ruthless intensity before he slides his scalding attention back to my face.

"It's you," I murmur.

"You expected someone else?"

I'm not ready for the onslaught of his perfectly calm, deeply rich voice. That voice does unpleasant things to me, like turning me absolutely obsessed to the point where I attempted everything under the sun just so I could hear it again.

Including watching and rewatching some old videos in which I was bugging him to speak more than a few words.

But that's neither for here nor now.

I take another step back. "Where am I? Where have you taken me?"

His expression, cold and callous, gains a sinister edge. "Somewhere no one can find you."

"W-what?"

"We're on a faraway island no one can reach. Not even your father and his gang of serial killers."

My lips quiver, but I force myself to remain calm. "Where's Cecily? What have you done to her?"

"Probably back to catch her classes."

"You...made her trick me?"

"No force was involved. She agreed to help on her own, though she thought I only wanted to talk to you. I told her nothing about this plan."

My limbs tremble the more I stare at his lifeless eyes. It's like I'm looking at a stranger, a person without a core, a heart, or morals.

A being that's designed for vengeance.

That's all Creighton ever wanted, and that's the only thing he's actively pursued ever since he found out about my family's involvement in his tragic childhood.

I was and always will be a tool with which he'll use to exact revenge on Mom and Papa.

And although I figured that out a long time ago, this is the first time it's slapped me across the face with enough strength to cause a sting in my eyes.

It takes everything in me to speak in a composed tone. "I want to go home."

"This is the only home you'll have. Get used to it."

"Creighton...this is called kidnapping."

"And you shooting me is called attempted murder, but you don't see me putting a label on that."

I flinch as if I've been punched in the gut.

And it's not only due to his words. It's the dispassionate way he speaks with, the coldness that coats his skin, and the cruelty that radiates off him.

I don't recognize the man who stands in front of me. He's a mash of particles with no heart or soul.

And I need to get the hell away from him before he does something we'll both regret.

I let my gaze stray sideways in search of an escape.

The door is behind him, and as much as I want to use that obvious option, there's no way I'd win against Creighton in the physical department. Not only is he bigger than me, but he literally pummels people for sport.

I'm not ready for what happens next.

I've been so caught up in my plans to escape that I completely missed when he started advancing toward me.

The moment I look up, it's too late.

His body traps mine and his hand wraps around my throat. He squeezes enough that my complete attention homes in on him.

The grip is firm enough to freeze me in place, allowing me only enough air to inhale him, and fall irrevocably into him.

"You don't need to busy that pretty brain of yours with thoughts of escaping, because that won't be happening. You're mine now, little purple, literally and figuratively."

My nails dig into his wrist. "Creighton, stop this, please…"

"Don't beg when we still haven't gotten to that phase yet." His fingers stroke my throat with no ounce of warmth whatsoever. "I'm going to need you to be real obedient for me, can you do that?"

I purse my lips.

"Answer the question."

"I'm not your plaything."

"You're more than that. You're the subject of my vengeance, Annika. You shot me and there needs to be retaliation."

I don't see it, but I can hear the sound of my heart smashing to pieces. The heart that I thought died the moment I pulled the trigger is obviously not completely gone. It keeps scratching, tugging, and attempting to burst out of my chest.

So I was right.

I had a tiny hope that the time we spent together would at least mean something to Creighton, but I thought wrong.

He's blinded by revenge and will never see anything past it.

Despite the pain that's breaking me apart at that bitter realization, I won't stay to find out what he has in store for me.

I stare at his impassive eyes that I once used as an anchor while my calm voice carries in the air. "You kidnapped Nikolai and forced my brother to come get him, then you made him watch his best friend get his own throat sliced. You forced me to watch you stab my only brother while I had a gun pointed at you. While I was high on emotions. I begged you to stop, I begged *you*, Creighton, but you made me pull that trigger."

Tension rolls off his body in waves as his harsh breaths fill the space, snatching mine, suffocating them, forcing me to breathe intoxicated air.

"I didn't make you do anything. It was *you* who pulled the trigger. It was *you* who chose your family. If we were to go back in time, you would choose your family again, wouldn't you?"

I would choose to shoot myself.

But I don't say that. Because I need to end this fucked-up charade and make him let me go.

This situation isn't about him or me anymore. It goes way beyond the two of us, and too many people we care about are involved.

Like his father and mine, who'll definitely clash if either of us is hurt.

"You're right. I already shot that bullet and killed us with it. We can't go back in time, but we can remove ourselves from each other's lives."

His hold tightens on my throat until I think he'll choke me to death. "That won't be happening."

I see it then, the determination, the decision he's already made about this.

He's keeping me.

Nothing I do or say will change anything. He meant it earlier when he told me that I'm his both literally and figuratively.

No.

No, this isn't how it's supposed to go.

I'm already suffering the fallout of my actions and going crazy in my attempts to move on. I'll simply not allow him to ruin everything by self-destructing.

Because that's what's happening right now. He might think it's payback, but he's shattering himself in the process.

I don't think about it as I lift my knee and hit him in the balls.

The moment of stunned silence is all I need. When his hold loosens around my throat, I push him away, dart around him, and run outside.

I have no clue where I'm going, but if I find the main road, a car, or a person, I'll be able to leave.

The sound of waves reaches me first and then as I run, I notice a shore, a rocky path, and a driveway but there's no sign of any cars.

The house is near the beach.

Surely, there are other houses around.

I don't stop running, ignoring the pebbles scratching the soles of my feet.

If I don't leave, my family will be dragged into this, and I can't... I just can't be forced to choose again.

It'll kill me this time.

Hard footsteps sound behind me, sure and composed, before his rough voice reaches me. "It's useless."

"I'm going home!" I scream without looking at him. If I do, things can only make a turn for the worse.

His steps get closer and I yelp when his closed voice sounds near my ear. "Then you better run. If I catch you, it's over."

I jerk but I don't stop.

I don't look back.

And I certainly don't think.

I speed in the direction of the beach. Surely someone will be there, like how Brighton Island's beach was never empty, even during the windy, cold days.

My heartbeat picks up when my toes get buried in the white sand.

Aside from the tropical-like water and plants, there's no one in sight.

I whirl around, my back to the water as Creighton closes in on me. He looks bigger than a god and as dangerous as the devil.

We're supposed to be strangers again, enemies even, but no

amount of bullets could kill the memories between us. If anything, it made them jaded, edgy, and full of tension.

"Stop it." I raise both hands. "Or I swear I'll scream."

"Do it." His voice drops as he strides toward me. "*Scream.*"

"I'm not kidding."

"Neither am I."

With his every step forward, I take one backward.

"Help!" I yell at the top of my lungs until my throat gets scratchy. "Someone help me!"

Creighton remains unfazed by my calls, absolutely detached. The more I shout, the closer he comes, the coldness on his face matching freezing ice.

"No one can hear you," he says, keeping up the cat and mouse chase. "This is a private island."

"A *what*?"

"Private island. In the middle of nowhere. No one will be able to save you from me."

I jump when something cold hits my leg. The water. I'm at the shore now, the sea of an island at my back and this emotionless man in front of me.

And I know exactly which option I'm willing to take. I dash in the direction of the water.

"Don't," his voice calls behind me.

But I'm not listening as I keep going on and on, despite the chattering of my teeth and the sting of the salty water.

"Annika, stop." The authoritativeness in his tone would've brought me to my knees once upon a time.

Now, other things are at stake, so I ignore it.

Water reaches my waist but I keep pushing forward.

"Annika! It's deep on this end—"

His words are cut off when I take another step and find no sand. I fall into the water with a sudden yelp.

I'm fully submerged within seconds. I try to swim up, but it's like an invisible hand is pulling me into the depths of nowhere.

Bubbles explode from my mouth, and panic explodes beneath the surface. I've never been a good swimmer and always held on to a float in the pool, which I should've thought about when I chose the ocean.

Shit.

I kick my legs underwater and fling my hands up, but the more I push, the lower I sink.

The light coming from above dims into a dark blue and my vision blackens.

If I'd known this would be the end, I would've…done something different.

I would've—

A hand grips me by the elbow and hauls me to the surface. I cough and splutter, unable to get the air in my lungs fast enough.

My blurry vision is half camouflaged by my hair, but I manage to focus on the man who's gripping me by the waist. With one hand and bold strokes, he swims us in the direction of the shore.

His clothes are soaked, his hair sticks to his forehead, and a muscle clenches in his jaw.

It's unfair that he looks drop-dead gorgeous. That he drips with feral masculinity without having to do anything.

It shouldn't be allowed, not when I'm trying my hardest to make him cut ties with me.

Once we're in shallow water that reaches our knees, I try to pull free. Not only does he not release me, but he also stops in the middle of the water and slams me against his front.

The breath is knocked out of my lungs as I stare up at his raging eyes. "Creighton…"

"Shut the fuck up, Annika. I'm so close to being completely unhinged. Don't test me."

"What's wrong with you now?"

"What's wrong with me? I don't know. You tell me. Since you thought it was a brilliant idea to jump into deep waters."

A map of shivers covers my skin, and it has nothing to do with the air and is more related to the lash of his voice, the worry in it, the care that he probably doesn't want to show it.

My voice softens. "I didn't know it was that deep."

"Did I or did I not tell you to stop?"

"Well—"

"Answer the fucking question."

"You did," I whisper out of habit, then glare. "But you were blocking me. I had nowhere to go."

"And you never will." His lips slam against mine, and for a second, I'm stunned.

For a second, I think I'm back in that cruel dream's clutches and imagining Creighton's full lips on mine.

That thought is soon dispersed when he thrusts his tongue inside. One hand fists in my wet hair and the other shoves me against him by the waist.

Creighton doesn't just kiss me, he ravages and devours me. It's a clash of teeth, lips, and tongues. It's an animalistic claiming meant to remind me that I've always belonged to him.

I plant both palms on his chest, trying to push him away, trying with everything in me to put an end to this madness.

But he delves deeper, kissing me harder, feasting on me in ways I thought would never be possible again.

And I just can't fight him.

Physically, emotionally, or mentally.

Still, I manage to pull back, breathing heavily. "Don't... Creighton..."

"Don't what?" His grip tightens on my hair and his other hand cups my breast through the transparent dress and pinches an achingly hard nipple. "Touch you? Own you like you're mine?"

A zap of pleasure starts where he's touching me and ends between my thighs.

It's been so long. And no matter how much I've touched myself, no matter how many times I imagined his face and his ruthless touch, nothing could bring me the unbound ecstasy only he can trigger.

"Just stop whatever you're doing." I dig my fingers in his hoodie. "Let me go home."

"So you can be your parents' perfect little doll and marry whoever they pick for you?"

"What if I do? It's none of your business."

"None of my business?" His voice darkens in sync with his eyes. They've become dim now, a pure imitation of a starless night.

He twists my nipple so hard that I gasp, but he doesn't stop there. He tugs on my dress's zipper and yanks it off me and then the bra follows. His hands are quick, meticulous, and so savage that I'm out of sorts.

My dress and bra are thrown to the shore, but my panties don't have the same fate. He all but shreds them, letting the massacred pieces scatter in the ocean.

When he pinches my sensitive nipple again, it's skin to skin, flesh to flesh, and with so much command that I melt. I'm so lightheaded that the crash of the waves against my legs causes me to sway.

"Everything about you is my fucking business." He releases my hair to unzip his jeans and pull out his hard cock. "You might have thought it was over, but it's not. Far from it."

He hooks his hands beneath my thighs and lifts me up so that I have no choice but to wrap my legs around his waist and circle his neck with a hand.

The moment I search his eyes, he rams inside me in one go. My head falls on his shoulder from the force of it, coupled with a strangled sound.

It's been only a month, but it feels like a year.

He stays there for a bit, unmoving for a second as we breathe each other in, fall into the lull of us. The sound of the crashing waves echo around us as we dig our fingers into each, both literally and figuratively. Just when I'm falling into the moment, he thrusts all the way inside until I physically jerk.

Then he does it again, and again, ramming his cock inside me in a ruthless rhythm, fucking me, owning me.

Punishing me.

My head falls forward and I dig my nails into his back.

It's a useless attempt to hurt him as much as he's wrecking my world apart. He fucks me with enough command and assertiveness that I have no choice but to let it happen.

I want him with so much desire that drives me insane. I want him as wildly as he wants me.

"This cunt is mine. *You* are mine, Annika. Nothing and no one will change that. Not your father." *Thrust.* "Not your brother." *Thrust.* "Not even you."

He's like a madman. There's no stopping him and certainly no reasoning with him. He drives inside me with a power that I've never felt before, and that says something since he's always been intense in some way.

This time, he doesn't even need to inflict any pain. He's the pain that's brimming with pleasure.

The sliver of light in the middle of the darkness.

He's both day and night and I have no escape from his orbit.

"Creighton..." I moan, shoving a hand against his chest. "Slow down...I can't take this."

"You can. You always did."

"This is too much."

"You know what's too much? Thinking you can marry some sorry fuck after I've claimed you. After I put my fucking mark on you." He slides his hand up to cup my jaw, tilts it back, then bites on my throat. *Hard.* So hard that I gasp. "It's believing I'd ever let you go."

"But you hate my family," I sob the words that have been plaguing me, the words that make this pleasure so screwed up.

"I can still fuck you." His tongue darts out and he licks my tears as he whispers, "Remember this, Annika. There's never been a day where you haven't been mine."

Then he drives so deep that he hits my sensitive spot over and over.

And *over.*

The moment his teeth find the sensitive flesh of my throat again, a powerful orgasm hits me and I release enough noises to disturb any living creature around.

Creighton doesn't slow down, doesn't take it easy, and he certainly doesn't stop.

He goes on and on like a machine that's bent on destruction.

He fucks and spanks my ass. He pulls my hair and bites my neck, my shoulder, the top of my creamy breasts, anywhere he can reach.

By the time he stiffens and spills inside me, I'm spent.

Completely and utterly done.

"Mine," he growls against my lips as he devours them again, rips them with his teeth, and fucks them with his tongue.

It's a possessive kiss.

A declaration of a savage claim.

I can't help the fresh tears that slide down my cheeks.

I hate myself for wanting the man who only sees me as a form of revenge.

I hate myself for not trying harder to run.

But I will.

Sooner or later, I will end this ill-fated relationship. This time, without getting my family involved.

THIRTY-FIVE

Creighton

ANNIKA HAS BEEN SILENT EVER SINCE I CARRIED HER TO the house.

She didn't release a sound when I put her down in front of the shower, but she did close the door in my face.

The chances of me breaking that door and claiming her against the floor like a savage animal were close to one hundred percent, but I repressed the compulsion.

One, I didn't like the sad look in her eyes.

Two, I'm spiraling out of control.

I feel it, smell it in the air, and can sense it crashing against my rib cage.

When I first came up with this plan, I thought of owning her, making her pay. Taking my vengeance while keeping her.

And while that plan is still up and running, something's changed.

I didn't count on seeing her again. *Really* seeing her.

In her purple dress, dainty shoes, and looking like sunshine and unicorns. I was blindsided by her violet perfume. Always violets.

Violets. Violets. And more bloody *violets*.

They seep beneath my skin, ripping the tendons apart and settling in the marrow of my bones.

I didn't count on hearing her soft voice, moaning, begging me to slow down.

To let her go.

That won't be fucking happening.

I strip and step into the downstairs shower, letting the icy cold water wash over me.

Every nook of my body vibrates with the feel of her soft skin, the sound of her whimpers that might as well be singing lullabies to my beast.

And violets.

Fucking violets permeate the air, clashing with the smell of the sea.

I've been imagining her naked and sometimes bound to my bed ever since I woke up in the hospital.

One fantasy turned to a hundred, then a thousand, overlapping and spiraling out of control until I became unhinged.

Which is probably why I acted in pure caveman fashion when I fucked her so mercilessly just now.

But she's the one who wouldn't shut up and kept talking about leaving and entertained the thought of another man.

Another. Fucking. Man.

I slam my fist against the wall, the cold water doing nothing to dissipate my blazing libido or simmering rage.

After a few more futile attempts to calm the fuck down, I step out of the shower, put on some shorts, and storm upstairs.

I turn the knob to the bedroom, only to find it locked.

My fist clenches around the damn object, but I force myself to sound neutral. "Open the door."

Nothing.

I bang on the wooden surface. "I know you can hear me, Annika. Open up."

No answer.

"If you think a door can stop me…"

"Leave me alone!" she shouts, her voice on the edge before it turns brittle. "*Please.*"

I don't like how she sounds.

It's pulling on that corner in my heart that has her name splashed all over it.

I've never heard Annika so broken, but ever since she pointed that gun at me, she's been slowly but surely losing her spark, her cheerfulness, and what made her who she is.

She doesn't even post on social media anymore, and when she does, they're no longer those happy, sunshiny, life-filled photos. They're more about ballet practice, shelters, and others.

She's more interested in posting about the homeless and the people who volunteer with her—including an older-looking fucker who's often super-glued to her side.

And she actually smiles at him.

And she called him her sanctuary in one of her posts.

I contemplated killing him before I flew her out of the US, but that would have hindered this plan, so I went with a priority concept.

The wanker is still at the top of my shit list, though.

"You have until the count of three to open the door before I break it down." My voice sounds harsh, cold, and nonnegotiable.

The type of voice I had before I let her in, before I allowed her to have a piece of me that she conveniently decimated.

"I just need time alone," her muffled voice comes from the other side.

"One, two—"

I'm about to ram my shoulder against the door when it opens and she appears at the threshold.

All small and broken. All sad and fucking petite.

She's wearing a bathrobe, her face makeup-free, which makes her look younger, and her half-damp hair falls over her covered round breasts.

And my necklace.

She's still wearing the necklace I gave her for her birthday. When I saw it back on the plane, I nearly lost it. For some reason, I thought she'd try to erase every memory of me, but maybe that's not the case.

I expect rage at worst and annoyance at best, but when her bright blue-gray eyes meet mine, there's nothing there. They're aimless, dim, and absolutely muted.

They look creepily similar to my eyes when I first escaped that hellhole as a kid.

Back then, I didn't look in the mirror for months, because the reflection I saw in there was no different than a monster and it rattled the fuck out of me.

"Shouldn't you try to not hurt your shoulder...?" Her dispassionate words trail off when her vision zeroes in on the souvenir she gave me.

Her lips part, trembling as she studies the gash on my chest. It's a red, ugly hole that Mum and my nan suggested I get plastic surgery for.

A suggestion I promptly dismissed.

I'm glad I did, if not for anything else, then for the whirlwind of emotions that dance in Annika's eyes.

She's no longer numb, dull, and lifeless now that her feelings pour out in a splash of colors.

Her shaking hand reaches out for the wound, but I grab her wrist, stopping her halfway.

"Who gave you permission to touch me?"

She jerks, lips pushing and falling in an *O* as she trembles. "I..."

"You're what? Trying to finish what you started by actually killing me this time?"

"I never wanted to kill you. If I did, you'd be dead already. I told you I don't miss, but I tried to, even when I wasn't thinking straight." A sob tears out of her throat. "I only wanted to stop you."

Using my hold on her wrist, I push her back, my chest rising and falling in harsh breaths.

Annika stumbles backward and winces, her face scrunching as she lifts her foot off the ground.

I pause, and all the anger I'd planned to unleash on her dissipates into a much more prominent feeling.

The need to protect her.

The fuck is wrong with me? She shot me and all I want is to

remove anything that hurts her. All I want is to keep her safe from the world.

But not from myself.

I inspect her foot that she's resting on her calf. "What is it?"

"N-nothing."

"Annika, don't fuck with me. What's wrong?"

She stares up at me with those round eyes, so big and tormented. "I think I cut my foot earlier, but it's not a big deal—"

Her words end in a yelp when I carry her bridal style to the bed. The moment I drop her on the mattress, she stands up again.

"I-I'm really fine."

"Sit the fuck down."

At my order, she flops down on the bed and that's when I go to the bathroom and retrieve a first aid kit.

A strange feeling grips hold of me when I find her in the exact position I left her in, her eyes focused on the bathroom door.

I kneel in front of her and place her leg on my thigh to inspect the sole of her feet. Sure enough, there are some bloodied cuts, and while they're not too deep, they would definitely be a hindrance.

Due to her ballet passion, Annika never, and I mean *never*, allows her feet to get hurt. She told me I could flog and spank her anywhere, but her feet were off-limits. The closest I could get to them was binding her ankles.

So to see her this fucking careless about them makes me murderous.

I retrieve a bottle of oxygenated water and clean the cuts on both her feet and then start to apply ointment.

"Next time you hurt yourself, I swear to fucking God..." I trail off at the strained sound of my voice.

The more I touch her, the faster pain and fucking rage consume me.

I feel the tremor in her body before her soft voice fills my ears. "I didn't mean to. I only wanted to..."

"Escape," I finish for her. "That won't be fucking possible."

"My dad will come for me," she murmurs, but it doesn't sound like a threat, more like she's informing me of facts. "He'll find me and you, and when he does, this will end badly."

"This island isn't on the map, and I left all your belongings back in the States. He won't be able to locate you."

Silence stakes claim as I continue lathering the cream on her cuts without looking at her.

After a moment, her gentle voice reaches me again, all elegant and melodic and made for me. "What do you plan to do with me, Creighton?"

"Keep you."

"And then?"

"There's no then."

"How long do you intend to keep me?"

"There's no time limit."

"So we'll live on the island for the rest of our lives?"

"If need be."

"You can't do that." Her voice becomes panicky. "We both have lives, families, friends, a future."

"A future where you'll be married to someone else will not fucking exist, Annika." I shut the first aid kit closed, about to stand up and cool myself before I act on the dark thoughts rushing wildly in my head.

A gentle palm falls on my chest, stroking the healed bullet wound, touching, trembling, exploring. "Does it hurt?"

"It does." I grab her hand and slam it on the thundering organ next to it. "Right fucking here."

"I'm so sorry." She lowers herself so she's on her knees facing me and I'm greeted by the pained tears that roll down her cheeks. "I know nothing I say would undo what happened and no excuses would justify it, but I want you to know that I hated myself every day since then. I couldn't sleep, eat, or breathe properly and was only able to survive thus far after knowing you were safe. I'm so, *so* sorry, Creighton."

"Apologizing isn't enough." I dig my fingers into the back of her hand. "You have to make it up to me for the rest of your life."

She breathes heavily, the sound echoing in the air. "If I do, will you let go of your grudge?"

"Don't worry yourself about that."

Her eyes shine with that irritating defiance. "You can take your rage out on me all you like, but I won't allow you to use me to bring my family down."

"You don't have a choice."

She starts to stand up, but I shove her back against the mattress.

And before she can move, I fling the side table's drawer open and retrieve my ropes and special toys I prepared specifically for her.

Annika's eyes widen and she struggles against me, but it's futile. "I did nothing to be punished for."

"Let's count what you did wrong. Aside from shooting me, you left." I strap her hands to the bedpost. "You up and disappeared, leaving me for dead."

Her fight slowly withers. "I didn't want to. Papa made me."

"I'm sick and tired of your father." I move to her ankles, binding them to the foot of the bed.

She tests the ropes but knows better than to pull on them since they'd only tighten. "Is that why you're so mad? Because I left? I wasn't really allowed to visit you, but I wanted to, Creighton. If it were up to me, I would've never left your side. Even if I was locked up for it."

"Is that why you went back to the States ready to marry the first son of a bitch your father chooses for you?" I stand at the foot of the bed and finger a toy, then turn it on. "Is he the older fucker you always smiled at and called a sanctuary?"

"What? No—" Her words end in a moan when I thrust the toy deep inside her cunt and push the vibrator extension against her clit.

The belt of her bathrobe comes undone beneath my ministrations. She arches off the bed and the ropes pull her back down. A pink tit teases from beneath the fabric, the nipple puckering and tightening for attention.

But that sight is not enough.

Nothing is enough when it comes to this girl.

I'm plagued with this need to brand myself on and beneath her skin, so she can't breathe without feeling me.

So she's unable to *breathe* without me.

Unable to exist if I'm not there.

I want her to feel the fucking pain I felt when I woke up and found out she'd left.

I retrieve the plug and her eyes widen as she fights against the ropes. My movements are methodical as I coat it against the juices that are gushing out of her cunt.

It takes everything in me not to replace the toys with my aching cock. But it'll happen.

In time.

"Bet your arse missed being spanked, little purple."

A moan is all the response I get as I plunge the plug into her back hole. The sound turns to a whimper when I jostle it inside, on and on just to fuck with her.

When she's gasping, her skin becoming pink in preparation for an orgasm, I release the toy. "Do *not* come."

I engrave my order with a slap to her arse then I go to the wardrobe.

Annika writhes, trying and failing to create more friction due to her position, but her gaze follows me.

My fingers splay around a leather belt and I do a slow show of rolling it around my fist as I stalk back to the bed. Annika's struggles come to a halt, her lips part at the object, and a flush covers her skin in red.

"You think you can move on that easily? You think I'd let you?" I expose her perky tits and bring the belt down on the hard tips.

She convulses, arching before she's held down by the ropes.

"Ack—" Her expressive eyes meet mine, pleading, begging, imploring. "Don't...Creigh..."

"Don't call me that." Two successive whips come down on her breasts and pussy, causing her to yelp and sob. "You lost the right to call me that."

Tears stream down her cheeks even as her holes open and close and stretch and beg against the toys. I bring up the intensity enjoying the sight of her cum all over the mattress. I'm going to make her drench the sheets on and on until she's all spent.

I whip her in rhythm with the vibrator and she cries out as the orgasm is wrenched out of her.

"You didn't deserve that, but I will torture you with it." I hit her across the pussy and turn up the speed of the vibrator.

Every time an orgasm is dragged out of her, she breaks out in sobs, writhing and causing the binds to tighten against her porcelain skin.

Skin that's filled with my marks, all red and angry and mine.

Her face is flushed, streaked with tears and sweat that rolls down her neck and coats her body.

With each orgasm, she grows lethargic, all pumped up to the brim with an overload of stimulation. Every time I think she can't come anymore, she does, with a low moan and a jerking of her hips.

But not once does she beg me to stop. She takes it, every depraved part of it. Her eyes even shine with desire whenever I whip and force orgasms out of her.

This girl was made for me. Her submissiveness is everything I've ever yearned for. Everything I wanted.

But something about her eyes bothers me. They've gone back to that sad state, the absolutely dim and lifeless state.

I undo her bindings and she flinches every time my skin meets hers. Considering the number of orgasms I pulled out of her, any touch must feel like lightning.

Annika slumps on the bed, her lips parted and dry. She's definitely dehydrated. Is that the reason she's lifeless?

I turn off the toys and remove them from her.

She whimpers but doesn't attempt to move, drowning in a puddle of her own arousal.

I planned to finish this by having her admit she's wrong, and saying she'll choose me this time, but something tells me this isn't the right moment for that.

"Are you done?" she whispers in a hoarse, raw voice.

"I'm only getting started."

"Stop this madness."

"Beg."

"Please." She sniffles.

My muscles tighten and the healed bullet wound burns. "You're begging for the wrong reasons. You're begging for your family when you should be begging for me."

"I can't just cut myself off from them."

"You can. I'll make it happen."

Her chin trembles and fresh tears stream down her cheeks. "This isn't the Creighton I know. This isn't the man I fell in love with."

Her sadly delivered words and the anguish behind them wrap a noose around my neck.

She hates that she loves me—or *loved* me. And I want to bathe in the blood of whoever changed her mind.

Of whoever made her dig a knife, or more accurately, a bullet, into my chest.

"The Creighton you knew was shot dead by you."

"Creigh…"

"I told you not to call me that."

"But—"

"Shut up and listen well, Annika. You'll never get rid of me unless you shoot me again. But this time, make sure you aim straight at the fucking heart."

She cries harder.

I pretend her tears don't affect me as I hydrate her, make her eat, bathe her, and let her fall asleep cocooned in my chest.

With a knife in the bedside table. A knife she can grab at any moment and use to kill me for real.

If she does, then so be it.

Because I meant it. Death is the only thing that will keep me away from her.

THIRTY-SIX

Annika

A WEEK HAS PASSED.

A whole week of being trapped on an island where it's only the two of us.

A whole week of being tormented by Creighton, brought to my knees in submission, stuffed with toys, forced to orgasm. Denied orgasms.

All of it.

A whole week of me fighting and negotiating and pleading. I tried to reason with him, to tell him that not only are my parents worried sick but his must be, too.

I tried to knee him in the balls again and run, but that only got me whipped until I cried while I orgasmed, and then he fucked me.

He punished me and brought me to the edge, where the only thing I could do was moan his name and hate myself.

Fully. Thoroughly.

I hate myself because no matter how much I want to leave, I want to stay, too.

I want to sleep cocooned in his arms, I want to be fucked by him to the point of insanity. I want to wake up all deliciously achy and marked.

I want him to put those marks on me and then carefully slather them with ointment. He'd kiss them, too, making me shiver in both pleasure and self-loathing.

Because how can I enjoy the company of a man who vehemently refuses to let us start anew?

How can I find pleasure in this situation when my family is probably suffering because of this?

I had a nightmare about my mom's mental issues declining last night and couldn't go back to sleep.

After I tossed and turned, Creighton woke up and he fucked me back to sleep.

He's been an insatiable beast since we got to the island. No matter what I do, he'd be breathing down my neck like a pervert with the stamina of a sex demon.

If I jog on the shore in the morning, he joins me and then fucks me on the nearest rock.

If I try to cook, he annoys the hell out of me, standing near like the Grim Reaper, and then after the meal, he eats me out on the kitchen table.

Sometimes, that happens during the process of making food.

If I'm trying to practice ballet to keep in shape, he sits across from me, watching my every move like a hawk. Then he tears at my tights and mounts me on the floor.

That one ends up being the most animalistic, with my cute purple tulle shredded and scattered on the floor.

I have no clue how he got my stuff here, but he definitely had them from back in England. When I left Brighton Island, I didn't pack everything.

A part of me hoped I'd go back.

That part never counted on this depravity.

I swear this isn't what I meant when I told the girls that my fantasy was to be kidnapped.

Or maybe it is.

But his reasons have left a bitter taste at the back of my mouth.

I place lamb soup and fish and chips Creighton made on the patio table that faces the bright sea and he brings my salad.

We've fallen into this domesticated routine that would be a dream under different circumstances.

We do our morning jogs or swims together, sometimes fully naked. He fishes by the rock and I try to help but end up making it worse. Then we shower together. He watches me practice, makes lunch, and then we hike on the island's mountains to the point that every day is an adventure. We talk about everything, or more like I do and he reciprocates. We discuss school, life, art, like when we were on good terms, but he completely closes off when I ask him if we're going back.

"I can cook sometime, you know." I sit across from him and wince at the discomfort in my ass.

It's impossible to move without feeling him inside me anymore.

A fact he notices and appreciates, considering the slight twitch of his upper lip. "I'll do the cooking."

"I thought you didn't know how."

"That was a month ago. I learned how."

I nod and take a bite of my salad. "Can I have some fries?"

"Chips?"

"Chips. Fries, whatever."

"You don't have to ask." He pushes the whole plate in front of me.

"Wow. You actually gave up your food. The first time we met, you almost killed me because I asked for a taste."

That event feels like ages ago. I was infatuated with Creighton at first sight. He was silent, stoic, and the perfect recipe to pull on my heartstrings. Despite his broodiness, I yearned to bring out the man that lurked inside him.

I yearned to sink my claws into his skin and yank the secret part free.

But maybe I should've heeded his and everyone else's warning and stayed away. Maybe I wouldn't be in the situation I'm currently in.

"You were a stranger back then," he says, scooping up a handful of fries and practically mounding them on top of my salad. "You're not now, so you can have my food any day."

I try and fail not to be touched, especially knowing how much he loves food and that he certainly doesn't give it up, even to the people closest to him, including his brother and Remi.

Clearing my throat, I say, "I can't eat all of that. If I didn't know better, I'd say you want to make me fat."

"You've lost weight."

"Not since I got here." I release a long sigh. "How come we never run out of stuff?"

He remains silent, seeming preoccupied with eating, but he just doesn't want to answer me.

"Does someone bring supplies? When?"

Silence.

"When I'm asleep?"

More silence.

"Creighton!"

Still clutching both his fork and knife, he lifts his head while chewing slowly. His look is unnerving, so absolutely blank sometimes that I'm terrified of the depths it hides.

Sometimes, he looks at me like he won't let me leave his side, ever, and if I try to, things will get ugly.

A secret part of me likes that. Too much. It scares me.

"Yes?"

"Do you have someone who comes over?"

"Not yet. I have a stock full of food that will last us for a few months. But even if we run out, you don't have to worry about it. Needless to say, if you have any plans to escape, you might want to abandon them."

My lungs deflate with a long breath as I let my fork stab into the salad without bringing anything to my mouth.

"Can I at least call my mom and tell her I'm okay?"

"So your father can track the call?"

"I'll just text her then."

"No. There are no phones here."

I release a groan of frustration. "What if one of us gets injured or sick and we have to call for help?"

"I'll think about that when it happens." He pours himself a glass of wine. No kidding, he drinks wine. At fucking twenty.

He's like an old man sometimes, I swear.

But I don't say no to a drink, so when he pours me a glass, I take a sip, too.

The bland stuff is starting to grow on me. Or maybe his family only keeps premium wine, because I never thought I would like it until now.

Creighton leans back in his chair twirling the glass of wine and watching me with a little smile.

I stuff my face with salad. "Why do you look so pleased with yourself?"

"Why shouldn't I?"

"Gee, I don't know. Because you kidnapped me?"

"You like it here."

"I do, but I don't want to be trapped in this place for the rest of my life."

"It's better than being surrounded by the outside world."

Oh.

It dawns on me then.

The outside world, the truth about his origins and my parents' involvement, is what tore us apart, so Creighton has purposefully chosen a place where they can't reach us.

I don't know if I should be touched or appalled by that fact.

"How about your parents?" I whisper. "They must miss you."

"They understand. Dad encouraged this plan."

"He *what*?"

Creighton lifts his glass in the form of a *cheers*. "Best Dad of the Year Award goes to Aiden King."

"Wow. I thought he might be unhinged from the time we talked, but now I'm sure."

One of his brows rises. "You talked?"

"More like he threatened me, but Papa threatened him, too, almost killed him, actually, so I pretended to faint and Papa had no choice but to take me back. He totally didn't believe my performance, though." I sigh. "I'm afraid some sort of a world war will happen if they meet again."

"Which is one more reason not to go back."

"Then we'd just be running."

"So what?"

I release a frustrated breath. "We can't just do that, Creighton. We have a life back at home. People waiting for us. People who love us."

He eats in silence and I think he's dismissed me, which is his modus operandi whenever he wants to change the subject.

I eat, too, feeling my heart shriveling up and dying inside my chest.

He really won't look past the grudge. It's already shaped who he is, and the more I try to make him get rid of it, the harder he holds on to it.

"What's his name?" The question he asks in a low tone catches me off guard.

"Who?"

"The man in black who's by your side all the time, looks twice your age, and whom you smile at. Constantly."

I frown. "Yan?"

Full-blown calculation covers his features. "*Yan*. Russian, I assume?"

"Yeah, didn't I mention him before? We're so close and he's a badass. A former member of the elite Russian Special Forces, ranked among the first, and one of the most merciless assassins in the Bratva."

"We will see how strong he is when I pummel him to death."

My lips part as the realization dawns on me and I burst out laughing.

He's jealous of him.

Creighton is jealous of Yan.

A dark look shutters in his unique ocean eyes. "What are you laughing at?"

"I'm sorry, but this is just too funny," I say, still fighting the remnants of my laughter. "Yan is Papa's second-in-command."

"And? Why is that information funny? If anything, it makes me hate your father even more for bringing this Yan into your life."

"My Tchaikovsky, are you for real?"

"I told you to quit worshiping that dead man."

I suppress a smile. "Yan is like my favorite uncle, totally more approachable than Kolya and Boris."

"There are more of them?"

"We have an entire army of guards. But don't worry, I was never interested in them in that sense. One, they're way older. Two, Papa would skin them alive. Also, he hates Yan with a passion."

"Why?"

"Because he's Mom's best friend and he kind of doesn't like that. Yan won't stop provoking him about it, though, so the whole situation is fun to watch."

"If your father dislikes him so much, why doesn't he get rid of him?"

"Because Papa knows how much Mom needs a friend." I grin. "I'm telling you, Yan will have a field day when he knows both you and Papa are jealous of him."

"I am not jealous."

"Yeah, right. Wait a minute, how did you see the picture I posted with Yan?"

He remains silent and flat-out ignores me by drinking from his wine.

"You don't have social media. Did you stalk me through Remi's account or something?"

"I tried, but he found out about it and exposed me in front of everyone in his super dramatic way."

I laugh. "I can imagine that. It must've been entertaining."

"No, it wasn't. And Remi is not *that* funny."

"He's hilarious. Don't be jealous."

He narrows his eyes on me but says nothing.

"Then how did you stalk me? The only alternative is through the others' accounts, but I doubt they would give you their phones unless...you made an account yourself?"

Silence.

I jump up from my seat and round the table to come to his side. "You did!"

"Sit down and finish your food."

"No, this is way more important. Does everyone else know you have a form of social media? What's the handle? Your profile picture? Your first post? Bio? I want to know all the things—"

My words die in my throat when he grabs me by the wrist and forces me to sit down. This time on one of his thighs so that I'm practically riding it.

Heat blossoms where my panties meet his jeans and spreads all over my skin.

His slightly stubbled chin rubs against my cheek as he whispers in dark words, "I said, sit down and eat."

"If I do, will you tell me your handle?" I don't recognize the thickness in my voice.

"That's not important anymore, considering we're not leaving."

"Or that's what you think."

His eyes, those gorgeous eyes that I'm sure once belonged to a fallen angel, turn to slits. "What is that supposed to mean?"

"Oh, nothing."

"Annika." I feel the vibration of his warning before I hear it and help me, Tchaikovsky, his authoritative voice is such a turn-on.

"I'm just saying." I shrug and grab a fry.

I'm going to convince him to let go of his grudge, even if it's the last thing I do.

And if I fail, then let it be the last thing I do.

"You have until the count of three to tell me or so help me God..."

I jump up from his lap and dart in the direction of the house. Adrenaline pumps in my veins at the thought of playing a cat and mouse game.

"Catch me first."

Creighton's eyes fill with unhinged animalistic power. The type of power that made me fall for him in the first place.

That's *my* Creighton.

The only Creighton that should be allowed to reign.

The other one who's bent on destroying us both is an asshole and I need to figure out a way to defeat him.

"Sure you want to play a hunting game, little purple? I always win."

"And I never lose."

Despite my confident tone, the moment he strides in my direction with that dark expression, thrilling fear courses through my veins.

I squeal, then turn around and run.

THIRTY-SEVEN

Annika

MY SPINE JERKS UPRIGHT AT THE SOUND OF EACH OF HIS strides.

They're slow, and measured, but they catch up to me in no time.

I'm not even one step inside the living room when I'm jerked off the floor, by my waist.

Hot breaths tickle my ear when he whispers, "You're fucked, little purple."

Red lava courses through my body and I fight with everything in me. I wiggle, trying to escape his steel arms.

While simultaneously wanting to fall into them.

"The more you push me, the harder I punish you." He throws me against the sofa. "Strip."

My breathing shatters and fogs against the leather of the sofa, but I stare at him over my shoulder. At his larger-than-life physique, at the ruthless virility behind it.

He's the man of my dreams and there will never be a day where I'm not attracted to him.

He lifts his T-shirt over his head, and I take in the veiny hands with long fingers and soak in the view of his rippled muscles and god-like physique.

A tinge of pain flashes through me at the sight of his bullet wound, a wound I gave him that neither of us will forget for the rest of our lives.

Me, because hurting him was worse than hurting myself.

Him, because the wound will remind him of how much he wants vengeance.

"If I have to repeat myself another time, things won't end well for you."

I turn around, propped up on my elbows, and meet his darkened gaze. I must be selfish, because all I want is to get lost in this moment. "Make me."

A low grunt slips from his mouth before he's on me. His fingers latch onto my throat and he uses it to haul me up, nearly lifting me in the air.

His hold isn't threatening, but it's controlling, and I have no choice but to look at him and drown in those eyes I thought I'd lost.

"As I said. Strip," he repeats again. "And that's ten."

My lips part. "You want me to strip in this position?"

"You don't want it to become twenty, now do you?"

My shaky fingers undo the zipper of my dress and I push the straps away until the piece of clothing hits the carpet.

Creighton's gaze falls to my lace bra and panties and he grunts. "Fucking purple."

I love how much I affect him.

The way he looks at me like he'll never look at anyone the same way.

The way he wants me with abundance and refuses to see anything past it.

"All of it, Annika."

It takes me several moments to unhook my bra, partly because of my unsteady hands and partly because of his hungry gaze.

When I take more time than needed to pull off my panties, he bunches the material in his fist.

"No, not Simone!"

A muscle clenches in his jaw but he pauses. "Who the fuck is Simone?"

"Simone Pérèle. The lingerie brand. Don't rip it." I push his hand away and try to finish the task.

The brute all but tears it to pieces.

"Creighton!"

"I'll buy you another one." His gaze darkens as he does a long sweep of my nakedness.

It's crazy how my body comes alive under his attention. How everything just...falls into place.

He doesn't need to touch me to provoke this feeling of irreversible belonging.

I was his even when I thought we were over.

I was his when I was trying to move on.

I'll always be his.

Just like he'll always be mine.

His free hand strokes my tight nipples, making me moan, then he pinches one with sensual brutality. His palm slides down, over the red fading lashes he left on my stomach. I hiss when he presses on them and then he moves to the handprints on my ass and cups me with it.

I get on my tiptoes, both due to the dull ache and the thrill of being utterly owned.

He wiggles the butt plug that he shoved up my ass this morning and I bite my lip.

"I bet this hole is all stretched and ready for me to claim it, isn't it?"

My teeth sink further into my lip when he glides his fingers from my ass cheek to the throbbing wetness between my legs.

The slap on my pussy comes so fast and without warning that I yelp and push farther into him.

"Shh, we haven't even gotten started yet." He slaps me again and thrusts three fingers inside me at the same time.

The friction from the pain creates a dizzying rhythm I can't keep up with. A hurricane of emotions that starts where he's touching me and spreads all over my skin.

His hold on my throat keeps me immobile so that he can do whatever he pleases.

I grab onto his bicep, not because I need balance, but more due to the inherent need to touch him. I'm as desperate for him as he is for me.

I want to be owned by him.

Only him.

"Do you feel how much your cunt is swallowing my fingers, little purple? Hear that sucking sound it's making to welcome me home?" His rhythm intensifies. "Because this is my home, *you* are my home, and I'll make you admit I'm yours."

A moan is the only answer I give. It's kind of hard to speak when spurts of pleasure shoot inside me, building, heightening, and wrecking me.

"You'll have no other home but me." He curls his fingers and thrusts. "You won't belong to anyone else but me, are we clear?"

My eyes droop and I let go, chasing the orgasm, the pleasure, that only his ruthlessness can bring.

"Are we fucking clear, Annika?" he repeats, his face a few inches away from mine and his fingers stopping their maddening rhythm.

I breathe harshly, but still have enough brain capacity to mutter, "This isn't the way to go about becoming my home, Creighton."

"Wrong answer." His eyes darken to become a deep hue of blue, a shade so terrifying, I'm rooted in place.

He wrenches his fingers out of me, and I resist the disappointing sound that's trying to claw its way out.

And then he pushes me back with his hold on my throat. My calves hit the edge of the couch, and I stumble backward, but before I can hit the cushion, he pulls me over and whirls me around.

I yelp as I fall to my knees and my achy breasts meet the cold surface of the leather. With Creighton's hand on my nape, fixing me in place. I don't see him, but I feel his presence magnifying, becoming absolutely frightening.

My body goes limp, and I'm not sure whether it's because of my survival instinct or due to pure unhinged anticipation.

The butt plug jostles before he wrenches it free, forcing a sharp moan out of me.

And then I feel something hard against my wetness. His dick. He's lubricating his cock with my arousal and I don't know why I find that so hot. More juices pour out of me, coating him and my inner thighs.

Creighton drives two fingers inside my back hole, causing me to scoot across the couch. I'm so stretched that I can hardly breathe or think.

"You've always been so tight, so small and breakable. No matter how many toys and plugs I shove inside this hole, it's barely stretching." He accentuates his words with merciless pounds of his fingers in my back hole and the up and down of his cock against my folds, teasing my opening but scarcely sliding in before coming back out.

Up.

Down.

Thrust.

Down.

Up.

Up—

I think I'll come from the torturous sensation alone. The shallow thrusts in my core overlap with the ruthless ones in my back hole until I'm lightheaded.

He's all I can focus on. His clean scent, large presence, and warmth.

It's his hand, all veiny and strong. His cock, all hard and ready to wreak havoc inside me.

It's everything about him.

Creighton keeps up the merciless, erotic rhythm. He thrusts, glides, strokes, and spanks. He grabs me in a figurative chokehold and I'm bucking my hips, writhing, panting, and whining.

Demanding that he take me.

Own me.

Make me feel alive the only way he knows how.

He removes his fingers and slaps my ass three consecutive times. A moan rips out of me as pleasure mixes with the mild pain.

And just when I think I'll come, he drives his cock inside my virgin hole.

The world stills as my earlier pleasure dims to excruciating pain. It doesn't matter that he's been prepping me for this or that he spent a lot of time stretching my hole or lubricating himself.

The fact remains, Creighton is huge and his cock shouldn't be anywhere near any back entrance.

It hurts, burns, and is downright suffocating.

Why do people love anal? This is torture.

I writhe and gasp and try to find reprieve from his savage hold on me.

Creighton doesn't thrust inside me, but he doesn't pull out either. His fingers dig into the flesh of my nape. "Relax. Don't push me out."

"I can't." Tears fill my lids as I strain. "It hurts. So much."

"Shhh. Don't fight me." He soothes, grabbing my hip, stroking all the way to my side, then my stomach, then to my back. His fingers on my neck draw comforting circles, all gentle and caring.

A trait that's not usual for him. Yes, he can be caring, but only after sex, not during.

He told me so himself once, that he knows how to take, and doesn't know how to give, which is why he's never considered relationships.

No clue if it's that knowledge, the fact that he's giving me this type of care so naturally or his appeasing touch, but I find myself relaxing, and my muscles loosen, slowly adjusting. I choose to focus on just how full he makes me.

So very full.

"Such a good girl," Creighton's deep voice might as well be touching me too. Or maybe it's that word, because I'm dripping between my thighs.

He holds my nape with the hand that was stroking my side and lowers the other to tease my clit.

The arousal that I thought had disappeared earlier returns with wrecking force.

When he starts rocking his hips, I fall into the slap of his groin against my ass, into the sounds of grunting, moaning, groaning. Slapping and slapping and slapping.

Sweat coats my skin and I melt into his touch, into his presence.

"That's it." His rhythm is slow, pleasurable. "You're taking my cock so well. You feel so good. So tight. So fucking mine."

A moan rips out of my throat and all the tension from earlier disappears. Raw, gritty pleasure pools between my thighs and I rock my hips, demanding more.

"You want me to fuck you harder? Want me to take your ass and ram into your virgin hole until you're unable to sit for days?" he asks, voice oozing with dark lust as his thrusts deepen. "Want me to tear into you and claim you as mine? Because that's what you'll always be, Annika." *Thrust.* "You can shoot me and run. You can push me and leave." *Thrust.* "But you are *my* girl, and you'll remain my girl despite your fucking parents." *Thrust.* "I'm the only home you'll ever have. My bed is the only bed you'll ever sleep in, so the next time I say you're my home, you say I'm yours, too."

I gasp and whimper and moan, unable to take in the load of emotions he's arousing.

Lust, despair, and sadness.

Complete utter sadness that stabs my bones, but I choose to fall into lust instead.

I choose to fall into the feeling of having him completely owning me.

Body, heart, and soul.

Pleasure shoots inside me in waves, starting where we're joined, where he's torturing my clit, and spreads through my whole body. The harsh slide of my hard nipples against the leather heightens it to the point of eruption.

The fact that his hold on my nape prevents me from fighting this, even if I wanted to, adds a sense of animalistic pleasure.

"Tell me you'll stay." He grunts from behind me as the slaps of flesh against flesh echo in the air.

Every hit on the welts on my ass causes me to drip into his hand.

Every inhale is filled with the smell of him, me, and sex.

Of us.

Still, I shake my head slowly, as much as his hand allows, and Creighton slaps my clit.

The hit is so sudden that I come in a long flood of…*holy shit.*

My eyes widen. Please don't tell me I peed myself.

Creighton becomes feral at the wetness that pours out of me and thrusts in with animalistic force.

I close my eyes and chase my orgasm, rocking my hips and adjusting to his rhythm.

He comes deep inside me with a growling, "Mine."

He doesn't seem done, though. After he pulls out, he coat my ass and thighs with his cum, as if he's marking me for the whole world to see.

When he finally releases my nape, I don't turn around and, instead, remain in the same position. In fact, I wish the world would open up and swallow me.

"Annika?"

I bury my face in the leather, my voice coming out muffled. "Leave me alone."

"Look at me."

I shake my head in the sofa, trying to ignore the process of my heart shriveling and dying.

"I won't repeat myself another time. Look at me."

I slowly do, shame and tears clinging to my eyes. "Can't you just leave me alone to deal with the fact that I peed myself?"

He frowns. "What are you talking about?"

"Just now when you… Ugh…give me a moment." A slow smile lifts his lips, and he looks so gorgeous that I want to slap him. "What are you smiling at?"

"You didn't pee, you squirted, and it was the hottest thing I've ever seen."

My cheeks heat. "Oh."

Hearing him call me the hottest thing he's ever seen makes me want to do it all over again. But maybe it only happens with strong orgasms.

A low gasp rips out of me when he lifts me in his arms. "Now, let's have a shower so I can fuck you again."

"But I'm so sore."

"Not in the cunt."

I release a long breath as his large strides eat up the whole distance to the stairs. Despite the peaceful moment, something still nags at me.

"I meant it, Creighton. I'm not staying."

His jaw clenches, but he soon schools his features. "I'll convince you otherwise."

My body falls slack against his. "That's what I thought I could do, too, ever since we came here. I thought I could convince you to let bygones be bygones, but that's not possible, is it? Aren't we both just fooling ourselves at this point?"

"Shut up."

It's two words. Merely two words and yet they hold so much punch that I tremble in his arms.

"Please…" I cradle his cheek, kiss his temple, his ethereal eyes, the ridge of his straight nose, the fullness of his lips, anywhere my mouth can find. "Please let go of your grudge, Creighton. Do it for yourself. Let that little kid go and stop being trapped in the past."

He doesn't say anything, doesn't even acknowledge me, and I want to cry.

Because I know, I just know that I've failed to change his mind, and now we're just on a path of self-destruction.

"I hate you right now," I murmur.

"I don't give a fuck."

"I wish I'd never loved you. I wish I could turn back time and unlove you."

A cruel smirk tugs on his lips. "But you can't. You love me, Annika. You never stopped."

"That might be true, but I will find a way to stop." I let my arms fall to my lap. "I'll never love a man who's intent on hurting my family."

THIRTY-EIGHT

Creighton

ANNIKA HAS SHUT HERSELF OFF FROM ME EVER SINCE I fucked her against the sofa. With my hand around her nape and my cock tearing through her back hole.

That was two days ago.

Two days of constant silence and cold shoulders.

She hasn't spoken a whole sentence to me since and the best thing I've gotten have been monosyllabic replies.

She hasn't run with me on the beach.

Hasn't even practiced her sacred ballet.

Hasn't touched food unless I force her to eat.

Silent treatment.

But this is completely different from when I wouldn't speak. That was part of my character, but whatever Annika has chosen to practice has nothing to do with her personality.

No one would accuse an annoyingly cheerful person like her of being quiet, but that's exactly what she's been the past couple of days.

She's been slowly but surely falling into a dark tunnel that I can't reach inside of.

Sighs have become her signature language and a lost gaze has been her standard look.

Every time I've tried to talk to her, she turns her face the other way. When I threatened to punish her, she told me to, "Do as you wish."

Whenever I've touched her, she pushes me away and tells me not to put my hands on her anymore.

I've been so tempted to fuck her until she screams my name so she knows not to pull this stunt anymore, but something stops me.

The mixture of disgust and indifference on her face.

Lately, it's veering more toward indifference.

People often say that hate is the most loathsome feeling, but that's because they've never been on the receiving end of apathy.

When the person who holds my world in the palm of her hand acts like I mean nothing.

Like I don't exist.

At first, I gave her space, tried not to push her too far, and thought she'd eventually come around.

Usually, there's no way in fuck Annika would stop talking. It's part of who she is, and the reason she got under my skin in the first place.

But the more time I've given her, the deeper she's withdrawn into herself.

And I need to put an end to it.

I open my eyes with the very intention of doing just that. Today, I'm going to shake the fuck out of her and make her talk, even if I have to resort to drastic methods.

Doesn't matter what lengths I have to go to in order to get actual sentences out of her.

I trace the spot beside me and freeze when my hand meets cold sheets. My eyes fly open, and sure enough, Annika is nowhere to be seen.

She tried to fight sleeping beside me at the beginning, but I wasn't having it, so she just lay stiffly beside me. It was either that or I'd sleep curled all around her.

We've kept that routine every night. Only, she's not here now.

I spring up from bed, pull on shorts, and throw on a T-shirt as I scan the room for her. The scent of violets permeates my nostrils, but they're not as strong or as prominent as when she's in my arms.

"Annika?" I call and head downstairs to the kitchen, to where she practices ballet in the hall, and then to the small library where she reads sometimes, or more accurately, makes me read to her since she's lazy to do it herself.

However, there's no sign of her.

My body tightens and a pungent taste fills the back of my throat. It's the closest I've ever felt to...panic.

Even back then, back when my mother hung from the ceiling, and I couldn't get air to my starved lungs, I didn't feel panic. I had an otherworldly determination to breathe.

I needed to fucking breathe.

Which was why I crawled and crawled and crawled.

I'm running now, down the street and onto the beach. She's not there.

Fuck.

She can't possibly go to the small airport at the other side of the island without a car. And she doesn't even know where it is in the first place.

Unless...she picked another way to leave.

My blood pumps harder and faster as memories of when she rushed into the ocean during a moment of despertion slam back into me.

No, no...

The clouds condense in the sky turning dark gray in full sync with my mood.

My breathing becomes deeper, less controlled, and absolutely chaotic.

"Annika!" I yell, but my voice is stolen and broken by the vicious wind.

The more I run and call for her, the less the chances of finding her seem to become.

Droplets of rain line the distance before it's proper pouring. Giant waves crash and shatter on the shore displaying the anger of the ocean. The tropical island is soaked in a second and so am I.

But I don't stop running, battling the wind, and scanning every nook and cranny.

I'm about to swim into the deadly waves in search of her when I see her.

Annika stands at the top of the rocky shore, arms spread wide and head thrown back. The rain has soaked her black dress, a color she's been wearing the past two days, and has glued it to her petite frame that's being swayed by the wind.

I storm in her direction, pumped by the worst-case scenarios that play in my head. For a second, as she sways violently, I think the wind will steal her away before I reach her.

That she will fall and drown, and I'll lose her for good.

You've already lost her. You just refuse to admit it, a bloody bastard who lives in my brain says, but I shut him out with plans to murder him later.

The moment I'm about two meters behind her, she turns around abruptly.

Streaks of her hair stick to her pasty pale neck, her cheeks are colorless, her lips are nude, and her eyes are so dim, I'd kill someone if it meant splashing color into them.

Including myself.

The rain soaks her, coming down so hard that she's almost blurry.

"What are you doing here?" I take a step forward and she takes a step back.

Toward the fucking edge.

I do it again and she does the same, her eyes never leaving mine.

"What the fuck are you doing?" I strain, the words nearly ripping my vocal cords on their way out.

She says nothing, and I have to inhale and exhale a few times to keep from reaching out and choking the fuck out of her.

"Whatever it is you're upset about, we can talk about it." I soften my voice—as much as I'm able to soften it under the circumstances. "Just come here, little purple."

Her lips tremble and a flash of light rises in the depths of her eyes before it's pushed right down.

She shakes her head.

"I swear to fuck, Annika—" I cut myself off and release a long breath, summoning patience I don't feel. "What do you want?"

"I want to go home," she says easily, assertively. The first sentence she's spoken in days is dedicated to her fucking parents.

"Anything but that."

She takes another step back. This time, her eyes are so lifeless, she looks like she's in a casket.

"Annika, stop!"

"*You* stop!" she yells back. "I'm tired. I'm so fucking tired of this, of *you*. You're not the Creighton I know. You're not the Creighton who made me feel safe and loved, you're not the Creighton who gave me the courage to go after what I loved. Creighton would never hurt me like this, he wouldn't rip my heart open over and over again no matter how much I beg him to stop. It's like I'm stuck with an imposter and I hate it. I hate it so much."

I grind my back teeth together and my jaw clenches so hard that I'm surprised no tendons are snapped.

"Is that why you refuse to talk to me or let me touch you? Because you think I'm an imposter?"

She nods.

I can hear the shattering sound of my world splintering to pieces. Pieces so small, I will never be able to find them, let alone mend them together again.

When I first brought Annika to this island, I thought we'd find what we once had. Yes, she fought me a little, but she also laughed and fooled around. She danced for me, flirted, and sighed contently in my arms. She loved laying her head on my lap and looking at my face when I read for her and then demanded more.

It felt as if she still loved me.

When she apologized for shooting me, I believed her.

I believed that she had to make a choice, but the bitter truth is that she'll never choose me over her family.

It's probably unfair for me to make her do that, but I wanted her to pick me like she picked her brother that time.

I wanted it to be *me*.

I just never thought that my fixation and my plan to bring us close would push us further apart. I never thought I'd rob her of light and leave her as this broken person.

She looks nothing like my Annika.

There's no trace of her cheerfulness, the constant mischievousness and innocence in her eyes, or the energy that bubbles from her pores.

She might have physically shot me, but I killed her.

And there's only one way to bring her back to life.

Even if it means sacrificing my own in return.

"Okay," I whisper.

Her brows crease. "Okay?"

"I'll take you home."

"You...you will?"

"Have I ever lied to you?"

She shakes her head frantically, some of the light seeping back to her eyes. Slowly but steadily.

Fuck.

The knowledge that I nearly broke her spirit makes me want to shoot myself and, this time, never wake up.

That would be better than hearing the sound of my crumbling insides or witnessing her live without me.

It'd fucking rip me apart.

"Now, come down from the edge." I offer her my hand, but she stares at it suspiciously.

We remain like that for a moment, her gaze sliding from my face to my hand and back again.

"Annika."

"Yeah?"

"It's raining."

"I know."

"Dance with me."

Her eyes widen, the blue and gray clashing for dominance. Despite her constant nagging about her hair and clothes, Annika loves when we dance in the rain. It brings out memories of our first date and kiss. Of the time I decided she'd become mine for good.

Her chin trembles and so does her voice. "But you don't dance."

"I do with you."

"I don't like the rain."

"You do for me." This time when I nod at my extended hand, she takes it.

I tug her so forcibly that she lands against my chest and her small palms fall on my shoulders. My hand grabs onto her waist and we sway slowly to the sound of the rain.

We're pressed against one another so closely that I want to stop time right at this moment. Lately, whenever we're this close, she pushes back or tries to put as much distance between us as possible.

But right now, she stares up at me with expectant eyes, eyes so full of light, I want to kick myself and throw my body into a ditch for ever tainting her with my darkness.

These eyes are only meant for light.

We continue swaying slowly, gently, and she doesn't stop staring at me. Whenever the rain gets in her eyes, she blinks it away to watch me closely, as if wanting to peel open my exterior and peek inside me.

"Does this mean you'll forget about the past?" she murmurs hopefully, expectantly.

And I hate to crush that hope, or decimate it, but that's exactly what I have to do to give her a new beginning.

One where I'm not tarnishing her life.

I was always meant to break Annika Volkov. I just didn't know I'd be the one broken instead.

"I can't erase my past."

Her feet come to a halt as everything shakes—her chin, her body, her lips. "What about your present and future?"

"I've already lost those."

"That's not—"

Her words are cut off when a commotion erupts on other end of the beach.

I frown.

No one is supposed to be here. This island is owned by Grandpa Jonathan and only he and Dad use it whenever they need a holiday. But they wouldn't come over, considering they both know I'm here.

Unless they decided to come uninvited. Maybe Mum and Nan pressured them into bringing them here to see me?

No.

Something is wrong about this.

"Stay here," I tell Annika and start to take the road down.

When I turn around to make sure she didn't go back to the rocky shore, I find her hot on my heels.

"What?" she asks. "I want to know what's going on."

It's useless to try to stop her and we don't have time anyway. The rain has stopped as abruptly as it started by the time we reach the beach.

Several men in black patrol the whole area like some special agent soldiers.

I don't hear footsteps, but I hear Annika's shriek as I'm hit from behind.

Pain explodes in the back of my neck and I fall to my knees. My wrists are wrung behind my back as a Russian-accented voice mutters, "Got him, Boss."

When I lift my head, I find none other than the man who murdered my childhood and bathed in its blood.

The man who gave Annika life.

Adrian Volkov.

And he's holding a gun to my temple.

THIRTY-NINE

Annika

I T'S STRANGE HOW THE WORLD CAN FLIP UPSIDE DOWN IN A matter of minutes.

A few moments ago, I started hoping again, pining, dreaming of convincing Creighton to give up on his vendetta.

And that was after two days of nightmarish, bleak surrender. Due to his complete inflexibility, my heart broke to pieces. I lost all hope and became a shell of my former self.

The thought of him turning into this heartless person who only sees vengeance has been ripping me apart and I couldn't withstand the torture. So imagine my surprise when he finally listened.

He stood there and heard me out.

He didn't attempt to antagonize me. He was even…scared. It was the first time I've seen that fear in his eyes.

Hell, even when I pointed a gun at him, he wasn't afraid. He was more like resigned.

He said he'd let me go home.

He embraced me in his safe arms and danced with me under the rain.

We were going somewhere and now we aren't.

Now, he's being held down by Kolya's massive hand as he stands like a wall behind him and Papa points a gun at his forehead.

And the worst part is, he looks ready to kill him, and not just in a normal way, no. This is the second time I've witnessed Papa's detached murderous face. The first was during my attempted kidnapping. His face is set, lips thinned, and his eyes are so dark, they're unable to reflect the light.

I've always known Papa killed people, but this is the first time I've seen him as a killer.

A cold-blooded, ruthless killer.

His men circle us with methodical stratagem, all tall, dressed in black, and with assault rifles slung over their chests. It's like they're out to snuff out a rival organization, not a simple college student.

I search every face, but there's no sign of Yan or Boris—the only two who might get on my side. They were probably left behind to protect Mom.

"You have the audacity to kidnap my daughter?" Papa's calm words reverberate in the gloomy air, but the amount of rage that bubbles beneath the surface leaves me panting.

Creighton stares him straight in the face, his gorgeous features sharpening, showing no hint of backing down.

Grown men beg and implore in his position, especially if they know who Adrian Volkov is and what he's capable of.

Not only is Creighton not panicked, but he also apparently has a death wish. Because he says, "Just like you had the audacity to take her from me in the first place."

Papa hits him with the butt of the gun, sending his face flying sideways, and blood explodes from his lips.

"Papa!" The blow might not have been directed at me, but I feel it deep in my soul, and I don't think about it as I run to Creighton.

To the gorgeously haunted man with demons who refuse to leave him alone.

"Stay back, Anoushka." Papa stares at me, still holding the gun to Creighton's forehead.

The way he looks at me is different from the way he regards the world. He's not an emotionless killer right now. He's a worried father with molten eyes and a rigid posture.

I can only imagine what he, Mom, and Jeremy have been through during the time they didn't know where I was.

"Did he hurt you?" he asks slowly, menacingly.

"No, Papa. Please let him go."

"I will do that after he's tortured to within an inch of his life. I'll hang him from the ceiling and lash his skin for every day he thought he could take you from your family."

A full-body shudder slashes through my limbs and it takes everything in me to remain standing. "Papa, please...don't."

"Do it." Creighton bares his bloodied teeth in a snarl. "Torture me. Kill me. Stab me to death then continue slicing my corpse like you did my father. You shouldn't have left me alive back then, but now is your chance to fix that mistake. If you don't kill me, I'll come back over and over, and fucking over again."

"What the hell are you saying? Shut up!" My limbs shake and a shiver skids through me and it has little to do with my wet clothes.

Papa tightens his grip around the gun, probably considering whether he wants to torture him first or just kill him and get it over with.

"Isn't this what you wanted?" Creighton speaks to me, but his cold gaze is locked with Papa's. "Isn't your family everything that matters? I'm making it easier for you."

It hits me then.

The realization is so fierce that I stumble a step back, my flip-flops sinking in the sand.

All this time, all those words, all that torture was because he thought I was choosing my family over him.

That I would always pick my family, the people who were behind his childhood misery, over *him*. That I would force him to either accept them or I wouldn't stay with him.

How did my attempts to free him from the past become falsified to the point where it's now the complete opposite?

"That's not..." My voice gets stuck in the back of my throat. I've always found it easy to talk about everything and nothing, but now I'm stunned into silence.

I can't find the right words to relay the explosive feelings whirling inside me.

"Your biological father was a scum and died like a scum. He assaulted my wife when he was clearly ordered to protect her, so I killed him," Papa says coldly with enough cool to make me shiver. "Your biological mother was of a similar breed, too. They both deserved their fate, and as I told your adoptive father, I will not apologize for protecting my family. However, you were only a kid and didn't deserve to suffer the downfall of their actions, which is why I made sure you were adopted into a good family."

Creighton's jaw relaxes and mine falls open.

"Papa, you…you made sure of that?"

"No." Creighton shakes his head. "You didn't know."

"Of course, I did. I followed Richard's family's downfall long after he was dead. I had men watching your house, recording your mother's desperate attempts to seduce the DA, an Italian mafia leader, a bank employee, anyone who could get her out of trouble. The night she lost all hope, committed suicide, and attempted to kill you, I was there."

"Shut up." Creighton's voice comes out so raw that I want to hold him.

"I found you passed out by the front door, face blue, and vomit streaked all over your face. I gave you CPR and carried your small body to the hospital. Once you were recuperating, I entrusted you to Rai so she'd get you out of the States and free you of the bloody pit your parents dug for themselves. That's how you got adopted into the current family you have. I might have taken your past life, but I gave you a new one. So even if you had a grudge, you should've come after me, but you were a coward who went after my children and I will not forgive you for that."

Creighton's breathing heavily, his chest rising and falling in a deadly rhythm. As if he's trying to expel a gloomy cloud that's been festering inside him for years.

As if he can't breathe hard enough or purge the energy bubbling inside him fast enough.

I tremble in sync with him, trying to see the revelations from his perspective.

He's devastated, even more than when I shot him or when he found out the truth. The fact that the man he hated with all his heart, my father, is the same man who gave him the precious family and life he currently knows is ripping him apart.

I inch closer, wanting, no *needing,* to hold him in my arms, but his cold words directed at my father stop me.

"Kill me," he spits out. "If you don't, I'll never stop."

"Foolish fucking coward." Papa clicks his magazine in place and I know I have seconds to react.

I don't think about it as I snatch a gun from one of the guard's side holsters. I'm so fast that when I grab it, he has no time to stop me.

Creighton's gaze finally falls on me, his eyes devoid of life, of that silent but caring Creighton I want back.

I'd go to unimaginable lengths to have him back.

Keeping my gaze on him, I point the gun at my temple.

"What are you doing, Anoushka?" Papa's calm voice carries masked anger.

"Let him go," I whisper with enough assertiveness that I believe myself.

It's strange how simple and easy things become when you make up your mind. Peaceful, too. Like it was always meant to be.

The wind caresses my cold skin, no longer swaying me. It's hugging me, holding my finger on the trigger and warming the barrel that's glued to my temple.

"Annika...give me the gun." Papa's warning tone would've made me do anything not so long ago.

Not today.

"Let him go, or I swear I'll shoot myself." I don't sound distressed, but more confident, because I'd do it.

I will not choose between them anymore. I won't survive it.

Papa slowly steps back, gun still by his side. "I did what you said, now stop this madness."

"Promise you won't hurt him anymore."

"I can't do that after what he did to you."

"That's between him and me. You have no place to interfere. I'm not a kid anymore. And you hurt him enough for a lifetime. It's time to stop it."

He purses his lips but doesn't say anything.

"Promise me, Papa."

"Fine, I promise. Now, come here, Anoushka."

I shake my head.

Creighton stares at me with the same fear he regarded me with when I was at the top of that cliff.

Only now, it's so much more prominent that I taste it with sea salt.

"Drop the gun," he whispers, voice strained.

"You asked me what I'd choose if you went head-to-head with my family again." I dig the gun farther into my temple. "This is my answer, Creighton. I'd choose *me*."

He struggles against Kolya's hold, and when my father's second-in-command pushes him down, he growls at Papa, "Let me the fuck go!"

Papa nods at his guard and when he releases him, Creighton all but runs in my direction.

I step back. "Don't come any closer."

He stops in his tracks, his body rigid, and it's the first time I've seen him look so helpless.

"Anoushka, I already released him. Don't do this." Papa's voice deepens. "Think of your mother, your brother. Me."

"I can't…" Tears stream down my face and I look at Creighton through blurry vision. "I can't live knowing you're full of rage and pain. I can't live knowing you'll always hate my parents, the same parents who gave me everything. I'd rather die than see that. Maybe if I do, you'll finally let go of your grudge."

"Listen to me, Annika." His voice carries in the cold air like a whip. "You're the only person who ever reached inside me, saw the ugly, rotten parts, but stayed anyway. You gave me yourself in spite of knowing how empty I am. You even filled me up with your endless energy, purple color, and fucking violets. I didn't understand how you liked me when I didn't like myself, how you fought to make me experience normal things despite my disinterest. When I found out the truth about my childhood, the only thing that broke me was knowing I couldn't be with you anymore. And when you didn't choose me and pulled that trigger, I became a bitter wanker with a death wish. I didn't care what happened as long as I had you, which is why I brought you here. But I realize now that it wasn't the right thing to do, which is why I chose to let you go. What you're doing isn't the right thing either. You might be able to live without me, but I won't survive a day without you, so your death won't solve any-fucking-thing. If you pull that trigger, mark my words, I will follow right after you."

My fingers tremble as an onslaught of emotions overtakes me. "You'd rather die than let go of the past?"

"I would rather die than live without you." His chest rises and falls with violent ferocity. "You don't complete me, you're a part of me. If you go, that's not different than erasing me along with you."

His words sink into the marrow of my bones and flow into my bloodstream. "It doesn't have to be like this, Creighton. Neither of us has to die if you just promise to try and leave the past behind. For you. For me. For *us*."

"Will you love me again if I do?"

A small smile grazes my lips as I lower the gun, place it in one of the guard's hands and walk toward him with purposeful steps.

He meets me halfway, his strong hands wrapping around my waist as my arms circle his neck. "I never stopped loving you, silly."

His eyes shutter slowly, and a long breath rips out of his chest. When he opens them again, they're clear blue.

Resigned.

"You win, little purple."

"I win?"

"All of me. My heart, body, and soul are yours. My grudge is also yours to do whatever you wish with."

"Including moving past it?"

"Including that." His hand falls on my hip and he strokes gently. "I lost to you a long time ago. I love you, Annika. I love you to the point

I see darkness without you and light only when I'm with you. You're my sanctuary and the one person who makes me whole."

A tear slides down my cheek. That's all I ever wanted from Creighton, to be the person he leans on, the one person he trusts to show everything inside him.

Because he's *it* for me.

He was the one long before I realized it myself.

I'm about to kiss him when the clearing of a throat stops me.

Shit.

I forgot Papa and the others were here all along.

Slowly, I release Creighton, but he holds my hand, interlinking my fingers with his when we face Papa.

This time, I don't try to run away or hide like when Jeremy found us. This time, I stand by his side and refuse to move.

"You're bold to think I'd let you have my daughter," he speaks to Creighton, but at least his gun is hidden from sight.

"I won't leave," Creighton announces point-blank.

"*Willingly*," Papa supplies. "I can find methods to make you leave."

"Papa!"

"We're going home, Anoushka," he announces.

"Like fuck—"

"You're coming with us," Papa cuts him off.

"W-why?" I stammer. Please don't tell me he's taking him back to kill him as he promised.

"I'm sure your mother would like to meet him."

"Oh… *Oh*!" I say again with a grin. "Does that mean you approve of us, Papa?"

"No," he says bluntly. "But I would rather have this little fuck under surveillance so I can end him before he attempts anything funny."

He glares at Creighton, who glares right back. As if this is some sort of a challenge.

Things won't be easy, but I'm ready to fight.

For him.

For us.

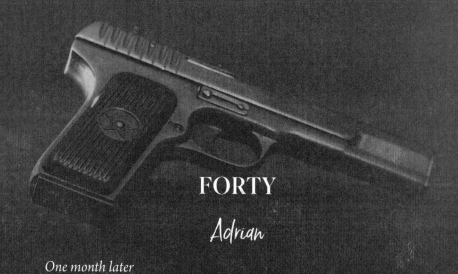

FORTY

Adrian

One month later

MY ATTEMPTS TO GET RID OF THE PEST WHO HAS snatched away my daughter have come to an irritating dead end.

I had hoped that with time, the young love haze would slowly fade and we'd have our sunshine back.

That slimy fucker had the audacity not only to steal her, but to also make her fall in love with him so deeply that she's become his designated defense attorney whenever anyone attempts to take a jab at him.

We wouldn't be in this predicament if I hadn't saved him that day seventeen years ago, but the fact remains that he was only a kid back then, and I would've upset the other important woman in my life if I'd left him to die.

What I could've done instead was send him to another nook in the planet he wouldn't have been able to crawl out of. An option my wife laughed at when I mentioned it.

"You can't stop fate, Adrian," is what she told me with that soft smile of hers that makes me look forward to new days.

"I can still try," I replied, and she just shook her head.

I meant it. Not only will I not stop trying, but I will win. Whatever way possible.

It's why I cut a meeting with the brotherhood's inner circle short and came home.

My daughter and her definitely-not-boyfriend are visiting today. Together.

After that shitshow on the island, Annika chose to continue with college in the UK. She didn't give up on ballet, but she's now taking it as a passion instead—something that's part of her that she doesn't necessarily need to go the professional route with.

A decision that made Lia happy. Even though she originally promised to support whatever choice Annika makes, I know that whenever Annika danced, my wife saw the demons of her past feasting on our daughter.

No matter how much we tried to convince her that they wouldn't share the same story, she just wouldn't believe it.

So the fact that Annika has willingly chosen to stay away from the spotlight has given her the peace of mind she constantly lacked before our daughter decided to have ballet as a passion.

I stop near the threshold at the sound of laughter coming from the back entrance.

I stalk to the joyful noise, something that's become a constant in my and Lia's life ever since Annika came along.

Jeremy was a quiet kid, and maybe that has to do with all the demons he witnessed me and his mother battle. He was nowhere as energetic as his little hellion sister who brought the whole house down from the time she was an infant, had my veteran ex-Spetsnaz guards chase after her as a toddler and lose, and had me, her mother, and brother wrapped around her pinkie finger.

Sure enough, when I reach the back garden, I find my daughter sitting beside the motherfucker, her hand in his, laughing at something Yan said.

My gaze strays to the beautiful woman who's also laughing, her features bright and welcoming.

A deep breath spills out of my lungs whenever I see her. It's a mixture of relief and wretched longing.

I've been married to that woman for over twenty-four years, and she's still the only person who's able to tame the chaos brewing inside me.

The only woman for whom I'm willing to sacrifice everything I have to see her smiling freely like that.

I just never thought I'd have to let go of my daughter instead.

Lia flat-out apologized to Creighton when we brought him with us that day. I wanted to kick the slimy bastard in the balls for pulling those twisted memories out of my wife.

She said she was sorry he'd had such a terrible childhood and parents and she regretted playing a role in that.

To my fucking surprise, he apologized back for being the biological son of the man who hurt her.

Annika looked proud as fuck. I narrowed my eyes, waiting for a scheme, a hidden motive, but there was no trace of either on his face.

Ever since then, Lia has basically adopted him as her third child. She easily fell in love with him and even started to make his favorite meals whenever he comes over.

The other day, they were texting back and forth about some stupid recipe. According to my daughter, he doesn't reply to texts from his own friends and family.

He apparently doesn't mind doing that with my wife.

Though Lia does have that quiet, spellbinding energy, where she'd capture anyone's heart without even trying. A fact due to which I tried my best to keep her shielded from the world once upon a time.

I still want to lock her up so no one but me can see her, where only I'm her world as much as she is mine, but I recognize how much she needs to be out there.

My reward is having her willingly come back to me every night, to willingly seek refuge in my arms, and willingly want to spend time alone.

That's the best gift I could ever receive.

"Try this, Creigh. I made it." Annika scoops out what looks like some sort of appetizer and places it near his mouth.

The fucker-on-borrowed-time actually opens his lips and eats. Without a change of expression.

It's Yan and Lia who wince, sharing a look.

"What do you think?" my daughter asks with expectant glee.

I'm ready to pummel him to the ground if he so much as changes that expression, but he nods. "Pretty good."

"I knew it!" She glares at Yan. "See? I told you someone likes my food. It's all about perspective."

"You really okay there, man? Want me to call an ambulance?"

"Yan!" my wife chastises.

"No, something is wrong with the kid, Lia. He actually eats the things your food terrorist of a daughter cooks."

"Wanna die?" my daughter asks with a murderous expression.

She got that one from me.

"Don't call her a food terrorist," Creighton says point-blank, earning a wide grin from Annika and a motherly smile from my wife.

"*Boom*," Annika says, unable to hide her boasting expression. "Mic drop."

"The sorry fuck is too in love to see how horrible your food actually is. Listen, kid, love won't save you when you're driven to the ER because of food poisoning."

"I'm going to kill you," Annika announces and proceeds to try and stuff him with her appetizers, but Creighton snatches them and starts to eat them all.

Christ.

The little shit might have a death wish, after all. In this house, we don't eat Annika's food or else there will definitely be some form of food poisoning. Or stomachaches. Or just plain inconveniences.

She tends to use what she thinks is beneficial for health out of context, like honey with spicy food or some nutriments with seafood. And she has no sense of how much salt she should put in any dish.

We know she means well, so Lia, Jeremy, and I usually tell her not to cook. Kolya and the other guards try to be diplomatic about it, too.

Only that fucker Yan told her the truth directly and has long since labeled her a food terrorist.

Creighton King is the first person who's eaten her food willingly and even compliments her for it.

However, I refuse to warm up to him due to that gesture. Or the fact that he's the one who made Annika abandon whatever suicidal thoughts she had on that island.

I haven't told Lia about that episode and ordered everyone not to. It would ruin her to know that dark thoughts have invaded our daughter's mind and we almost lost her.

But we didn't.

Because Creighton was there and managed to tug her from the edge of nothingness.

It's mostly because of him that I still have my daughter in one piece. But it's also because of him that she got to that state, so I will be considering that incident neutral.

"How is that girl?" Lia asks Creighton while Annika chases Yan with a flower because he keeps calling her a food terrorist.

"Girl?" he echoes with a hoarse throat—definitely not as unaffected with the food as he claims to be.

"The one who told us about where you took Annika."

"Cecily?"

My wife nods.

"Do you really want to know?"

She inches closer, her soft features creasing. "Why? What happened?"

"You do realize that Jeremy didn't get that information out of her by being a good sport, right?"

My wife swallows. "I figured as much. He…can be cold-blooded, he takes that after his father, but they do have a heart beneath it all, I promise."

"That's what my mother says about my brother, and the worst part is that she believes it, but we all know he's a functioning psychopath."

"Jeremy isn't a psychopath."

"In view of what he's done, he's probably worse."

"What did he do?"

"I promised him I'd stay out of his way if he stays out of mine, and I'd like to keep that truce. Not for self-serving purposes, but for Annika's sake. She doesn't like it when we clash."

Lia nods in understanding, and I want to haul my son back from the other side of the ocean and shake the fuck out of him.

He's not supposed to accept Creighton this easily, or fast, no matter what type of deal they struck.

Though after Annika shot Creighton to save him, his disapproval was slowly subsiding anyway.

"I hate to see her go, too, but maybe we should let Annika make her choice this time, Dad," is what he told me the last time we saw each other.

That's obviously because of whatever deal he struck with this little shit.

Said little shit gets up, whispers something to Annika that she pauses her antics with Yan to hear, then she smiles widely at him.

He walks toward the house and I hide out of view as he goes into the bathroom, probably to wash his face or throw up whatever she fed him.

When he emerges, I don't bother to hide and he pauses before he heads in the direction of the garden.

I block his path and he stops, raising a brow. "Is this my welcome? Or do you have a gun hidden somewhere to threaten me with?"

"You're awfully talkative today."

"And you're suspiciously not threatening me with bodily harm."

"We'll get to that point in a few."

"By all means. Let's get the tedious chore over with."

"Was that sarcasm?"

"Was it? Annika is rubbing off on me."

This little fucking shit will be buried six feet under before my wife and daughter wake up tomorrow.

He takes a step toward me, all nonchalance vanishing from his face. "I'm happy to indulge in whatever threatening kink you have going on, and I won't tell Annika or Lia about it, but I'm telling you right now that you won't be able to get me away from what's mine."

"What the fuck did you just say?"

"Mine. Annika is mine, and no one will change that fact, not even you."

"Annika will get over you eventually."

"Keep dreaming, Adrian, and while you're at it, I'll become your son-in-law. We'll work hard to give you beautiful grandchildren."

"Not if you somehow end up dead before that. And who gave you permission to call me by my name?"

"I don't like Mr. Volkov. Too long."

Either this fucker is bold or he has no care whatsoever for his life. Or probably both.

"Also, if you're so territorial, how come you still haven't done something about *him*?"

I turn around so that we're both facing the scene in the garden. Annika splutters on water and Lia bends over laughing at something Yan has said while he grins like an idiot.

"He's a fucking clown who doesn't know his place," I mutter under my breath.

"Which you should've taught him a long time ago," Creighton says with an equally displeased tone.

"You think I haven't tried? He bounces back up like a parasite whose sole purpose is to piss me off."

"Annika mentioned that you've often threatened to ship him to the Special Forces back in Russia. Is there a reason that hasn't happened?"

"See that woman?" I tilt my head in my wife's direction. "That's the reason."

"You can still do it now."

"He's too old."

"Could he be put in an administrative post?"

"Possibly." I share the first look of understanding with the little fucker. At least we both can't stand Yan.

Or more accurately, how close he is to the two women out there.

When we walk upon the scene together, Yan doesn't even bother to stand up and continues sipping from whatever cocktail Ogla has made for them.

It's Annika whose expression lights up like fireworks upon seeing me with her still-not-her-boyfriend and not actually threatening to throw him into the nearest ditch.

She's been his spokesperson, manager, and PR specialist ever since the island and has used every trick under the sun to make me warm up to him.

Such as mentioning his protective episodes and that he's worse than me and Jeremy combined. Or how he learned to cook because he doesn't want her to get tired—more like he doesn't want to go through the torture of consuming her food.

Or how he slowly mended her relationship with the friends she made in the UK by telling them that they'd lose him, too, if they reproached her about what happened.

I still plan to give him hell. Even if, deep down, I know he genuinely cares for her.

My daughter jumps up from her chair and runs into my arms. "Papa! I missed you."

I stroke the top of her hair as she squeezes me tight. As much as I hate to admit it, Annika has grown into a responsible adult ever since the fucker on my right came into her life.

She needed the pain of loss and real-life experiences to shed that naiveté and actually grow into her own person.

"Are you sure?" I ask when we break apart. "Because you barely text me anymore."

"Oh, please. You don't even like texting, Papa, and I FaceTime you all the time when you come to steal away Mom."

She runs to Lia's side and hugs her. "She's also my mom, you know."

"My wife first."

"Sorry, unlike you, I'm related to her by blood. That gives me more privileges." She grins like a little daredevil.

"Stop it, Anni." Lia laughs, but she hugs her back. That little spoiled brat was always a mommy's girl. When they're next to each other, they look like sisters instead of mother and daughter.

I sit down with a grunt and glare at Yan.

"What?" he mouths.

"I'm going to kill you."

"Whatever for?"

"The little show you just put on."

"I wasn't touching anyone."

"Still counts."

"Stop being jealous of my charming qualities and the fact that I can make Lia laugh while you can't, grumpy old man," he murmurs back, then swiftly gets up before I choke the fuck out of him.

He's also saved by the fact that Lia disappeared inside, probably to see if she can help Ogla with anything.

I catch up to her and pull her by the elbow before she reaches the kitchen.

My wife slams against me with a gasp. My cock throbs as she stares up at me with those huge, absolutely mesmerizing eyes.

I love when I reflect in those eyes, when I'm the center of her world as much as she's the orbit of mine.

When she looks at me like she never wants to leave.

"Adrian…" she breathes out. "What is it?"

"I didn't get my welcome home kiss. Have you forgotten about me now that Annika and the little shit are here, wife?"

"I wouldn't dare." Her voice lowers as she pulls me down by the lapel of my jacket, gets on her tiptoes, and brushes her lips against mine.

Lia's kiss is gentle, but it's imploring and passionate.

It's nowhere near my brutal claiming, but it's an invitation for it. My wife knows full well that I get off on her softness and the knowledge that she wants me to seep inside and break it.

Every night.

Every chance I get.

Her lips release mine too soon and she gets back on her feet, licking her lower lip, chasing my taste in a way that gets me even harder. "Welcome home, Adrian. I missed you."

"Didn't look that way when you were laughing with the two fuckers outside."

"I can't believe you're still reproaching Yan after all these years."

"He's a provocative motherfucker and you know it."

"That's because he's trying to mess with you and you kind of let him." She smooths an invisible wrinkle from my jacket. "As for Creighton, you're being unreasonable. We wronged him, but he loves our daughter enough to let all of that go. You need to let go of your imaginary grudge, too."

"Like fuck I will. The bastard just threatened me that he'll become my son-in-law and give me grandchildren."

She laughs. My wife's head tips back, bearing her pale throat as my ears fill with the delighted sound of her laughter.

"How is any of this funny?" I try to sound stern, but I love the sound of her laughter too much to actually be mad.

"Looks like he learned how to mess with you, too. Good for him. I really like that kid."

"Which makes me like him even less."

"Oh, stop it, Adrian. He's the best thing that's ever happened to Anni, and if you weren't so judgmental, you'd know it, too."

I grunt but say nothing.

Lia skims her fingers over the dip in my brows, her voice dropping. "I hate it when you're all upset. How can I make you feel better, husband?"

A groan spills out of me when she rubs her stomach against my growing erection.

"Repeat that."

"Husband," she says again and I tighten my grip on her hip, feeling her shudder.

"Upstairs. Now."

"But the kids are here."

"They can wait."

When she hesitates, I carry her in my arms bridal style. Lia yelps even as her arms encircle my neck.

Her fingers stroke the short hairs on my nape. "Did I mention lately that I love you?"

"No."

"I think I did this morning."

"I must've forgotten."

She grins as she whispers, "I love you, Mr. Volkov."

"And I love you, Mrs. Volkov."

I might have partially lost my daughter, but I'll always have my wife.

The woman who accepted me as her villain and fell in love with me in spite of it.

EPILOGUE 1

Annika

I HIDE BETWEEN THE CARS IN THE PARKING LOT, BREATHING heavily.

If I'd known this is what we'd be returning to, I would've voted for skipping classes and staying the whole week with my parents.

But no, Creighton had an important thing to do.

Like today's match.

Against my brother.

I wince at the reminder of their threatening stares when they jumped into the ring, looking no different than walls of muscle ready to pound each other into oblivion.

And since this happens to be the most awaited final of the current championship, both REU and TKU students are swarming the place, cheering and shouting and thirsting for blood.

Both Jeremy's and Creighton's blood.

Yikes.

I stare at my watch and groan when I find it's been only ten minutes since I kind of escaped from the club.

So no, I wasn't going to watch them go at each other's throats. I begged them both to stop this or for one of them to forfeit, but neither of them is a quitter.

Besides, Jeremy said he can't trust anyone to protect his sister if he can't beat him. Something that got Creighton even more riled up for the fight.

Men and their testosterone will be the death of me.

So here I am, all alone in hiding, waiting for the ordeal to be done with.

Glyndon was keeping me company because she doesn't like manifestations of violence either. Despite our objections about attending, we were all dragged by Ava anyway—she's all for fights and is probably cheering for Creighton at the top of her lungs as we speak.

It took her some time and a few shopping trips for her to actually forgive me for shooting Creighton, and only because she knows how much we mean to each other.

Glyndon was the nicest of the bunch and talked to me soon after I got back to college. And since she's a sweetheart, she opted to escape with me and was busy showing me her latest paintings. But alas, Killian interrupted us a few minutes ago and kidnapped her to God knows where.

"I still don't forgive you for making her cry," is what he told me as he swooped her away.

That psycho is incorrigible. Aside from Creighton, he's the most territorial.

Actually, Creighton is in a league of his own. Not only is he possessive of me to the point where he's constantly glaring at Tiger whenever he lies on my chest, but he's also so consistent about it that no guy comes close to me in fear of his wrath.

Even Harry, who's gay and has a crush on Creighton and is the leader of his fan club, isn't safe from his lashes of jealousy.

I lean against my car and opt to roam social media. I pause at the picture I see on Creighton's account.

He actually used the one Remi and I created for him a long time ago, but he changed the password and everything because Remi was planning to post 'weird shit' on his page.

Creighton's profile picture is the same as his first post. It's a selfie he took when I wasn't even aware. I'm asleep in his lap, head tucked in his chest so that my face isn't visible and only half of his is.

His veiny hand grips me possessively by the waist and the caption says:

My girl. My woman. Mine.

That was during the month we were apart. Exactly a day before he kidnapped me to that island.

How romantic.

Not.

The second picture is another selfie he took after we got back to college. He's carrying me with a hand beneath my ass, my legs are wrapped around his naked waist, and my head is buried in his shoulder.

Did I mention that she's all mine?

The third—the one I'm currently looking at that's making me struggle to breathe—is one he posted just earlier.

Before the fight, I kind of slipped into the locker room for one final attempt to dissuade him from going against Jeremy.

Big mistake.

Not only did he look at me like a hungry predator, but he also oozed with savage adrenaline.

Needless to say, I didn't stand a chance.

Creighton fucked me senseless against the bench in the pussy and then in the ass while he bit my throat and spanked me.

My core throbs and the welts on my ass sting at the reminder. I should feel demented that I get off on the pain as much as I get off on the pleasure, but I've learned to accept that about myself and us.

I've learned to own up to what makes us who we are, because I realize just how lucky we are to be so compatible despite having such different personalities.

Like a puzzle, the good and bad parts fit together perfectly.

The picture he posted is from the neck up, when he kissed me soon after we finished. My eyes are closed and his are open as he stares at the camera with chilling possessiveness.

Reminder: She's mine.

A tingle ripples through me and dances at the base of my spine.

He's simply impossible.

I still like the picture anyway. What? I've got to stake a claim, too.

Next time I catch a girl flirting with him, I'm going to forward her to his Instagram account.

That he made for me.

No kidding, the other day, he was like, "Didn't you say you'd un-follow all the guys if I make an Instagram account? Do it."

I reminded him that I said he should have social media to follow me, not that he'd cut me off from the world, but he's not having that.

Anyway, I'm so going to send this to Harry and his ever-growing fan club when he taunts me.

"Can't you stop this?"

The very familiar voice filters from a few rows ahead. I let my phone slip into my dress pocket and sneak along the cars.

Sure enough, Cecily stands in the shadows, her silver hair flying in the wind as she grips her phone tight.

Oddly, her shirt is a simple black one with no quotes on it.

"You don't understand. I just can't do this," she whispers in a shaky voice and I want to reach out and hug her.

She's been distressed for a while, and even Glyn expressed her worry about it the other day.

I must make a noise in trying to get close to her, because she faces me with a deer-caught-in-the-headlights gaze before she removes the phone from her ear and hangs up on whoever she was talking with.

"Annika?" Her tone is cold, a little bit wrong, as if it's not the same Cecily I know. "What are you doing here?"

"Uh, I kind of couldn't watch my brother and my boyfriend fighting. Especially since they have a *grudge*." I air quote the last word.

"Oh, I see." Her voice softens.

I approach her slowly, scared any sudden movement will make her bolt. "Are you okay, Ces?"

She nods soundlessly.

While Jeremy has been insufferable since he learned Cecily helped Creighton abduct me, I don't hold a grudge against her.

One, she didn't know and really thought he only wanted to talk to me before she was thrown out of the plane.

Two, she's suffered from Jeremy enough as it is. I know how harsh my brother can be, and he's never really liked Cecily.

It's mutual, but still.

And sometimes, I catch them looking at each other in a way I can't put my finger on.

"I'm always here if you want to talk," I tell her softly. "Even if it's about Jer."

A visible tremor goes through her limbs and she stares at me, hard, as if trying to figure out if she should trust me.

I think she decides she can, because she takes a step forward. "Anni, you can't tell anyone about this."

"Cross my heart and hope to die."

She inhales sharply, her eyes darting sideways. "I made a terrible mistake and I don't know how to undo it."

It's the first time I've seen her so lost, so scared. Cecily has always been the most confident one, the assertive one, the crash-into-the-problem-head-first one.

But she looks so terribly confused that I want to hug her.

"What is it? Tell me and I might be able to help."

"It's—"

Her words are cut off when I feel a presence behind me and then my nostrils fill with his distinctive scent mixed with adrenaline and sweat.

A strong hand wraps around my waist and I shiver as I'm slammed against his side, where his body heat overwhelms mine.

"Hi, Creigh," my friend murmurs, then slides her dejected attention to me. "I'm going back."

"Cecily, wait," I call after her, but she's already gone.

I glare up at Creighton's gorgeous face with the thick brows and busted lips, and it's hard to be mad at him. "Ces was going to tell me something and you screwed it up."

"Don't get involved in Cecily's business when she doesn't even know what she wants." He pushes a stray hair that the wind stuffed in my face behind my ear. "Were you hiding, little purple?"

"I didn't want to see you guys fighting." I swallow. "Who won?"

"It was a draw."

"Thank God." I release a breath.

"We'll have a rematch next week."

"Seriously?"

"Next time, don't hide or I'll draw it out more." He flicks my forehead teasingly and I massage the spot, glaring up at him.

"Aww. And I'm so going to hide again."

"Don't be a brat."

"Oh, please, you love it when I'm a brat."

"Seems the appetizer from earlier didn't teach you a lesson."

"That was…just an appetizer?"

"More or less."

"What's the main course then?"

"You'll find out if you're a good girl."

My panties soak at the promise in his voice. I love it when he keeps me in the dark about his plans and then I find myself all tied up and fucked to within an inch of my life.

Or when he introduces new toys that I swear are manufactured so he can torture me with them.

"Will you take a picture and post it on IG this time, too?"

"No. They only need to be reminded in another two weeks or so."

"You're so over the top, but I still love you," I whisper. "So much, it's insane."

"Good, because I'll make sure you always love me as much as I love you."

And then he's lifting me by the waist and kissing me.

EPILOGUE 2

Creighton

One year later

WHOSE IDEA WAS IT FOR US TO COME HERE?

Right, my brother's.

I'm left wondering why I haven't punched him in the face as I glare at him from across the table and he smiles widely, even winking like the little twat he is.

The thing is, we're at a family dinner, as in, with Dad and Mum. We finished eating, but there's still dessert.

The worst part? This is only the first season. Tomorrow, in part two of this family saga, we'll be joined by my three grandfathers—who like to bicker for sport, Nan, Uncle Levi, and Aunt Astrid. The twins and Glyn may join, too, since it's a holiday.

If—when—Glyn brings Killian along, we'll have a bloody circus on our hands. One, Lan still can't stand him, Uncle Levi barely tolerates him, and Grandpa Jonathan still views him as the thief who took away his cute granddaughter. Two, Kill and Eli have grown a bit close, demolishing all the parents' attempts to keep them apart, and, therefore, are always stirring up trouble.

I'm definitely kidnapping Annika the hell out of here before the circus begins.

If she hadn't been so quick to accept my parents' invitation, we wouldn't be here in the first place.

Thing is, it was hard getting my folks to warm up to her entirely after the shooting episode. Mum was a bit difficult at the beginning because she couldn't stand the thought of anyone hurting me.

Annika actually spent months on end bribing her, calling her, and talking to her about everything and nothing. She even offered to be her designated spy in college.

Dad, on the other hand, was suspicious of her, considering her background. He didn't believe she or her father wouldn't hurt me. Not to mention that Dad and Adrian met exactly two times, and everyone in the room had to stop them from murdering each other.

The fact remains, after I got back from the island, Dad said he was proud that I went after what I wanted, because that's the right 'King' way of doing things.

However, no matter how many difficulties Mum and Dad posed, my girl still managed to win them over with her cheerful personality and ability to empathize with anyone.

Besides, unlike her father, who acts like he doesn't like me—but deep down does—my parents are happy when I'm happy. No questions asked.

I tilt my head to the side and watch as she helps Mum clean the table. We have staff, but Mum dismissed them today because she wanted the 'homey' experience. This time, Dad cooked—thank fuck.

My gaze follows Annika as she moves with the grace of a feather. She's wearing a purple-and-white floral dress, and her hair is held up in a ponytail with a fluffy purple butterfly that matches the ones on her flats.

Annika always complains about how I tear her clothes, but I can't resist when she looks like a present I have to unwrap. And I'm too impatient to do it properly, so her clothes have to pay the price.

The more I watch her, the harder my cock strains against my jeans. I discreetly readjust myself and force my gaze away from her.

And that's when someone hits me upside the head. "Pussy-whipped."

I glare up at my brother. "Sure you want to say that?"

His eyes darken, but he soon smooths his expression and runs his fingers under my chin. "Did I mention you're so adorable lately?"

I try to push him away, but he's no different from a parasite sometimes. I have a deep appreciation for my relationship with Eli and how he's always been there for me, but I can't get used to him being a wanker whenever he pleases.

"Leave your brother alone," Dad chastises as he strides from the lavatory and sits at the head of the table.

Eli squashes my face between his fingers. "Look at his adorable cheeks."

"He's not a baby anymore."

"Unfortunately." Eli lets out a bored sigh and releases me, then focuses on our father. "And don't be jealous, Dad."

He gives him a blank stare. "Of what?"

"Our beautiful relationship."

Dad snickers and Eli's eyes narrow. "What was that for?"

Dad says nothing.

"What was it for?"

"Are you guys bickering again?" Mum strokes Eli's hair and touches my cheek, then she kisses Dad on the lips. "Can we not? Just for tonight?"

Dad wraps his arms around her waist, pulling her against him. "Do I get a reward later?"

"Dad!" I protest.

"Seriously?" Eli echoes.

"What?" He stares at us innocently. "She's my wife."

"And our mum," I say.

"We didn't need that image," Eli mutters.

"Maybe the problem is you, not me. Get that image out of your heads, sons," Dad tells us as if the topic is completely normal.

"Aiden, stop it." Mum smiles and tries to slip free. "Let me go help Annika with dessert."

"Eli or Creighton can do it. You worked hard tonight."

My brother is ready to bolt, but I'm out of my seat before he blinks.

"I can't believe you abandoned me, you little fuck!" he shouts behind my back.

"Should've brought a date!" I smirk, and he flips me off.

I find Annika in the kitchen, fussing over some ice cream.

"I'm almost done!" she calls out and I grab her by the elbow and wrench her small body back.

Annika gasps, slamming the glass of ice cream against my chest, spilling it on me. "You."

"*Me.*" My voice lowers and she understands the meaning quite well, because she shakes her head.

"Not here, Creigh."

"Why not?"

"Everyone is waiting for dessert."

"Everyone can come get it themselves."

"They're right outside."

"They're preoccupied."

I pull her behind me into one of the storage rooms and she yelps when I push her onto the table and fling the dress to her hips.

"You're always walking around with pretty little dresses that beg to be removed." I tug on her underwear, ripping it. "And these fucking things that keep me from my pussy."

A moan is the only reply I get and she doesn't fight or protest when I take the glass of ice cream from her hand. It isn't until I spill it all over her pussy that she gasps, arching off the table slightly to stare at me from the shock of it.

"What are you doing?" she whimpers even as her pupils dilate.

"Eating dessert." And then I'm devouring her. I lick every drop of ice cream off her folds and swallow the taste of chocolate that's mixed with her arousal.

Annika writhes, pants, and demands more as her fingers get lost in my hair. Once I'm done licking up every drop while slapping her arse now and again, she comes undone, squirting against my mouth. This time, she doesn't pause or hide as she drenches my face.

I taught her to never be ashamed of her pleasure with me, that she can take everything and more.

Just like she licks every drop of me when she sucks me off, I drink her, my cock becoming rock-fucking-hard as she chants my name.

Then when she's still riding her orgasm, I pull her up so she's sitting and bury myself in her to the hilt, until my groin slaps against hers. I grunt and she moans while flooding my dick with her arousal.

Her head tips back, eyes half closed. One hand on her hip, I catch her jaw with the other and direct it to where we're joined. "Look at how I fuck you. Do you see how your cunt was made for me? It's mine, isn't it?"

"Yours..." she whimpers, watching me fucking her with absolute fascination.

And I swear my dick hardens further the more she releases those noises and tries to adjust herself to take me all in.

She still struggles with my size sometimes because she's too tiny and I'm too big, but I have all sorts of toys to prep her, to make her enjoy this as much as I do.

There are no toys now, and she's fully lubricated, but the slight pain is her aphrodisiac. She's a glutton for pain, my Annika, just like I'm a glutton for inflicting it.

So I bite her throat. "Such a good girl. Come for me."

She does, shattering around my cock, milking it and grinding against me.

I go for a few more strokes, fast, hard, and absolutely animalistic. I break her with my cock, but she takes everything I dish out and more. Then the words that are my undoing spill out of her lips like a chant.

"I love you, Creigh, I love you."

I come then, hard and long and with a deep grunt that anyone on the other side of the door could hear.

Once I've emptied inside her, I hold her against me and whisper, "I love you, too."

She sighs into my neck, her breathing fluttering against my skin, and we remain like that for what seems like an hour.

When we pull apart, I can't resist fucking my cum back into her cunt, making her whimper and release soft moans.

"One day, you're going to marry me and let me fill this cunt with my babies, aren't you, Annika?"

Her breath hitches as she rocks against my hand, her arousal coating me. "We're still too young for marriage."

"Age is just a number, and you'll marry me, Annika. I'm the only one you'll marry, right?"

She sighs. "You are."

"Good." I grin. "It's time I turn my threat to your father into a reality."

"You're so bad." She strokes my cheek but is smiling. "But my kind of bad."

"And you're my very good girl."

She shudders at that, and I kiss her lips, sealing our future.

Then I take a picture to post as a reminder for the whole world.

THE END

Next up is *God of Wrath*.

You can check out the books of the couples that appeared in this story.

Aiden & Elsa King: *Deviant King*.

Adrian & Lia Volkov: *Deception Trilogy*.

Jonathan & Aurora King: *Kingdom Duet*.

Killian Carson & Glyndon King: *God of Malice*.

For more news about future audiobook releases, please visit rinakent.com.

WHAT'S NEXT?

Thank you so much for reading *God of Pain*! If you liked it,
please leave a review.
Your support means the world to me.

If you're thirsty for more discussions with other readers of the
series, you can join the Facebook group,
Rina Kent's Spoilers Room.

Next up is a complete standalone in Legacy of Gods series,
God of Wrath.

ALSO BY RINA KENT

For more books by the author and a reading order, please visit:
www.rinakent.com/books

ABOUT THE AUTHOR

Rina Kent is a *USA Today*, international, and #1 Amazon bestselling author of everything enemies to lovers romance.

She's known to write unapologetic anti-heroes and villains because she often fell in love with men no one roots for. Her books are sprinkled with a touch of darkness, a pinch of angst, and an unhealthy dose of intensity.

She spends her private days in London laughing like an evil mastermind about adding mayhem to her expanding universe. When she's not writing, Rina travels, hikes, and spoils cats in a pure Cat Lady fashion.

Find Rina Below:

Website: www.rinakent.com

Newsletter: www.subscribepage.com/rinakent

BookBub: www.bookbub.com/profile/rina-kent

Amazon: www.amazon.com/Rina-Kent/e/B07MM54G22

Goodreads: www.goodreads.com/author/show/18697906.Rina_Kent

Instagram: www.instagram.com/author_rina

Facebook: www.facebook.com/rinaakent

Reader Group: www.facebook.com/groups/rinakent.club

Pinterest: www.pinterest.co.uk/AuthorRina/boards

Tiktok: www.tiktok.com/@author.rinakent

Twitter: twitter.com/AuthorRina